ECHOES OF AN ALIEN SKY

James P. Hogan

By James P. Hogan

ECHOES OF AN ALIEN SKY

James P. Hogan

ECHOES OF AN ALIEN SKY

Copyright © 2007 by James P. Hogan

A Baen Books Original

Baen Publishing Enterprises
P.O. Box 1403
Riverdale, NY 10471
www.baen.com

ISBN 10: 1-4165-2108-9
ISBN 13: 978-1-4165-2108-2

Cover art by Bob Eggleton

Distributed by Simon & Schuster
1230 Avenue of the Americas
New York, NY 10020

Library of Congress Cataloging-in-Publication Data:

Hogan, James P.
  Echoes of an alien sky / James P. Hogan.
      p. cm.
  "A Baen Books original"—T.p. verso.
  ISBN-13: 978-1-4165-2108-2
  ISBN-10: 1-4165-2108-9
  I. Title.
  PR6058.O348E25 2007
  823'.914—dc22

                              2006035270

Printed in the United States of America

10 9 8 7 6 5 4 3 2 1

Dedication:

To the first great-grandchild, Kaileigh Marie Hogan,
and with fond congratulations to the proud parents,
Vanessa and Mark. May there be many more to follow.

CHAPTER ONE

The long-range supply ship *Melther Jorg* was named after a deceased Venusian statesman from the island state of Korbisan, who had been a pioneer figure in marshaling political support for space exploration. Twelve weeks after lifting out from orbit above Venus, it entered the terrestrial magnetosphere at a distance of 90,000 miles from Earth, where the interplanetary plasma of charged particles organizes itself spontaneously into the form of an enveloping sheath that isolates the charged body of the Earth from its electrical environment. As the vessel shed the artificially sustained charge that its engines had maintained to ride the electric field gradient extending from the Sun to the periphery of the Solar System, magnetic decelerators braked it into a descent path that would bring it into a matching orbit standing ten miles off from Earth Expedition Headquarters. The orbiting HQ was still referred to as *Explorer 6*, although structural extensions and additions had greatly increased its size and altered its appearance beyond recognition from the Scientific Operations Command ship that had been on station for half a year now.

Half an Earth year, that is, Kyal Reen reminded himself—an Earth year being equal to a little over one and a half Venusian years. The local system of reckoning was used here. It was one of the things he was going to have to get used to.

He sat with a mixed group of newcomers in the midships cabin on C-Deck, used by crew and passengers as a general dayroom and mess hall, staring in fascination at the slowly enlarging view of Earth being presented on the screen dominating the end wall. The world of blue, broken by brown and green coastlines showing through curdled whorls of white, with its fantastic geography and astounding climates so different from the juddering lava plains and steaming swamps of Venus, was familiar to all of them, of course. They had read the volumes of exploration reports, followed popular news features, and seen pictures going all the way back to the views captured by the earliest unmanned probes. But the image they were looking at now instilled awe in a way that was different from any previous experience. Right now as they contemplated it, beyond the thin walls of the hull containing them and the bubble of air that had carried them across millions of miles of space, the world that it represented was really out there.

Yorim Zeestran, Kyal's junior colleague from the International Academy of Space Sciences, took in the view, sprawled untidily in an easy chair next to him. He had a lean but broad-shouldered, loose-limbed frame, and his chin had sprouted a fringe of yellow growth in the latter part of the voyage. "Imagine, a planet five-sixths water," he murmured. "Who'd ever have believed so much water? It amazes me that the Terrans weren't fish."

Yorim had a casual attitude toward protocol and custom that sometimes raised eyebrows with strangers, but he and Kyal had worked together long enough for informality to be natural between them. For all of those present except Kyal, this was their first time off-planet apart from the short training flights that had formed part of the mission preparation program. Kyal's work in electrical space propulsion research had sometimes involved him in protracted space trips, but never before over interplanetary distances. Hence, all of them were first-timers to Earth.

"Look, over to the left," Emur Frazin said, gesturing. "That thin, curving shape showing through. I think it's part of the double American continent that extends almost from pole to pole. The spine of mountains running all the way down has peaks miles high, and fissures that could swallow a city. What kind of violence did it take to do things like that?" *It was on a scale that our world has never known*, Kyal completed mentally. After a twelve-week voyage, they all knew each other's standard lines. But this time Frazin didn't voice it.

Short in stature, balding, and sporting a short beard, Frazin was probably the oldest among them. He was a psychobiologist, come to join a team at one of the surface bases who were investigating evidence for planetwide calamities early in the Terrans' history, and the effects the experiences may have had on their enigmatic psychology. He was one of those fussy but meticulous workers whose refusal to commit to a conclusion until he had satisfied himself three times over could be irritating at times to some— especially those like Yorim, who had never managed to cultivate the art of patience as a principal virtue. But then again, people like Frazin could save a lot of time and money back home to somebody who was, say, contemplating buying a car or deciding where to look for a home. If Frazin had done the research, it was a foregone conclusion that the option he had come up with couldn't be bettered, and one could proceed to follow it with confidence. From what Kyal had gathered, Frazin was also a family man and something of a creature of habit and fixed routine. Kyal marveled at the dedication to work, or maybe it was the fascination with new discovery, that could induce such a person to come on a mission like this, over such an immense distance, and probably of indeterminate duration. Yorim had offered the more pragmatic opinion that perhaps life could sometimes get to be too much a matter of families and routine.

"And that's the way it is now, after thousands of years of wear and erosion. Imagine what things must have looked like when it was all newly formed," Drekker added. Drekker was a climatologist, pursuing what had emerged as something of a new science, since the ever-turbulent squalls of Venus, driven by the hot equatorial belt with its permanent pall of smog and fumes, produced little in the way of a structured "climate" to be studied. He was young and independent, happy to let domestic considerations wait until he had satisfied his curiosity and appetite for adventure a little more, and was ready to go back to them.

"Ice," Quelaya said, staring at the view dreamily. "Natural ice. . . . Caps of it miles thick. A white fantasy world with floating islands. Have you seen pictures of the polar regions? And animals live there. They will be the first places on my list to visit, if I ever get enough time off." Born an Altian, trim and petite, with cropped red hair, dark eyes, and swarthy skin, she was the archeologist among them, and as such faced the prospect of more than enough work for a hundred lifetimes. She and Yorim had developed a friendliness that could hardly be disguised in the confined conditions of a long voyage, and somehow managed to disappear for periods that politeness and discretion precluded comment on. Kyal made it his business not to notice.

He let his gaze drift over the others as they sat spellbound and oblivious of his staring. Arissen, the zoologist, like Kyal himself, a Ulangean, and as with Quelaya, looking ahead to no end of work to be done. Ooster, an entomologist, drawn to the source of Terran insect specimens he had examined that had been brought back to Venus. Naseena, a geologist, her face mirroring Frazin's awe at the panorama of Earth's surface. Sartzow, the microbiologist. And besides scientists, already a flow of early colonists had begun from among the more adventuresome, drawn by the cleaner, clearer climate, by the opportunities available with the industries and farms springing up to support the scientific influx, or simply by the excitement of starting anew, somewhere among the astounding variety of environments that Earth had to offer, each a world in itself.

It had dense equatorial forests, where the huge trees created a shadowy underworld beneath a green canopy that effectively became a false surface supporting animal forms that lived their entire spans without ever descending to the ground. The more temperate belts contained vast grasslands—arid seas of windblown waves that in turn gave way to dry deserts, hot and cold, and the towering ranges of snowy mountains. Most awesome of all were the oceans, contiguous over the whole planet and extending all the way north and south to Quelaya's fantasy realms of white fairylands and floating mountains.

Every region, even the deserts, teemed with its own fascinating, uncannily adapted mix of life. There was not one among the excited scientists arriving with the *Melther Jorg* who had not seen at some time or other some of the specimens transported back to Venus, or at least been captivated by the documentaries and studies that had been produced of just about every form of Terran life, recorded in their natural habitats.

Every form of Terran life, that was, except one.

Besides researchers of natural phenomena, the teams aboard the orbiting *Explorer 6* and down on the surface also included engineers, architects, historians, scholars of sociology and the humanities, and other specialists like Kyal and Yorim, whose interests lay in artifacts, structures, art forms, and languages. The new arrivals in those categories were eager to get down to the surface of Earth too, and play a part in reconstructing a picture of the world and history of the vanished humanlike race that had once lived there.

The image on the screen changed to show a telescopic preview of *Explorer 6*. As the *Melther Jorg* drew nearer, the lines of the original ship became vaguely discernible amid the clutter of communications antennas and instrument mountings, bulbous projections housing astronomical and surface observatories, and surface lander and supply craft docking ports, that had transformed it into what would now be a permanently orbiting command center for Earth-centered activities. An announcement sounded from the room's address system. "Attention, please. We are about to commence our final approach and closing. Docking in thirty minutes."

CHAPTER TWO

The first manned mission to Earth had arrived fifteen years previously. Before that, the tantalizing neighbor world had long been an object of intermittent study from the few parts of Venus that enjoyed clear skies long enough to allow astronomy to emerge as a serious science, and eventually of exploratory visits by robot probes. *Explorer 6* was largest and latest in a series of manned craft built specially for Earth research following the initial explorations and establishment of surface bases. Of its predecessors, *Explorer 1* was now based above Venus as a training facility—in fact, it was the one that the arrivals aboard the *Melther Jorg* had been introduced to before their departure. *Explorer 2* had been cannibalized at the end of its final voyage to Earth to provide most of the extensions to *Explorer 6*. *Explorer 3* had been diverted from Earth operations and sent on a survey of Mercury and the closer solar vicinity to test theories of the electric field configuration and plasma discharge phenomena. *Explorer 4* was back home undergoing a refit, while *Explorer 5* had been subjected to major design changes to bring it up to the standard of 6, which had actually put 6 ahead in construction, and as a consequence it had been able to depart first.

The Terrans, too, had ventured into space, establishing a presence on their enormous moon, and—if the plans contained in some fragmentary translations that had come to light had been carried through—sending at least one and probably two manned

7

reconnaissance mission to Mars. However, although their civilization had spread to become planetwide, in contrast to the relatively patchy distribution of habitable areas on Venus, and their technology was for the most part at least as advanced—if not more so in areas of military applications—their ambitions for expanding more vigorously into space had been hampered by a curious deficiency in scientific knowledge that had persisted into the latter days of the time for which their culture had existed.

The theories of astronomy that they promulgated were based on models restricted to electrically neutral bodies moving only under the influence of gravity. It was true that this did accurately describe the motions of the Solar System during a quiescent period, when the planets had found stable orbits sufficiently circularized and separated to keep their magnetospheres from coming into contact. Under such conditions, the sheaths that formed at the boundaries of the interplanetary plasma and shielded bodies from electrical effects were never broached, and gravity was left as the sole effective force to influence them. So although practical enough in the shorter term, the theory was flawed in that it obscured a more complete understanding of the nature of celestial events.

Ironically, a major reason for this seemed to have been Earth's clearer skies, which had made possible the detailed study of the motions of heavenly objects from the earliest historical times, when only a primitive understanding of mechanical dynamics had been available to explain them. By the time more advanced knowledge became available of the nature of matter and how it interacted, traditional ideas had become too entrenched to be superseded. On Venus, by contrast, astronomy hadn't really started coming together as a comprehensive science until the advent of balloons, rockets, and other means of basing observations above the all-but-ubiquitous clouds, with the result that the later findings in physics and electrical sciences found ready application naturally.

As a consequence of their gravity-only celestial dynamics, the Terrans were led to believe that the stability they saw in planetary motions represented a permanent state of affairs that could be extrapolated back indefinitely. It produced a myopia that made them unable to recognize the evidence for the role that events of cosmic violence had played in shaping their own early history— evidence that was clear to Venusians, even with their limited knowledge of things the Terrans had found records of and not understood.

The other major consequence of this deficiency in Terran science was that through most of their time as a spacegoing culture, they had concentrated on reaction-mass methods of propulsion, depending on hopelessly inefficient chemical rockets in its formative years, and progressing later—in typically Terran fashion, only when military demands so dictated—to nuclear. To a Venusian propulsion scientist like Kyal, such an approach was akin to tackling the problem of flight with gliders and ground-based catapults and cannons, instead of utilizing onboard power. The Terrans had never, until they were in their final days, grasped that the Solar System is a vast plasma discharge circuit focused on the Sun, and that by suppressing its isolation sheath a craft carrying an artificially sustained charge could harness the unshielded electric field for interplanetary travel.

However, recent discoveries at what had been some kind of Terran base or research facility on the far side of Earth's moon seemed to indicate that in the time running up to whatever calamity finally overcame them, some elements at least among the Terrans had started to appreciate and explore the electrical possibilities for space travel that the nature of the universe offered. Some of the outlying structures that had been found there looked suggestively similar to launch and test facilities familiar to Venusian propulsion engineers. These were what Kyal and Yorim had been brought out to investigate.

Explorer 6 seemed even bigger inside than it had looked from the viewing port when its metal booms and surfaces loomed out of sight all around in the final moments before the *Melther Jorg* docked. Plans of the layout had been made available during the voyage, along with all kinds of other information that newcomers might need, but like most, Kyal and Yorim had continually put off studying them until they were closer to arrival, and in the end never got around to it at all.

The first item on their agenda was to meet for lunch with Borgan Casselo, who ran the physics side of the Earth Exploration Expedition, of which they were now to become part. After that, Kyal was due to meet Director Sherven, the overall scientific head. Casselo had hoped to meet them off the ship personally as would

have befitted someone of Kyal's seniority, but just as they were
disembarking he had called to apologize and say that one of those
"things" had come up that was unavoidable and would detain him
slightly.

"You would hardly have been sent to Earth if you weren't the
kind of person to be busy and in demand," Kyal replied.

"The Master is too generous." As the occasion demanded, Casselo
used Kyal's professional title: Master of Engineering. "One of our
people here can stand in for me. But she will be a few minutes."

"It isn't necessary. We'll learn more seeing something of the
Explorer 6 than waiting. Why don't we meet you at the place where
we're having lunch?"

"Are you sure?"

"Absolutely."

"It's the staff dining room called Patagonia. I can give you
directions. You've been given deck plans already, no doubt?"

"Of course," Kyal affirmed confidently.

"Very well. Here's the one you need, on your screen now. What
you do is go through the double doors you'll see ahead of you at the
far end of the disembarkation hall . . ."

After checking at a reception point inside the docking port, they
were soon lost in the labyrinth of galleries, shafts, and metal-walled
corridors with color-coded floors leading off in all directions. They
followed a terrace above an open area described as the Central
Concourse, with staircases going up and down, and spaces opening
off, and after negotiating a couple of communications nodes marked
by emergency isolation doors where major sections of the structure
joined, found themselves coming back into the Concourse again
from a different direction. After asking directions, they eventually
found the entrance to the Patagonia set a short distance back behind
a sitting area part way along a pedestrian thoroughfare traversing
the outer parts of the structure. This was where Casselo was to meet
them, but he had apparently yet to arrive. They settled down in a
couple of the broad, padded chairs to wait, watching the
intermittent flow of figures in work clothes, casual gear, and
occasional crew uniforms going about their business. The section of
roof above the pedestrian way in front of them was formed from
curved window sections. Through it, framed on one side by the gray
metallic lines of other parts of *Explorer 6*, was Earth itself. Not on a

screen this time. Not electronic at all, or any other kind of reproduction. But real.

Kyal had harbored a fascination toward anything concerning Earth since his student days. It had been recognized as the only other planet in the Solar System that showed signs of supporting life long before the first probes were sent, making it an object of widespread curiosity and speculation. Then had come the excitement of the first pictures transmitted back from orbit, followed shortly thereafter by the incredible scenes captured by surface landers. Ever since those first days of actual exploration, Kyal had devoured the news from the first manned expeditions and reports of findings that had poured forth subsequently as a major interest aside from his own principal work. And now it was really out there, shining above his head, and he was a part of that work.

He picked out the bulging coastline of the southern continent that had been known as Africa, home of the darkest Terran race. Farther north, reconstructed more from memory than visible among the curving ranks of cloud, would be Europe, which along with the northern part of the double continent America, lost in the curvature across the ocean to the west, seemed to have originated most of the lighter skins. How the various groups came to be as mixed as they had was not yet clear. There were different types on Venus as well, but they tended to coexist in their own areas. Occasionally—more so in the past—there had been instances of conflict between some of them, but nothing like the wars that raged on Earth, with enormous industries dedicated to supplying and promoting them.

On the basis of what had been found, views of the Terrans were mixed. On the one hand, they seemed to have been a callous and violent people, producing societies based on enforced conformity and obedience, and holding conquest and the exploitation of others as their dominant imperative in life. Yet at the same time they could be highly artistic, creative, and sensitive to the misfortunes of others. They had devised weapons horrible enough annihilate whole cities and ruthlessly massacred deviants from their own dogmas of belief. And yet some of their architecture and paintings were stunning. Nobody knew what had wiped them out. Many Venusians theorized from the records of progressively more destructive and insane wars that the Terrans must have brought it on themselves, but there was no direct evidence for such a conclusion.

Yorim looked up from the screen of the phone that he had been consulting. "Well, that's some good news," he announced. "Our bags have made it across from the ship okay. I figured it wouldn't do any harm to check."

"Better than finding out when they're halfway back to Venus," Kyal answered without turning his head.

Yorim followed his gaze across and up to the viewing windows. From the extent of the polar caps and the ice fields covering the higher mountain regions, Earth seemed to be going through a cool period compared to the time of its final habitation by humanoids. "So that's how they think home will look one day," he commented. It was generally established that Venus was a much younger planet than Earth, still shedding excess heat. "Cool and fresh, and lots of water. You know, Kyal, I think maybe we were born too soon. Somehow I feel more at home already."

"A lot of people who've been down there say that."

"The beaches. That's where I'm heading before we start work." It was usual for new arrivals to get a break at the end of the trip. "Have you seen the pictures? A mild Sun in a blue sky, and water clean enough to swim in as far as you can see. How about you?"

"Oh . . ." Kyal returned from his reverie of contemplation and looked up and down the gallery, scanning the faces of the people scattered along it. A squat, bearded figure in a dark blue tunic appropriate for occasions midway between casual-working and formal was just coming into view around a corner at the far end, walking quickly. Because of their appointment, Kyal and Yorim had put on neater attire than the sloppy shirts and sweaters and crew fatigues that had become normal during the voyage out. "Probably more academic and historical stuff."

"I could have guessed."

"I'll probably try and take in some of the ruins and cities."

Yorim made a dubious face. "More off-duty females on the beaches. Who are you going to find in the ruins?"

Kyal straightened up in his chair and indicated the direction along the gallery with a nod of his head. "That looks like him, coming this way now."

Casselo had already spotted them. They stood up as he approached. He had dark, curly hair and bright black eyes set in a knobby face with a nose perhaps a size too large for it. His manner as he approached seemed lively and energetic. Kyal made a short, half bow, which Yorim followed—although he sometimes stretched the normal familiarity bounds among compeers at times, he wouldn't overstep the line at the first meeting with a new boss. Casselo returned an inclination of the head, held briefly enough to denote seniority.

"Deputy Director Casselo?" Kyal said.

"My pleasure indeed. We meet finally."

"My colleague, Fellow Yorim Zeestran."

"The pleasure is doubled," Casselo said.

"But mine the honor," Yorim completed.

"Once again, I must offer apologies," Casselo told them.

"Greatly appreciated, but unnecessary," Kyal replied.

"Again, you are too generous." Casselo raised his eyebrows momentarily in a way that signaled a relaxing of formalities. "What can I tell you? We had a slight accident with some equipment just at the wrong moment."

"Nobody hurt, I hope?"

"Oh, no-no. . . . Well, since I've held everyone up, why don't we go straight in? They should be ready for us."

Casselo ushered them toward the doors, which opened on their approach. Inside was a traditionally arranged dining room with cloth-covered tables and draped walls bearing pictures of Terran landscapes. The place was fairly full with lunchtime diners, business or professional dress being seemingly the order of the day. A steward conducted them between tables to a corner booth that had been reserved. The ceiling contained a series of large shutters that were closed at the moment. The alignment of the room with the gallery outside suggested that they could be opened to give an outside view when required.

"This is something I hadn't expected," Kyal remarked, motioning with a hand to indicate the room as they sat down. "The standard you maintain here. It's very impressive."

"We try to do our best," Casselo replied. "Can't afford to let anything more deteriorate. Enough has gone to ruin on Earth already."

Kyal smiled. "Is this where you eat every day?"

"Oh, not at all. The laboratory section has a cafeteria that goes better with regular working days. But this place does make a pleasant change when you're in the mood. And of course there are times when the company or the occasion requires it."

Yorim was studying the menu on one of the view pads provided. A short silence ensued while Kyal and Casselo consulted their own. The fare was mixed, with a number of sections dedicated to various types of Terran food, fish, meat, poultry, and vegetarian. Kyal decided he would postpone any such experimenting until another time and decided on a good, familiar Venusian dish that he hadn't tasted since before boarding the ship. The steward returned with impeccable timing and took the orders. When he had gone, Casselo looked across and spread his hands.

"So, welcome to Earth and to *Explorer 6*. And to my modest domain aboard it. We might not be here at all, but for the efforts of your father, Master Reen. Did you know that Director Sherven was a friend of his?"

"No, I didn't." Kyal was genuinely surprised. But if it were true, he hoped that it hadn't figured in the process of his being selected for this job. "That will make it even more of a privilege to serve here. Did they work together at some stage?"

"The Director can tell you about it himself when you meet him, if he wishes," Casselo said.

For Kyal, the assignment to the Earth Expedition carried more than just academic and professional significance. His father, Jarnor Reen, had been a prominent scientific and philosophical figure on Venus, who had played a major role in the development of space electromagnetics and been a driving force for mounting an Earth exploration program when probes sent back the first pictures telling of a former civilization there. Being a part of that exploration now was a fitting way of paying a tribute to his father's work.

Casselo turned toward Yorim. "Well, we've heard about the son of Jarnor Reen from Ulange. What about yourself, Fellow Zeestran? You are from Gallenda, I understand?" Gallenda was a nation in Venus's mid-temperate northern continent. The northern and southern oceans didn't connect.

Yorim nodded. Although he'd had the ship's barber trim his hair, he rather liked the look of his facial growth, he had confided to Kyal, and so had declined shaving. The sight of Casselo's luxuriant beard had probably put him at ease on that particular score. "From the southern part. A small town along the coast from Beaconcliff."

"I know that area," Casselo said. "I taught a course in nuclear generating at the National Engineering College in Beaconcliff years ago. You're from one of the places that's lucky enough to have a coast."

"The part that isn't swamp, anyway," Yorim agreed. "I captained the college first-league longball team at Beaconcliff. That was where I took electrogravitics."

"I'm well aware of your qualifications in electrogravitics," Casselo went on. "You wouldn't be here now if they weren't exceptional. We'll have to show you the *Explorer 6*'s polarizing system while you're up here. Maybe after lunch, while Master Reen is talking administrative matters with the Director."

"I'd be interested to see it. If it's no imposition."

"None at all. A pleasure."

Casselo was referring to the layers of "hi-polar" material built into the floors of Venusian spacecraft and orbiting platforms. Gravity emerged as a residual effect of the electrical nature of matter. Although atoms were neutral as a whole, they deformed under stress to form electrostatic dipoles, in which the charges were not distributed uniformly but concentrated in distinct regions. Within a system of atomic dipoles—for instance, a piece of ordinary matter—the like parts repelled and the unlike parts attracted, but arranging themselves in such a way that the two effects didn't quite cancel. The mutual attraction ended up slightly greater than the mutual repulsion. Very slightly. The resultant force was forty orders of magnitude smaller than the unneutralized electrical force between the same particles. The effect was self-reinforcing, yielding a force that intensified with the amount of material present—in other words, its mass. On the basis of that principle, another branch of the same technology that had yielded electrical space propulsion had developed, enabling such forces to be induced artificially.

"*Explorer* has a free-fall gym here as well," Cassello informed them. "The G-polarizers switched off." He looked back at Yorim. "Perhaps you'd like to see that too?"

"Yes, I would," Yorim said. "We've seen videos of it. There wasn't room for anything like that on the ship. It looks like fun."

"Well, we'll see what we can do," Casselo promised.

Terran spacecraft and orbiting stations had been free-fall gyms everywhere, Kyal reflected. Sometimes it had taken months for them to recover normal muscle tone and bone strength after extended tours. They must have been a tough bunch.

"You don't waste very much time," Yorim commented to Casselo.

"Wasting time would be robbing the old man who will one day have my name." Casselo said.

Kyal smiled. "I see that my father wasn't the only philosopher."

Casselo thought about it for a second or two. "I don't know about that," he said finally. "Now is the only time in which anything gets done. Everything else is either already done, not done, or yet to do."

A philosopher and yet a pragmatist, Kyal thought to himself. He had the feeling they would all get along just fine.

CHAPTER THREE

The office of Filaeyus Sherven, Scientific Director of the Earth Exploration Expedition, was located on the highest of several administrative decks contained in a prominent superstructure on the main section of *Explorer 6*, termed the Directorate. Kyal's first impressions on being shown in after he had left Yorim and Casselo to go their own way were more of a control room—which, he supposed, in many ways it was. The walls in front and to the right of the immense concave desk seemed to consist mainly of panels and screens, with the section of the right-hand wall immediately opposite the desk opening through as an arch to a small private conference area. The wall along the left side was practically all glass. Beyond it was the Earth and its moon partly obscured behind, both halflit, and a starfield of density and brilliance that after twelve weeks in space was now familiar. In the foreground, a craft that looked like a surface shuttle had just detached from the docking port section protruding below the Directorate and was coasting to distance itself before accelerating away.

Sherven was tall, probably in his sixties, but still holding himself upright, Kyal saw as the Director rose to greet him. He had steel-gray hair, receding at the temples above hollowed but firm-lined features with high cheeks and a prominent chin. His bearing and manner as they went through the formalities conveyed self-assurance and the composure that comes from a long and successful career, an established social position, and solid reputation. He would hardly have been made scientific head of the Earth Exploration Expedition had things been otherwise. After they sat down, he opened in a way that sounded a bit set-piece, either because he had rehearsed it or it was his standard line for welcoming newcomers.

"I'm very happy to have you join us, Master Reen. I expect both of us to benefit from your stay here. You will find it a unique opportunity to play a key part in what is undoubtedly the most exciting scientific venture of our times. There is a whole new world to be opened up, immeasurably rich, varied, and vibrant in itself, and yet with the added fascination of a lost race and its history to reconstruct. We have lots of work ahead of us. Let me add my personal thanks to you for being willing to take a share of it."

"The thanks are all mine for being permitted to," Kyal answered.

Sherven tossed out a hand vaguely in the general direction of one of the groups of screens, and his manner lost a little of its stiffness. "Something new turns up every day here. A report came in only this morning of a part of a library that's been uncovered in a city of the large southern continent—Australia. The linguists there and up here are all excited. We're already getting requests for some of the material from translators back home on Venus. It's ironic that Terran paper records are among the most sought-after. Isn't it strange? With the right spectral analysis, all kinds of invisible things can be made to appear. Electronic media turn out to be all but useless. Degradation has wiped most of them clean. And in the few cases where there is anything detectable, it's impossible to decode. You'd need the original equipment. The things that were carved in stone by earlier cultures thousands of years before actually lasted the best. Maybe they weren't so backward."

Kyal smiled and acknowledged with a nod.

"Anyhow . . ." Sherven sat forward, bringing his elbows onto the desk, "to more immediate matters. Deputy Director Casselo moves around a lot. He's nominally based here, but also spends a lot of his time down at Rhombus." Rhombus was one of the main surface bases, in the center of the main Euro-Asian-African land mass. "You'll be running your own operation out at Luna, alongside the ISA people there who conducted the preliminary diggings and survey. They'll provide whatever support and services you need. At present they're headed by somebody called Brysek, a good man I'm told. Any questions on any of that?"

Apart from naming Brysek, it was a reiteration of the arrangement that Kyal was already familiar with, and he had nothing to add. The International Space Authority was the umbrella organization under whose auspices the entire Earth Exploration Expedition was coordinated. It had been formed primarily for that purpose. Several months before, a reconnaissance survey team had landed at a site known as Triagon on the lunar Farside to investigate some strange constructions showing in pictures obtained from orbit. At first, the facility was thought to have been some kind of an observatory, perhaps located there because of the radio screening from Earth. But on closer examination, some of the forms suggested power focusing guides and concentrators of the kind used in space propulsion, which the Terrans were not supposed to have possessed. Kyal had long been looking for an excuse for an Earth trip, and although his name would certainly have carried weight had he chosen to push, his line of specialization had given little reason to justify it; on the contrary, it provided plenty of pressing commitments to keep him on Venus. But the Triagon findings changed all that, and suddenly made him an obvious choice. Yorim had needed no second asking, and they had concluded the bureaucratic procedures barely in time to join the next ship heading out. Since then, the original ISA survey team had been moved on to other things, leaving the group that Sherven had described to carry out exploratory excavations and generally prepare things for Kyal and Yorim's arrival.

Sherven sat back in his chair and rubbed the center of his forehead with a fingertip, as if giving Kyal a moment longer to consider any further business details. Then he resumed in a different tone, "As I said, it's going to get busy. But before we plunge you in, you're due some time out to acclimatize and relax after the voyage. Most new arrivals here are eager to get down to the surface and see something of Earth. I assume that would be the case with you also, yes?"

Although Kyal was more than curious to see what was at Triagon, the pull to set foot on the world that had captivated his imagination all these years was stronger. "What did you have in mind?" he asked.

"A week before you go on to Luna. That's a local Terran week, measured their way as seven days. We use local time cycles, so you might as well get used to them. I'd recommend going down to Rhombus. It's a good location for getting to anywhere else that takes your fancy."

Kyal had no problem with that. "Sure," he agreed. "If we can afford the time."

A thin smile warmed Sherven's features. "Oh, that moon has been there for a while now. I can't see that a week is going to make much difference."

"Then . . . fine. When?"

Sherven bunched his mouth briefly. "Why not later today—if that's agreeable? A week isn't that long a time. Why waste any of it?"

Kyal gestured to show that he could find no fault with that.

"I didn't go ahead and set anything up beforehand, because I wasn't sure how you would want to play it," Sherven said. "Would you like us to find someone to show you around down there? Or would you rather make your own way? Communications are good everywhere these days."

Kyal got the feeling that Sherven was probably operating with his staff and resources stretched to the limit, and that the offer was made as a courtesy. "There's no need to go to the trouble," he replied. "Fellow Zeestran and I are old friends. We'll manage fine on our own. As you say, there's plenty of help available if we find we need it." This time it was Sherven's turn not to be inclined to argue.

"If I could just ask one thing in the meantime," Kyal said.

Sherven spread his hands. "Please."

"The forms of some of the Farside structures suggest functions that should require significant generating capacity. There wasn't any mention of the kinds of thing I'd have expected in the survey report, so during the voyage, out, I sent a request ahead to Deputy Director Casselo to have the ISA people carry out some deep sonar scans of the site while they were still there. He did so and beamed the results back to me. They show some interesting things." Kyal took his phone from his pocket and indicated one of the blank screens on the section of wall by the arch. "May I?"

"Go ahead."

Kyal used the phone to access a file in his work area on the general net and directed it onto the screen. It listed a set of images. Kyal selected several of the early ones and stepped through them. They showed a lunar landscape of gray dust and ridges under a black sky, with the cluster of domes, pylons, and other Terran constructions viewed from different directions. "Surface shots of Triagon," he commented. Sherven nodded. Damage was evident in certain places, but in the absence of weather or erosion, everything was preserved virtually unchanged.

The next view was a schematic of a vertical cross section of the ground, with the forms of the constructions depicted recognizably on the surface. "Here's a vertical slice of the subsurface," Kyal said, although there was no need to. He entered some codes to superpose the results of the sonar scans, which he had analyzed while aboard the *Melther Jorg*. They appeared in reversed color as green patches indicating hollow spaces. Although the details were indistinct in places, the general pattern of rectangular forms in a regular array was unmistakable.

"There is a lot more to Triagon than what you see on the surface," Kyal said. "A whole complex of deeper levels that the ISA team never suspected."

Sherven's eyes danced alertly over the image, taking in the details. "Interesting indeed," he pronounced. "Does it look like the kind of thing you'd expect?"

Kyal frowned. "I'm not sure. It seems to consist of too many small spaces. And why so many levels? It doesn't look right. And it seems strange that the ISA people didn't find it. Why would a large power generating installation be hidden?"

"Hm. I see your point. It does seem odd, doesn't it?" Sherven agreed.

"Maybe Brysek's people can do some deeper digging while they're waiting for us to arrive," Kyal suggested. "I can give them the precise locations. In fact, here they are." He added a second layer of superposition giving the details in red. "A week might not be so long. But as you yourself just said, Director Sherven, why waste it?"

Sherven nodded. "Yes, of course. It will be done. I'll make sure that Borgan passes this information on, and has them make a start. You may forget the matter for now and enjoy your well-earned vacation."

"I'm most grateful."

Silence fell for a short while. On the far side of a gap outside, in the shadows at the base of a wall of windows and metal culminating in a turret bristling with antennas, Kyal noticed a group of figures in yellow EV suits restrained by safety tethers, floating around an opened housing. Sherven got up and moved to the window, standing for a while with his back to the room, hands clasped loosely behind him, as if prefacing a change of subject and allowing time for the mood to change. Evidently there was more.

"There's a maintenance crew outside down there," he commented. "Looks as if they're doing something with one of the cosmic ray monitors."

"Yes, I'd noticed."

"Did you know I was a friend of your father's?"

"To be honest, I hadn't, sir, until Deputy Director Casselo mentioned it only now, over lunch."

"The privilege was mine, to have known him. You have a first-class record of career background and credentials too, Master Reen. Every indication of being a solid, and reliable addition to the enterprise here. A piece of the old Jarnor Reen, without doubt. He would have been proud, I'm sure."

The tone and use of the informal second person signaled a relaxing of protocols, inviting closeness and frankness. It was a gesture of trust from a senior rare for a first meeting. Kyal said nothing, wondering where this was leading. Sherven turned and moved back to the desk. He sat down again, picked up a blue file that had been lying with some papers to one side, and opened it to turn briefly through the top few sheets of its content.

"About this Gallendian . . . Fellow of Applied Sciences, Electrogravitics, Yorim Zeestran." Sherven looked up. "He would appear to have, shall we say, a more volatile history and temperament. How much do you know about him?"

"I've worked with Yorim for over five years now, sir. I've always found him totally dependable. His scientific approach is first class, with a solid grounding in engineering practice. I would trust him without reservation."

"Hm. Very commendable," Sherven complimented. All the same, he didn't seem very happy. "I'll be frank. I wasn't in favor of this selection, you know. I went along with it on the strength of your own insistence—if that's not too strong a word—and out of respect for your father and his work. We are a small community, isolated and far from home, held together by dedication to our common goals. Maintaining an atmosphere of stability and harmony is one of the first imperatives to facilitate getting the work done." Sherven set the file down and leaned back in his chair, propping his elbows on the rests and steepling his fingers under his chin. "Nevertheless, signs of the radicalism that has been disturbing all facets of existence back home for some years are starting to make themselves felt here. I trust that I make myself clear."

Kyal nodded that there was no need to spell anything out. Sherven was referring to a social-political movement known as the "Progressives" that was gaining ground internationally, particularly among younger elements of the population. Essentially, the Progressives were questioning the traditional pattern of letting social and professional institutions, and the organizations that dispensed learning structure themselves in whatever ways reflected the loyalties and recognitions of merit displayed by the individuals who composed them, rather than conform to any notions of hierarchy imposed from above. According to the Progressives, such reliance on the "emergent dynamic"—to use the term employed by those who studied such matters—was wasteful and inefficient, and discriminated against people who were not gifted with popularity or a flair for attracting professional support. Stronger coordination and control, under the direction of more clearly designated authority, would, they contended, not only produce results faster and more efficiently, but broaden opportunity by making appointment and advancement more accessible to those judged to be deserving rather than being left to chance and whim.

Sherven went on, "Your colleague has the kind of profile that one can't help speculating might lead him to become active in such a respect here." He indicated the file briefly. "For instance, did you know that he helped run a college newspaper that made a case for panels of scientific peers having a say in what kind of research ought to be published and funded? The piece argued that only specialists are fit to decide within their own discipline." Sherven shrugged as if nothing further needed to be said. "We all know that by the time experts qualify as professors, they're likely to have become walled in by their assumptions and lost their ability to think creatively. I'm not saying that Zeestran wrote it, but it gives an indication, perhaps, of the direction his inclinations point in." It sounded like Yorim, sure enough, Kyal thought. But you had to know him to understand that he was about as far from being driven by ideology as it was possible to get, and would happily take either side of any argument just to test the reactions. Sherven's brow creased. "He was also mixed up at one time with a political advocacy group that seemed to think that matters of private relationships should be coercively regulated by the state, and that a standardized code of personal ethics should be included in the educational curriculum."

Kyal couldn't mistake the thinly veiled hint that such an association might not have the most desirable effects on those whose reactions might affect his own image and prospects. One of the unfortunate things of life was that what drove events was not reality but people's perceptions of it. Sherven was just doing his job and trying to honor a loyalty.

"I appreciate the Director's candor," Kyal replied. "And I understand your concerns and responsibilities. However, from my own experience, I know Fellow Zeestran to be simply his own free person. He explores all of the world and is curious about everything. With all respect, I would regard the things you mentioned as due to that nature, rather than anything that should cause concern."

Sherven gave Kyal a searching look and nodded finally, but still seemed dubious. "You do see my point? We have a vitally important mission to think of, far from home, with never enough people and slender resources. We can't afford the kind of agitation that we see in the news from back home. We don't bring people this distance to spend their time promoting disruptive agendas that have no place here. I trust that we can count on you to watch for any signs, and if necessary impress whatever cautions are necessary to nip them in the bud."

"Of course." Kyal nodded that he understood.

His own position on such matters was divided. On the one hand, who could disagree with the suggestion that more efficient use of resources in a harsh environment like that of Venus, and a fairer recognition of talents constituted desirable aims? He didn't see that concerted moves to bring about improvement could ever be a bad thing. At the same time, he couldn't deny holding a certain respect for the values enshrined in the traditional principles of open debate, freedom of individual choice, and in the end letting everyone follow the direction that their reason and their consciences dictated. Such things hadn't come to be accepted lightly, but only after generations of trial and experience. They shouldn't be thrown away lightly or impetuously either. It was the kind of attitude that Jarnor had brought to his science: using the tried and tested methods for as long as they seemed favored, but not hesitating to abandon them when facts, evidence, and not uncommonly feelings and an indefinable intuition too, said the time had come to move on. It was also the way he lived his life—and no doubt, too, one of the strongest influences that had guided Kyal in forming his own view of the world.

CHAPTER FOUR

Although there had apparently been some who tried to point out the obvious, the mainstream of Terran science had refused to recognize that Venus was a much younger planet than Earth—even after sending down surface probes of their own when its surface and atmosphere were still forming. The maturer conditions of Earth had proved so much more hospitable that several Venusian researchers had suggested, not always jokingly, that they should consider moving their whole culture there.

The Terrans' error was another consequence of their assumption of gravity being the sole means of shaping the Solar System, and missing the importance of electrical forces involved in causing ejection of lesser objects from gas giants by fission. This led them to construct a theory in which all bodies had formed together out of a collapsing dust cloud, and hence had to be the same age. When data started coming back from Venus clearly telling of the hot, primordial conditions there, they invented a notion of a runaway atmospheric greenhouse to account for it.

In this they revealed an extraordinary capacity for self-delusion that resulted from their tendency to twist the evidence to fit a theory that they had convinced themselves had to be right—as if fervency of belief could somehow affect the fact. This typified the negation of science as it was taught on Venus, and as Kyal had learned it from Jarnor, where one of the essential disciplines to be mastered at the outset was learning to recognize and suppress desires and preconceptions, and simply follow where the evidence led.

Emur Frazin, the psychobiologist among the company on the ship out, had held this to be the most significant psychological difference setting Terrans and Venusians apart. Looking for reasons for it was a big part of the work that had brought him here. The same underlying philosophy pertained too to the managing of Venusian political and social affairs. Or at least it did traditionally. And this would explain Sherven's reservations toward militant demands for changes in public policy from quarters he saw as allowing thinking to be dominated more by ideologies of how things ought to be, instead of by the simple and practical lessons that experience taught of what worked and what didn't.

Even though the views from orbit had prepared them, the pageant of detail unfolding as the lander descended toward the surface awed Kyal and left even Yorim speechless. Despite all the images they had seen, to fully grasp the extent of Earth's oceans, you had to actually see one down there, through an atmosphere as clear as crystal, stretching all the way to the rim of a quarter of a planet and beyond. As the landscapes of colored daubery rose, expanded, and resolved into plains, valleys, rifts, and snow-topped mountains of stupefying dimensions, the age of the planet became visible too. They could sense the aeons of history written into every fold, river channel, and crumbling ridgeline taking shape among the bastions of ancient rock.

"It makes home look a bit like a factory slag dump," Yorim offered finally.

Rhombus, by now a small if cluttered and somewhat inelegant town, had grown from one of the earliest surface bases. The most geographically widespread Terran language, de facto standard for business and most other international dealings, and hence the one that Venusian linguists were concentrating on, had been that known as English. It took its name from the dominant of a diverse collection of squabbling tribes who inhabited a group of islands off the northwest of the main planetary landmass, where it had emerged as an impossibly irrational amalgam of various ancestral languages brought by successive waves of foreign invaders, all of whom added to and further complicated the makeup of the final population. Untangling the history was still a bewilderment to Venusian scholars, but it appeared that the English had inherited their various contributors' proclivities for conquest as well as their languages, for they went on to establish an empire of their own that for a short time girdled the entire world. Either the language itself somehow instilled a tendency toward aggression—or perhaps was an expression of it—or there was some peculiar genetic connection between the two. One of the principal regions colonized by the English—after invasion by a number of rival groups and virtual extermination of the natives—was the northern part of the double continent Americas across the ocean to west. Having adopted the language, the Americans then became the major world power and proceeded in turn to begin attacking and invading everybody else.

Rhombus was situated in what had been known as Iran, part of an area called the Middle East. The initial consideration of the first Venusian explorers was proximity to a wide range of geology and climates. However, this was followed by rapid expansion to accommodate just about every line of research when the region was recognized as having been where many of the major Terran cultures and racial divisions met. Perhaps not coincidentally, it had also been the focus of the Central Asian War, which had been one of last great conflicts to be fought before the Terrans died out.

The town derived its name from the shape of the main building of the original base of fifteen years previous, still discernible among the sprawl of launch and transportation installations that formed the outskirts on the east side. That was also where most of the scientific complexes were concentrated, having grown from the first field cabins and laboratory shacks. Subsequent development became more orderly as it spread westward and now constituted the central district, with residential precincts, services, amenities, and supporting industries that had quickly come into existence to ease the burden on the supply ships from Venus. On the western periphery was an animal- and plant-breeding station, where attempts were being made to redomesticate what were thought to be the descendants of former artificial Terran strains that had reverted to wild.

A white, dust-covered bus brought Kyal, Yorim, and a batch of other arrivals to a reception building in the service area clear of the launch areas. It was their first taste of being out of doors since leaving Venus. Kyal had never seen a landscape of such dazzling clarity under the clear blue sky. The Sun was noticeably smaller than he was used to, but impressively radiant. Venusian days were hazy even when the cloud cover broke, which was seldom. The other striking thing was the dryness of the terrain, extending away as a brown, dusty plain on the far side of the launch area to craggy hills rising in the distance. Venus was humid and soggy everywhere. Supposedly, Earth had been like that once. He tried to imagine the surroundings without the launch gantries, servicing hangars, or any of the other constructions, empty and desolate, as it had been fifteen years ago when Armin Harra set the first Venusian foot on the surface of Earth. There wasn't a Venusian who had never seen the recording of that memorable moment, or a schoolchild who couldn't recite the immortal line that had gone down in history. It was only years later that the diligent research of a zealous student journalist established that the first words actually uttered on the surface of Earth had been, "Is the camera running yet?"

Inside the building, a knot of people were waiting to meet the incoming arrivals, and the two groups dissolved into a flurry of pairs and more finding each other, and a few lost souls looking around for sources of information or inspiration. Casselo had arranged for Kyal and Yorim to be met by a clerk from the local admin office named Vereth, who had called them shortly before they boarded to let them know he would be there, identifiable by a red cap and a light blue jacket. Yorim spotted him first as they halted and looked around.

"There's our man, over there—in front of the wall with the map and the posters. I think he's seen us."

"Yes, he's coming over." Kyal sent a confirming nod and raised a hand. Vereth was somewhere in his twenties, lean and bony, with short-cropped hair and dark skin that set off his teeth when he smiled. He took off his cap and made a short bow. Kyal and Yorim inclined their heads.

"Master Reen and Fellow Zeestran?"

"Our pleasure," Kyal returned.

"A pleasant voyage and a comfortable descent, I trust? Welcome to Earth." Vereth replaced his cap.

"Decidedly so. May life be as kind to you."

"Nice hat," Yorim said.

Vereth didn't seem sure how to respond and looked around. "The staff in here are all going to be tied up taking care of people with prearranged schedules," he said. "But I've talked to somebody in the

Site Operations Support office who has been making arrangements for you. It's just a short way along the block outside. Please come this way."

He led them from the reception hall and out through some doors on the opposite side of the building to that where they had entered. The bus had delivered them to a glass-fronted dock, so this was their first real exposure to Terran air. It was invigoratingly fresh and clean, but cool. The oxygen content was higher than on Venus.

Yorim drew in a slow breath as ambled beside Kyal in long, easy strides, the bag he had brought with him for the week slung over a shoulder. "Say, this feels *alive!*"

"Chilly, though" Kyal said. "I'm not so sure I could go for this swimming idea of yours."

"Aw, I don't know. It's pretty high up here," Yorim said. "And it'll be warmer farther south. I'll find a spot."

"Very dry too," Vereth said. "Best to use cream on the skin until you get used to it. Especially the lips."

They had come out onto a roadway running between the reception building and an adjoining shed that looked like a vehicle depot. A couple of side roads opposite disappeared among a conglomeration of metal and plastic buildings butted together in ways that spoke of sporadic additions and extensions in whatever way was expedient, intermingled with shacks, communications masts, storage tanks, and tangles of pipes. Apart from a slow-moving truck a block or so away, the traffic just at this moment was all pedestrian. The higher buildings of the central area of Rhombus some distance away were visible above the roofs ahead of them. Kyal found himself feeling mildly agoraphobic at being unenclosed by walls for the first time in months, but it would no doubt soon pass. Yorim slowed several times to draw a toe of his boot wonderingly through another novelty spread out under their feet: *sand*. Vereth looked amused. Kyal had the feeling he'd seen all this before.

"Where are you from?" Kyal asked him.

"Korbisan, originally."

"You look on the dark side for a Korbisanian."

"The Sun here will do that," Vereth replied.

"How long have you been on Earth now?"

"A year."

"What brought you out here?"

"I came to join my older brother. He's with an excavation party working over in the east at the moment, in China. My family were pressuring me to find a wife and get married."

"Oh." Kyal didn't want to get too personal. "What brought your brother out here?"

Vereth's teeth flashed in a quick grin. "Same reason."

The Site Operations Support office was located in a two-story building on a corner across the street, announcing itself under a larger sign that read ARMIN HARRA SPACEPORT. Vereth brought them to a room with some chairs and a counter. A plump, middle-aged woman in tan work fatigues appeared through a doorway from an office to the rear at the sound of their entering. "You found them, then?" she said to Vereth, and nodded jovially to the arrivals. "It's a long trip out, isn't it? Glad to have you here."

"This is Olin," Vereth said. Kyal and Yorim inclined their heads. "What have you managed to come up with?"

"A week, and then going to Luna."

"Yes," Vereth confirmed.

"It's a bit difficult. The hotel rooms and the short-term apartments were all taken by prebookings. It's always like this when a ship arrives."

"Olin doesn't mean just the regular commercial hotels," Vereth explained. "It's what people here also call the quarters that ISA manages for professionals visiting Rhombus."

Olin looked at Kyal and Yorim anxiously. "The best I've been able to do is a double room in the hostel. It's where people like technicians usually stay for a few days when they come down to the surface. But it's comfortable and clean. And you'll probably be away seeing other places for most of the time anyway."

"It wasn't decided until lunchtime today," Kyal said. "We're very grateful. The hostel will be fine."

"You make life too easy."

Yorim was studying a wall adorned with notices, timetables, and a large map of Earth showing the main surface bases and areas of ongoing exploration. Rhombus was marked prominently, sitting in the middle of it all. "Here are your cities, Kyal." He pointed at areas to the west and north. "Europe and Russia. Those are the areas you wanted to see right?"

"A lot of work is going on in those areas," Vereth said. "Huge old cities, millions of people. They even built them in colder climate where the precipitation falls as snow."

Olin shivered. "I'll just stick to watching the pictures," she said.

Kyal moved closer to the map to look at the region Yorim had indicated. It was where the latest Terran civilization seemed to have originated, the one known as Western, which the Americans took over and carried worldwide. A number of other major civilizations had come and gone before the rise of the Western, but none had attained a significant level of technology. The Venusians had gone unerringly from simple beginnings to industry to air flight and space travel with no such diversions in other directions, as if they had been predisposed in that direction. No particular explanation had been offered as to why there should have been such a difference, or seemed called for. It was just one of those things that was accepted.

"What other kinds of things are there to see closer to home?" Kyal asked, turning back toward Olin. "Here in Rhombus, for instance—for the first day or two, anyway. A lot of things happen here too, don't they?"

"Many of the scientific labs and academic offices are concentrated here," Olin said.

"They can give you a list of what's where," Vereth interjected.

Olin went on, "There's a shop not far from here that bits of Terran machinery are brought back to for assessment and cleaning up. Some of it gets refurbished and shipped back to Venus. A lot of the language work is centralized in Rhombus, correlating inputs from all over. We've got biology and microorganisms, and a big geological lab with all kinds of departments. Between them, they can give you a good guide as to what's going on in other places. And Rhombus is a good center for transportation to any of them. There are flights coming and going all the time, and getting rides is usually not a problem. One benefit of being in the hostel is that you'll meet plenty of people who'll be able to give you pointers. And you know my name: Olin. If you need any more, or get stuck, you have my number on the net. Is there anything else I can do for now?" Kyal and Yorim looked at each other. Both shook their heads.

"Sounds just fine," Yorim said.

"You've been more than helpful," Kyal told Olin.

"We try to please our guests."

"Shall we go, gentlemen?" Vereth asked. He acknowledged Olin with a nod. "I'll show you the way to the hostel."

"Enjoy Earth," Olin called after them as they left.

CHAPTER FIVE

The hostel was situated a few blocks farther on in the direction of the Central District, where already the surroundings began to feel more like a town meant for people than an industrial suburb of trucks and machines. Although the effect was marred somewhat by the profusion of overhead cables and communications antennas everywhere, the place did make the effort to look more like a residence than an office block or factory shed, and even sported some color in the form of planters containing strange red and orange Terran flowers standing along the foot of the walls on either side of the entrance. Vereth regretted that the hostel didn't have a restaurant in the manner of the hotels, but he pointed out a cafeteria adjacent that he said was "interesting." Terran steaks tended to be on the chewy side, he told them, but they tasted wonderful.

A clerk at the lobby desk greeted them with the customary pleasantries and confirmed the details that Olin had given. Vereth saw them to their room, where they deposited their bags, and they walked with him back to the lobby. Was there anything else he could do? No, he had been more than helpful already. It was his privilege. Echoing Olin to remind them that they could always feel free to call him on the planetary net, he made his parting bow and left.

The hostel lobby had its notice-board wall complete with a map too, but embellished with poster-size prints of Terran ice cliffs, mountain peaks, and deserts, and giving details of local entertainments and activities that would help newcomers meet their neighbors and make some friends. A quick perusal revealed a couple of longball teams, a drama group, a class for Terran art and architecture studies, a debating group hosted by the Progressives, a club devoted to a Terran game of positional strategy called chess, which was becoming popular back on Venus, an organized sightseeing itinerary, and several musical groups. There was also the usual collection of ads describing items for sale, lost and found, attempts to match skills for hire with work in demand, and shyly disguised pleas from lonely hearts looking for company.

"That place that Olin was talking about sounded interesting," Kyal remarked.

"You mean the shop where they bring the machines and things?" Yorim said over his shoulder as he scanned the board.

"Yes. If we've only got a week, we might as well make the best of it. What do you think?"

"I say let's get something to eat next door first." Kyal agreed, and they turned to head back out the door.

"Try a Terran steak," the desk clerk tossed after them as they left. "The chicken bird is good too."

Yorim had the steak. Kyal tried the chicken. They sat on opposite sides of one of the long, eight-seat tables, munching in silence as they experimented. "What do you think?" Kyal asked finally.

"Okay . . . but a bit bland compared to a good flank cut. Better when you spice it up." There were some home-imported sauces on the table. "How's the bird?"

"Okay, I guess."

"I read somewhere that the domesticated variety the Terrans had didn't fly. Maybe it was better."

"Oh, really?"

"Your face looks a bit funny. Kind of distant. Are you feeling okay?"

"A bit muzzy-headed," Kyal admitted. "But I don't think it's the food. The air, maybe."

"It could be the gravity," Yorim said. "You're feeling the effects of a whole planet for the first time in months. A ship's G-polarizers are localized. It produces a subtly different effect. Some people are sensitive to it. It'll wear off by tomorrow. Did you feel dizzy on the first day or two out in the ship?"

"I can't remember. . . . Could be, I suppose. Let's hope so." Kyal took a sip of water. It tasted sweet and clean. "How was the tour of the G-system in *Explorer 6*? You never told me."

"Interesting. They're not under drive in free fall, so you can't divert power from the charge generators the way you can when you're in Venus transit. So they extract it from orbital momentum with periodic reboosts."

"Casselo could tell you everything you wanted to know about it, then, eh? So you think he's okay too?"

"As good as we'll get," Yorim agreed. "My take is that we picked ourselves a good boss here, chief. I don't see any problems."

Kyal chewed silently for a while, then asked nonchalantly, "Did he bring up any political angles? You know, feelers about attitudes and views about different things? . . ."

"No. We just talked about longball and technical stuff."

Kyal felt relieved. It seemed that Casselo didn't represent an extension of Sherven in that respect, which would intrude into their working relationship. The findings on lunar Farside sounded too intriguing for the work to be marred by concerns that belonged back home, and as far as Kyal was concerned, were better left there.

Others had been drifting in since they sat down, mostly younger people but with a few older ones among them too. A girl detached herself from a group who were finding seats at one of the other tables and came over. "Well! Two familiar faces. This huge world is becoming smaller already." It was Naseena, the geologist who had come with them on the *Melther Jorg*.

"Naseena!" Kyal exclaimed. "And you seem to be making a good start in getting to know people already."

"Hey," Yorim greeted.

"I thought you two were going to that place on Luna," Naseena said.

"We're taking a week's break to look around a little down here first," Kyal replied.

"Where are you staying?"

"Next door."

Surprise showed on Naseena's face for a moment. She probably expected them to be in one of the hotels. "Me too," she told them. "I'll be leaving in a couple of days." They already knew from their time on the ship that she would be working in the huge mountainous region to the east known as the Himalayas. She took a step back and explained to the others, "These are Kyal Reen and Yorim Zeestram, who were on the same ship. Space electromagnetics. They'll be going on soon, out to Luna."

"Involved with those Terran constructions that were discovered on Farside?" one of her companions guessed.

"Exactly right," Kyal said.

"I've read about them." The speaker was stocky and rounded, wearing a padded work vest over a red shirt, his white hair showing beneath a flat peaked cap. "And I'm curious. Any ideas yet?"

"The place is a lot bigger than it looks," Kyal said. "We've had some sonar scans done."

"Already?"

"While we were on our way out. It goes a lot farther down below the surface."

"Really? Now I'm *really* curious."

Naseena sighed. "Oh dear, I'm doing this all the wrong way round. This is Mowrak, the person I'll be working with. I've only just met him today too." The white-haired man tilted his head. Naseena gestured to the younger man next to him. "Whylen is an excavation engineer, soon to go back to digging up cities in . . . Where was it, Whylen?"

"China." Whylen was dark-haired and sinewy, his face shadowed by several days of stubble. He rose briefly from his chair. "My privilege, I'm sure."

The man who had sat down next to him was about the same age, thirtyish, muscular and lithe, with a florid countenance that complemented a head crowned by a thicket of copper-red hair. His features were drawn in intense, angular planes about a sharp nose, thin but firm mouth, and a pointy, determined chin. He was wearing an open black shirt and a brushed leather jacket that was at the same time stylish and durable.

"And this is Jenyn," Naseena completed the introductions. "Just back from being in the Americas for a while. He's next door in the hostel too, waiting for permanent quarters. That's right, isn't it? . . . I'm not sure what he does, though. What do you do here, Jenyn?"

"Linguist." Jenyn answered. He didn't concede to any courtesies, but regarded Kyal and Yorim unsmilingly with pale blue eyes. Kyal had the discomforting feeling of being evaluated for some prospective purpose. Jenyn cocked his head to one side. "Where are you people from back home?"

"I'm a Ulangean," Kyal replied. "Fellow Zeestran is from Gallenda."

Jenyn nodded. The coolness and distancing implied by Kyal's use of the titular form didn't make any visible impact on him. "How were things there when you left?" he inquired.

Yorim's brow furrowed. "What kind of things?"

Jenyn answered in a careless drawl. "Oh, life in general. The usual things people talk about. Prices and taxes. Who makes the rules. Are they happy with the way things are being run?"

Naseena threw in, "He's becoming the local Progressive organizer in Rhombus already. You're running for the leadership nomination among the Terran bases, Jenyn, yes?" She looked back at Kyal and Yorim. "I suspect that probably had more to do with what he was doing in the Americas."

Mowrak had registered that Kyal and Yorim were not responding warmly to the turn of conversation. "There's a workshop where they clean up pieces of Terran machinery and things," he said. "We were going there after we've eaten. Want to join us?"

"We had exactly the same idea," Kyal said, happy to move the subject along.

"Great," Mowrak said. "They've got a Terran war tank that's just been brought in, dug up out of the desert not far from here. It's going to be sent back home as a museum exhibit."

Kyal and Yorim looked at each other and exchanged nods. "Sounds good," Yorim said for both of them.

CHAPTER SIX

It stood in an open yard behind one of the workshops. The angled planes of its squat, heavy bulk seemed sinister and menacing—which was hardly surprising, considering the purpose for which it had been built. Though little more than a corroded hulk, it was better preserved than most similar vehicles from its times, thanks to the dry desert conditions. Fastened to a board on a nearby wall was a print of an engineering isometric drawing reconstructed from various sources of how it had originally looked.

The mobile steel burial vault had run on belt tracks similar to those found on heavy construction machinery, and been powered by a hydrocarbon-fueled engine. It carried a crew of four. A somehow ghoulish swiveling turret with sloping sides like a truncated pyramid carried an enormous cannon fired by chemical explosives, along with a lighter secondary weapon. It had been destroyed by a projectile that melted a hole through its armor on impact and spewed white-hot metal liquid into the interior.

Kyal found himself disturbed and unsettled as he stood staring at it in a silent semicircle with the others. He was thinking of the lives that had begun somewhere in some unknown alien mothers' arms, grown and flowered through all joys, pains, and dreams to become those miracles of creation called persons . . . all to be vaporized in an instant, for what? From the strained silence and somber looks on their faces, it seemed to be having a similar effect on others.

41

"There's something . . . I don't know, something horrible about it," Naseena whispered finally. "Can you imagine what it would be like shut up in a machine like that?"

"Especially with people trying to destroy it," Whylen said. "Imagine being trapped and incinerated in there."

"Oh, don't!"

"How old would you say that is?" Yorim asked, addressing the words to no one in particular. There was controversy over dating the sequences of the events that had taken place on Earth. Estimates made by Venusian scientists based on the methods they employed back home disagreed with reconstructions based on the Terrans' own records.

Mowrak, the geologist that Naseena would be working with in the Himalayas, shook his head. "I don't think anyone can be sure yet. Our own estimates give results orders of magnitude different from what the Terrans believed. Where we infer tens of thousands of years, they claimed millions." He shrugged. "It's difficult to argue too much. They were on their own planet longer. Maybe rates change more than we think as planets get older. That's one of the lines we're investigating." He turned and called to a technician from the shop, who was carefully removing encrusted sand and rock from a corroded object at a bench outside the workshop door. "Excuse me. Do you have any kind of date for the tank here?"

"The experts are still arguing about it. Some say thousands of years, others say tens of thousands. If you extrapolate the system that the Terrans used, it comes out at a lot more than that. Take your pick."

Mowrak gave the others a look that said that made his point. "You see? What more can I tell you?"

"You sound as if you're involved in that kind of thing yourself," the technician remarked.

"Yes, I am a geologist. Back at Rhombus briefly, but working out east. I'm the tour guide today. We have some people here new to Earth, just down from orbit."

"I hear the *Melther Jorg* is back in."

"That is where we're from," Naseena said.

"Welcome to Earth. I hope it treats you all well." They returned short nods. The technician took them all in with a glance. "We've got some more interesting things inside. Come on, I'll show you."

"I've got another question . . ." Yorim moved up alongside the technician as he turned to lead the way through the doors. As the others began following, Kyal stayed back to look once more over the drawing of the Terran war tank mounted on the wall. The heat and noise in such confinement, hemmed in by machinery above, below, and on every side, must have been fearsome. He wondered if they actually found volunteers for such tasks, or if the crews had to be forced to accept them. All in all, he decided he'd take agoraphobia.

A movement nearby made him turn his head. Jenyn had also stayed back and was standing beside him. He regarded Kyal questioningly, then half turned to look back at the Terran tank. After a moment or two, he said, "They were a violent and destructive breed, yes. But couldn't that have been a manifestation of other qualities too, Master Reen? They understood the power to effect change that comes from having order and discipline. They stood together to bring about the things they believed in, instead of letting themselves be carried along by the herd. And yes, they would fight to the death if they had too. They didn't just passively accept whatever lot fell to them by other people's whims and preferences, the way Venusians would. It could cause grief in the short term; but there was something magnificent and stirring about it that perhaps we could use a little more of at times. Don't you think so?"

Jenyn's tone was soft and exhorting, but at the same time his pale blue eyes had a challenging light in them. Kyal recognized the Progressive line and shook his head. "Save it for the language students. Politics isn't what I do."

"It's the future, the way things are going to be. You won't change it. Why be left behind?" Jenyn didn't expect any instant conversion, Kyal knew. He was trying to plant seeds.

Kyal resisted the impulse to be blunt. "Well, we are being left behind, aren't we?" he answered. "I think it's time to catch up with our friends."

Inside, they found the others clustered around a large wooden table, where pieces from the tank's engine had been laid out after painstaking etching and cutting to separate what was left of them from masses of corrosion like others lying on a bench by the wall. There were also parts of its instruments and control gear, along with several conical objects that the technician said were tips of the projectiles fired by the cannon. Yorim was examining a plate from one of the tracks. Looking around at the rest of the shop, Kyal picked out the hub and rim of a large wheel that looked amazingly like one from a Venusian agricultural tractor; a couple of shelves of electrical devices and components; an assortment of helmets, belt buckles, other oddments of clothing; knives, cutlery, and various hand tools. The technician was showing Whylen some long objects that could have been firearms.

There were also a few other items that didn't fall into the category of "equipment and machinery" but had ended up here anyway, including some surprisingly well preserved pieces of wooden furniture. Kyal stopped to inspect a sitting, cross-legged figure about a foot high, carved out of stone, on a shelf to one side. Mowrak saw him looking at it and came over, at the same time gesturing to Naseena, who was watching. "You'll see a lot of these farther east, where we're going," he told her.

She moved over to join them. "Who is he?"

"Some kind of religious deity from an earlier culture—earlier than the one that produced the tank." Mowrak looked at Kyal. "How would you and Yorim like to come and see them too, while you've got the chance?"

"The sculptures?"

"No, I meant the mountains—the Himalayas. Five miles high, summits of ice. We were planning a few days of hiking around and showing Naseena some of the sights there before getting back to work. Whylen and Jenyn and some others are coming too. Why not make a party of it?"

"When did you plan on leaving?" Kyal asked him.

"Later on tonight."

Yorim had sauntered over and been listening. "What do you think?" he asked Kyal. The expression on his face said he could go for it.

"I thought you were set on sunshine and beaches?"

Yorim shrugged. "That was just a thought. I could live with this too."

"What's the problem?" Mowrak asked, seeing Kyal's hesitation.

"Oh . . . Kyal was thinking about seeing places to the north and west from here," Yorim told him. "Where the Terran Western civilization originated."

"The European cities," Kyal said.

"Wasn't that where Terran science finally came together?" Nassena put in. "Is that what you're more interested in?"

"That. And the history," Kyal said.

The technician and Whylen had come over and were following. "There'll be a supply flight going up to Foothills Camp first thing in the morning," the technician said to Kyal. "That's in the mountains north from here, between the two big inland seas. They're doing a lot of excavating at one of the Russian cities up there." He patted one of the pieces of wooden furniture and indicated some other objects that looked like household pieces. "That's where these pieces came from. I could probably get you a place on it. You shouldn't have much problem getting a connections west from there. The colonists are starting farms in Europe. A lot of the traffic from Rhombus uses that route."

Kyal considered the option. There probably wouldn't be another chance like it in the week that they were here. And there was no way of telling what kind of time he might have to spare the next time he was back from Luna and found himself in this vicinity—whenever that might be.

"Look, why don't you go with these people tonight?" he said to Yorim. "I can meet up with you back here in Rhombus before we shuttle back up to the *Explorer*. That way neither of us will be a drag on the other. After twelve weeks we could probably both use a change of company anyway."

Yorim gave him a dubious look.

"Hey, I like being on my own sometimes," Kyal said. "It's when I do my best thinking."

Yorim took in a breath and raised his eyebrows, which Kyal knew was the nearest he would come to making a fuss over it. "Okay," he agreed.

"You're sure?" Mowrak asked Kyal.

Kyal nodded. "Sure." And to Yorim, "You go ahead. I'll be okay."

"Well, I guess you can count me in," Yorim said, looking around to take in the rest of the company.

"Great," Naseena said enthusiastically. "But we'll miss you, Kyal. Are you sure we can't twist your arm?"

"Be quiet," Kyal told her.

Jenyn had drifted a short distance away, where he was looking over one of the wooden objects. It was of a peculiar construction, giving the impression of having been a flat, rounded cabinet of some kind. The remains of a metal frame and tatters of strings lay among the splintered woodwork, along with numerous long, rectangular, white objects. "What's this?" Jenyn asked, looking up and turning to the technician.

The technician moved closer to join him. "It was a kind of keyboard musical instrument, from what the Terrans dated as their early twenty-first century. All these pieces were unearthed from ruins covered by a layer of dried anaerobic bog. It seems to have been formed by sediments from a temporary lake or flood. A big war that took place around those times is believed to have begun in that region."

"The Central Asian War," Jenyn supplied. He looked around as if he were lecturing. "I have studied it. The democratic Western nations were defending the world against international lawlessness and aggression instigated by backward-looking tyrannies who were losing their control over people who wanted Western freedoms for themselves."

The technician paused politely for a second or two, but seemed obliged to make some comment. "Well, that was what they told the people, anyway," he agreed. There was a moment of silence. "Let me show you what one of their computers looked like. Or what's left of one, anyway. This way, over here...."

As the group moved away, Kyal turned to look again at the relic from a lost world, a lost age. What kind of sounds, he wondered, had once been evoked from it? Decoding and reproducing Terran music had so far defied all attempts. He stared at it in fascination, trying to picture in his mind the place to the north that it had come from, among the mountains between the central Asian inland seas. Who was the long-dead Terran whose hands had played it? he wondered. What events, now forgotten forever, had been taking shape then? What story could this strange, alien instrument have told of those times?

CHAPTER SEVEN

The somber chords of a Rachmaninov concerto tumbled through the rooms and out through the open windows into the gardens of a large house nestled in a fold among the hills overlooking the town. In the distance, the peaks of the Caucasus mountains shone white in the early summer sun. But the mind of the player, Leon Ivanovitch Borakov, brooded on things that were far from the music. The wars to the south and east that had followed America's latest bid to control the oil regions were spreading. Some saw a deeper motive and interpreted the moves as furthering a strategic encirclement in preparation for an inevitable clash with China.

The tragedy was that there was no need for any of it. Borakov and a few others like him who knew but were unable to make themselves heard could give the world all the energy it needed—indefinitely. The potential was there, in catalyzed nuclear reactions that he had analyzed and seen demonstrated repeatedly. Fusion and all that it promised, without the brute force approach that had been failing for half a century. But oil-focused global financial interests and academic politics had caused the research to be ridiculed or suppressed. Greed, paranoia, suspicion, and the disastrous combination of mediocrity in possession of authority were in control everywhere. Humanity had the knowledge, the ability, and the resources to solve its problems at a fraction of the cost it would expend fighting over them, which would solve nothing. But all efforts to stop the madness were in vain against the ignorance and ambitions of deluded egos leading compliant masses who delivered their families to their nightly electronic brainwashing just as surely as their ancestors of earlier centuries had marched theirs to be harangued from pulpits. "Fanatics are the cause of every evil," a British member of the House of Lords had once observed to Borakov. "They should be ruthlessly hunted down and exterminated."

The phone rang on a side table. Borakov stopped his playing and reached to take the call. He would not have been disturbed without some good reason. His secretary spoke from the office downstairs in the house. "Greganin is asking to talk to you. He says it is urgent." Josef Greganin was a presidential aide in Moscow.

"Put him through," Borakov said.

"Leon?"

"Yes. Hello, Josef."

"Have you heard the news?"

"What?" There was a hollowness in Borakov's voice. A premonition told him it was something he had been expecting but refused to acknowledge consciously.

"The Chinese are landing on Taiwan." The situation had been escalating for two weeks. They had threatened to dismantle the new missile installation there themselves if their demands for removal were not met.

"The talks?" Borakov said. Negotiations had been going on behind the scenes that the public never saw.

"It sounds as if they've given up," Greganin told him. "The word is that the Chinese were rebuffed. The Americans were never serious. They went through the motions for the historical record. But China won't let itself be seen as being cowed in the eyes of the world."

Borakov was horrified. "But this is exactly what the Americans want, Josef! We both know that those missiles were only put there as a provocation."

"But the West doesn't know. Their media are already shouting about naked aggression. President Rafton was on fifteen minutes ago, spouting the usual claptrap about defending freedom and values. The naval battle group that they've got in the area is moving in. There are unconfirmed reports of aircraft engagements already."

Borakov felt his mouth going dry. "This is it, then?"

"It looks like it. I would advise you to get out, my friend. The first place it will spread is across into central Asia from the Gulf. You'll be in a prime war zone there. It could be in a matter of days."

Borakov and his family evacuated their home when American bombers begin attacking local targets. The town below was pummeled in the fighting that followed when the southern battle lines drew nearer, and the house was reduced to rubble by artillery fire. Later, when a counterattack came, the pocket that the ruin stood in was inundated by an emptying lake when a cruise missile carrying a tactical nuclear warhead destroyed the dam in the valley above.

CHAPTER EIGHT

It was as well that Kyal had thought to find a general store and equip himself with some warm clothing and sturdy boots before leaving Rhombus. His twinge of agoraphobia had passed, and the feeling of openness and freedom when he emerged from a twin-rotor chopper at Foothills Camp was exhilarating after the enclosed, artificial worlds of the *Melther Jorg* and *Explorer 6*, and the concentrated bustle of Rhombus. The only human habitation to be seen was the scattering of shacks and tents fringing the archeological excavations beginning a short distance away on one side of the airstrip. On the other, rolling wooded hills rose toward the distant peaks of the Caucasus, white with snow against a clear sky. Kyal had never seen snow before. The freshness of the breeze coming from the east was intoxicating. After consulting with the site office at the airstrip and obtaining a photocopy of a crude map of the area, he decided to postpone looking at the diggings until later and get some exercise for legs that hadn't been used enough for a while by hiking a few miles up into the hills. The sunbaked soil and rocks, and tall, slender Terran trees with their strange needlelike leaves were unlike any scenery on Venus. As he gained height and the vista below expanded, he began to think that perhaps he would stay on here until tomorrow. It was already becoming obvious that a week would be hopelessly inadequate for the kind of plans that he had envisaged.

After an hour or maybe more, he stopped to rest on the trunk of a fallen tree. Sitting there, he could make out the general form of the town that had stood in the valley below from the lines of the archeological cuttings and trenches. According to the notes that he had pulled from the net and read during the flight up, it had been attacked first by one side and then by the other in the Central Asian War, and the ruins that were left were submerged when a dam higher up in the valley that Kyal had followed was destroyed. The ensuing geological conditions proved unusually conducive to preservation, which was what had attracted the archeologists. Although the particular town that had stood here was abandoned because of the flooding, other towns destroyed in the Central Asian War had been rebuilt, only to be razed again in the even greater war that came later. Seemingly a continuation after a period of recovery, with some shifting of alliances, it had gone to even greater extremes, involving weaponry and combat in space. There were even some indications of its spreading to the Moon.

Kyal was beginning to feel cooler now that he had stopped climbing. He pulled the hooded parka closer around him over his sweater and stared down over the bare valley where a town had been, trying to picture in his mind the things that had happened here long ago. Large white birds with black markings were wheeling lazily over a stream winding a rocky course between deep banks of green. It was all so quiet and peaceful and tranquil now. Yet how many lives had ended horribly in this very place, screaming in terror and agony amid carnage, flames, noise, and violence that he was probably incapable of imagining? The folly and the waste of it all still sickened him.

The Terran Western civilization had emerged out of a confused pattern of rivalries and wars that the exohistorians were still far from being able to agree over. After being weakened by endless strife among themselves, the original core nations of Europe were invaded from the east by Russia, which had come to dominate a large part of Asia, and by America from across the ocean to the west. An enigma here was that America's principal partners in this were the same British whom the Americans had rebelled against and evicted not long before; but the British seemed to have had a history of fighting either against or alongside just about everybody at some time or another, so their far-flung empire probably expired from exhaustion.

Another conundrum was the Japanese, who while overrunning the Europeans' possessions in Asia were fighting the Americans, while the Americans were at the same time invading Europe in the west. Whatever the explanation of that was, the overall situation appeared to make the Americans and the Russians allies. However, they turned out at the end of it all to be ferociously opposed to one another, and world's main fear for some time became that of a major nuclear conflict between them, with the Europeans now aligned with America.

And the confusion didn't end there. After a series of escalating local conflicts, the big clash when it came was with a late but rapidly developing China—which had previously sided with the Americans and the Europeans against Japan.

By now, Kyal was not only chilly but getting hungry. In the last-minute rush to make the morning flight, he hadn't eaten anything yet that day. He stood up, waved his arms and stamped to get some circulation moving, took a last look around at the serenity where he had rested, and began the easier trek down. He was intrigued to see his breath condensing into a white stream of vapor. That never happened on Venus either.

Back down at the site of the town, he spent some time as he had intended, touring the archeological excavations and talking with some of the workers. One sector consisted of practically a whole street of unearthed shops that had yielded collections of items ranging from electronics devices and kitchen appliances to clothing, shoes, and children's toys. One of the walls had a door still attached, with several panes of glass intact.

From there, he followed a track to a repository back near the airstrip, where items were sorted and catalogued, and saw some examples of Terran jewelry and decorative art. The Terrans seemed to have been able to devote more of their lives to such things than was possible on Venus, where the harsher conditions made eking the essentials to staying alive a constant struggle. By comparison, the Terrans had been endowed with a garden capable of providing everything they needed in abundance. So did people compete and fight when they could have plenty for all, but work together and share in the face of scarcity? It seemed paradoxical.

Alongside the repository was a cabin devoted to classifying and copying written material, and treating precious originals for preservation. Although it was a trove of books and other documents, translation was not performed here, and Kyal had to content himself with browsing through some of the images that skillful electronic manipulation had extracted from the fragile ancient sheets.

He found some views of the town as it had been, with high square buildings and streets busy with people and amazingly many cars. It was bright and colorful compared to typical towns on Venus, and had evidently been laid out with more consideration given to space and aesthetics. Another consequence of having unlimited habitable land and more time to spare for leisure, Kyal supposed. There were other images of the Terrans themselves: groups posing; children laughing; heads and shoulders; faces smiling, frowning, looking solemn; what appeared to be prominent figures making speeches, shaking hands in the Terran custom. Kyal found that by being here, seeing the land they had lived in, contemplating things they had made and used, and now gazing at their likenesses, he was developing a growing fascination for this strange, lost race. On the one hand so impulsive, cruel, violent, irrational. On the other, so ordinary. Would it be possible, ever, to really understand them? Why did he care?

He realized suddenly that he was not alone. A young lady was standing at one of the other tables across the room, like him, poring over some of the sets of pictures. He wasn't sure if she had been there all along or had come in after he. He hadn't noticed anyone when he entered—but she could have been there and moved around from one of the other sections. If so, she moved quietly. She seemed to notice him at the same time as he did her. It was hardly a situation in which they could comfortably ignore each other. Kyal bowed his head by the correct amount. She inclined hers a fraction less—the female's privilege. They held each other's eye questioningly for a moment. "Kyal Reen," he said. "A pleasure, I'm sure."

"Lorili Hilivar. Full of *is*." Her manner was immediately easy and direct. The hint of a smile played on the corners of her mouth as her eyes interrogated him silently. "You don't waste very much time, Mr. Reen. Just down from orbit, and traveling the surface already. I'm suitably impressed."

Kyal reciprocated by permitting a grin. "We used the tanning booths on the ship. How can you tell?"

"Oh, the sweater and parka are new. The shirt is the floppy ship's fatigue kind that they issue on the trips out. The collar has a little *MJ* motif on it, and the *Melther Jorg* docked at *Explorer 6* yesterday."

"That's amazing, " Kyal answered in a distant voice. After the solitude of the morning, his mind hadn't fully adjusted to the sudden company, and he was still taking her in. She had rich black hair reaching to her shoulders with just enough of a curve not to look stark, and a pleasantly tapering oval face with a narrow chin, full mouth, and a slight turn-up to the nose. Her complexion was pale, whether naturally or from some cosmetic he couldn't tell, adding a contrast that set off her features and her hair.

"Where will you be heading eventually?" she asked.

"Luna, after a short break to cut my teeth down here. Checking out some unusual Terran constructions on Farside. They look as if they might be connected with space electromagnetics. That's what I do."

"That's interesting. I didn't know the Terrans were into things like that," she said.

"Neither did anyone else. That's why they're unusual."

Cordiality being satisfied, it would have been acceptable at this point for Lorili to return her attention to whatever she had been studying. She didn't, however, but continued looking at him with an easy directness that invited conversation. It was flattering but at the same time mildly disorienting. "I suppose it's my turn," he said, searching hopefully for a lead to reciprocate her power of divination. She was wearing an open gray coat over a lightweight tan sweater and work slacks; but it left him with nothing to go on other than her slight accent. "Gallendian?" he guessed.

"Close. Korbisan." The island nation off Gallenda was traditionally a friend of Ulange, where Kyal was from. "How about you?" she said. "Ulangean?"

He grinned a capitulation. "Right again. Have you been on Earth long?"

"A little over four months now. I came out on the *MJ* too."

"So what do you do here?"

"I'm a microbiologist—from the Korbisanian State Institute. Of Biochemistry and Cell Biology, that is. I do nucleic acid sequences and genes, and wet sticky things like that. Not like electromagnetics at all. Based at Rhombus."

"There was a microbiologist with us on the trip out who was going to Rhombus," Kyal said. "Gofel Sartzow."

Lorili nodded. "Yes, I know the name. We're expecting him. He'll be joining a group in the same section. But I don't think he's down from orbit yet. You must be a VIP. They usually get moved through first. Who will you be working under, Sherven?"

Well, Naseena seemed to have done all right, Kyal reflected; but it wasn't worth quibbling over. "Borgan Casselo," he replied. "He runs the physics part of the operation."

"Yes. I've heard he's very good."

It was rare for Kyal to feel so comfortable and at ease with a stranger so quickly. After just a few minutes they had fallen into using the familiar voice, and it seemed as natural as talking with an old friend like Yorim. "So what brings you out here among the relics and ruins?" he inquired. "Did you decide it was time to take a break too?"

"Yes, exactly that. A small group of us are doing the rounds. We've seen the mountains and the deserts, so we thought it was time to balance things out with some of the serious stuff."

"So where are they—the others?"

Lorili made a tossing motion with her head to indicate the door and the world outside in general. "Oh, they set off early to hike up and see the remains of a power plant and dam in a valley up above the town. Machines and pipes. As I said, I'm more molecules and culture dishes. Anyway, you get to see enough of the same people, shut up in labs and around the base all the time."

"Tell me about it," Kyal agreed with feeling. He pointed toward the image prints that she had been looking at. "What have you got here? Mind if I look?"

"Sure."

Kyal moved across to the other table. The pictures were from Terran wars: military aircraft in action; missiles being launched; defense works with dug-in artillery; some tanks very like the one he had seen the previous day. From the backgrounds and landscapes, they could have been from this area. He pursed his lips while he thought for the right words, but then saw from Lorili's expression that it didn't matter; she was waiting for it. "Unusual interests for a lady," he commented.

She paused for a moment before answering, as if she were weighing up the tack it might be best to take. "It isn't so much military things in themselves. More the spirit that they represent. Underneath all their madness, there was something fine about the Terran spirit, something . . . indomitable." She seemed to wait for a reaction. Kyal hoped he wasn't about to get another Progressive pitch. Lorili indicated the images with a wave. "Do you know about the war that destroyed the town that was here?"

"The Central Asian one. A little."

Lorili looked down at the images again and sighed. "The very tribulations that they inflicted on themselves forged qualities of courage, resilience . . . the ability to endure against hopeless odds in ways that few of us could match. That war began when the West moved to defend a tiny island over in the east that was being invaded by a giant power. All for honor and to protect the rights of the people who lived there. Don't you think that's wonderful?"

"I know some people think so," Kyal answered. He sought for a way to sound neutral without being too concessionary. "But then, I'm not sure how far you can trust their own accounts. It wasn't unusual for their governments and news media to lie to the people. They worked for powerful elites, not for the general good. Even in systems that claimed to be run by majority decisions, and where the majority clearly didn't believe them." He felt it needed spelling out, because such a state of affairs would have been unthinkable on Venus. Government positions were seen as privileged opportunities to serve the people on behalf of the heads of state. Few worse crimes were imaginable than abusing such offices for personal gain.

She eyed him for a moment longer and then dismissed the subject with a nod. "Maybe so, I suppose. But it's something to think about, isn't it?" If she had been sounding him out, she had better radar than Jenyn. Kyal decided that he was getting to like this person more and more already.

"Is there anywhere near here where you can get something to eat?" he asked. "It was an early start this morning. I haven't had breakfast yet."

"The airstrip chow shack is practically next door," she replied. "They've always got something going."

"Care to join me?"

Lorili summoned just the right touch of hesitation to be proper, but at the same time letting her eyes say she was glad he'd asked. "Sure," she replied simply.

They left the cabin and headed toward the huddle of buildings at the end of the airstrip. Some loaders with a mobile platform lifter were working amid a litter of crates, bales, and pieces of machinery. The supply chopper that Kyal had traveled in from Rhombus was just lifting off to make its return trip. As they walked, a silver metal pendant hanging outside Lorili's sweater flashed in the sun and caught Kyal's attention. It was in the form of the Venusian "katek" character, also a traditional symbol of good luck.

"I see you look on the optimistic side of life," he remarked, nodding toward it.

Lorili glanced down and smiled. "Oh, my mother gave it to me just before I left. You know how mothers can be. It was so I wouldn't forget them, and to remind me to look forward to coming back. Nice, isn't it?" The katek was also associated with homecoming.

"There's an old story about the katek," Kyal said. "Do you know it?"

"No . . . I can't say I've heard it. How does it go?"

"I heard it from my father a long time ago, when I was a boy. I'll tell you inside. Let's get some of that food first."

CHAPTER NINE

Kyal watched intently across the table as his father tied a line from a mast to the bowsprit of the model sailing schooner they had been making intermittently together for the past two months or more, and snipped off the end. His mother had explained to him how his father was always busy and in demand somewhere or other with his work, which made it all the more significant that he made the effort to spend times like these with his family. They were among the times that Kyal treasured the most. It still amazed him that a man's thick, strong fingers were able to perform such delicate tasks.

"There," Jarnor pronounced. "Just tight enough to be tensioned. You did a neat job with the rigging while I was in Korbisan."

"When are we going to paint the bow ornaments?" Kyal asked.

"Oh, that comes later. Patience is one of the most important virtues for boys to work at, you know."

Kyal moved a tray of cut parts that were still to be added, and inspected the drawing of the bow that was given in the plans. "A fish and a bird holding a katek between them," he said.

"Yes. Do you want to use the colors it says, or shall we pick our own?"

"I'd like more blue."

"Very well." Jarnor began sorting out the pulley accessories.

"And what do you think about gold for the katek?"

"I think that would look very nice. . . . Have you heard the legend of the katek, Kyal?"

"No. What is it?"

"Oh, it goes back far into the past. It's supposed to hold an important secret. One of the great mysteries that we philosophers and scientists debate all day and write long books about that most people have better things to do than worry about is life and how it began, and where we come from."

"Who? You mean humans?"

"Yes. All of us. Supposedly the answer is there, contained in the katek. But nobody has ever been able to decode it."

Kyal looked at the character with a new interest.

But nothing obvious jumped out and hit him. "I thought it was just something that people hang on doors or write on labels when they wrap presents," Kyal said.

"That too. It also stands for good luck. . . . Can you start painting these pulleys? They need to be matte black. It means be safe, and come home safely."

"Is that's why there's one in the bow emblem of the boat?"

"Yes, very likely that's the reason. It says something about life too, you know."

"How?"

"Oh, the importance of things that are trusted and familiar. You hear these people today who are in such a hurry to change things they don't understand. They think anything new and different is exciting and must be better. And sometimes it's true. But it's also true that things came to be the way they are for good reasons. You should judge people who try to sell you their ideas and theories the way you do a cook. It's what comes out of the pot that matters, not what he says he's going to put in."

Kyal reflected on it while he unscrewed the cap of the paint bottle. "Is that the same legend as the Wanderers?" he asked.

"Yes. According to the myth, it was supposed to have been the Wanderers who wrote the secret code into the katek. But then people forgot what it was."

"How does it go, again?"

Jarnor grunted and smiled despairingly. "The Wanderers were the earliest people, but they didn't like the ways of the world, so they went to live on the Sun. But the Sun was too hot, so they went to live on the stars. But the stars were either too cold, or too small, or too hard, or too bright. . . . Always there was something. Eventually they came to a Place of Death that was the worst of all, and so in the end they came back home."

"Before there was a moon," Kyal put in.

"So the story says. Froile was born later, out of hurricanes and floods, when the sky fell, and the seas moved over the land. During their travels, the Wanderers had annoyed a lot of inhabitants of other places. On their way home, they frightened a dog so much that he ran away. But the people they had annoyed caught it again, and they sent it after them as a watchdog over the world to make sure they stayed home." Jarnor picked up the plans of the schooner and unfolded them to study the next part. "So perhaps that's all the katek really means, but everyone is looking for something profound and complicated," he said. "Maybe it just means that when you've been everywhere and seen it all, coming home to the things you know isn't so bad after all."

CHAPTER TEN

The chow shack was a utilitarian affair of wooden tables and benches, where a cook deposited the offerings of the moment into warmed pots and dishes on a counter at one end, and the patrons served themselves. The fare was plain but appetizing, blending Terran with imported foods into concoctions that maybe one day would acquire names and be celebrated.

"No, I never heard that story," Lorili said again. "I gather nobody has ever figured out how to decode it?"

Kyal shrugged without looking up, the bulk of his attention, just for the moment, being taken up by the food. "Not as far as I know."

Lorili looked at him for a second before commenting, "You talk about your father fondly. You and he must have been close."

It took Kyal a moment to catch the implication. He hadn't said anything about Jarnor's passing on. So Lorili must have made the connection from his name—a reasonable inference, now that he thought about it, since Jarnor Reen had been known for his contributions to space electromagnetics. But she had refrained from saying anything, allowing Kyal the right to be himself, on his own merit, and not simply "Jarnor Reen's son." He accorded her the same respect by leaving it unsaid now.

"We were," he replied. "But all things have their span. He had a constructive and rewarding life and was appreciated during his time. That's more than many could say. He was a friend of Director

63

Sherven's, apparently. I only found that out myself yesterday. . . . But enough about me. Tell me more about you. What kinds of things are you finding out in microbio?"

Lorili finished her mouthful of food while considering how to answer. "Well . . ." she said finally. "Earth is more diverse in climate and geology. And it's a much older planet. Yet there's a strange thing about it."

Kyal completed it for her. "It only has quadribasic life."

She looked surprised. "I thought you were electrons and amps."

"Oh, somebody on the ship was talking about it."

Life forms on Venus, as any reasonably well-read Venusian would have known, fell into two broad classes that were distinguished by the number of nitrogenous bases available for the structure of their DNA: quadribasic (four base, comparatively rare) and hexabasic (six bases, common). The six-base structure was more versatile, able to specify a more complex coding system and hence, in principle, to blueprint a greater and more complex variety of plant and animal forms.

"So you know about the way things back home seem to be backward?" Lorili queried.

"As far as I know, hexa forms are the most common and should theoretically have more potential. But it's the quadri forms that you don't find so much that are more varied and advanced." The gap between the two groups was quite marked—although it would have taken a biochemist to appreciate it—and had mystified biologists since they first began sequencing giant molecules. The Venusians themselves were quadri.

"That's right," Lorili confirmed.

Kyal picked up her original point. "But it turns out that *all* Terran life is four-based. There are no six-base kinds at all."

"Exactly," she confirmed.

"Mm." Kyal tried to look businesslike about it, but the significance eluded him. As far as he could see, it was just one of those many apparently strange things that the universe turned up that could only be acknowledged and accepted. "Does anyone have any idea why, yet?" he asked.

"There are a lot of speculations . . ." Lorili hesitated for the briefest of instants, ". . . not all of them intellectually fashionable." She was testing him again. He decided to rise to it.

"Well, what can you say? It's just the way things are. Vizek knows best, I suppose." He met her eyes over the top of his mug as he sat back to sip his drink, challenging her to make an issue of it. He wanted to know at this early stage if he was dealing with someone who couldn't let it go. Charming and intelligent, maybe . . . but a fanatic was still a fanatic.

But she opted for a tactful withdrawal. "Maybe. We'll see what more turns up. But anyway, that's the kind of thing we're into."

Kyal was inwardly relieved. Yes, he would like to get to know her better if circumstances should move them in such a direction, he told himself. An obligation was also now on him to acknowledge the truce by changing the subject. "What are your plans from here?" he asked, returning to his meal.

"The group I'm with is divided. Some want to get back to Rhombus. Others are talking about detouring via the Himalaya plateau first. I've seen enough of mountains. I'd like to see something of the European cities, but I think I'm outvoted."

"That's exactly where I'm hoping to go. . . ." Kyal started to answer automatically but fell silent as an implication of what he was saying became clear. He paused to wipe his mouth with a chow shack paper towel. No, it was too outrageous a thought. They had only just met.

He looked up. Lorili's eyes had an impish light. "How long did you say you were down for?" she asked.

"A week. A Terran week, that is."

"I'm not due back in Rhombus until Tenday." Evidently some Venusians stuck to their own fourteen-day cycle. Back home, a longer working spell was preferred, followed by enough days off to go somewhere or do something useful. Lorili let things hang for a moment—just enough not to be indelicate. "What would you say to going our own way together?" She shrugged lightly. "Seems simplest to me. And eminently sensible."

A woman putting a proposition to a man? And she hadn't even asked if there was a Mrs. Reen back home, or some such. That clinched his suspicion.

For form's sake, Kyal made a pretense of having to mull over it, then grinned. "So long as I don't have to listen to any Progressive propaganda," he said. Better to be clear about that from the outset, he supposed.

She neither questioned, confirmed, nor denied anything, but took a phone from her jacket pocket and punched in a code. Before Kyal had fully registered what she was doing, he heard her say, "Hello, Iwon. How's it going? . . . Did you get to the dam? . . . Oh, just fine . . . Yes, very interesting. Look, I've decided on a change of plan. We've all got different preferences, and there's only a few days left. I've met someone here who has the same agenda that I was hoping for. Why don't we go separate ways for now, and I'll see you back at Rhombus on Tenday? . . . Of course I'm sure. . . . Well, we can always call each other about that, can't we? . . . Yes. . . . Not really. . . . I'm not sure yet. It depends on flights and things. I'll let you know. But if not, then I'll see you back in Rhombus. . . . Well, have fun there. . . . Whenever." She flipped the unit's cover shut and looked back at Kyal. "No problem," she announced.

CHAPTER ELEVEN

Kyal had intended giving Moscow, the former Russian capital city, a miss. It had been obliterated by nuclear bombs in the Central Asian War and never rebuilt thereafter. Hence there was little to be seen there other than a small geological drilling and weather station, and some scattered excavating to probe the ruins. But a supply ferry on its way there from Rhombus and due to make a stop at Foothills Camp was less than an hour away when Kyal checked, and a repair crew would be returning from Moscow to the central European region the following morning. Kyal called them, and yes, they would have room for two extra. The ferry's stop at Foothills Camp was a brief one, and Kyal and Lorili left aboard it before Iwon and the other friends had returned.

En route to Moscow, they put down again to drop somebody off at a small settlement of colonists at the site of what had been another Russian city called Volgograd, situated by a wide river. Apparently it had been the scene of large battle in the worldwide conflagration the historians were still trying to make sense of, that had happened before the Central Asian War. There was little to see, since it was getting dark by then. Kyal was beginning to wonder if there was anywhere on Earth that didn't have a battle associated with it from some era or another. Killing each other seemed to have been the Terrans' main preoccupation. There was certainly no denying that they became very proficient at it.

If Kyal was a VIP, the style of life that went with being a notable personage had changed markedly in the day that had elapsed since his coming aboard *Explorer 6*. The reception party at Moscow took the form of two site workers with a truck, and supper came as meat stew and bread in a prefab hut lit from a noisy motor-generator in an adjacent shed. But the chance to meet some of the field archeologists and geologists, and talk face to face with them around the stove until late in the night more than made up for the conditions. Kyal didn't particularly mind roughing it a little in any case. It felt like some of the expeditions to wilder parts of Venus in his student days. Lorili seemed to thrive on it.

The drilling station was one of a chain strung across northern Asia and the top of the Americas. The huge deposits of graded sediment, silt, amorphous muck forming a band of hills, plains, and swamps around the polar regions, filled with the fossil remains of millions of animals, told of flooding on an immense scale, in which the oceans had surged poleward and then retreated. The most likely explanation seemed to be one or more close encounters between Earth and another massive object—and not too far distant in the past. Significant in this connection was the fact that legends and myths going back to the earliest period of recorded Terran history contained vivid descriptions of skies filled with fiery objects and spectacles of violence unlike anything seen in the present heavens that were consistent with just such happenings. There were even suggestions that the most terrifying and destructive encounters have been with primordial Venus! However, the Terrans of later times refused to accept what Venusians already had no trouble seeing, and wrote it all off as fanciful invention.

Investigations into these and related matters indicated that the old Venusian myths about Froile appeared to have substance after all. Terran astronomic records showed that at the time of their presence on Earth, Venus had no moon. Also, its rotation had been slow and retrograde then, giving it a day that was longer than its orbital period—in contrast to the current rotation giving it a little over seventy-five days to its year.

Such speeding up as a young planet aged was consistent with the accepted electrical model of Solar System dynamics. Since planets carried electrical charge, any small initial rotation would constitute a current that would produce a magnetic field, which according to calculation would interact with the solar field in such a way as to enhance the effect and spin the planet faster. The general observation that planetary rotation rates correlated with magnetic field strengths seemed to support it—although Mars stood out as an anomaly. A newer proposition was that the capture of Froile some time after the Terrans became extinct was responsible, but it was hard to see how an object that small could have imparted the required angular momentum into a body the size of Venus, and the suggestion had not found many takers.

What had come out of it all, however, was that Froile could have caused the kind of havoc that the old Venusian legends implied when they talked about a time of hurricanes and floods, the seas moving over the land, and the sky falling. If, then, the much earlier Terran catastrophe had indeed involved Venus, the scale of the devastation and the terror induced by it were probably beyond the powers of imagination. The wonder, surely, was that anyone could have survived it at all.

CHAPTER TWELVE

There wasn't a lot of time to be spent at Moscow. They did drive out with some of the drilling engineers the first thing the next morning, but the operations were concerned primarily with obtaining samples of materials melted in the nuclear blasts, offering little to see. The surroundings were bleak, somber, and depressing, the feeling perhaps intensified by the knowledge that millions of people had been wiped out here, along with their city. They were happy enough to return by mid-morning to catch the small, twin-motored service plane taking the repair crew back to Europe.

The "room for two extra" turned out to be a couple of folding jump seats in the rear compartment of the craft, cramped between toolboxes, cable reels, and assorted gear and tackle. Soon they were flying above a monotonous landscape of gray plains and marshes cut into patterns by sullen, winding rivers. Even the sixth of the planet that was supposedly land looked to be half water, Kyal thought to himself. Lorili was less talkative today, staring out at the landscape, absorbed in her own thoughts. Fatigue was no doubt taking its toll. Kyal pulled the hood of his parka up around the back of his head as a cushion and settled himself as comfortably as it was possible to get against the bulkhead and the wall ribbing. Within minutes he was dozing.

✧ ✧ ✧

Living things had fascinated Lorili since an early age. One factor that had no doubt contributed was her growing up on the island of Korbisan, in Venus's northern mid-temperate region. "Temperate," that was, as the term was understood there. Hot and humid, covered with dense vegetation, and teeming with life, it would have qualified as tropical by Terran standards. The equatorial zone was too hot and dark from heavy, ever-present cloud cover for comfort. Life there was sparse due to sulfurous gases and pollution from liquid and vapor hydrocarbons, and it was generally avoided.

From their observations of the complexity of life and the intricacies of the universe, Venusians had always considered it obvious that the reality they found themselves part of owed its existence to a powerful creative intelligence of some kind, which made its presence felt through the very functions of consciousness and spirituality and life. If it acted for anything that could be understood as reasons, they would be its own reasons. Since there was no obvious way of knowing what such reasons were, or of doing much about them in any case, the sensible reaction seemed to be to accept that the span of existence called life was there, and get on with making the best of it. Although various speculations were sometimes aired, nobody claimed to really know the nature of the implied intelligence, its motives, the extent of its powers, its mental state, or much else about it. It was simply acknowledged as an organizing principle that defied the physical laws of inanimate forces and matter and caused impossible things to happen. In everyday speech it was referred to in such vague, general terms as "the Scheme of Things," which in latter times biochemists unraveling the genetic codes carried by the immense nucleic acid molecules had whimsically personified as "the Great Programmer." Sometimes, as when dealing with children or simply as a convenient shorthand, it was given the name "Vizek."

The Terrans had arrived at similar conclusions too. But in following their fashion of molding reality to suit their wishes, they had taken things to an absurd extreme by projecting their own fears, desires, likes, and dislikes into various forms of divine beings that concerned themselves with day-to-day human affairs, and judged, rewarded, or punished them as if the universe existed for that sole purpose. The cults founded on these beliefs proved an effective means of social control, enabling a few to exercise power and control over the many. A number of Venusian exohistorians, pondering skeptically on the discrepancies they uncovered between the ideals the cults preached and the reality of how they behaved, were led to wonder just how sincerely the professed beliefs were held. Strangely, it had never seemed to concern more than a minority of Terrans.

Venusians accepted that some restraint on individual behavior was necessary too, of course—but as a practical, common-sense aspect of making communal societies workable, not out of obedience to some supernaturally handed-down law to be coercively enforced. To Venusians, external conformity obtained through coercion was meaningless and in the end, self-defeating. Behavior that emerged freely from following their own internally adopted standards was what said something worthwhile about people. Politeness, a mindfulness for decorum, and respecting others through observance of simple social etiquette were examples.

Along with the Venusian worldview came the generally noncontroversial notion that the immediately apprehended material aspect of reality represented just a part of something vaster. Although some theorized on such things as the possible nature of the rest of it, and whether consciousness of some kind continued beyond death, the prevailing attitude was that, as with anything else, things happened in their own time and they would all find out soon enough. Lorili had never been particularly interested, having a more practical outlook on life that she brought also to biological matters.

In this connection, there was one aspect of Terran belief systems that intrigued her. With their characteristic compulsion to polarize around extremes, they had reacted to the irrationalities and antics that went with humoring their vengeful, imaginary gods by constructing an ultrapurist concept of science that insisted everything could be accounted for in terms of material phenomena capable of being observed and quantified, and denied the reality of anything else. Not surprisingly, this brought them into conflict with the cults and politics based on anthropocentric gods; in fact, some Venusian historians were of the opinion that irreconcilable differences between the two camps had been at the root of most of the Terran wars.

While such an outlook might have been overly rigid and restricted by Venusian norms, it had led the Terrans to a theory of life originating and developing via purely naturalistic means that, whatever else might be said, was striking in its originality. Lorili wasn't sure how far, if at all, she was convinced by it yet. But it had an audacity and appeal that made it irresistible as an object of study.

She had always been motivated by curiosity about new hypotheses and an inclination to test them by experiment. Also, she had to admit to a certain delight in prodding institutions that were getting too staid, and challenging them to stir themselves not simply to seeking new discoveries—which happened of their own accord anyway, when the time was right—but to entertain new *ideas*. It followed that by instinct and nature, she had become attracted to the Progressive movement. It wasn't so much a case of believing it could achieve the things its proponents claimed, or opposing the detractors who said it couldn't work. She didn't know. None of them knew. That was the whole point. As with the questions that guided her experimental designs in the lab, it was a new idea that made her curious enough to want to find out.

The more scientifically inclined among the Progressives quickly absorbed Terran-inspired ideas of the natural evolution of life into the philosophical underpinnings of the movement. It gave them a means of questioning the traditional notion of existing as parts of some vaster, unintelligible scheme, and advancing instead the claim of being accidental products of the universe, unconstrained by any role, free to assert themselves to whatever extent they were capable of achieving. If the traditional views could be wrong about something as fundamental as this, they could be wrong about a lot of other things too, which would legitimize much of what the Progressives had been saying. As a professional, Lorili appreciated that emotional appeal could have no bearing the scientific fact of the matter, in the way that some of the Progressive campaigners seemed to imagine. But she couldn't deny an irreverent side to her nature that found it amusing to see traditionalist scientists spluttering and rushing to the defensive, instead of making lofty pronouncements.

She looked across at where Kyal was by now asleep, and smiled to herself. But here was one who seemed refreshingly different. He was definitely from a traditional type of background—what else with a father like Jarnor Reen?—raised to the correct mores and acknowledging his own conservatism. But unlike so many, he didn't seem to feel he had to be proving his case all the time. It was an uplifting feeling for Lorili to be not just tolerated by such a person but accepted unconditionally; to be recognized as a person with a right to be herself, as she chose, without being categorized or judged.

A rap sounded on the door leading forward to the crew cabin. It opened, and one of the repair team in coveralls stepped through, bringing a couple of mugs containing hot drinks. The noise and movement caused Kyal to stir and wake up.

"I thought you two people could use these. Sorry about the accommodation. We're less than an hour out now."

"Don't worry about it," Lorili told him. He handed the drinks over, nodded, and disappeared back up front, closing the door.

"Well, a fine amount of sightseeing you're doing," Lorili commented while Kyal rubbed his eyes and straightened up.

"There's not that much to see just at the moment. . . . Oh, my. . . ." Kyal set his mug on a ledge and flexed his arms. "I guess it all catches up with you after a while."

"Feel better?"

"Yes. I needed that. You just keep going and going, eh?"

"I didn't arrive here from Venus the day before yesterday."

"At least I've got the sense not to go straight off running up some Himalayan mountain somewhere, like Yorim."

"Is he the one who came out with you? The electrogravitics expert. A Gallendian, you said."

"Right."

"What's he like?"

"An old colleague. We've worked together for years. Solid and dependable. The kind of pal you'd trust anywhere. If I was going to climb a mountain the way they do with ropes and things, he's the kind of person I'd want to have at the other end."

Lorili asked, just to see how Kyal would take it, "Is he kind of traditional too?"

He endeared himself more by merely smiling in a way that seemed to say, *Good Try.* "He's easygoing with either side. What you might call an ideological eclectic. Rides with the flow. The pragmatic kind—and so are you deeper down, if you want my honest opinion. He says it was their fixation on ideologies that messed the Terrans up." Kyal paused to sip his drink appreciatively. "I need to call him. He'll be interested in that business about Froile that they were talking about last night."

"You mean whether it contributed anything to Venus's spin rate?"

"Right. That's more his department."

"How come you haven't called him before?" Lorili asked.

"What for? If he needed anything, I'd have heard."

"How do you know he hasn't fallen off a mountain?"

"If he has, then there wouldn't be any point in calling him, would there?"

Lorili shook her head despairingly. "Guys!"

Kyal grinned, took his phone from an inside pocket of his parka, and flipped it open. "It should make you feel appreciated. You see, we need females around. The reason there are two sexes has nothing to do with producing children. The biological part's easy. It's to *raise* them. They need a bit of both of us. . . . Ah, it looks as if we're through. They've certainly got the net up and working here."

"Can I say hello to Yorim?" Lorili asked.

"Sure. I was hoping you would."

"Really? Why?"

"Oh . . . just to see his face, I guess."

"What do you mean?"

"I'm supposed to be so traditional. Remember?"

CHAPTER THIRTEEN

The group that Yorim was with had changed their plans at the last moment and gone westward from Rhombus instead of east. Wearing an open bush shirt with britches to just below the knee, and a floppy-brimmed hat that a site worker he'd stopped to talk to had given him, Yorim was sitting not far from Jenyn near the top of an immense weathered pyramid. Naseena and Mowrak were clambering about a short distance above, around the summit. The others were below, exploring tunnels that had been discovered, going deep into the structure.

The pyramid was the largest of three, standing between flat grasslands that disappeared to the horizon in one direction, and a broad river running south to north in the other. According to the geologists, the area had been a dry desert once. A strange effigy of an animal in repose with a human head stood near the pyramids, which along with other constructions in the surrounding area dated from a civilization far older than the Western technological one. Many great cultures had evidently arisen on Earth and been gone and practically forgotten by the time of whatever the final calamity had been that ended all of them. It brought home just how young Venus was in comparison.

"You know what this reminds me of?" Yorim said, still squinting out at the distance. "You remember the guy that I was with in Rhombus, who went his own way, Kyal? He's an electropropulsion specialist. We went to some trials once, that they were conducting back home, of an experimental model of a high-power interplanetary drive they're talking about that would land you right down on the surface. But to do that, an incoming ship would need to lose its excess buildup of charge. The attractor they used was this kind of shape—a pointed artificial mountain. It focuses the field, like a lightning rod. You'd need something like that even more here on Earth. It's more active electrically than Venus. Doesn't have the same amount of cloud blanket to act as an intermediary distributor between space currents and the surface."

"Technical matters don't concern me," Jenyn answered. "My subject is languages."

Yorim hadn't formed an impression of him as the friendliest of people, but there was nobody else nearby to talk to just now. Jenyn seemed to be of the kind who never smiled, as if he preferred keeping others at a distance. Maybe he felt that setting expectations of amicability conferred an obligation to live up to them that put him at some kind of disadvantage. Yorim didn't particularly care why. "Is that what you were doing across in the Americas?" he asked.

"Yes. In the north they spoke mainly English, which is the principal language that we're studying."

"But England was over this side, right?"

"True. But more sources are turning up over there." Jenyn looked across at where Yorim was sitting. "It was a legacy from the times when the English were a nation of conquerors. They had a huge empire for a time." Yorim got the feeling he was looking for approval.

"If you say so," he replied noncommittally.

"Don't you think Venus could learn something from Earth?" Jenyn persisted. "How to stand up and fight for the right to be independent, for instance. To reject these constraints we have to live under, that say you can only be what the approval of others allows you to be." His tone moved a notch toward being conciliatory. "I would have thought that would appeal to someone like you. You seem like an independent kind of spirit. I'm pretty good at sensing a potential rebellious streak in people—the instinct to be one's own person."

Yorim showed his teeth, drawing a plant stem between them that he had picked up somewhere and was still chewing. "What are we talking about here, Progressives and traditionals? That kind of stuff?"

"Yes. It's no secret that I believe very strongly in the Progressives. Naseena said it in Rhombus, when we met."

Yorim shook his head. "You've got me wrong. I just get on with my life and try to enjoy it without spoiling anybody else's. There's probably some truth on both sides. I figure it will all come together in its own time without people needing to blow each other up the way the Terrans did."

Jenyn was not put off so easily. "You must be the adventurous type at heart, who has to test limits. Why else would you come to Earth?"

"I'm just on my way to Luna with Kyal to do a job. We're electromagnetics specialists. Propulsion and gravity. That's what interests me. The other business isn't worth getting tension sickness over. Life's too short."

"But it's not quite that simple, is it? Holding back when you could play a part is no different than working against us. Changes are going to happen. Will you be happy to just sit on the side and accept the freedoms and rights that others won?" Jenyn paused for an instant. "Maybe even died for?"

Yorim looked at him disbelievingly. "Died for? You're not seriously suggesting that what's going on back home could come to armed conflict?"

"Who knows?" Jenyn shrugged. "Anything is possible. Terrans wouldn't have shrunk from the thought of it. . . . But tell me, out of curiosity, if it did come to that, where would you stand, do you think?"

Yorim sighed and shook his head. "You just don't give up, do you?"

Jenyn's face remained serious. "The Terrans taught us never to give up. Study their history. In any social order, the top level eventually becomes complacent and idle, set in their ways. When that happens, somebody else displaces them. Venus is ripe for such a change today. So now it's our turn. But it took the Terrans to show us. They were attuned to it. They created a world of ideas, passions, crusade, and conflict that makes ours look tame and timid."

Yorim snorted. "Sure. And look what happened to it."

"We don't know that they were responsible for whatever happened."

"Oh, I wouldn't think there's much doubt about it from the way they were heading." Yorim smiled crookedly. "Tell me, just out of curiosity, if you had to, which way would you bet?"

Jenyn was unfazed. "Even if so, it doesn't change anything. Nothing worthwhile comes without its risks. They knew it too, but they were prepared to take those risks. They didn't shrink from them. The lives they lived, they lived to the full."

Just then, Naseena and Mowrak appeared, clambering carefully back down from above to rejoin them. "These constructions are incredible!" Naseena exclaimed as she perched herself by the pack that she had left earlier. "They're from long before there were any machines. How did they build them? And Whylen says there are others with even bigger blocks in them at other places."

Yorim sat back and stretched his legs, happy to change the subject. "Well, maybe it wasn't as difficult as you think," he said. "It looks as if Earth's gravity might have changed several times in the past. So things might not have been so heavy then."

Mowrak sat down heavily by Naseena and wiped perspiration from his forehead with a handkerchief. She was looking at Yorim as if what he had said was new to her. "Through electrical discharges in encounters with other bodies," Mowrak told her. "Gravity changes with charge." He looked at Yorim. "Is that right?"

"Uh-huh. Exactly. And we know Earth had more than its share of them. There are arc discharge scars all over the surface. They gouged some of its most spectacular features. And there were huge animals and birds in earlier ages that couldn't function here today. The gravity must have been less in earlier times."

Naseena finished drinking from a bottle of fruit juice that she had taken from her pack and passed it to Mowrak. He took a sip and offered it to Yorim. Yorim shook his head. Jenyn reached a hand out and nodded.

"The Terran scientists knew about them too. But they never made the connection," Mowrak said.

Yorim shrugged. "Well, that was Terrans, wasn't it?"

"I wonder what made them that way," Naseena mused.

"Trapped in deductive logic," Yorim said. "It can't tell you what's true, only what has to follow from your assumptions."

"You have to experiment," Mowrak supplied. "That's the only way to know what's true, what works, and what doesn't. Call it experience."

Yorim looked pointedly in Jenyn's direction. "But the Terrans made everything follow from principles that couldn't be questioned. They got hung up on ideologies that became more real than the reality in front of them, and ended up fighting wars over them." Even as he spoke, he wished he'd let the subject lie, but the gibe had been irresistible. He saw Jenyn squaring to pick it up again . . . and then the phone in Yorim's shirt pocket chimed and saved him. He pulled it out, snapped it open, and acknowledged. The caller was Kyal.

"Say!" Yorim glanced around at the others. "It's Kyal—the guy you met in Rhombus. So how's it going? Where are you?"

"Across in what they called Central Europe. It's all a bit funereal, but educational. How are the Himalayas?"

"Oh, we had a change of plan and ended up going the other way."

"Oh. . . . Okay, I guess. So where are you?"

"At the southern end of the Mediterranean. There are some fantastic constructions here. In fact I'm sitting on the top of one. They remind me of the discharge attractor that we worked on at Dakon—but much bigger."

"You're not telling me the Terrans had field riders?"

"I doubt it. These things date back to long before the Western culture. Nobody's sure what they were. Mowrak thinks they might have been some kind of religious monument. There must have been a huge amount of work in them, though. Let's see if I can get you a shot of the one next to us. . . . There, are you getting it? The one we're on is even bigger."

"Wow! Looks like you found yourself some mountains after all."

"And sun and beaches too. But haven't I always told you Vizek works for me? So what's new with you?"

"That was really what I called about. We were up north at Moscow yesterday, and met some people who said a few things about Froile that you should hear. . . ."

"We?"

"Yes. That was the other thing. I've a friend here that I met after I left Rhombus. She's heard all about you and wants to say hello."

Yorim made no attempt to conceal a smirk. In fact he deliberately emphasized it. "*She?*"

"Quit it. Her name's Lorili. Here."

Yorim murmured at the others, "He's met a friend. They're up in Europe somewhere." Then louder, "Lorili? Hi, how are you doing? . . . Yes, this is he. I just can't let Kyal out of my sight for a day, can I? . . ."

A few yards away, Jenyn had caught the name and was staring across fixedly.

CHAPTER FOURTEEN

They were walking among the ruins of what had been a major metropolis on the western side of Europe. It had not been devastated by war or buried by time, but decayed gradually into a broken landscape of overgrown concrete and remnants of walls, among which jagged pinnacles of concrete and twisted steel clawed their way skyward like fingers in the final spasms of somebody drowning. In his mind, Kyal tried to picture the city of life and lights that once had been, as he had seen in the images gleaned from faded Terran prints. Moving through the avenues of crumbled paving and mounds of rubble, he almost expected to see ghosts rising of the crowds who had flocked in thousands along boulevards of busy stores and the impossible congestion of mass-produced automobiles that anyone from schoolchildren to geriatrics had driven in the carnival of carefree mayhem that was their way of living. But all that disturbed the silence of the encroaching trees and weeds were birds and the movements of other curious animal life, evidently devoid of fear of humans.

In front of them was part of an immense steel arch that had once formed the base of a tower of girders and latticework dominating the city, now lying scattered and corroding amid the undergrowth of surrounding trees.

"So what was the attraction in coming to Earth?" Kyal asked. "A change from life's regular, boring routine? You hear that a lot from women. I suppose it's understandable in a way."

Lorili gave him a reproachful look. "Life doesn't get bo*ring*. People let themselves get bo*red*. I've never found it short of interesting things. . . . But very well, yes, I suppose there might be some truth in that. Mother was the traditional image, shaping her life to her own choosing: a few friends and activities outside the home that she pottered around with, but firstly dedicated to the family."

"She was the one who gave you the katek, right?" Lorili was still wearing it, tucked inside her sweater. It was warmer here, and they had come without jackets. They had found their way the previous day to a small experimental farm by the river upstream from the ruins, where colonists were trying to recreate the strains of domesticated grass that had supplied much of the Terran diet. Such food was unknown on Venus. The main vegetable foods there were tubers, fruits, and various legumes.

"Yes. . . ." Lorili hesitated. "There was another reason too. You ought to know, I suppose. I was involved in one of those relationships that can make you lose all common sense and reason until it all goes wrong. Have you ever been in that situation? Is it the same with men?"

"I know the kind of thing you mean," Kyal said. He wasn't sure how to answer the direct question. He had married at a fairly early age, soon after graduating. But the meeting of minds that followed hadn't lived up to the promise that seemed implied from the meetings of epidermises, and after a few years they had agreed to call it a day. Since then he had tended to focus mostly on his work. Typical engineer, he supposed. "What went wrong?" he asked.

"Oh. . . ." Lorili jerked her head briefly, as if shaking of the remnants of a bad dream. "He was tyrannical . . . one of those control fanatics who has to prove he can make you do everything his way, even when it doesn't matter. He was the one who got me involved with the Progressives. I was intrigued and infatuated with the idea, but I confused it with the person. He wouldn't let it go when I said it was over. It was a bad time all round. When the Institute offered me a place to come here and study Terran biochemistry, I took it."

Kyal waited, but she didn't volunteer any more. He didn't want to press. "What does your dad do?" he asked.

"Did. He's retired now. A solid and respectable ex-maintenance administrator of roads and bridges. He goes to his club on

Froileday, plays hegely with the same friends every other weekend, thinks the Progessives will be the ruin of all of us, and has unshakable confidence that Vizek arranged everything the way it is for reasons that will work out for the best in the end. And before you ask, one older sister, who's a teacher. A brother the same age—they're twins—a hydrocarbons extraction engineer. He spends his time in appalling places in the Smog Belt, building plants and sinking pipes. And a younger brother who's a musician. He plays a full-key polychord. He would love to have seen that Terran instrument back at Rhombus that you told me about." Lorili turned, spreading her arms. "And there it is, potted: the wild, exciting saga of the Hilivars of Korbisan."

They had come to the scene of some workings that had evidently been going on earlier, around the opening to a shaft cleared beneath fallen masonry and dead trees. A sign with an explanatory caption left by the archeologists marked it as an entrance to the Paris Metro system.

"You know, maybe you shouldn't dismiss it all too lightly," Kyal said. "The Terrans had all this, yet look how they ended. We may have had less of a world to work with, but our ways of getting along with each other seem to make more out of what there is. It wasn't through people like your control fanatic forcing his own ways on everyone else. It was people like your folks all doing what they did as well as they were able, because they knew they all depended on each other."

Lorili was nodding before Kyal finished speaking. "I wasn't meaning to sound unappreciative of things like that. Just making the point that doing things the way they've always been done, for no other reason, can stop you finding a better way. . . . But how about you? I'm familiar with the name but not the family history. Are there any other Reens?"

"A few cousins and such, but I was an only son," Kyal answered. "There's even less to tell a story about, really. The usual student stuff—physics, and then propulsion engineering. An attempt at marriage soon after that showed me I wasn't very good at it. Some work with space contractors that involved a few flights. Accepted by the International Academy of Space Sciences. Then here—the first time truly off-planet."

"Isn't your mother alive either?"

"No. She died less than two years before Jarnor did. They were very close and devoted. I often think that had something to do with his going downhill as rapidly as he did."

"My father would say Vizek works for what's best," Lorili said.

They moved on, away from the shaft opening. A brown four-legged creature with white patches and large eyes that had come out from some greenery to investigate them from a distance changed its mind and retreated. Kyal glanced at Lorili curiously.

"Is there anything you don't ask questions about?" he asked her.

"It's supposed to be a healthy sign. Why?"

"Even the Great Scheme of Being that we play a part in?"

Lorili took a few seconds to compose a reply. "I think the Terran theory is interesting," was the most she would concede.

"How does that go? You mean this business about matter assembling itself into living things accidentally?" Personally, he thought it was preposterous, but he left it at that. He didn't want to sound like another control freak.

"The possibility that purpose might be an illusion projected by the intelligent beholder," Lorili replied. "What if they were right, and in time, everything will turn out to be explainable in purely natural terms?"

"Doesn't it sound more like another case of faith in something they'd already made their minds up about?" Kyal suggested. He knew the Progressives were attracted to the idea.

"I didn't take it seriously until more of the Terran science was translated," Lorili answered. "They had it all figured out. It was fresh and exciting, like the air here. A whole new way of looking at something, that showed just how stifled we've let ourselves become, bogged down in old ideas."

As an electromagnetic space propulsion specialist Kyal didn't feel so bogged down in old ideas compared to Terrans, but he let it pass. He'd looked at some of the Terrans' arguments too, but been unimpressed. It was common knowledge that all living organisms possessed a limited capacity to adapt to stress and change—given the nature of real-world environments, they would hardly have been viable otherwise. But the whole Terran theory was based on hypothetical extrapolations of the principle that strained credulity and had never been observed in attempts to accelerate the process experimentally. But once they had settled on the dogma that only a naturalistic explanation was permissible, it was the only theory they had.

"So if life results from a selected series of accidents, how do we and Terrans come to resemble each other so closely?" Kyal asked. It was one of the standard criticisms. "Not even Progressive naturalists could accept that amount of coincidence from two different, isolated biosystems, surely." Traditionalists had no problem with it. Maybe it was even to be expected. Having produced a system that worked well enough in one place, why would Vizek do things any differently in another?

"Suppose we're not two isolated biosystems, the way it's assumed," Lorili replied.

"How else could it be?"

"Suppose we're genetically related ancestrally."

That was a new one for Kyal. "How?" he asked her again. "The timescales don't match. The Terrans were extinct long before there was life on Venus."

"Oh, I didn't mean as direct ancestors. But evolved from the same genetic codes. Organic material is detected everywhere you look in space. There are many mechanisms that could transfer it from one body to another. I meant that Venusians and Terrans could both have originated from the same seed material somehow."

"Hm . . ." Kyal had to think about it. Lorili stopped to pick a luxurious, bell-shaped flower of yellow and purple growing among some leaves and grass, and held it up admiringly.

"Isn't it gorgeous? And oh, the scent! Try it."

"But if that's the case, and you're still selecting accidents, wouldn't you expect them to have diverged more?" Kyal asked finally.

"I don't know. Maybe that's what we should be researching instead of making our minds up about in advance." She stole an amused look at him. "Who's doing it now?"

"Okay, you got me." He thought some more while they walked on. "But it still wouldn't work. Venus is too young. The kind of mechanism the Terrans talked about was driven by random mutations of the genome that took enormous amounts of time to work through and be selected as established traits. A lot of Terrans weren't happy that it could have produced them even in all the time Earth had. Venus had a lot less."

"You do know something about it, then," Lorili observed.

"I said I'd always been interested in Terran things."

Lorili sighed. "Yes, you may have a point. But it's too early for conclusions yet. There's a lot of uncertainty about timescales and whether the Terrans' got it right. The rates of change that we infer are much faster than what their science taught. And then again, another possibility is that there could be some other aliens out there somewhere that we're both descended from."

"Are you serious?"

"I'm just saying that there are other answers that are consistent with the idea. You can't rule it out as impossible. . . . Anyway, what about that legend of the Wanderers that you told me the other day? Doesn't it talk about our ancestors coming from the sky?"

"Yes. And it also says they rose from the dead."

"How do you figure that?"

"The last home they tried was the Place of Death. How else would you read it?" Kyal clapped her lightly on the shoulder as a way of conceding that he was being facetious. "But seriously, you have to admit that the enthusiasm the Progressives have for all this is fueled by other factors too. It appeals to their political agenda. But that's not science, is it? It's making the case for the wrong reasons."

"The Terrans thought they had evidence for it," Lorili said.

"Well, we know what they said they thought," Kyal agreed. "But it's like the reasons they told the people for why they had to have wars. Can you accept it at face value?"

"In science? Are you saying they might have distorted it deliberately? Lied about it? That would be inconceivable." Lorili sounded genuinely shocked.

Kyal couldn't contain a laugh. "On Venus, maybe. But this was a different world. Be honest yourself, now. Don't you think the Progressives' picture of Terrans might be a little fanciful and oversimplified?"

"In what way do you mean?"

"You can't assume the same primary values we hold to, that set the tone for all else. The Terrans elevated self-serving above everything, regardless of the cost to others. What else were their wars all about? They saw buying and selling as the sole purpose of existence. Things that were desperately needed didn't get done if they weren't profitable to the minority who controlled things. And yet these are the qualities that the Progressives are saying they want to import to Venus. Well, I can't help having reservations. Even if our ways do seem a bit stodgy for some, they've proved pretty robust and benign compared to a lot of things that happened on this planet. I think we should think long and hard before risking an erosion of our values."

"I think maybe I hear a little of Jarnor Reen speaking here," Lorili said.

Kyal nodded candidly. "Very likely so. He used to say that the young and the restless would spend their energies better by getting off the planet and into space. That probably had a lot to do with why he pushed so strongly for the Earth exploration mission."

"It could be a way of getting the awkward ones out of the way, too," Lorili observed. Kyal wasn't sure how serious she was being. But she could certainly give as well as she got. She glanced across as if checking his reaction. "Do you not think that their way would permit better rewarding of ability and talent to those who deserved it?"

Kyal made a face. "How can anyone be sure? Well, we know what they *said*. But the ones who received the rewards would have more control over what people were told. And of course *they* would say that. But to those who didn't benefit from any rewards, it would look like exploitation by a parasitical minority, wouldn't it? So you get the periodic crises, wars, and revolutions. On Venus we've got the opposite. We're raised to believe that the most valuable way you can use your talent is serving the community. I don't think that's such a bad system."

Lorili sniffed, evidently not conceding anything, but at the same time not needing to take it further at that point either. "Do you think you're perhaps being a bit unduly cynical?" she said.

Kyal replied in a way that accepted the truce. "It all depends on how you conjugate the verb. *I* am healthily skeptical; *you* are suspiciously cynical; *he* is psychotically paranoid." Lorili laughed delightedly and squeezed her arm through his. "Healthily skeptical is what seekers after reliable knowledge are supposed to be," Kyal pointed out.

A tone sounded from his phone. He took it from his shirt pocket and answered. It was Borgan Casselo, calling from orbit aboard *Explorer 6*. "Master Reen. How are things down there? To your satisfaction, I trust?"

"I'm honored that you should concern yourself. It's proving very welcome after the voyage."

"Where are you now?"

"In the western region of Europe—the city that was called Paris. There's lots to think about here."

"I have been there. I understand your sentiments." Casselo pause for an instant. "Kyal, I've heard from Aluam Brysek at Triagon. He confirms that there are large underground spaces there as the scans indicated. But it seems you were right. They don't appear to be connected with power generation. I want to go out there and see things for myself. We have a transport leaving *Explorer 6* for Luna tomorrow. If you and Fellow Zeestran can arrange your schedule to catch a shuttle up from Rhombus, we'll be able to travel on to Triagon together."

"He's elsewhere just at present, but I'll call him right away and see if we can coordinate things."

"It shouldn't be a problem. Shuttles up from Rhombus are pretty frequent.

Vereth was waiting again to meet Kyal and Lorili when they arrived at Rhombus. Yorim's group had also returned from the Mediterranean coast. The vessel that would take them on to Luna was already docked at *Explorer 6*, and they were on a tight schedule to make the shuttle up. In fact its liftoff was being held at Sherven's request. Vereth had a site car waiting to rush Kyal straight across from the airfield to the launch service area. Lorili went with them to see him off. Yorim was already there, waiting.

Kyal just about had time to say, "Well, so you two meet face-to-face finally. Lorili, this is Fellow Zeestram. Yorim, Madam Hilivar."

"Hello, Yorim. Delighted."

"Lorili. My pleasure."

"Gentlemen, my apologies but they are waiting to close the door," Vereth interjected anxiously.

Kyal and Lorili looked at each other for a second or two, and on the same impulse hugged each other hurriedly—and awkwardly; Kyal was holding his bag.

"Stay in touch," Kyal murmured.

"Of course I will."

"And thank you for all your help, Vereth," Kyal said as he turned to follow Yorim through the gate to where a van was waiting to take them out to the pad.

"My privilege."

Lorili watched the van cross the open boundary area and waved after it halted, even though she couldn't make out their figures in the clutter of gantries and service structures around the nose of the shuttle protruding from its silo. As soon as the van had cleared the blast zone, the shuttle slid upward amid a wreath of flame accompanied by a roar the rolled over the base, and disappeared skyward balanced on a column of light.

She turned away, finally, and saw that Vereth had been waiting a short distance back. "Can I offer you a ride back into town?" he said.

"Oh! You're still here, Vereth. I hadn't realized. Yes. . . . Yes, that would be appreciated. Thank you."

"My privilege."

As they moved away through the mix of people toward the entrance outside which Vereth had parked, a lean, muscular figure with copper-red hair who had followed Yorim emerged from behind a pillar on the far side of the hall, where he had been watching. The name had not been just a coincidence, Jenyn now knew. If she was here in Rhombus, she would be working somewhere in the biochemistry labs. It would be a straightforward matter to find out the rest.

CHAPTER FIFTEEN

Lorili felt deliciously—in her imagination she would have liked it to be outrageously—*chic* in a close-fitting sleeveless navy dress cut daringly low, and her black hair worn loose. The image captured the spirit of the new wave of youth, wild and independent, shaking itself free from stuffiness and suffocation.

Jenyn was the Man of the Moment. The party was being thrown by the local chapter of the Progressives to celebrate his appointment as editor-in-chief for *The Commentator*, an influential Korbisanian news journal noted for its opinion columns on public affairs. The move would be a significant step forward in popularizing and advancing the Progressive political platform. All of their close friends from within the movement were there, along with numerous faces of campaign helpers from outlying areas that Lorili had not met personally before. The dance music was wild and free too, stirring them into the swaying, twirling abandon of things like the "catwalk" and the "rotary," which threw aside patterns and steps that bewildered seniors had learned for generations. A plentitude of high spirits was in evidence, of both the temperamental and the liquid kind.

Muso, the self-appointed clown for the evening, emerged unsteadily from the throng and raised his glass in Jenyn's direction. "I drink his health. Our future commentator in *The Commentator* . . . Have you got a job saved for me there, J?"

"When I get them to add a comic-strip section," Jenyn said. Others who were nearby roared delight and approval. Lorili clung more tightly to his arm.

"I think we should all drink a toast to Lemaril Aedua," another of the group cried out. "With ice . . ." In the highest of Venusian traditions. "To . . . to . . . avarice and corruption!"

"Avarice and corruption!" they chorused.

"May they continue to serve us well," Jenyn said solemnly.

Lemaril Aedua was the editor of a rival paper and had been Jenyn's leading rival, tipped as the front-runner when word trickled around the Korbisanian publishing grapevine that the head-ed slot at *The Commentator* was being vacated. An outsider in Jenyn's position would not normally have ranked highly as a contender, but his case had gained enormously when Aedua's practice was exposed of buying works from contributors who agreed to giving her kickbacks in the form of a cut of the payments they were made. It was hardly coincidental that the Progressives had been instrumental in uncovering the facts. Jenyn had exploited the politics of the situation skillfully, and his recognition as a champion of integrity and honesty was now confirmed.

"It's unbelievable that it could happen in a reputable journal!?" Lorili heard somebody say behind her. "Scandalous. What did Aedua have to say when it came out?"

"Oh, she denied it. Totally brazen. But testimonials were produced. Jenyn will soon restore the standards there. You can count on it."

A man approached them that Lorili recognized vaguely as being from somewhere within the trade. "You've got a great opening for your Progressives now," he said to Jenyn. "And I know that someone like you isn't going to let the chance go by. So what's first on the agenda, eh? What are you going to be pushing us for?"

Jenyn answered without hesitating. "The widening of academic entry standards by direct grant awards. Basing it on somebody's ideas of performance is too restrictive. Who knows how much ability is squandered as a consequence?"

"Hm. Of course, it would extend your base of popular support a lot as well, now, wouldn't it?"

"Yes, there is that too," Jenyn agreed evenly.

"But won't it lower standards in the long run? Open positions to bribery and favoritism?"

Lorili had heard Jenyn answer this one many times. "It is anyway, by those who decide what qualifies as merit. So the process is hidden," Jenyn replied. "This way things will be out in the open, where they can be controlled by responsible authorities."

"We need to go electronic, Jenyn," one of the campaign workers urged, joining them. "Become a voice all over Venus, not just on pages that intellectuals read."

Jenyn had in fact been thinking in just this direction. However, he didn't involve himself personally in technical matters. "Do you have any ideas on how to go about something like that?" he asked the speaker.

"It's what I do. I've got lots of ideas."

"Good ones too," somebody threw in.

Jenyn eyed him for a second or two. "Let's talk," he said. "But this isn't the time. Call me in the next day or so. What's your name?"

"Horan Ikles."

"Ikles," Jenyn repeated, nodded, as if committing it to memory. "We should try to develop a dialog with the scientists involved in the Terran discoveries," he said, addressing Ikles but speaking loudly enough to take in the company in general. "They use electronic media all the time. It will spread everywhere eventually. The history of Earth that's starting to unfold is fascinating. It was a world of Progressive ideas."

"I read somewhere that they had a much greater diversity of languages than we do," a young woman the other side of Jenyn said.

"Jenyn is broadening his study of Terran languages, precisely to become better acquainted with their ideas," Lorili told her.

"That's wonderful!"

"You have to go to the original sources," Jenyn said.

Lorili thought he looked resplendent and debonair in a semi-formal evening suit, with his rugged features and red hair. Life for her had taken some exciting turns recently. She could count on a successful career ahead as a cell biologist, and had been accepted by State Institute as a research project leader. Now she was acquiring some interesting social and political connections, along with a forceful, charismatic man to add some zest to it all. The contrast with the life she had grown up knowing at home couldn't have been sharper. She was still fond of them all, and they would doubtless continue to get along well enough; but a hidden part of herself seemed to be awakening that delighted in anything new and shocking. She looked at Jenyn again as he talked to the group, pretending not to notice the envious looks that she caught on the faces of one or two of her friends. He was Man of the Moment; and Lorili was Woman of the Future.

Later in the evening they found a moment alone together, when Jenyn steered them to the buffet table to sample some of the snacks and delicacies. They were both feeling heady and exuberant, intoxicated as much by the mood and the atmosphere as by the liquor. She sensed him looking at her thoughtfully while she ran an eye over the table's offerings. "You know, you're just what my life needs to make the image complete," he said.

She turned her head. "Well . . . I'm glad. What else should I say?"

He leaned closer, still looking at her. His voice fell. "This needs to be a full-time thing. I can't afford any divided loyalty."

"What are you talking about?"

"Birds fly when they're ready. You have to move away from that house. Let's set up together. I'll show you the person you really are, and make you everything you can be. But it won't happen while half of you is still in that old world."

"I've never heard anything so outrageous!" Lorili's tone was jocularly reproachful. Inwardly, she was thrilled. But it would have been unbecoming for a lady to seem too eager. "We'll just have to wait and see," she said. But she could read in his eyes that he knew already he had won. "Shall I get us some more drinks?"

CHAPTER SIXTEEN

The central complex of the original Terran facility at Triagon consisted of several interconnected domes and superstructures hiding among a jumble of broken crags and dusty ridges. Some blobs of color had been added to the scene in the form of the huddle of portable domes and huts that the Venusians had set up adjacent to house their operations. In addition, there were a number of outlying latticeworks and dishes, which had first given rise to the idea of its having been some kind of Farside astronomical observatory. The constructions that Kyal and Yorim had been brought in to investigate were spread over a more open area designated the "South Field," extending for roughly four miles on one side of the central complex.

After the hours that Kyal had spent studying ground and overhead shots, close-ups, and measurements, they were easily recognizable as the lander from the orbiting transport braked into the final stage of its descent. The nearest took the form of a cluster of bunkers sprouting finned housings and pylons capped with domes, suggestive of a large electrical research facility. Beyond, partly sunken in the surface like immense donuts surrounding towers of curious metallic contours, were two toroids braided with helically wound bands of guides and conductors that looked suspiciously like variable-phase launch boost resonators. And further out were an assortment of shapes that could have been approach guide retro arrays and point attractors. For Kyal it was like seeing some of his own speculative design sketches come to life.

"It's like that pyramid I was on when you called," Yorim said, leaning forward to peer through on of the ports—a lunar transport surface lander didn't boast the luxury of cabin wall screens. "Parts of it look as if they could be from Dakon." That was the test ground on Venus where they had worked on experimental models of some advanced space propulsion ideas.

"Why would they come all this way to do it?" Kyal asked.

"Secrecy?" Casselo offered. "Terrans were obsessed with it. Very likely it had some military connection. Everything did."

Watching the large toroidal radiators flatten out as the expanse of gray desolation outside rose toward the lander put Kyal in mind of the difficulties the Terrans had caused themselves by taking the fundamental entities of physics to be point particles. Any communications physics engineer knew that an antenna has to have some physical extent in space to radiate energy. Elementary particles were ring-structured.

Luna was substantially larger than Froile, and far closer to spherical than Froile's peculiarly elongated, knobby shape. Its surface features, pattern of deep-running cracks and fissures, and evidence of residual heat—which would have been even more evident when the Terrans existed—all spoke of its having been involved in the catastrophic encounters that had affected Earth. Nevertheless, the Terrans managed to see it as having been a dead body for billions of years.

One of the attractions that had brought Venusian researchers to Luna when it was discovered that there had been a Terran presence there—mainly on Nearside—had been the prospect of its yielding artifacts and structures better preserved than anything to be found on Earth itself. And sure enough it turned out to be so. Some items were so unchanged as to look as if they had been made practically yesterday. Triagon possessed all the facilities that would be expected for a remote research and engineering facility: accommodation and living areas; an administrative and control center, workshops and storage space; a launch area and depot building for local ground and short-range surface-hopping vehicles. Abandoned vehicles and equipment, and the nature of damage evident on some of the structures, testified to violence in the final days of whoever had occupied the place, and a hasty departure.

That much had been known since the preliminary visit by the ISA survey team, and since then the existence of deeper levels as Kyal had inferred from the sonar scans had been confirmed—which was what Casselo had called him about. It turned out that more had come to light while they were on their way from Earth and *Explorer 6.* Aluam Brysek, the head of the ISA crew left to carry out a more detailed exploration, updated them over hot drinks inside the largest of the huts when they had completed the greetings and introductions.

"There are Terran corpses out on the South Field. We've found twelve so far, a few together, the others strewn out over a wider area. There are more in some of the vehicles." He had an athletic build, with sharp, clean features, dark curly hair, alert eyes, and a lively yet economic style of speech and manner that gave Kyal confidence. The kind of person who knew his job and would get things done with a minimum of talk and fuss, he thought to himself. That would be Yorim's kind of person too.

"Corpses?" Casselo repeated. The three arrivals from the crawler still connected to the hut's air lock exchanged questioning looks. This added a new dimension to the job, which would probably call for some new expertise to be brought in.

"How come they weren't spotted sooner?" Yorim asked.

"They're a fair distance out," Brysek replied. "We've been concentrating mainly here, around the base. Their suits are the same gray as the dust, which doesn't help. You'd think they were meant as camouflage."

"Military," Casselo said.

"What kind of condition are they in?" Kyal asked.

"Shot to pieces," one of the technicians threw over his shoulder from a table by the wall, where he was reading something. Brysek nodded confirmation.

"We've got some clips. Here, I'll show you a few." He got up and led the way across to a bank of communications gear. The others closed up around as he activated one of the screens and brought up a series of indexed frames showing the remains. They made his point about the difficulty of spotting them. Even from what must have been tens of yards, the twisted gray forms lying amid the dust and boulders could easily have been mistaken for rocks and shadows. Close-ups showed the damage as ranging from lacerated suits and shattered helmets to scattered body parts and fully dismembered torsos. The corpses themselves were not reduced to skeletons, as was universally true of human remains found on Earth, but still possessed their solid softer tissues as dried, shriveled husks covering the bones. All the same, this would make them prize trophies for the biologists.

"We haven't attempted moving any of them," Brysek said. "They look pretty fragile. Probably best preserved out there, anyway. I figured we'd leave that to the specialists."

Casselo nodded approval. "Good man." He sent an inquiring look at Kyal. "What do you want to do? Go and see them now, while we've still got the crawler attached outside? Or get settled in and have a look around here first?"

Kyal couldn't see that it would make much difference either way. "Whatever you prefer," he replied. "You're the boss."

Casselo shook his head. "Not here, Master Reen. This will be your patch now. You might as well get used to it from the beginning."

It took Kyal a few seconds to adjust to the feeling—like trying on a new coat. Yorim was looking at him with a mixture of amusement and curiosity. "Let's get our bearings here inside the base first," Kyal decided. "A day more won't make any difference to the time the corpses been lying out there." He licked his lips pensively and looked at Brysek. "The last thing we had to eat was a quick snack in the docking bays on the *Explorer* when we changed ships. How about starting with the canteen, after we've stowed our things?"

"We can eat first, right here," Brysek said.

"I was hoping you'd say something like that," Casselo told Kyal.

Although the interior of the Terran structures had been pressurized to a comfortably breathable level and seemed to be holding, they put on back harnesses with air bottles, and respirator masks close at hand clipped to the straps, before proceeding through the surface tube and connecting lock. Full suits would have been too cumbersome. In the event of any failure short of explosive—which was hard to visualize as likely—the respirators would get them back to the huts on the safe side of the lock. The precaution would be relaxed once the structure had been fully examined and pronounced safe.

Walking on the one-sixth-normal-gravity lunar surface was unaffected inside the huts and the Terran sectors, which had been "carpeted" with strips of Venusian G-polarizer panels. Power came from a small fission reactor sunk in a silo by the landing area, which also supplied the rest of the base. They followed Brysek and Irg, a communications specialist who had joined them at lunch in the hut, through into the first of the Terran domes. Somebody called Fenzial, the foreman of the excavating crew below, was due to meet them farther down, where the way had been opened through to the lower levels.

It was a very different feeling from that of walking among the ruins of ancient Terran cities. There, the effects of time had faded and blurred the once-sharp images, distancing the events that they spoke of and the people who had lived them to remote ciphers. The reality of their having existed was something that was merely acknowledged without any sense of being apprehended directly. It was not so in the rooms and corridors of the buildings that constituted Triagon. With no breeze even to carry in dust, no atmosphere to bring corrosion, and not a microbe to initiate any process of decay or decomposition, the surroundings were as clean and unchanged as if they had been lived in yesterday. Brysek pointed out more instances of damage as they passed: a door broken off its hinges in one place; holes and gouges in the inner walls in several others. There had been further signs of unrest in the form of upturned furniture, abandoned utility items such as tools and kitchenware, and clothes and other personal effects scattered over the floors. These had since been catalogued, and either stored or shipped away for further study by archeologists who had been here earlier.

They came out from the bottom of a stairwell into the vault that the original survey team had taken to be a storage cellar, and shown on their drawings as the lowermost level of the complex. However, when Brysek, on receiving Kyal's directions based on the sonar scans, had his people cut through some heavy steel shutters at the far end that the survey people had decided probably wouldn't justify the labor of tackling at that early stage, they found the connection to a whole deeper extension of Triagon, which up until then nobody had suspected existed.

The formerly bare outer vault had become something of a staging area for exploration of the lower levels, with boxes of hardware and materials everywhere, and switch panels controlling bundles of cables snaking over the floor and into the opening where the cut-away shutters stood propped against the walls on either side. A couple of technicians were busy at a worktable littered with tools. Brysek and Irg picked up hand flashlamps from a rack as the party came to the entrance between the shutters. "It's huge down there," Brysek explained. "We don't have permanent lighting fixed up everywhere yet. Still a lot of shadows and dark areas. It's easy to trip over things." Kyal, Yorim, and Casselo followed suit and picked up a lamp each.

"Is this the only way down to the whole lower section?" Casselo asked, looking puzzled.

"As far as we know," Brysek said.

"Seems odd."

"No other way in, at the back, maybe?" Kyal suggested. "If it's that big, you'd think there would be some kind of emergency exit somewhere."

"Maybe there is," Brysek answered. "We haven't gone all the way through yet." They moved on into a corridor lined by doors and strung with overhead lamps converging away for what must have been hundreds of feet. Even Kyal, who had been the first to study and measure the sonar scans, was surprised by the sudden feeling of roominess.

Fenzial, the excavating foreman, was waiting as arranged. The introductory formalities were completed, and he took the lead from there. Everything here was more spacious and lavishly fitted than the levels they had passed through above—not anything that would have qualified as luxury, to be sure, but a definite step up from utilitarian concrete floors and painted walls. First were what had obviously been offices, and then beyond them, larger rooms that appeared to have been for day use or sitting areas, with large chairs, tables, and collections of books—another priceless find for the linguists—and cupboards containing things like games, household oddments, and children's toys. Next was a large communal dining area and kitchens. Unlike the levels above, which had been primarily functional, with limited living space to accommodate the occupants, the space here seemed to have been devoted mainly to habitation. All very strange.

A difficulty in exploring the lower complex, which had slowed things down considerably, was that stairs from the surface only extended down as far as the vault on the far side of the steel shutters. Below the level they were on, the only access was by means of elevators, and the elevators were not working. Hence, Brysek's workers had been obliged to rig up a system of makeshift stairs in one of the shafts. The next level down contained various workshops, a pharmacy and medical center, and a section at one end containing communications and computing equipment. This was Irg's specialty, and where he had been spending most of his time since the lower complex was opened up.

Despite their lag in space technology, Terran electronics was astoundingly advanced. If anything, it had been ahead of the state of the art of Venus. The technical historians attributed it to the combined effects of the subordination of just about everything else to military demands and the ferocious competitiveness of Terran economics. Ironically in some ways, the greater lifting power and onboard cosmic supply tapping of Venusian spacecraft had made the need for extreme miniaturization less pressing. The Terrans' ultra-dense and fast circuitry had also given them computers of phenomenal power and complexity, but none of the remnants discovered on Earth were in a condition that would allow much to be learned from them. But here was equipment that had been preserved in a deep-lying, radiation-protected, sterile environment, and if the intricacies could only be unraveled and decoded, looked as if it might well still be functional.

Irg patted the side of a cabinet that had been opened up to reveal rows of tightly packed racks and assemblies. More similar parts were strewn across several of the countertops, connected to tangles of Venusian instruments and monitoring screens. "If we can work out the powering and operating protocols, I'm certain we can get this working," he declared. "It's like new."

"You mean we might get to hear some of that Terran music finally?" Yorim said.

"And more. I'd say there's a good chance of accessing bulk storage media that hasn't deteriorated. Think what that could mean! Whole libraries of information at once, instead of things having to be reconstructed from fragments scattered all over the place."

Kyal thought about the still images that he and Lorili had looked at in the collection at Foothills Camp. "You might even be able to bring some Terran movie clips back to life," he mused to Irg.

"Exactly."

The next two levels they clambered down to were all sleeping accommodation—both small private rooms and dormitories. That was as far as they had penetrated, Fenzial told them as they came back out into the corridor from another of several identical rooms. The lighting here was sparse, and they were having to use their hand lamps to move around. There was more below, but the stairs down were still being constructed. Fenzial waved a hand to indicate the direction into the shadows and darkness ahead of them. "We've only just got to the end that way.

"Well, we think it's the end." "More of the same?" Brysek asked.

"And a couple of bigger rooms. They look like a playroom and a gym. Showers and baths, and what probably a laundry," Fenzial told him. Brysek scratched his head, looking baffled, and looked at Casselo. Casselo looked from Kyal to Yorim.

"What do you make of it?" he asked them.

Yorim shrugged. "It beats me. How come all this living space and comfort? It feels more like a hotel than a moon base."

Kyal stared at Casselo with an odd, thoughtful look on his face, then turned to take in the surroundings again. Finally, he brought his gaze back to the others. "How about a survival shelter?" he suggested.

CHAPTER SEVENTEEN

In the Molecular Biology section of the ISA Laboratories at Rhombus, Lorili checked through her incoming mail. A smile brightened her face when she saw Kyal's name among the list of senders. They had arrived on Luna without mishap, he informed her, and he was working with a good team there. The stillness and desolation made Moscow look like the center of Thagar—the principal city of Ulange back on Venus. The feeling of newness about everything in the Terran installations was eerie. You found yourself half expecting a live Terran to come around a corner or out of a door at any moment. The electrical constructions that he and Yorim had gone there to study were an enigma. There was much to do yet, but what they had seen so far seemed to reinforce the original impression of an experimental facility built to test a technology that the Terrans weren't supposed to posses. It was all very intriguing. Anyway, he hoped she was settled back in and being creative after her vacation. Oh yes, and there were hopes here of reactivating some of the Terran electronics; so they might actually see some of those cities that they visited brought to life before very much longer. Wouldn't that be something? He signed the message "Fondly."

Lorili read it again. It was a warm and reassuring feeling that he had found time to remember her in the middle of all that seemed to be going on up there. She moved the file to her Reply queue and

105

opened the next. It was from a research group on Venus that she contributed to, and contained the results of comparisons of a selection of Venusian bird DNAs with those from Terran species. All Venusian birds had quadribasic DNA. The similarities to the Terran types were uncanny. Lorili spent some time going over the details. Then she called Iwon, her colleague in the adjoining lab, who had been with the group that she split off from to go her own way with Kyal.

"Are you busy, Iwon?"

"I could use an excuse for a break. What's up?"

"I've just got something in from Venus that I'd like to show you."

"Sure, come on over."

Iwon inclined toward the traditionalist outlook, but he was easygoing about it in the same kind of way that Kyal had been. Lorili liked him for that reason. He made a good sounding board for her to bounce thoughts off and know she wasn't going to end up in an argument. Their current topic of amiable dispute was the Terran notion of unguided natural evolution, driven by chance mutations. Having little in the way of Progressive views that it would appeal to, Iwon was not attracted to it. His main objection echoed the conventional line that the timescales the Terrans had used to make it appear workable were vastly exaggerated. Whether it had been a result of genuine scientific error, their tendency to erect unquestionable dogmas, or a manifestation of some deeper psychological need was still being debated.

But whatever the reason, the result was the same. In earlier days, the Venusians' first inclination had been to accept that maybe the enormous epochs that the Terran sciences talked about were a possibility. Venusians' only direct knowledge of such matters was that derived from their own planet, after all, which had a different history. Shouldn't the Terrans have been the better judges of the one they had actually lived on? But the evidence was piling up, and there no longer seemed any doubt. The Terrans had gotten it colossally wrong.

She found Iwon sprawled at the desk at one end of his cramped lab, surrounded by bottles, glassware, analytical instruments, and a centrifuge. The desktop was barely visible beneath a litter of papers, micrograph prints, and a monitor screen showing a table of protein folding parameters. He was tall and loose-limbed, with clear gray eyes, sandy hair, and a ragged mustache. Mustaches were something the Venusians had copied from Terrans. Early researchers returning from Earth had started sporting them to let people know where they had been, and it caught on as a fashion. Lorili had never seen him looking anything but at ease and relaxed; never tense or flustered. He was one of those enviable people who could sit talking for an afternoon at a table outside one of the cafes in Rhombus, managed to read the piles of books most people always had set aside but never seemed to get around to, had seen every movie that was talked about, and yet all the things that he needed to do got done.

He pulled a stool from under the bench by his desk, cleared away a box of data disks balanced on some journals, and pushed it forward for her to sit down. "You never told me you read minds. The timing's perfect. I'm wearing my brain into a rut." He gestured at the screen and the rest of the mess around him, then pushed back his own chair. "Did you ever try coffee? It's a Terran drink made out of crushed dried beans. One of their addictions."

"Yes. They've started serving it at the Blue Planet. I heard somewhere it's one of the things they're trying to grow back home."

"I've got some here. Want to try it?"

"Okay."

Iwon got up and moved to the bench, where a section of the shelf above was reserved for jars and mugs. "Sweet?"

"You know I am."

"When have you known me argue? What about your coffee?"

"Please."

"I think they put cream or something in it, didn't they? I've only got this powdered stuff you mix for dessert sauce."

"That's fine. It's okay black too."

"Really?" Iwon contemplated the mug he had been about to fill. "Maybe I'll give it a try."

Lorili took a look around. "You look busy enough," she remarked.

"Oh, just staying out of Nostreny's way, really. He's running around in a panic over something." Garki Nostreny was the section chief. "So, anyway . . . what have you got?"

Lorili set down a sheaf of printouts that she had brought. "The results of those bird DNA studies just came in. The parallels are striking. You can have a look at them for yourself when you get a moment. It's just the kind of pattern you'd expect from a common ancestry." She meant descent from common ancestral genetic seed material in the way she had described to Kyal, which had somehow found its way to both Earth and Venus.

Iwon was already shaking his head as he immersed a net bag of the crushed beans into a flask to boil. But he didn't smile. Another thing Lorili liked about him was that he wasn't condescending. It was nice to think she was being taken seriously, even when their fundamental premises were at odds. "The timescales just aren't there for anything like that to have happened on Venus," he said. "And it's looking pretty certain now that it wasn't much better on Earth either, whatever else the Terrans thought. Have you seen what's coming in from the geologists? There are fossilized trees here, extending intact through layers of coal and limestone that the Terrans dated as millions of years apart." He turned briefly and tossed up his hands. "How could they be? The trees didn't stand there for millions of years being slowly buried in sediments. They were obviously buried rapidly. . . . And the boundaries between the sediment layers are clean, with no signs of tracks, roots, worm burrows, or any of the other biological activity you'd expect to find if the surfaces had been exposed for any length of time."

Lorili had expected this much. They had been over it enough times. "But we know that organisms can vary over time." She was simply staking out the ground, not saying anything new.

"Nobody's disputing it," Iwon agreed. "There has to be some ability to adapt over a range of changing conditions. But the same would have to be true whatever its origin. And extrapolating noncontroversial variations about a theme to account for major differences between types is an act of faith, not an inference from any evidence. Even the Terrans never stopped arguing over it. The universe doesn't possess enough probabilistic resources for the number of trial combinations it would need."

Lorili held up her palms in a restraining gesture. "Okay, if it will save time, I accept that the Terran idea of major change through selection of random variations doesn't work. But here's another angle."

Iwon sat back down and handed her one of the mugs. He looked interested. "What?"

Lorili separated out several of the sheets that she had laid down. "Twenty-five years ago, a population of finches was introduced into Abarans—they're not native there." The Abaran Islands were a remote group in Venus's embryonic northern ocean, well to the east of Korbisan.

"Uh-huh."

"Already, several distinct types of beak morphology and plumage have appeared. See what it means? The programs to produce the different types didn't come together a step at a time through trial and error in twenty-five years. They were already there, in the genome. We know that most DNA doesn't code for protein. It's the same thing as Julow has been saying in Ulange, from those experiments with bacteria. Gene changes aren't random, the way the Terrans insisted. They're cued by changes in the environment."

Iwon shrugged. "Which fits with what the traditional view has always said. It's what you'd expect from the explanation that we're part of some purposeful scheme that nobody pretends to understand. I can't put it better than what they told us at school: Vizek knows best."

"It isn't an explanation," Lorili retorted. "It's just a label to hang on not knowing the answer. But what I'm suggesting could give you faster, directed evolution without the label."

"How so?" Iwon invited, sitting back down and stirring his own drink.

"We've been hearing a lot of speculation about what the purpose of reverse transcriptase is," Lorili answered. It was an enzyme discovered some years previously that wrote information into DNA. This was in the opposite direction to that believed until then to be the rule for genetic information flow: originating in DNA and ending up in proteins. Hence the name. "The information that it carries seems to originate within other cells of the body."

"Okay," Iwon agreed. For a while there had been a flurry of activity among researchers on Venus following a false trail that attributed it to an external virus.

Lorili went on, "Suppose that a lot of DNA coding comes about in this way. Maybe even most of it. What you'd have is a feedback system from the body for creating a repository of acquired survival-related information. Valuable lessons learned in an individual life can be written into the germ-cell DNA for transmission to future generations. So the genome carries an accumulating history of the race that programs the descendants to deal with situations that have been encountered in the past."

"Like the immune system." Iwon was clearly thinking about it.

"A good example. So evolution doesn't have to be a process of blind trial-and-error groping over countless generations the way the Terrans thought." Lorili nodded to concede a point. "It *is* directed, as the traditional view maintains. But not for the reason we were told at school." She concluded, "It's not driven by random factors that would take forever to come up with something useful. And so the long timescales that the Terrans constructed aren't necessary."

Iwon stared into the distance while he turned the proposition over. Then he sipped his drink experimentally, sucked his teeth, and smacked his lips.

"What do you think?" Lorili asked.

"Hm . . . Stronger. But more flavor. I think I like it."

"About what I was saying."

"I see your point. . . . But I don't agree there's a need for it. I don't have any personal motive for wanting to put Vizek out of a job. Everything you've said could be true. In fact, it makes a lot of sense. But what I said before is still true too. It's equally compatible with both theories. It doesn't prove one or the other."

"I never claimed that it did. I was simply making the case that a faster form of natural evolution is plausible without the need for huge, fictitious Terran timescales. And if it takes the form of the same basic genetic program responding to the same kind of environmental cues, it might explain why us and Terrans, and some of the other living things from both places, turn out to be so similar."

"Okay, I'll grant you that much," Iwon conceded. "But even so, you've still got a huge *difference* in times. Earth has been around far longer than Venus, even if it isn't as old as the Terrans thought. Maybe the process of evolving from whatever this ancestral genetic material was to humans was somehow telescoped enough to have happened there. But surely it couldn't have happened on Venus. We've barely cooled from being incandescent."

Kyal had made the same point. It was a valid one, and Lorili had no delusions otherwise. It was a good place to agree to leave things for now.

Iwon seemed to read it that way too, and eased back in his chair. "Well, time will no doubt tell, I guess. Anyway, I'll have a look at these papers as soon as the hysteria abates. . . . So, you haven't told me yet how the European cities were, after galloping off and leaving us."

"Interesting," Lorili said.

"Worth the trip, then?"

"Oh yes."

"Good."

"Especially Foothills Camp—where a city was destroyed in the Central Asian War. Some of the things there are amazingly well preserved. They have a wonderful collection of restored Terran images. In some ways I think it's inspiring—the tenacity and resilience they could show against impossible odds and not give up. And sometimes even win."

Iwon shot her a glance of mock reproach. "Be careful that you're not falling for the official propaganda versions of their history. . . ." He pushed the side of his mouth with his tongue as if he were trying to stop himself, but couldn't resist adding, "Like their science."

Lorili had heard this from Kyal too and ignored it. "We were at the nuclear ruins of Moscow too, but there's not a lot to see there. It's just a drilling site."

"Oh yes. Tell me more about this lucky person who carried you off. The Ulangean space-propulsion expert. What's he doing here?"

"He was on his way to Luna. In fact he's there now. He and a colleague of his are investigating some Terran constructions on Farside. You'd probably get along with him, Iwon. You remind me of his friend—although I only met him briefly. He's son of Jarnor Reen."

"Who, the friend?"

"No, the person I went to Europe with. His name's Kyal. Kyal Reen."

"You mean the son of the famous Ulangean statesman—the one who pushed for the Earth program?"

"Yes."

"You're joking."

"No, I'm not. They were sent here by the IASS and just arrived on the *Melther Jorg*. It was their acclimatization break before going on to Luna. The friend had done the same thing as I did and gone off with another group."

"Hm." Iwon looked as if he were suddenly seeing a new side to her. "I'm surprised you got along," he said. "I'd have thought someone like that would be solidly freethinking and traditional. Not exactly your authoritarian radical."

"Well, yes," Lorili agreed. "But he doesn't get defensive and dogmatic about it." She motioned with her half-empty mug. "A bit like you."

"So what am I doing wrong?" Iwon spread his hands in appeal and grinned unapologetically.

"Isn't it obvious? You knock down my pet theories." Lorili finished her drink and stood up. "But don't imagine you've heard the last of it. I've been working on some further thoughts that haven't quite crystalized yet."

"I'll be here when you're ready to talk about it," Iwon said.

It was starting to get dark when Lorili shut down her system for the day, tidied her work space, and left the ISA laboratory buildings. The evening was cool, making her glad she'd brought a coat. After deliberating whether to stop on the way back, she decided on eating in and a quiet evening at home. Although there was a shorter route to the residential sector where her apartment was situated, she detoured via the Central District, both for the lights and the life, and to get a little air and stretch her legs after the day. It also meant she could pick up a few groceries.

It was a pity that her few days with Kyal had been restricted to archeologists' camps, workmen's trucks, and ruined cities, she reflected. It had to have been a strange itinerary for a member of the IASS who was the son of Jarnor Reen. But he had acted all the way through as if he felt perfectly at home. It made her feel all the warmer toward him. Maybe he would be able to spend some time in Rhombus when the work on Luna was done, she thought to herself. Before he went back to Venus . . . But Lorili found herself not wanting to dwell on that part of it.

She came to the block where her apartment unit was located, and followed the path between prickly Terran shrubs to the front door, standing on a small patio beside an outside storage closet. Ufty, a neighbor in an upstairs unit across the way, was cooking something out on the balcony. He saw her in the light above her door and waved. She managed an awkward wave back while balancing the bag of groceries and finding her key, and let herself in. Closing the door with her back, she took the door direct through to the kitchenette to deposit the bag on a worktop, then went on through the arch to the living area to close the drapes.

"*Ahh!* . . ."

It was only when she turned from the window that she saw the figure in the shadows, stretched out in one of the armchairs. In that split second, the fright had sent her heart pounding. She recoiled into the kitchen archway and fumbled for the light switch.

Apart from raising his rugged, copper-haired head a fraction to look at her, he didn't move.

"Hello, Lorili," Jenyn said.

CHAPTER EIGHTEEN

For the first few seconds, all Lorili could do was stand there, fighting the surge of adrenaline that turned her into a wound spring ready to fly at him or back out the door. The reflexes subsided slowly.

"How did you get in?" she heard herself whispering. It was a pointless question; more a mechanical reaction while she was still striving to bring herself under control.

"Oh, come on. You know I have my ways." Jenyn's eyes were mocking, enjoying his moment of domination.

Lorili braced herself. "I don't care. . . ." Coherent words refused to form. She shook her head violently. "I don't want to know what it's about. Just . . . get out."

"Hey, aren't we being just a little bit hasty? I mean, do I look threatening or something? And this a long way from home. Don't you even want to know what I'm doing out here?"

"No. It's not my concern anymore. Please . . . just leave."

Jenyn shook his head as if disappointed. "That's not really called for, you know. We had a great thing going back there . . . at one time. It's not good to throw it all away the first time there's a problem." He raised a hand and motioned to indicate both of them. "You and me . . . we were never quitters. Remember all those good times? There were a lot of them too." He bunched his face in the kind of expression that says everyone regrets things. "Oh, okay . . . I know I

115

can be a bit overbearing at times. I admit it. But knowing something like that is the first part of fixing it. You get older. Being out here at a place like this makes people see things differently. I've changed now."

For a moment Lorili felt herself falling under the same charm that had captivated her before. Somewhere inside her there was still a vestige of the raw student who wanted to believe it. Jenyn could cast the kind of spells that on Earth had moved armies. He would have made a good Terran. Maybe that was why he idealized them. The scientist who dealt in realities rescued her.

"You'll never change, Jenyn. The world and everyone in it exist to serve your ends. I was expendable when it suited you, and that said it all. I'm my own person now. I plan on making my own life, not being an accessory in someone else's. It's all over. Forget it."

"It's not just me and us. That's the sauce on the meal. There's a whole future too, that's bigger than both of us. Have you forgotten the movement and what it means? It used to be the most important thing in our lives. I've been across in the Americas, just back. It's a different, vibrant feel. You've got a critical mass of younger people here at Earth, open to new ideas and excited by change. A chapter built out here, with this kind of energy, could go back, take over the whole Progressive organization on Venus, and become a real political force there. *That's* what I'm working on out here. It could use your kind of help. And that's what you could become a part of again." Jenyn was reading Lorili's face while he spoke. "Have you forgotten about things like order, organization, the power of authority to enforce equality for all? Don't those things matter anymore?"

Lorili didn't want to be drawn in. Arguing politics with Jenyn was like walking into a web. "I still believe any new idea should be tried and not prejudged," she said. "But being out here has clarified a lot of things for me too. Venus *does* have equality. Of opportunity. If you're good enough, you can make it anywhere. It's not the whims of unregulated institutions that keep people out. It's their own inabilities. You can't demand equality with high performers. You can only earn it. What you really want is an army of followers who believe they can take by force what the world isn't prepared to pay them in any other way. But what that really means is power for you—because you won't get people to follow you in any other way."

"Boy, who have you been talking to?"

"What does it matter? The point is, it's a fraud. You tell people it's for them, but it isn't. It's really for you. They don't matter. They never did. Lies, treachery, deceit—anything goes if it might get you what you want."

"Harsh words, Lorili." Jenyn's tone was assuaging but his brow furrowed uneasily. It was one of the rare moments when Lorili had seen him look taken aback.

"The world you'd deliver would be very different from the one they thought they were sacrificing themselves for," she said.

Jenyn shook his head. "Now I don't understand. What would make you say things like this?"

Something snapped then. The anger flared up that Lorili's initial fright and confusion had been holding in check. "Did you think I'd never *know*?" she burst out. "That I'd be too stupid to find out? I have eyes and ears and a brain, Jenyn. I do talk to people."

He made a play of being at a loss, eyes wide, hands upturned. "What? . . . What are you talking about?"

"That whole scheme of yours to discredit Lemaril Aedua. It was a setup. She never split any payments with writers to run their works."

"What do you mean?" Still, he was brazening it out. "The evidence was there. You saw the testimonials."

"*Oh, give me a break, Jenyn!*" Lorili shouted. "That woman who did the series on game-playing psychology was a former lover of yours. You blackmailed her into giving it. That kind of involvement with a Progressive activist wouldn't have looked very good if it came to the attention of her very traditional patron, would it? And I never believed that guy with the piece on topology and sculpture. He was a plagiarist. He couldn't have written it. He didn't have the credentials. So what does that say for *his* standards? What was the angle there, Jenyn? A straight cash deal?"

The mask turned itself off, and Jenyn's face hardened. "Oh, you were busy, weren't you. Quite the little spy, eh?"

"When rumors like that start coming around, you follow them up. Did you expect me not to *care*?"

"Yes, to care about the movement, the idea, the big picture. We got a say in *The Commentator*. Sometimes it's what you have to do. It got the results."

Loril stared at him incredulously. "But you *lied*! What kind of better world is supposed to come out of that? A world where everything is turned into manipulated images. Where nobody can believe anything anymore. And what would you have to turn people into for it to work? A world of mindless sheep?"

Jenyn checked the flash of meanness that had started to show, and became mocking again. "Now you're almost sounding like a trad. Just who *have* you been talking to, Lorili?"

"There are just some basic values that you don't try to change. The idea was about building a better world on the old, not tearing it down."

"Sometimes, to build a new house, you have to dig new foundations."

"Not your kind of house, where it's all right to bend everything if it serves an immediate need. The principle has to come first."

"Everything changes with time. Those values were appropriate to a small, struggling society in a harsh environment with limited resources. We're a growing civilization now. It can afford to be less self-sacrificing. In fact, it's going to have to learn to be. The ones who learn to compete are going to come to the top now. Those are going to be the new rules. You either play by them or go under."

"Well, you came to a planet with the right history to learn about all that, didn't you?" Lorili said. She couldn't refrain from adding sarcastically, "Or was it because they were onto you back home? How come you're still not on the editorial board at *The Commentator*?"

Jenyn was on his feet. For an instant Lorili thought he was going to strike her, but she squared to him, daring him to try it. "So what made *you* run here and hide?" he asked her. "Were you one of the ones who put them up to it?"

They stood glaring at each other for several seconds. She saw the anger flaming in his eyes, and then abate gradually as he fought it under control. He could be violent and impassioned, she knew, but he was not stupid. He knew there was nothing to be gained here now, just at the moment.

Lorili let her voice fall to defuse the tension. "I think you'd better go."

Jenyn stared at her for a second or two longer, as if seeing it too, but unable to back down. She held her breath. Then, mercifully, he moved away, toward the door. "Think about it when you've calmed down," he said. "It wasn't a bad thing we had going. And we will again. You know I never give up."

"Just go," she repeated.

He opened the door, stepped through, then turned and looked back. Lorili stood staring stonily. "Why make life tough on yourself, when you could be riding with it?" He closed the door, and was gone.

Loril swallowed and sank down into one of the chairs. She put her hands to her mouth and found that she was shaking. His ego was at stake. The only thing of importance to him now would be that he win. No other matter, nor anybody else, would be of importance. She realized that this wasn't going to go away.

CHAPTER NINETEEN

New discoveries followed quickly on lunar Farside. The heavy power generating plant that Kyal had looked for beneath the main Triagon complex was found in a subterranean extension of one of the larger outlying bunker constructions on the South Field. Tracing the distribution grid, and further study of the other structures spread out across the area, as well as their associated equipment and control rooms, confirmed the site to have been an experimental facility for developing and testing electrical space propulsion technology. Why it should have been hidden on the remote rear reaches of the Moon, permanently out of sight from Earth and conceivably defended against overflights by unwanted observation satellites, could only be left as matters better comprehended by minds schooled in Terran military mystique and paranoia.

Opening up the newly discovered lower levels at the main part of Triagon revealed a whole, hitherto unsuspected section of the base, with access from the familiar part apparently restricted to the one steel-shuttered corridor. It was as if the two sections had served different purposes and been kept functionally separate. They were designated, accordingly, the Upper Complex and Lower Complex.

When the exploration crew pushed to the farthermost extreme of the Lower Complex, they made a further discovery. An internal lock chamber—a standard feature of Terran lunar constructions, affording emergency isolation like bulkhead doors in a ship—led to a further, smaller extension consisting of some rooms and corridors and larger space that seemed to have been a depot for vehicles, with a ramp going up to a lock that opened to the outside. So there was indeed another entrance to the whole place that could be used in emergencies, as Kyal had speculated on the day he and Yorim arrived. Egress to the surface was concealed in a steep-sided gully in the broken terrain on the far side of a ridge running behind the main facility, which was why it hadn't been found from the outside. The extension beyond the Lower Complex was named the Rear Annexe.

The internal lock connecting the Lower Complex to the Annexe was closed when the exploration crew found it. Testing before opening it up, however, showed hard vacuum conditions on the far side, which turned out to be due to both inner and outer doors of the surface access lock at the top of the vehicle ramp having been opened. It could only be presumed that this was how the Terrans had left it. Going through the various parts of the Rear Annexe yielded more Terran corpses, scores of them this time—sixty-eight, to be precise, male and female, including children. Unlike the corpses found earlier on the surface, there were no indications of their having died violently. They were laid out in rows in several of the rooms, transforming them into oversize, improvised morgues—as if the whole place didn't have enough of a macabre side to it already. Brysek decided not to extend the sealing and ventilating operation into the Annexe, but to leave the finds in the original conditions of lunar vacuum in which they had been discovered. The biologists would know best how they should be handled, and he didn't pretend to be a biologist.

The size and nature of the Lower Complex, with its lavish provisioning for storage and self-sufficiency, reinforced the notion of its having been a survival center—perhaps a refuge for some kind of privileged elite from the endless and progressively more destructive Terran wars. The space had obviously been intended to accommodate far more people than the number of bodies found, and ubiquitous signs of day-to-day wear, along with the variety of clothing and personal effects found throughout testified that at one time the facility had been used to capacity. Its coexistence with the propulsion research installation represented by the Upper Complex and the South Field structures suggested a connection between them. The most likely conclusion seemed to be that a new, embryonic technology had been seized upon and developed to support an evacuation program involving numbers beyond the capability of the conventional chemical propulsion methods in use at the time. When the emergency had passed, the evacuees—or conceivably their descendants—had used the same means to return. Indeed, what other means could they have used, since Luna would have been incapable of supplying the fuel required for chemical rockets, even with its relatively smaller gravity well? Such an interpretation was supported by the fact that there was no trace of any vessel employing the electrical techniques that the South Field constructions pointed to, and the landing and launch area contained no other kind of functional Terran craft. The several wrecks found in the vicinity were all conventional, chemically propelled, short-range types suitable for surface ferrying.

Walls and columns at strategic points around the interior of Triagon had charts showing the levels and floor plans. Other signs marked the entrances to certain rooms and sections. Whatever the specific details, they all carried the generic heading: "Terminus." Some documents, still readable, recovered from a crashed Terran vessel ten miles or so out from the base yielded references to "Terminus Ground Control frequency," and a "Terminus beacon," along with some numbers that hadn't been interpreted. This led to the not unreasonable conclusion is that "Terminus" had been the facility's Terran name.

In an endeavor to find further support for the conjecture, Brysek had, fairly early on, sent a request to the Linguistics center on *Explorer 6*, who were coordinating inputs from translation groups at Rhombus and in other places, for a search to be run for other references to "Terminus" in such a context. In this, the linguists had an ambiguity problem to deal with, since "terminus" was also a regular Terran word meaning "endpoint" and sometimes "railroad station," so it could be expected to appear in all kinds of contexts that were irrelevant. But that was all part of the job, and the task was run with as many constraints as possible to filter out wrong leads.

One of the first responses to be flagged was from an archeological base on the western side of the northern American continent. Among the excavations of what had been identified as a Terran military space launch center, some pieces of shipping crates had been found with the word "Terminus" marked as part of the destination code. Another item came from a report detailing the investigation of an abandoned Terran base on lunar Nearside. A chart had been found that mapped the various Terran lunar sites and showed Terminus at the correct location on Farside. Interestingly, the accompanying summary description showed it as a research facility only, with only the subsurface levels that formed the Upper Complex. There was no indication of the extensive Lower Complex, which from engineering considerations and the general layout could not have been excavated later. It all added to the impression of secrecy and deception at work. Whatever had gone on at Terminus had not been for the world in general to know about.

After all the jaunting out from the main base area in open surface buggies, and poking around among metal structures and concrete foundations, Kyal was getting to feel quite at home, finally, in a surface and extravehicular suit. Being confined in one added to the feeling of isolation and desolation about everything in this dead and silent world. Yet the Terrans had brought their compulsion for violence and conflict with them this far. Even here, where one would have thought that the knowledge of being fellow creatures from the same distant home should have assumed a significance that would override all else, still they hadn't been able to desist from killing each other.

He voiced the thought when he was out with Yorim and Casselo at one of the large Terran toroids on the South Field, loading equipment and samples into a buggy before heading back. They had been out at the site for twelve hours, initially with a work crew who had departed earlier. Kyal was looking forward to a hot shower in the huts that served as living quarters, the evening meal, and an evening of face-to-face company and conversation without suits. It was his turn to send Lorili a letter too. The regular phone net did connect to Luna, but most people found the two-and-a-half-second round-trip signal delay from Earth and its vicinity disconcerting. It was difficult to resist the impulse to jump in with another line before the response to the last one came back, with the result that conversations tended to get hopelessly out of synch. Having to say "over" and wait all the time was stinting and tedious.

Casselo hoisted a pack containing a portable waveform analyzer into the rear of the buggy and then rested himself back against a stanchion securing the end of a tension line to an antenna mast. His breathing sounded from the speaker in Kyal's helmet. Although things might weigh less in lunar gravity, they still had normal inertia; maneuvering massive objects like test gear and pieces of machinery about in ways that involved velocity changes could still take some effort. The trick was to avoid stops and starts and keep them moving along steady curves rather than around corners, but it took practice.

"They were all psychotic." Yorim's voice came over the circuit. He was still inside the control room in a sunken area at the foot of the mast, packing away the last of the tools they had been using. "Who can ever know why psychotics do what they do?"

"There might have been reasons," Casselo said in a curious voice.

Kyal turned from where he had been standing with an arm draped along the side of the buggy's rear section, staring out across the waste of rock and dust. "Reasons? Why Terrans were the way they were, you mean?"

"Yes."

"What reasons?"

Casselo brought a gauntleted hand up to brush something off the sleeve of his suit. "Somebody from Rhombus was up at *Explorer* talking about it while you were in Europe. He thinks it might have to do with the different way they saw the organizing power that's responsible for life."

"You mean Vizek?"

"That's what we call it for convenience, anyway. But what do we mean by it, really? What would be your definition?"

Kyal shrugged to himself inside his suit. It was a common enough question. "It's just a way of acknowledging that there's more going on behind it all than we see. We're a part of something bigger, that's no doubt being acted out for reasons. What else can you say?"

"Do you know what the reasons are?" Casselo asked.

"No," Kyal said. "I know some people think they know, but I've never been convinced. We might get to find out one day, after checkout time, the way other people say. . . . If so, I can wait till then."

Yorim, wearing a yellow EV suit and carrying the tool bag, appeared at the opening from the bunker below. Brysek's crew had cut the lock door away, since the Terran power source to open it had long since died. "I knew a guy back home who said the reason was to test social systems," Yorim's voice came in. "He figured that

Vizek is really plural, and they're not as smart as most people assume. They have their own problems in getting along too, so they seed all these planets with genetic prototypes and let them develop to see if they come up with something that might be the answer. It's like the best way to get a good computer program or solve a lot of problems is often to let a thousand people loose and just leave them to it." Yorim made the top of the steps in a series of slow bounds and added the tool bag to the items in the back of the buggy.

"He can't *know*," Kyal commented.

"I never said he did. *He* said he did."

Casselo came back in. "But the Terrans had a very different view, that was practically universal. Even Yorim's friend wouldn't have thought that Vizek—or I suppose I should say these 'Vizeks' of his—concerned themselves with his own personal day-to-day business."

"Not at all," Yorim said. "Why would they? Like I said, it was just to see what different kinds of social dynamics came out."

"But the Terrans imagined wrathful, vindictive supernatural beings who *did* concern themselves," Casselo said. "Who judged, punished, and rewarded what humans did. From some of the things that Terrans said, you'd think that worrying about the antics of humans was their prime preoccupation. Why the difference, do you think?"

Yorim turned back and swung from side to side, checking for stray items left lying around. "Who knows? They were an older race, I guess. Maybe they just had longer to get paranoid and work on it."

"Different origins? Genetics?" Kyal hazarded.

"We don't think so," Casselo said. His face turned to gaze skyward inside his helmet. He half raised an arm. "Look at those stars up there," he invited. "People come to Earth and see clear skies for the first time, and they talk about how fantastic it is. But down there, it's nothing like this, is it?" That was one of the first things Kyal had noticed on setting foot outside at Luna. The stars were unwavering and brilliant, crowded everywhere in uncountable numbers greater than anything seen on even the clearest of night on Earth. Casselo went on, "The planets are insignificant pinpoints. Most people couldn't find them. And yet, from what we've put together of old Terran legends from the beginnings of their history, they saw the planets as objects of awe and terror. Practically universally. It was the same across peoples and races everywhere. Early Terrans thought they were the supernatural beings that decided the fate of individuals and nations. They built temples to them, and had whole priesthoods that dedicated their lives to watching them and plotting their movements. Why should those tiny, remote specks have become objects of such obsessions?"

Kyal looked back over the moonscape and up at the starfield again. He had never thought about it that way before.

"Well, I guess they must have lived in one of the unstable periods," Yorim said. He meant of the Solar System, which Venusians accepted as occurring irregularly but the Terrans hadn't appreciated. "Disruptions happen. We've only just found out Froile wasn't there when the Terrans were around."

"You're on the right track, Yorim," Casselo said.

Kyal thought back to the evening that he and Lorili had spent talking to the archeologists and geologists at Moscow. They had spoken then about enormous cataclysms in Earth's past, unleashing death, destruction, and violence on a scale beyond anything Venusians had ever experienced. The most recent had occurred during Earth's early historic period, they had said, and the survivors had left records in their myths and legends of the things they had seen. The strange thing was that the symbolism was obvious to Venusians, even from the fragments they had found aeons afterward. But Terrans, who lived in the aftermath, with not only the records in abundance but the physical evidence all around them, couldn't see it. Lorili had commented that their ability to see only what they wanted to see went all the way back to their beginnings, and wondered if it was a genetic trait.

"You're saying the planets came closer to Earth and to each other at one time," Kyal said. "Close enough to interact. The Terrans could see them clearly."

Casselo's beard bobbed up and down behind his helmet visor. "Yes."

"Some people that Lorili and I met at Moscow talked about that. They said Venus could have been one of them—when it was a white-hot protoplanet."

Casselo straightened up from resting. Kyal climbed into the buggy's open cab and slid onto the bench seat spanning it. Yorim got in from the other side, as on the outward trip taking the driver's position, which was in the center. "The early Terrans lived under a different sky. They saw the planets as apparitions in the heavens, bringing death and terror and devastation," Casselo said as he followed Yorim. "With arc discharges going on between them, and all kinds of plasma effects. Volcanoes, earthquakes, storms of meteorites coming down. The whole climate in chaos. But being at a pretechnical stage, they were unable to understand what they were witnessing. They interpreted it as wars between celestial gods. The devastations on Earth itself became retribution on the inhabitants for transgressions of their laws." The buggy moved away, throwing up a small shower of dust that fell back promptly with no lingering cloud. Casselo went on, "The terrors handed down from those times were ritualized into religions fixated on obeying and appeasing wrathful deities. Later, when the planets receded and sorted themselves out into remote, nonthreatening orbits, the memories of what had started it all were repressed."

Yorim was looking more thoughtful now as he navigated them back across the gray wilderness of dust and rubble. "So what are you saying? That the same thing happened that you get with individuals sometimes after something traumatic? A kind of collective amnesia? The literal meanings were forgotten?"

"Something like that," Casselo agreed. "Although I'm not so sure there's any collective mechanism that could produce actual amnesia. More an unconscious cultural consensus would be my guess. You know the kind of thing. If you all don't talk and don't think about something that's too painful, it ceases to exist."

"Somebody who was on the *Melther Jorg* with us was into all this," Kyal said. "Emur Frazin. He's done a lot of work on Terran mythology."

"I know," Casselo said. "He was the one I got all this from."

Kyal smiled faintly and nodded. "And so the ancient accounts were dismissed as myth and fable. Which would make sense of why they would be obvious to us. We'd never been through it."

"Exactly," Casselo said. .

"What about Froile?" Yorim queried.

"Yes, our own miniature version, maybe," Casselo agreed. "But from what I've been able to make out, it would have been a pretty tame affair compared to what happened on Earth. Sherven has a theory that it might help explain this big difference in timescales— why the Terrans appear to have fabricated huge epochs that never existed."

"How?" Kyal asked, turning his head to look across. "What's the connection?"

"The evidence for massive catastrophes in their past was there all around them. But seeing it would be to accept what had happened, which would mean acknowledging that it could happen again. That was something that the shocked Terran unconsciousness was unable to face. So they persuaded themselves that slow, gradual change, working over immense spans of time, could account for everything that they saw in the world. They created an illusion of a safe, secure place in the universe, where everything was stable and predictable, always had been, and always would be. All that was violent and threatening was banished to remoteness, either light-years away from them in space, or billions of years back in time."

They arrived at the main base area, and Yorim parked by the other vehicles in front of the huts. The entry lock to the hut they used as the mess room could only take two suited figures at a time. Casselo and Yorim went ahead. While Kyal was waiting for the pumps to complete the cycle, he turned and stared out again across the stillness, replaying in his mind the scenes of conflict that had taken place here on this very landscape long ago.

Finally, maybe, he was beginning to understand the strange inner conflicts that had made the Terrans what they were. As often happens with an individual who is in denial, the trauma and terrors they had experienced found release in other ways. The brutality and carnage of Terran wars reenacted mass extinctions they had suffered, and represented symbolic human sacrifice to their bloodthirsty gods. Their obsessive pursuit of ever-more-powerful weapons echoed the violence on a cosmic scale that they had seen in their sky. And what else were their entire political and economic systems but expressions of the craving for the dominance that would bring security? All were manifestations of a bewildered psyche struggling to face a future that it feared and distrusted. For the first time, Kyal found himself moved by something akin to compassion for them.

He thought back to the side of the Terrans that Lorili had seen, and he looked up again at the stars. The Terrans had talked about one day going out there. Some Venusians were of the opinion that they could have done it. Yes, it was true: Much that was disturbed and had gone wrong was eradicated from the universe when the last Terran eyes gazed sightlessly up at the skies they would never conquer.

But something extraordinary that had come into being, and tried for a while against hopeless odds to grow and become what it could and flourish, was lost too.

CHAPTER TWENTY

It was springtime in Maryland. In a walled estate situated twenty miles from New Washington, crocuses were coming into bloom on the grassy slope leading down to willows by the lake. Sandra Perrin-McLeod sat at a wicker table on the patio outside the open French windows from the summer house, watching a pair of mockingbirds hopping among the branches of the large elm and chattering noisily as they teased a squirrel. The peaceful hours that she had spent here alone on fine days, confiding her thoughts to her journal, were among her most pleasant memories. Soon now, she would be seeing it all for the last time.

It was an island of tranquility among the storm clouds that were gathering to engulf the world. The American-led western alignment had emerged victorious but battered from the war with China that had culminated from beginnings around Taiwan and in the Middle East. Schooled and bred to the tradition of loyalty to her social class, she would utter no aspersions regarding her country's publicly stated position: Having saved its friends and been betrayed by them, America would defend its honor. But she knew enough to despise it inwardly and deplore the fraudulent history that was being taught in the schools and presented through the popular culture. There was no honor nor virtue nor glory to any of it. By definition, war was the business of mass killing, destruction, lies, and deception. All the victors proved was that they were the more ruthless and better at it.

The Euro-Russian monolith that had consolidated while America recovered had aligned with the Muslim bloc to expel American influence from the Asian continent. Ironically, the new China, rebuilding itself from the ruins, was turning now to America for security and defense. All the familiar mechanisms for manipulating public perceptions, from the demonizing of the future enemies by means of stereotyped images in the mass entertainments, to slanted news reporting, silencing of dissent, and the handpicking of approved appointments in academia were in evidence again. As always, the weapons had grown more fearsome, with near-space dominated by the military and outposts on the Moon. Alexander said it would be much worse this time. And he should have known, if anyone did. Universally hailed scientific genius, master-level chess player at high school, an architect of the alliance's defense strategy, with a seat on the Inner Security Council; and she the daughter of one of the leading financier families. Their position should have gained them the world. Instead, its only tangible worth would be to get them out of it.

She shook the thought away and returned her attention to the journal. After reading over the last paragraph she had written, she appended:

Humanity has invented much and learned nothing. There seems to be something deep in the subconscious of our kind that compels nations to orgies of violence and mutual annihilation. . . .

The sounds of scampering mixed with children's voices came through the open windows from the house. Moments later, Allan, who was ten, and Marie, eight, appeared on their way to the stable, dressed for riding. Sandra rested her pen on the book and forced a smile. "All ready to go, I see. You have a perfect day for it."

"What are you doing out here all by yourself?" Marie asked.

"Oh, writing down my thoughts. It's better to be alone when you want to do things like that. The quiet helps."

"Why do you have to write them down? You already know what they are."

Sandra smiled again, wider and this time genuinely. "To remind me a long time from now what they were. When I'm older and probably won't remember what I was thinking today."

"I didn't think grown-ups forgot things. You always have to remind us when we forget. How can you, if you forget them too?"

"There's Maggie," Allan said. "She's waiting for us."

Their riding instructor came out from the stable below and called up toward the house. "*Marie. Allan.* We're ready to go. You can come down and bring your horses out yourselves. I'm not the groom here, you know."

"There." Sandra nodded at them. "Quite right too."

"We've got to go," Allan said. "Can you come too?"

"Not today. I need to finish this. Anyway, I'm not dressed for it. I'll see you both at dinner. Run along, and have fun."

"Will our dad be here for dinner?" Marie asked plaintively as Allan went on ahead. "Is he back yet?"

"No, I'm afraid not, Flower."

"When will he be back?"

"It will be a while yet. Go on now. Don't get Maggie cross."

Sandra watched them mount up and depart at a slow canter toward the trail leading to the wood. Then she lifted her pen again and resumed.

The children miss their father already. I dread to think how much we will miss our home, our whole way of life, possibly forever. In his last letter, Alex talked about getting us out via a launch base somewhere on the West Coast in the next week or two. I'm not really sure why I bother to write this and keep the journal up to date. I won't be taking it with us to Terminus. Oxstead, before he left to follow after Alex, warned me that it wouldn't be wise to bring any evidence of our discussing things that are this sensitive. I really would have preferred not knowing that Robert and Vera are not on the list. The thought of never seeing them again is harrowing . . . and of what might become of them.

I know now how foolish I was to have talked about any of this to Gorman. But the man is so persistent. I will leave this account with family things, where it belongs. More foolishness, perhaps? But it gives a certain sense of completeness to life, knowing one's affairs were left finished and in order. I wonder if anyone . . .

. . . will ever read it.

Casselo set down the copy of the translation. The image of the original document, fragile and faded, restored by a delicate treatment with infrared and dyes, showed on the screen next to him. It had been discovered among a carefully packed and preserved collection of picture albums, letters, and cards in a family burial vault in the eastern part of northern America. The search being run for references to Terminus had pulled it up, and the details transmitted up from Earth via *Explorer 6.*

"*Launch base somewhere on the West Coast,*" Casselo read again to Kyal and Brysek, who were with him in one of the lab huts. "Which we've seen mention of before. And it's a 'sensitive' subject. People being moved out to a secret location. Sounds like this place, doesn't it? It all fits."

"The whole planet would have had to have been threatened," Brysek muttered.

"Who are these other people that it talks about?" Kyal asked, leaning forward to peer at the translation again. "This Oxstead . . . And then there's Robert and Vera . . . and Gorman. Do we have any idea who they were?"

"I've put all the names through for another search," Casselo replied. "But don't hold out too high hopes of much turning up. The linguists tell me that Robert and Vera were both popular given names that could have referred to just about anyone. And Gorman was a fairly common family name. They're giving it a try. But as I said, don't expect too much to come out of it."

CHAPTER TWENTY-ONE

Jenyn sat at his work station in the Linguistics offices of the ISA laboratory complex at Rhombus, contemplating a screen showing the translation of a Terran political tract that he had worked on during the time he had spent in the Americas. It was the president of that region's exhortation before the final war that had followed the Central Asian War. The words were stirring, a call to unite a nation that had inspired millions to courage and duty and sacrifice. Their cadences reverberated in his mind, bringing visions of huge armies mobilizing and moving to their positions, formations of aircraft sweeping across the skies, ships putting to sea. "We will defend our freedoms and our honor to the last one of us that is left to stand. We will never surrender." How could such passions and determination be instilled into dull Venusian minds? he asked himself. There had to be a way. His being thirsted and cried out for it. He felt the natural instinct for power in his veins. The great Terran leaders had faced the same challenge and risen to it.

It needed organizing and direction. As with the cutting edge of a tool, or the combined work of the swing of a hammer and the point of a nail, the secret lay in concentrating all effort on the place where effect was to be achieved. Every distraction and diversion of a resource was to the same degree to detract from the plan and render attainment of the goal that much less likely. It really was as simple as that. The pusillanimous Venusian reluctance to resort to force would have to be overcome. His shock troops would be the disaffected and envious, who, once they were awakened, could always be spurred to demand as rights what the traditional anarchic ways of undirected individuals muddling through had failed to confer. The scattering of loosely affiliated Progressive initiatives behind the labor strikes and student demonstrations that the news channels were reporting from Venus were groping around the right idea, but in their implicit expectation that they themselves only partly recognized, that energy and direction would somehow emerge under its own dynamic, they were adopting the same assumptions as the system they criticized. It needed a *leader*, who would *make* it happen. In some ways, the time he had been obliged to spend out here at Earth while the fuss at *The Commentator* cooled down had not been a bad thing. It had given him time to reflect and to plan. Like a general from a distance, he had been able to see the full scheme of the battlefield with all its strongholds, weaknesses, and openings for opportunity. By rallying the young and adventurous, undulled minds that he had found here, far from home, he could light a flame that would ignite the world when he brought it back to Venus.

But first there was Gaster Lornod to think about. While Jenyn was on the far side of the planet, Lornod had come to the fore in Rhombus and among the professional cadre up on *Explorer 6* as the prime contender for coordinating the Progressive groups on Earth. He called himself a Progressive Moderate, taking the position that the traditional system had grown complacent in some ways over the years, and perhaps some looking to itself to put its house in order would not be a bad thing. The pure meritocracy upon which it was based was a fine thing in theory, he conceded, but it left many ways whereby deserving people were being left behind through no fault or failing of their own, creating needless personal distress and a loss of their services to society as a whole, which society had within its power to put right. It was a soft line that, while possibly effective in attracting initial support, missed the whole point of power by mistaking the means for the ends. Even the name "Progressive Moderate" was a contradiction of terms. But it was getting attention, not only from intellectualoid invertebrates who would never show strong Progressive mettle, but now also among the younger contingent, eroding what Jenyn had looked to as his potential recruitment base. Even Sherven was on record as remarking that the Moderates might have some valid points.

Yes, he would have to do something about Lornod.

Elundi Kasseg, who worked in the same room, in his own niche on the far side of a large, shared table covered with papers, file folders, and references, interrupted Jenyn's thoughts. "Got a second, Jenyn?"

"What?"

Elundi gestured at the screen that he was using. "This latest that's come through from *E6*. I need an opinion."

Jenyn copied the text to one of his own screens. It was another search request from the group at Triagon on lunar Farside. "Okay," he said.

"The name Oxstead is rare enough, but there aren't any hits. Robert and Vera are too vague. We can forget them. But it's come up with a number of Gormans."

"Wasn't that a pretty common Terran name too?" Jenyn queried.

"True. But look at number twenty-eight. It has an association with Terminus."

Jenyn followed the link and read the reference. It was to an indexed catalogue of names that listed a Herbert Gorman as a New Washington journalist. Several entries related to him. The one Elundi had highlighted described him as having written some articles on the mysterious disappearances of a number of scientists, senior administrators, and other key figures.

"This one, about the missing people?" Jenyn checked.

"Yes." Elundi leaned across the table separating them and passed over a hard copy of a file from one of the big translation facilities on Venus that included a piece by Gorman restored and scanned from a Terran periodical called *Insider*. Jenyn read through it quickly. The official story was that the names Gorman had drawn attention to had been commandeered for secret work relating to the war that was threatening—other sources said impending. Gorman wasn't convinced by the explanation. He didn't see how many of the skills and background represented were relevant to such ends. Power and influence seemed to him to be a more significant common factor.

"I'm still not seeing the connection," Jenyn said.

"Here." Elundi handed him a further sheet that he had been holding. It was a letter from Gorman to somebody called Kathryn— the translator had added parenthetically "Barnes"—asking her if she knew anything about a code word *Terminus*. He thought it might refer to a secret evacuation center somewhere for the privileged.

"This isn't out of any published document," Elundi elaborated. "It's just from some private papers found in a different city. So the connection is pretty thin. Just the name, Gorman, and the mention of Terminus." He looked across dubiously. "What do you think."

Jenyn read over the letter again. "Did Gorman ever get an answer, do we know?" he inquired.

"There's no way of telling. The thread ends there. He was killed shortly afterward."

"How?"

"There's one mention of it being an assassination by some Asiatic terrorist organization, but no further details."

Jenyn sighed. Everything that was wrong with the world was due to people being too timid and cautious. He was in a mood for playing the odds today, he decided. "I think it's good," he pronounced. "Yes, send it up to the people on Luna."

"Will do," Elundi said.

By the end of the day, Jenyn was still in a restless, unsettled mood. He was nurturing plans for building and controlling a political movement that would take over a world. Yet he had been unable to assert his will with one obstinate female who couldn't see what would be best for her in the long run. The power of a strong team working together scaled much faster than the sum of its number. The team would need a solid nucleus to form around. Lorili and he could provide such a nucleus. They had proved it years ago, on Venus. He wasn't going to let this beat him now—the first major target he had set himself since arriving back in Rhombus.

He went down the corridor to an empty office, closed the door, and called her number in the Bio Sciences complex. She didn't look pleased when she answered.

"Yes, look, I know," he told her before she could say anything. "I'm sorry that went the way it did, too, okay? We both lost it a bit. I'm not saying it was all you. I'll meet you halfway over the bridge. How's that?"

"What do you want?" Lorili asked tightly.

"Just to talk. I just want you to hear me out. We could still do such a lot together. Out here . . . its a huge opportunity that I think maybe you don't fully understand. I just don't want to see it thrown away, that's all. I know I made mistakes before, but all that's changed now. I've got great plans that I want you to hear about. We could still go places when we get back home. Big places, big time."

"I think it's you who doesn't fully understand, Jenyn," she said. "I've already told you all I have to say. I have plans of my own now, and my own life. And right at this moment, I have my work to do."

"I just want to talk, that's all."

"I don't think that would be a good idea."

"An hour. It doesn't have to be anywhere private, if that makes you uncomfortable. I could meet you somewhere in town."

"Please stop bothering me."

For a moment Jenyn felt an impulse to lash out about the man he had watched her seeing off at the launch port, but he held it in check. "Look, Lorili, you know me," he said. "I don't quit. If you're really serious about ending this, the only way will be to hear me out."

"It's already ended."

"Not on my terms, it hasn't."

"Still laying down the conditions. You just have to be in control, don't you? Oh boy, yes, you've really changed."

"I could make you one of the best-known names on Venus one day."

"*You* could *make*. Is that all you think people are? Things to be put together and used and thrown away."

"You know what I mean. . . ."

"Good-bye, Jenyn."

He was still in a sour mood when he came back into the office. Elundi was backing up files and tidying papers in preparation for going home. "You were right on with that piece about Gorman," he greeted. "I got a reply straight back. It was just what they're looking for. They asked us to look out for anything more on the survival center angle."

Jenyn nodded but his mind was elsewhere. "Got any plans in particular for tonight?" he asked.

"Not really. I was thinking about dropping by a couple of friends who are into Terran chess, but it's no huge thing? Why?"

"I feel like hitting a couple of bars down in the Center. Could use some company. Interested?"

Elundi rocked his head first to one side, then the other. "Sure, why not?" he said finally. "In fact, the more I think about it, the better it sounds." He shut down the system, stood up, and took his jacket from a hook behind the door. Jenyn retrieved his own coat from his side of the table.

"Ever try it?" Elundi asked as they came out into the corridor.

"What?"

"Terran chess."

"Can't say I did. Never had the time."

"One of the kinds of games I like. You can learn the rules in ten minutes. But it'll take the rest of your life to learn how to use them. You know . . . the opposite of these games where they spend all their time looking up more rules and tables than there are in the Terran translation libraries."

"I think there are better things to do in life," Jenyn said.

"That's a shame," Elundi told him. "The Terrans called it the Game of Kings. Apparently, it was devised as a stylized form of warfare in miniature. I would have thought you'd have loved it."

CHAPTER TWENTY-TWO

The Magic Carpet bar-restaurant in Rhombus's Central District took its name from an old Terran fairy tale relating to the region. It was reasonably busy that evening. The dining area at the back was doing a brisk trade with its mixed menu of traditional Venusian food and a choice of Terran dishes based on foods from different climate zones. The dance floor to one side of the bar was starting to warm up with couples from the younger set working through the latest crazes with the added dash and daring that comes with being a long way from home. Alcohol was an accepted relaxant on Venus, along with other stimulants comparable to ones that for reasons the psychologists had never quite been able to explain had driven the Terran authorities into fits of repressive hysteria. The general rule on Venus was that what a person did with their own body in their own time was their business, so long as the effects didn't spill over the line of harming or endangering anybody else. Maybe the difference had something to do with the Venusian reliance on internally assimilated disciplines to curb excesses of behavior, rather then having to resort to external means. It was unusual for them to take things to the kind of extremes that seemed to have caused social problems among Terrans. Human nature being what it was, and nothing in the real world being perfect, infringements of custom nevertheless did occur, of course. An assortment of uniformed national organizations known as provosts existed to step in on such

141

occasions as circumstances required, but their role was essentially one of passive response to transgressions of a relatively few limits that few questioned. There was nothing resembling the attempts at thought control and forcible imposition of others' creeds and personal tastes that seemed to have been practiced by most of the Terran "police" forces—the term "force" said a lot in itself. Being a diverse social organization in its own right as well as a scientific and exploration endeavor, the Earth mission also operated a modest-scale Office of Provosts, headquartered in Rhombus.

The company in the bar area was the usual evening mix of workers from the ISA labs and the town unwinding with one or two before going home; early stalwarts set to make a night of it; and couples and groups meeting and planning what to do from here. Although locales on Earth offered virtually unlimited space for expansion compared to the restricted niches typically occupied by Venusian towns, Rhombus's growth had reflected the pattern and ways that were familiar: functional; ugly; and crowding lots of variety and activity into a small space. That was a part if its legacy from being one of the first bases. Some of the newer habitats in places like Europe, the Americas, and Asia were starting to spread out more and find time for experimenting with airiness and aesthetics in the ways that Terran environments seemed to call for.

Jenyn and Elundi found themselves a table below stairs leading up to a function room used for meetings, private parties, musical performances, and the like. As Elundi had half guessed would be the case, it didn't take Jenyn long to get into politics. He had sensed that Jenyn was in a belligerent mood ever since they left the office. But he was enjoying the atmosphere and decided he could live with it.

"Appealing to decency and reason will never bring about any significant change," Jenyn said. "Nobody who has power ever gives it up voluntarily. The Terrans knew that. They have to be made to. In the end it comes down to force. Don't you agree?"

Elundi tried to evade being pinned down. "Oh, I don't know if you can make general rules about things like that. Depends on the circumstances."

Jenyn held his glass up in front of him and shook his head from side to side. "Not good enough, Elundi. You have to make a commitment. Are you with what I'm saying, or against it? It has to be one or the other."

Elundi sighed but forced a grin. "Well, I'm not so sure that all that force solved very much for the Terrans. There were still flagrant injustices on Earth. A lot of people were robbed and exploited by force. Maybe it was necessary there. But I can't see that it applies so much to Venus. Most people seem happy enough with what we've worked out in our own messy way."

"Pah!" Jenyn made a contemptuous gesture. "Give them a shirt on their back, a bowl of soup for the day, and a mattress for the night, and they'd be happy. A pig in a pen full of mud is happy. Don't you think that a life's work should be worth more than that? They're happy because they've been conditioned not to see it; to docility. There are thousands out there who deserve better than they're getting, and they don't even know it because we rely on this touching faith that individual judgments and freedom of choice will somehow magically produce better answers. Abilities that should be positively acknowledged and rewarded get shut out."

Elundi didn't want this to turn into an argument, but he couldn't let it pass. "I'm sure you're right there," he said. "But it doesn't follow that force is the only way. Look, I'm not trying to tell you how you should think. But you know . . . it might pay to take a look at the way Gaster Lornod is approaching those same issues."

"Lornod! All talk . . ."

"But people are listening to him, Jenyn. And he makes some valid points. There *are* too many people hiding behind collective rulings and putting out decisions made by nameless committees. He's right when he says projects should be headed by an individual who will stand up and take the responsibility. They can use all the expert advice they want, sure, but at the end of the day somebody has to be prepared to say, *I decided.* . . . You've got the answer to half our institutional problems right there. There's no need to start shooting people. All it will do is create people who want to shoot you back." Elundi saw the dark look coming onto Jenyn's eyes. Just as he was telling himself he'd gone too far, and was searching for a tactic to back out gracefully, a voice called out from nearby and rescued him.

"*Jenyn! You're back!*" They turned their heads.

A tall, well-built girl had emerged from among the gaggle of figures along the edge of the dance floor and was coming over to the table. She had yellow-orange hair styled in wavelets and was wearing a loose sleeveless top with a short, black, braided leather skirt. Elundi would have described her appearance as "formidable," though with nose and chin perhaps a touch on the prominent side. Another girl was with her, shorter and petite, with long dark hair tied in a tail behind her back, and less ostentatiously dressed in a light sweater and casual pants.

"Tyarla. Well, hey." Jenyn smiled; but just at that moment, Elundi got the feeling he would have preferred to continue talking politics.

She stooped, put her arms around Jenyn's neck, and kissed him, making an exhibition of it. "I had no idea! I thought you were still in the Americas. How wonderful! How long have you been back in Rhombus?"

"Not long. I'm still waiting for a permanent place." Jenyn detached himself sufficiently to gesture. "This is Elundi, who works with me. Elundi, these are two old friends from a while back. Tyarla. . . . And this is Derlen."

Oh, so Jenyn knew both of them. From the way Tyarla had monopolized him, Elundi wouldn't have guessed it. "Hello," he said.

"Hi, Elundi," Tyarla gushed. For a moment, he thought she was going to subject him to the same treatment as Jenyn but she held it to a smile that merely invited him to admire her. Derlen just smiled and nodded. He got the impression that Tyarla liked making other girls jealous. She seemed to be succeeding.

Tyarla did accounting for the base administration at Rhombus, and was good at it—because she told them so. But her talent was undervalued. She also painted pictures of Terran landscapes, designed her own interior decor, and danced "correctly." Derlen was a hairdresser and dermatician. They were both from Korbisan, like Jenyn. It soon became apparent that Tyarla was also an ardent Progressive, which perhaps explained a lot.

"Is that when you two met?" Elundi asked Tyarla, nodding toward Jenyn. "When he was here in Rhombus before?"

"Actually, it was back on Venus," she said. Jenyn gave her a puzzled look. She sipped hastily from her glass—Jenyn had bought them all a round. "Well, we got to *know* each other in Rhombus, didn't we, darling?" Jenyn made as if he hadn't heard. "Venus was where I first saw him. . . . But he wouldn't have known about me then. I was just one of the many distant admirers, slaving to play my part in the campaign. He was the big name, you see. Posters with his face on; top table at all the dinners. And *very* charming and splendid in formal attire, if I may say so." She looked at Jenyn for acknowledgment. He smiled obligingly. Tyarla emitted an exaggerated sigh. "But of course he didn't notice any of us poor phone-canvassing and envelope-stuffing peons in those days. He had this black-haired siren clinging to his arm all the time." She turned her head toward Jenyn. For an instant her voice took on a tone of forced nonchalance. "Is she still around, Jenyn?"

"That all ended back on Venus," he replied.

"Oh." The remark was throwaway but the eyes betrayed something deeper.

Elundi figured that the person she was referring to had to be the biochemist that Jenyn had been telling him odd details about. If that were the case, then it didn't sound exactly all that ended from his latest comments—not if Jenyn had any say in things, anyway.

"How about you?" he said to Derlen to steer them off that particular tack and bring her more into the conversation. "Are you an old-time Progressive from Venus too?"

"No. I'm just finding out about it from Tyarla. It sounds interesting." Derlen looked away suddenly, cocked her head, and began swaying. "This is one of my favorites." She meant the song that had just come on. "Do you like to dance?" she asked, looking back at Elundi.

"Maybe . . . In a minute?"

"Sure."

"What brought you out to Earth?" he asked.

"Oh, you know how it is. Good money, something different, a chance to get away from boring everything. I guess we're mostly all going to settle down to it anyway, sometime. So see what you can, while you can, eh?"

"You like it here?"

"Sure, why not?"

"Is she your regular friend, then—Tyarla?"

"Sort of, I suppose." Derlen glanced aside. Tyarla had moved her chair closer to Jenyn and had her hand draped on his shoulder, teasing the side of his neck with a fingertip. They were talking in lowered voices. Derlen leaned closer. "Sometimes she can be a bit . . ." She left the sentence unfinished and motioned with her eyes. It seemed they were on their own as far as further conversation went. "But when you're out at somewhere like this, you make the best of whatever friends you get. Know what I mean?"

"Still, I'd think she's the kind who would make it easy to meet people," Elundi said.

"True, but . . ." Derlen paused, as if weighing what she had been about to say. She let her voice fall almost to a whisper. "Some of them are not exactly, how would I say it . . . the most respectable people you'd want to meet . . . if you know what I mean. Yes, okay, this is a long way from home and all that, but there are standards. You're still who you are."

Elundi decided she was interesting. And his life had been distinctly lacking in companionship of the distaff kind of late. The way her eyes were flickering over him, taking in the details, was not unfriendly. *If you don't buy a ticket, you don't get a prize,* he told himself. "You know, ah, you don't have to rely on her to find you friends all the time," he murmured. "I think you're kind of nice. How about getting together for a drink ourselves here sometime? They don't look as if they'd exactly miss us anyhow."

Derlen shrugged and nodded. "Sure, why not?"

As simple as that? Elundi realized he wasn't sure how to follow on now. "You'd better give me your call code, then," he said.

"Okay, I will before we go."

He grinned, feeling that maybe they were being too serious. "But you have to promise not to talk about the Progressives and all that stuff."

"Suits me. I'm not sure I really buy the things Tyarla talks about, anyway. To be honest, I have more time for somebody like Gaster Lornod. What he says makes a lot of sense."

Elundi looked warily toward Jenyn, but Jenyn hadn't overheard. Elundi raised a hand to cover his mouth. "Look, I'll tell you why next time, but for now, I don't think it's a good idea to mention Gaster Lornod. Okay?" Derlen nodded, sat back in her seat, and picked up her drink.

The music has switched to a slow, quiet number, allowing snatches of Jenyn and Tyarla's talk to filter through.

Jenyn: ". . . What kind of a party? . . ."

Tyarla: "An *interesting* kind. You'd like it. . . . tomorrow night . . ."

" . . . don't know for sure . . ."

". . . could call me later anyway . . ."

Elundi caught Derlen's eye. She looked uncomfortable. "How about that dance?" he suggested.

She danced easily and naturally, making eye contact and smiling, with none of that bored wooden look focused on infinity that could make a guy feel like a moving hall stand—just there to fill the empty space. Elundi sometimes had a problem staying in time with the rhythm, getting jerky and uncoordinated, and then feeling conspicuous. But tonight everything was smooth and relaxed, and he congratulated himself inwardly that he wasn't doing too badly at all. Maybe it just took two. Some of the couples were showing off with the new body-hugging style of dance that was raising eyebrows back home. Elundi was not up to being that forward, and kept it open and styled. Before returning to the table he wrote Derlen's call code into his phone's directory, and was gratified when she asked for his. Another good sign.

Tyarla had her purse on her lap and seemed to be getting ready to leave when they arrived back at the table. "Going already?" Elundi said, disappointed. "It was just getting to be fun."

"We only meant to stop by for one," Derlen said. "We're supposed to be going to a play the ISA group is putting on. It's going to be tight making it now. Give me a call."

"You've got it."

Tyarla seemed a little out of sorts, as if things between her and Jenyn had not gone entirely to her liking. Elundi got the feeling that her ego had taken a dent, possibly from not having swept back into the celebrity's life with the full accord that she expected. Overripe things dented easily.

"Well, *so* sorry to deprive you of my company, guys, but we do have to rush," she told them as she stood up. "Oh, is it really that time? We may have to miss the first act, Derl. Lovely meeting you, Elundi. . . . Jenyn, I can't *tell* you what an unexpected delight it is." And louder as the two girls moved away, making a public announcement of it, "*Do* remember to call me."

Elundi got himself and Jenyn another drink. Jenyn was broody and not very talkative—which at least kept them off politics. His naturally florid countenance seemed to have taken on a deeper hue, and his eyes had a hard glint to them. A meanness was coming to the surface that Elundi hadn't seen before. He thought he sensed the conflict. Tyarla's overtures were tempting, but Jenyn felt inhibited by the other situation he had talked about with the biologist.

Elundi acknowledged a wave from some people grouped by the bar. "Sulvay and a couple of others from the translators' section are over there," he remarked.

"Uh-huh."

Elundi waited for a few seconds. "Shall I call them over?"

"Ah, they'll only be talking shop as usual. I'm not in the mood."

"Okay." Another silence. Elundi sipped his drink and then observed neutrally, "Something seems to be bothering you."

Jenyn didn't respond but shot glances this way and that around the room, as if looking for an escape route. Then, suddenly decisive, he tossed back the last of his drink and set the glass down with a thud.

"You leaving?"

"I've got some unfinished business to attend to," Jenyn's growled. He was spoiling for a fight. "It's time to clear some air."

"Do you mean with the one in Molecular Bio? What was her name? Lorili?"

"Yes. It needs to be brought to a head." Jenyn braced his hands on the table to rise.

"Er, look . . ." Elundi felt he had to say something. "I don't want to pry into your personal business, but is this really the best time?"

"What are you trying to say?" Open belligerence, directed at Elundi now.

Elundi raised a restraining hand. "Easy. . . . Just that it might be better left until tomorrow. You know, let it cool a little. You've had a few tonight, man."

"I don't remember asking your opinion about that."

"Okay, okay. . . ."

"I'll see you tomorrow." Jenyn got up and stalked out.

Elundi sat staring uneasily at his drink. He knew somebody over in the Molecular Biology labs. But would it be overreacting?

The group at the bar had seen he was alone now, and were coming over. "We saw your friend leaving, so we thought you could use more company," Sulvay greeted. Elundi made his decision and rose from the chair. Sulvay halted. "Oh. Are you going too?"

"I just have to make a call," Elundi said. "Sit down. I'll be back in a moment."

He went up the stairs to the hallway outside the function room, which was not being used that night—it was quieter, besides having more privacy. What was that guy in Molecular Biology's name? He checked his phone register. Iwon, that was it. He flagged the code and pressed the Connect button. Iwon's face with its ragged Terran-style mustache appeared in the window after a few beeps.

"Hi, Iwon, do you remember me?"

"Oh, right . . . from the Linguistics office. I enjoyed the chat. Good to hear from you again. What can I do?"

"Do you know a person in the Mol Bio section by the name of Lorili?"

"Lorili Hilivar? Sure, I work with her."

"So you'd be able to call her?"

"Yes, naturally. Why? What's up?"

"Look, I may be overreacting here, but I'd rather play it on the safe side. I think there might be trouble heading her way right now. Can you call her and tell her that Jenyn's on his way, and he's in a mean mood. I think she'll know what that means. Whatever she wants to do about it is up to her. But I thought she ought to know."

"'Jenyn.'" Iwon repeated. Thankfully, he didn't seem to be the kind who wanted details and explanations.

"Right."

"I'll call her right now."

Lorili was in her neighbor Ufty's apartment upstairs, across the way, by the time Jenyn arrived at her door. Keeping back in the shadows behind the window fronting the balcony, the light turned off, they watched as he jabbed repeatedly at the door chime, and then banged loudly on the door, calling out her name. He swayed back a few steps to survey the place, stalked around muttering, then went back to the door again and banged some more. Faces appeared in some of the nearby windows. Finally, he left.

"It happens that way with some people," Ufty commented, shaking his head. "He's just had one too many. He'll be okay in the morning."

"No, you don't know him," Lorili replied. A sick, sinking feeling had taken hold of her. "This isn't going to be the last of it."

A block away, Jenyn stopped on the corner and stood glowering along the street for a while. Then he took out his phone and called Tyarla. She seemed surprised and also pleased.

"So soon! We decided to miss the play. Derlen has gone on home. Changed your mind?"

"Would you still like to be envied and famous?"

"Well, whatever comes to us naturally, you know . . ."

"I could have a job for you that would be a big step in the right direction." Jenyn looked at the image pouting out at him. "And maybe the rest too," he said.

CHAPTER TWENTY-THREE

The Special Task Committee met in a room of the military command complex on the west side of New Washington known as the Hexagon—its architects had had to go one step better than their predecessors. It functioned under the auspices of the Joint Services Internal Security Office but its name didn't appear in any of the official departmental listings. It was chaired by an Army general known to the others and written up in the minutes simply as "Polo."

"Okay, that's settled." He shuffled the papers that they were done with to the bottom of his folder. "Moving on to item three." The sheets that came to the top referred to an article by Herbert Gorman that had appeared two days previously in the left-sponsored political incitement journal, *Insider*. Polo allowed a minute or so for himself and others to refresh themselves. It was the latest in a series that Gorman had been putting out on mysterious "disappearances" of key people. Apparently, the attempts to send him a discreet warning were having no effect. If anything, his tone was even more defiant and militant. It was inexplicable to Polo that the obvious talent Gorman displayed in one direction could be accompanied by such foolishness in another. Gorman *knew* how the system worked, yet he seemed unable to apply the obvious implications to himself. Polo didn't believe in willingness to sacrifice oneself for a principle. That was the stuff of uplifting stories as fodder for the sheep pen. But it could have no place in the mind of any realist.

"I thought this rag was going to be shut down," somebody halfway along the table murmured.

"It's being worked on," another voice said.

"What's this note about Perrin-McLeod?" Polo asked. He looked up. "It says Juggler has something."

The officer that he had addressed read from a laptop. "Gorman has been talking to the wife, Sandra, trying to track her husband. According to a source who's close to her, he asked her if she knew anything about a code word Terminus. She told him she didn't."

Polo frowned. "How in hell did Gorman get hold of that?" he asked, looking around.

"More to the point, how did he connect it to the disappearances he's been writing about?" someone else added. Nobody responded.

"This has gone too far," Polo declared. "He's already run the stop sign. I think the case goes to Removals. Anyone disagree? . . . Any further points? Okay. Cymbal, will you take care of this?"

A broad, gray-headed, unsmiling figure in a plain tunic without insignia nodded.

Polo moved the sheets to the bottom of the folder. "Okay, moving along. Item four . . ."

Three days later, the media carried the story that a New Washington journalist called Herbert Gorman had been killed by a car bomb outside his home. He had been a controversial writer with outspoken views on a number of inflammatory topics that had earned him enmity from many quarters, including unstable political regimes and international terrorist groups, so such an incident wasn't entirely unexpected.

Not long afterward, the story surfaced that Gorman had been working on a piece to expose secret plans by Muslim governments in Southeast Asia to destabilize the situation in parts of southern China that were wavering over Beijing's leaning closer toward America. Experts duly appeared, expressing suspicion of Southeast Asian political terror groups believed to be infiltrating the country. Their connection with Gorman was corroborated by the production of a threatening note warning him off that line of research. It was said to have been found among Gorman's papers. There was even a security camera clip from a gas station not far from Gorman's home, allegedly taken early on the morning of the murder, showing an Oriental filling the tank of a car, acting suspiciously, and checking the trunk before departing.

None of this caused any great surprise. After all, everyone knew that terrorists from that part of the world were everywhere and were likely to do things like that at any time, anyway.

CHAPTER TWENTY-FOUR

The short-haul service flyer skimmed low over the terrain of lunar Farside. Yorim was at the controls, Kyal beside him. Some familiarization with piloting came as part of the training package for lunar environments. They were both suited up and had the cabin evacuated in preparation for outside work on arrival. Casselo had left Triagon to return to *Explorer 6*. The discovery of the sixty-eight Terran corpses, intact and in an unprecedented state of preservation, was getting the biologists excited, and Sherven was considering setting up a more comprehensively equipped biological laboratory at Triagon to study them.

Yorim was intrigued by this woman at Rhombus who seemed to communicate with Kyal more frequently than he thought a mere casual acquaintanceship would call for. It intrigued him because over the years he had always known Kyal as being reserved and conservative in his ways, focused on his work, and not of an inclination to involve himself in such things. And now, all of a sudden, he's being publicly hugged at the spaceport by this person he's met only days before who has come out of her way to see him off, not only striking in all the eye-catching ways that would have gotten Yorim's attention at any time, but from some of the oddments he'd heard since, pretty interesting and unconventional in herself as well. He wasn't letting Kyal off the hook until he'd learned more.

"So are you telling me you didn't have this set up all along? That wasn't why you ducked out at Rhombus and went your own way?" he challenged.

"How could I have? We'd only just arrived on Earth," Kyal retorted. "I told you, I met her in that city up in the Caucasus. It just turned out that we have the same kind of interests."

"That's it, eh?" Yorim looked sideways inside his helmet with an expression that said maybe he believed it but many wouldn't.

"And okay, yes, she's different as a person from most that you meet," Kyal said. "Curious about things. Thinks for herself and forms her own opinions. I like that."

"Is she a Prog, out of curiosity? Brysek says there's a lot of interest in it around Rhombus."

Kyal waved a gloved hand vaguely. "She thinks that some of what they're saying is worth thinking about—maybe we've gotten a bit too set in our ways and could give youth and diversity more openings. . . . Apparently she was mixed up with it for a while back on Venus."

It wasn't something that Kyal wanted to go into, Yorim read, so he didn't ask about it. "I thought you said she was into that Terran theory of life appearing by itself, out of chemistry," he said instead.

"She's curious about it. But simply as a scientist—trying not to prejudge anything until she's had a chance to look at it and think about it. That's the way it ought to be. See what I mean? She'll figure out for herself what she wants to believe. Nothing wrong with that."

The monotony of dust, rocks, and crater rims rolled by below. They were about a hundred miles from Triagon.

"Why are the Progressives so keen on the idea?" Yorim asked.

"You mean that extrapolating selective adaptation without limit can explain everything?"

"Yes. I mean, whether it's true or not is a matter of objective fact. Whatever they, you, me, or anyone else thinks isn't going to change it. What does it have to do with their politics?"

"I suppose maybe if you're not a scientist, you don't think about it that way. If you can convince people it's true, then you can point to it as validating your ideology." Kyal held up a hand before Yorim could respond. "Yes, I know that doesn't make it true. But in politics it's what people believe that matters."

Another short silence fell. Yorim glanced over the flight processor and status displays while he thought about it. "So what is there about it that appeals to their ideology?"

"The notion of unrestrained striving and competition. Being able to go all-out and use any means to get what *you* want, with nobody and nothing to answer to—as opposed to existing as part of something larger that you have to learn to harmonize with. It fits with their platform of changing the system by demands and coercion—and some of them say violence if need be."

As with many things, Yorim had dabbled in Progressivism for a while, but found that he couldn't relate. Maybe things on Venus did change slowly enough to try the patience of some, but were they really any worse off at the end of it all than the Terrans with their frenetic pace of building things up, when they devoted as much energy and industry to knocking them down again?

"Emur Frazin said the general Terran belief was that there really wasn't any choice if you wanted to change things," Kyal recalled. "At the end of it all, nothing else worked. Force was the only way."

Yorim made a face. "If that's what they thought, I guess it explains a lot."

"They believed that whoever had the power never let it go voluntarily. They had to be made to."

"The Progs say the same thing."

Kyal tossed up a hand. "Well, there's your answer. That's how their ideology fits. Maybe they got it from the Terrans." He mulled over it some more and then went on, "Their leaders were very different from ours. Maybe there's another part of your reason too. We think of political and social leaders as belonging to the same family. They work to try and get what's best for everybody, right?"

"Well . . . yeah." Yorim had never thought about it being any other way. After all, what else were they there for?

"But with the Terrans it was different," Kyal went on. "The leaders were an elite class among themselves—across-the board, even on the opposite sides of wars. The rest of the people were just expendables to be exploited. Of course that wasn't the way they were told. They were kept divided against each other in ways such that they always thought some other group was the cause of their problems. So they were never able to unite against the real common enemy of all of them."

Yorim was having trouble picturing it. A people's leaders working against the people? It sounded like a self-contradiction. He shook his head. "But . . . they didn't *know*?" he objected.

"The business of their mass communications was to indoctrinate, not educate," Kyal replied. "Dissemination of official lies. The media were owned by the ones who stood to benefit."

"But it must still have been obvious that the leaders were doing a lousy job. How could the Electors stay in office? Or are you saying they owned the Electors too?"

"They didn't have Electors. The people appointed the leaders direct."

Yorim frowned across as if to make sure that Kyal wasn't joking. "But that's crazy. It would be like . . . like expecting someone on the street to pick who should design the *Melther Jorg*—instead of the people at ISA whose job it is. You and I wouldn't be here."

Kyal shrugged. "That's how the exohistorians figure it was."

"No wonder they had lousy leaders," Yorim said.

Kyal looked at the control panel clock. "We must be getting close," he commented.

"Almost." As if on cue, an alert beeped to tell them they were coming onto final approach. "I think I see it," Yorim said.

Kyal peered ahead and picked out the pointed tip among the sunlit crags and ridges ahead. "There was something else, deeper down, that made Terran social structures different," he said. "Ours work together, to try and make the quality of life better for all. Oh, yes of course they have differences at times, but the whole art is to resolve them. Terrans worked against each other. The aim all the time was to 'win,' which meant someone else had to lose."

"Which *they're* going to try and put right as soon as they get the chance," Yorim said.

"So it would be best to make sure they're not around to try. . . ." Kyal's voice trailed away for a second. "There, you've got it. 'Survival of the fittest.' Their theory of biology captured it exactly. Or maybe it was the way they were that shaped the theory. But whatever, there was some fundamental difference between us and them psychologically. Lorili thinks it might be genetic." He shook his head. "I don't know any more than that, Yorim."

The pyramid had escaped notice until methodical scrutinizing of orbital pictures covering the environs of Triagon revealed it as an artificial form in a remote area of overlapping crater ridges and humps. The analysts who carried out the first cursory checks had been looking for engineering constructions like those found Triagon itself. Then it was found that something down there was highly reflective to ground surveillance radar.

The flyer landed close to the craft that had brought Brysek and a reconnoitering party ahead some hours earlier. Brysek and a couple of other suited figures appeared from among the boulders and mounds at the base of the pyramid as Kyal and Yorim climbed out.

"It's even more interesting close-up," he greeted as they joined him.

"Not just another Terran tomb, then—for a king that liked solitude?" Kyal quipped.

"Burns and discharge scars. It seems you were right on."

"Let's take a look."

Brysek and his two companions turned, and the group made their way to the pyramid's base. In size it was nothing like the one Yorim had climbed back on Earth, but the side facing them was catching the sun full-on, making it a mountain of whiteness above them, dominating the surroundings and dazzling against the black sky.

With no wind to carry eroding dust, and micrometeorite infall not worth talking about, its laminated structure and vertical lines of conductive ribbing were still clearly defined. The whole form was tantalizingly suggestive of the discharge attractors that Kyal had conceived in speculative theoretical studies he had produced for heavy lift, long-range transportation systems. The charge accumulated by electrically energized vessels on extended journeys would need to be dissipated before landing on a surface or docking with any sizeable body possessing a significantly different potential—which would generally be the case with a spacecraft arriving from a distant electrical environment. The pyramid's dimensions suggested that it could have been intended for quite large craft.

"Now where did you see something like that before?" Kyal asked as they stopped and looked up to take stock of it. He meant his own tentative design sketches, which Yorim was familiar with.

"I wonder," Yorim replied.

In his mind, Kyal ran through the findings they had amassed so far. References to Terminus implying a secret survival shelter for a large number of people; disappearances of leading scientists and other key figures; an all-too-convenient assassination of a journalist who knew too much and was getting too close. The deeper parts of the Triagon Lower Complex, adjoining the Rear Annexe with its own entrance from the surface, had revealed animal pens and cages, and some kind of hydroponic botanical facility. And now, here was evidence for a development program involving heavy, long-range transportation. Was Triagon *just* a survival shelter? He was beginning to wonder. Or had it been part of a more grandiose undertaking? Evacuation to somewhere else, maybe?

Yorim seemed to be having the same thoughts. He swung from side to side to take in the base of the pyramid, then gazed back up at summit. Finally, he turned and scanned the surroundings, as if they might furnish more clues. His voice came over Kyal's radio. "I don't know what to make of it. What kind of weapons did they have that would make them come all the way here? Even Terrans couldn't blow a whole planet up."

"I know," Kyal agreed.

"So are we talking about just a survival center? Or was it an operation to get them away? That could be one reason why they'd hide it out here."

"You tell me."

"Maybe Terminus meant the *other* end of the line. The beginning, not the place where it ended."

"That's just what I was wondering too."

"A staging base for shipping one to somewhere else."

"Yes. It fits."

"But where?" Yorim turned back toward Kyal and spread his arms.

"There isn't anywhere else in the Solar System they could have gone for any length of time," Brysek came in, tuned to the same channel.

"Not now, anyway, that's true," Yorim agreed. "But the Solar System isn't a constant place. It changes. Maybe there was somewhere else that was suitable then."

"Their records don't say anything about anywhere like that," Brysek pointed out.

"Not any that we know of. But they weren't supposed to have electric propulsion either."

Kyal had to agree with Yorim. "Perhaps things were different then," he said.

CHAPTER TWENTY-FIVE

Garki Nostreny settled back behind his desk to listen as Lorili got to the point that she had come to his office to discuss. He was the section head of Biochemistry, genial in a fatherly kind of way, with a long, creased face that looked as if it no longer quite fitted a head that had shrunk a little, and wispy, graying hair. Lorili had found him consistently open, receptive, and easy to work with since her arrival at Rhombus.

"They're unprecedented," she said. She was referring to the Terran remains found out on the lunar surface at Triagon, and then later, the unmarked bodies in the Lower Annexe. Tissue samples had been taken to *Explorer 6* for analysis and yielded more information on Terran biochemistry than anything available before. "Iwon thinks we might be able to reconstruct the cell metabolism in detail. This could be the break I was looking for to establish just how close we are genetically."

"You're still looking for a common ancestral link?" Nostreny said. He didn't mean directly, but in terms of some remote spaceborne seeding that might have originated both races, as Lorili had elaborated on earlier occasions.

"It's a something that should be followed up," she answered.

Nostreny smiled. "You still like that idea, don't you?"

Lorili had long learned that trying to hide anything would be futile. The clear, gray eyes, ever-mobile behind his metal-rimmed

163

spectacles, seemed to see into heads and read brain patterns. "Yes," she admitted. "The Terrans seemed to combine a fascinating combination of conflicting qualities. Having a better idea of how close we are to them might tell us things about ourselves."

"But I thought we went through all that with Iwon. The timescale on Venus has been too short to have gotten from some primordial ancestor to us and the other quadribasics by any mechanism of the kind the Terrans postulated—even with your environmentally cued mutations to speed things up. And even if you did somehow telescope the process into Venus's life span, you've still got the morphological similarities to explain. Skeletally it's practically impossible to tell the difference between us and Terrans. And so far, the soft-tissue specimens from Luna are telling us the same thing." Nostreny spread his hands. "Two independent sequences, both resulting in virtually identical end products? It's too much to accept as a coincidence, surely."

"That's what I wanted to talk about," Lorili said. "Maybe the cued mutation idea in the form I've been stating it might be too weak. I think there's a stronger form that could explain it. These latest Terran finds could be our chance to test it. But it would need a full biolab investigation."

Nostreny grinned and shook his head. "You just don't give up, do you?"

"Maybe it comes from studying Terrans. As I said, it's important to me."

"A stronger form of the theory?"

"Yes. It occurred to me when I was thinking about undifferentiated cells in a growing embryo."

Nostreny interlaced his fingers and sat back in his chair. "Okay, go on. Let's hear it."

"Their plasticity is an astounding example of how sensitive biological systems are to environmental cues. Any cell can become bone, muscle, nerve, or any other kind of tissue. The potential to be all of them is inherent in the common genetic program that they all carry. The cues merely determine which parts of the program are switched on." She knew she was hardly telling Nostreny anything that he wasn't aware of. It was more to set her direction.

"Okay," he agreed, opening his fingers briefly.

"Mightn't the same principle operate at a higher level? We still only know a tiny fraction of what genomes do. Perhaps the reason they're so huge is that they carry the potential to become anything over a far wider range than has been supposed."

Nostreny inclined himself forward, evidently taking the point. "You mean more than just the potential to differentiate into different kinds of cell?"

"Yes, exactly. The potential to be totally different organisms. Not just to produce different beak shapes and body sizes. But all of it already in there, contained in a common program. So the forms they come to actualize and express could be determined not by the kind of selection that the Terrans talked about, but by *selective activation* of already existing genetic potential." Nostreny nodded that he was following. Lorili warmed to her theme. "On that basis, the first life to appear on a hot, recently formed planet would be of a primitive form not because it represents an early stage of evolving information, but because it's *appropriate* in terms of what a primitive environment can support. A young planetary surface cues the appearance of microbes because nothing else could live there. Microbes initiate processes that transform the environment. The transformed environment provides new cues that switch the genetic programs to producing new types of organism. And there you have it."

Nostreny looked intrigued, to be sure. But that was just his way. It didn't meant that he bought it. His willingness to consider new things on their merit was one of the things that made him easy to work with. It mirrored Lorili's own inclinations. "So as soon as the conditions are right, you can have complex organisms that are appropriate to it appearing right away," he summarized. "Without involving enormous timescales."

"That's right. One of the things that baffled Terran evolutionists was the sudden appearance of complex life-forms in their fossil record, already fully differentiated and specialized. They never could explain it to their satisfaction. But this might."

"Of course, if it's all part of some bigger scheme in the way we've been taught, then there's probably nothing that needs explaining anyway," He wrinkled his nose and rubbed the end with a knuckle. "To be honest, it's the kind of answer I'd be more inclined toward. But then at my age, I'm not going to change now, I suppose."

"What I'm saying is that maybe we have a unique opportunity to find out," Lorili replied. "Who knows? It could even lead to some kind of reconciliation between the traditional and evolutionary views. Fast, preprogrammed repopulation to new conditions, but originating from a Vizek-like common source. The philosophical implications alone could be enormous."

"Hm." Nostreny stared at her in silence without really seeing her as he turned it over in his mind. Lorili waited. She had said what she had to say. Anything more would have been repetition. If Nostreny needed clarifying on any point, he would say so. "And this is what you want a full lab setup to look into more deeply," he said.

"Right."

"What are you proposing, more specifically? Can you give me more of an outline?"

Lorili had come prepared. "A biochemistry group from *Explorer 6* is moving out to Triagon," she replied. "That means there will be some lab space freed up in *Explorer 6* with the kind of equipment and support that I'd need. What I'd like to do is have a few of the best-preserved Terran corpses, say half a dozen, shipped to *E6* for detailed sequencing studies of some of the frozen inner cells."

"You'd be carrying this out yourself? So are you saying you want to transfer from Rhombus to *Explorer 6*," Nostreny checked.

Lorili nodded. "For the duration of the project anyway. It would be a lot simpler that way."

"Hm . . . What about Mirine?" Nostreny asked. Mirine Strass was Loril's assistant. They had come from Venus together.

"If she decided she wanted to come too, she could take care of selecting and shipping the specimens from Triagon while I was getting things set up on *Explorer*." Lorili said.

"Have you mentioned this to her yet?"

"No. I thought it best to run it by you first. But I don't think there'll be much doubt about it. She's as interested in this as I am. And we've always worked well together."

Nostreny was looking favorably impressed. He nodded absently, at the same time studying her curiously. Lorili had the feeling of the pale gray eyes reading through her skull again. "What's your real reason?" he asked finally, in a light tone. "Purely to test the theory? To simplify the logistics?" He paused pointedly. "Or could it be something more personal?"

Even with her experience of him, Lorili was taken aback. A news item had recently broken on the Earth-local net concerning Gaster Lornod, Jenyn's principal rival for the Progressive nomination. Allegedly, the real Lornod was a very different person from the restrained and respectable public image that had been getting attention, with a secret life that involved bar girls, use of stimulants to excess, and certain kinds of parties. A general rule of Venusian politics was that if one chose a life as a public figure, setting an acceptable tone in personal standards was part of the job. Public figures were expected to be models of the principle of internal restraint that the society based itself on. In short, this could be ruinous. An intuition told Lorili that Jenyn's hand was behind it. He was already dragging her into his machinations. And it was going to get worse. She didn't want to be around.

"Why should you think that?" she asked Nostreny guardedly.

"One hears rumors." He regarded her challengingly.

If he already knew something of her situation, denying it wasn't going to help matters, she told herself. In any case, it wasn't her style. She looked him back in the face.

"Personal reasons," she said.

"In that case, yes. I'll see what can be done. Leave it with me, Lorili. I'll talk with Sherven to get his approval on the use of the space up there. If he goes along with it, I'll authorize the arrangements right away. . . . And you'd better talk to Mirine."

CHAPTER TWENTY-SIX

A stranger was waiting for her with Iwon when Lorili returned to the lab. He looked to be somewhere in his late twenties, with straight dark hair worn shoulder length and a smooth, olive complexion. His expression was serious, though not unpleasant. Iwon introduced him as Elundi. He was a linguist who worked with Jenyn. Elundi was the person who had alerted Iwon on the night when Iwon had called Lorili, warning her that Jenyn was heading her way and likely to cause trouble. "We need to talk privately with you, Lorili," Iwon said.

Lorili's mind had still been on her meeting with Nostreny when she walked in the door, and she was momentarily disoriented.

"It would probably be best if we weren't seen talking together, if it can be avoided," Elundi told them. The lab was otherwise empty just at that moment, but anyone could have walked in.

"There's a storage room downstairs," Iwon suggested. "We keep equipment just down from orbit there, before it's distributed." Elundi nodded.

Mystified, Lorili walked with them a short distance along the corridor outside the lab, and through a side door to the rear staircase of the building. Something in Elundi's quick, tense pace telegraphed an urgency about the business that had brought him.

"I apologize for this intrusion into your personal affairs," Elundi said to Lorili after Iwon had closed the door. "But there is reason to believe that a scandalous injustice is being done. We would be failing in our duty by not delving deeper if that proves to be the case. You might be able to help us."

"Well, of course . . . if I can," Lorili said.

Elundi came straight to the point. "I understand that you have known Jenyn for some time."

Lorili nodded. "Yes. For quite a number of years—back on Venus."

Elundi took a moment to compose his words. "I take it you've heard the story that's been going around concerning Gaster Lornod, who is standing as a nominee to represent the Progressives?"

"Yes." Lorili looked from one to the other. "It would be difficult to miss."

"What's your reaction?" Iwon asked her.

"I was surprised. I don't know Lornod, but it's out of character with the impression I'd formed of him." Lorili hesitated for a moment, then added, "If you want my honest opinion, I think the world goes too far in making things like that its business. If Lornod is at fault, it's in showing poor judgment, considering his position. But it's society's customs that make it that way."

"Some of us think the story is false," Elundi said. "And that Jenyn is behind it. Have you had many dealings with him since you came to Earth?"

"Not since he began bothering me again recently. You obviously already know about that. I've only been here for four months, and for most of that time I believe Jenyn was in the Americas." Lorili made an apologetic shrug. "So I'm not really sure that I will be able to help you. I don't know very much about what he's been doing. If he is mixed up in this thing that you're talking about, I don't know anything about it at all."

"Oh no, I wasn't meaning to imply anything like that," Elundi said hastily. "I'm just looking for some sort of corroboration from someone who knows him better that my suspicions are at least believable, before we go jumping in and making it even more noisy."

"We?"

"There are others involved, who feel equally concerned. The allegation about Lornod that started the whole thing came from a person called Tyarla Yiag."

"Yes, I'm familiar with the name from the news reports," Lorili said.

"I've met her," Elundi said. "But more to the point, she's obviously known Jenyn for some time. If I may be permitted to be critical in someone's absence, she strikes me as a somewhat naive person, also vain, and ambitious. She appears to idolize Jenyn and believes he is the key to a lifestyle that she evidently craves."

Lorili laughed, humorlessly and bitterly. "Believe me, I do understand."

Elundi gestured in a way that conveyed there was no more to be said. "I work with Jenyn, and I know something about how he thinks. I have seen him and this lady together, and the way they act. And what I immediately find myself thinking when I hear these things about a rival who has been sounding very threatening is that Jenyn put her up to it. I have shared these thoughts with certain others that I trust, and we agree that the subject must be pursued. So that is what I am doing. We have no desire to compound the situation further if my fears are groundless. So I'm collecting as much background information as I can. Jenyn has mentioned your name on occasions, which is how I was aware that you knew him. So what I am asking from you is a 'character assessment,' if that's the right way to put it. From what you know of him, could the kind of thing that I've intimated could be true, would you say? Is it plausible?"

Lorili was already ahead of him and answered without having to think about it. "More than plausible. It's exactly his style," she said.

"Be careful, Lorili," Iwon cautioned. "This is a pretty serious matter. You're sure of what you're saying?"

She nodded. "Oh yes. In fact something very like it happened before, on Venus. He framed a rival contender for an important editorial position, using a girl who was a former lover. But it blew up in his face. It wouldn't surprise me if that was what made him decide to get away from Venus for a while."

"I see." Elundi drew a long breath, looking from her to Iwon and then back again. "Thank you. I'm sorry to have had to ask such questions. But I think you've done the right thing."

"So what are you going to do?" Lorili asked him.

Elundi gave a helpless shrug in a way that said there was no choice. "Confront Jenyn and try to persuade him to admit it."

"He won't," Lorili said flatly.

"From what I've seen, you're probably right," Elundi agreed with a sigh. "But as a first step, it has to be tried."

"What then?" Iwon asked.

"I suppose we decide that when and if we come to it," Elundi answered.

Lorili bit her lip while she thought, wondering how this might impact her own plans. "Are you going to want me involved in this?" she asked Elundi. She shifted her gaze to take in Iwon. "You might as well know this now. I've just been talking to Nostreny. There's a good chance I'll be moving out very soon, going to *Explorer 6*. I put a proposal to him about setting up a sequencing lab there for the Triagon finds. He's for the idea and is putting it to Sherven."

Iwon raised his eyebrows. "Oh dear! You'll be leaving?"

But Lorili knew he wouldn't be totally surprised. She had confided something to him of the situation she was in.

"Were you pushing the preprogrammed universal genome line?" he asked.

"What else?"

"So what did he think?"

"He didn't make his mind up about anything ahead of the evidence. Just agreed it should be tested."

Iwon nodded, but his mind seemed more on other things just then. "What made you put it to him? Did this situation with Jenyn have something to do with it?" he asked her.

"Yes, a lot," Lorili admitted candidly. She looked back at Elundi. "Or should I start thinking it terms of maybe needing to stay on down here for a while longer?"

Elundi was looking uncomfortable. "Really, I don't think there's need for that," he said. "You've been all the help that you can, and I'm grateful. I only wanted your opinion, off the record. I don't want to implicate you in any of this. It sounds as if life is complicated enough for you as things are. We can handle things from here. If we do find we need you for anything further, we'll contact you."

CHAPTER TWENTY-SEVEN

Counselor Corrio Weskaw was a senior member of the Korbisanian governing congress back on Venus. A staunch traditionalist, he was known for his outspoken opposition to the Progressive movement. He particularly ridiculed their demand for direct universal franchise, which he compared to letting popular celebrities design bridges and teach mathematics. And the herd continued in its placid, unquestioning way to let others do their thinking for them by repeatedly returning the Electors who appointed him to office. But it seemed there were elements of the population who were running out of patience. The news from Venus reported that the Counselor Weskaw's offices had been destroyed in a serious fire that had gutted part of an official building. Although the material damage and loss of records was severe, the blaze had taken place over a weekend, when the premises were unstaffed. More alarming, however, was the conclusion by police and insurance investigators that the fire appeared to have been the result of deliberate arson. That public affairs could descend to such a level was causing widespread shock, and the media were clamoring with demands for the speedy uncovering of whoever was responsible.

Jenyn reread the account with satisfaction. He still had a cadre of loyal and capable associates back home who were preparing the way. The trail the forensic experts would put together contained some apparently careless failures to obscure the evidence and would point to the campaign group supporting a certain Torag Ryalees, who happened to be the Progressive nominee for southern Korbisan and potentially Jenyn's biggest obstacle when he returned from the triumph he would have scored at Earth.

One of the benefits that came with working in the Clearing and Correlation section of Linguistics was the access it gave him to examples that had been collected of the Terrans' mastery of political subterfuge and pragmatism. So-called "false flag" operations had been one of the standard ploys used by virtually all groups and nations, so simple in concept, yet one of the most consistently effective. An outrage calculated to provoke fury and calls for retaliation—the assassination of a popular public figure, maybe, or a bomb planted in a public place—would be made to look like the work of one's opponents and depicted as such in lurid terms by the controlled media. And the average Terrans, even with their centuries of experience to draw on, had seemed incapable of noticing that it was the alleged perpetrators who stood to lose in terms of image, sympathy, support for their cause, and in just about every other way, while their accusers made all the gains. Yet nobody had asked the obvious questions. Perhaps it showed the skill of the Terran perception-management industries in conditioning the masses to accept as real only what they were officially told was real.

Yes indeed, Jenyn conceded, there was much that he could learn from the Terrans. He faulted himself for still having too much of the inbred Venusian tendency to moderation. The great things that he planned would never come about through half measures. A fire in some empty offices over a weekend was pretty tame fare compared to the examples of boldness and audacity that he read in some of the translated files. Terrans would have blown the whole building up— with Weskaw and his entire staff of prattlers and muddlers inside it!

The door opened, and Elundi came in. He hung his coat and went to his desk on the other side of the room without saying anything, depositing the document folder that he was carrying. He seemed to be preoccupied. There had been a tension and remoteness about his manner all day. He sat down and turned to look across the table separating them. Jenyn sensed something about to come to a head and raised his head inquiringly.

"This business about Gaster Lornod," Elundi said.

"Moderates!" Jenyn retorted derisively. "I've always said he was a hypocrite. The quieter and more reasonable they try to sound, the more they've got to hide."

Elundi ignored it. "The girl who's making the accusations is the one we met in the Magic Carpet—Tyarla Yiag. Your old friend. A very close friend, by the sound of it."

"I know. She was trying to get me involved too." Jenyn met Elundi's gaze evenly. "It says something about the veracity and good judgment of the opposition, then, doesn't it? Also about the loyalties of some seeming followers. I was right to keep her at a distance."

"I've talked to a number of people who have known Lornod for a long time. They don't believe it. I had one of them call Ms. Yiag. She couldn't even describe Lornod. That story was fabricated." Elundi stared at Jenyn pointedly. "Wasn't it?"

Jenyn returned his gaze coolly. "How would I know?"

"Wasn't it, Jenyn?"

"If you're trying to say something, then come out and say it. Don't sit there hiding behind innuendos."

"I heard the way she talks. She thinks you can make her a big name one day, back on Venus. She's the kind that your line appeals to: delusions of unrecognized abilities that aren't there, being held back by a system that isn't affirmative enough. But you'll change the system. I'm saying I think you put her up to it."

"You think? So it's just some wild idea that's come into your head? Why shouldn't I 'think' that maybe you're just jealous because you don't get invited to interesting parties? Where's your proof?"

"Look, Jenyn, this isn't because I *want* to take it any further. I'm just asking you to admit it. And if you can't bring yourself to do that, call it off, now, before the consequences get serious." Elundi waved a hand. "I don't want to know, okay? Just get her to retract. Tell her to say it was a stupid bet or something. That'll be embarrassing, sure, but there's no totally clean way. Letting it go on will be worse."

"How can I admit what I don't know anything about?" Jenyn replied obstinately. He gave Elundi a long, hard look, then went on to add, "And even if it were true, I wouldn't apologize. As you say, it's a serious business. Results are what counts. You can't evade problems forever by pretending that Vizek will take care of them. Sometimes the real world just isn't for the squeamish."

✦   ✦   ✦

Elundi met Iwon near the ISA complex later that day. "No good," he announced. "It's just the way Lorili said it would be. Jenyn isn't going to admit anything. And he wouldn't back down, even if he did. It's his idea of astute politics."

Iwon didn't look especially surprised. "It had to be tried," he said.

"Then we have to approach Tyarla directly ourselves," Elundi said. It was what they had agreed as the next step. "I've been thinking, it would probably be better if we had Lorili in on this. Is she still here?"

"Yes—they're still waiting for approval from *E6*," Iwon said. "But it could come at any time, and then she'll be up to her neck. Best to get this out of the way now, while we still have the time."

"Will you talk to her—if I set things up with Tyarla?"

Iwon nodded. "Of course. No problem."

"I'd better call her right now," Elundi said, reaching for his phone. He had obtained Tyarla's call code from Derlen. He flagged and activated it while Iwon waited. A moment later Tyarla's face appeared on the screen.

"Yes?"

"Tyarla. Do you remember me? Elundi. We met at the Magic Carpet not long ago. You were with Derlen."

"Right. And you two are going out together now. She told me."

"I need to talk to you."

"What about?"

"It's kind of personal. I'd rather not go into it now."

"Is it about this Lornod thing?"

"Yes, as a matter of fact. I have a couple of friends, too, who would like to ask you some questions. One of them is a former campaign associate of Jenyn's from Venus."

"What does Jenyn have to do with it?"

"We think he has a lot to do with it."

Tyarla's manner became defensive. "I'm not answering any more questions about it," she said. "I'm already tired of people poking and questioning."

"Tyarla, you've already set yourself up," Elundi persisted. "You're going to be asked a lot of questions now anyway. Would you rather it was by us, in private, who just want to straighten a few things out? Or wait until it gets really tough with people who'll do it in public?"

Tyarla started to object, but then faltered and shook her head, looking cornered. She really didn't seem to have thought the thing through. "When?" she asked in a sullen voice.

Elundi glanced at Iwon. "Soon as you can," Iwon murmured. "Lorili could be gone at any time."

"It's going to have to be tonight," Elundi told Tyarla.

CHAPTER TWENTY-EIGHT

Brysek stepped aside, grinning, and gestured for Kyal to go first. "Take it easy," he warned. "The floor's not polarized." Kyal stepped through into the elevator, moving gingerly in response to the feeling of sudden lightness. Brysek followed. He pressed one of the buttons on the panel, and the doors closed. "We think they were automatic, but that part's still dead," he said. He pressed another button, and Kyal felt the car start to descend.

It was uncanny. After it had remained idle and unattended for unknown millennia, Brysek's engineers had cleaned up the workings of the Terran elevator, rigged a connection to the Venusian power system up on the surface, and managed to get it working again. It was plain and utilitarian as elevators went—little more than a metal-walled box that the paint had powdered and fallen from long ago. But then, this was hardly a commercial hotel or one of the more stylish residential complexes on Venus either. The walls were scarred and gouged to the rear on one side, and part way along the back. "What do you think happened here?" Kyal asked, gesturing.

"Damage by firearms," Brysek answered. "Have the translators come up with any leads on what the trouble was about here?"

Kyal shook his head. "Nothing that I've heard."

The car halted at one of the intermediate levels of the Lower Complex. A technician who was in the process of taking a couple of the newly arrived biologists on an introductory tour stared in amazement as the doors opened, and Kyal and Brysek emerged.

"How long has that been working?"

"Only since today," Brysek told him. "Kyal was the first guest passenger."

"I *wondered* what they were doing up on the roof, with panels opened up and all those cables," the technician said to his charges.

"We'll have the kitchens and the showers going by tomorrow," Brysek informed them cheerfully. "It'll be the spot of choice on Luna—just the way the Terrans had it."

"Not *totally*, I hope," Kyal said, remembering the bullet scars.

"Oh, excuse me." Brysek said to the newcomers, and gestured. "Master Kyal Reen. He's the man that IASS sent out to look at the electrical constructions on South Field." The technician introduced the two biologists. They were with the group just in from *Explorer 6* to assess the Terran biological facilities and conduct further tests on some of the bodies, along with animal and plant remains that had been found in the section with the pens and cages.

"We heard they were to do with an experimental space propulsion program that the Terrans were running here," one of the biologists said.

"It seems that way," Kyal confirmed.

"Nothing more on what it was about?" the other inquired.

"Just that it seemed to have involved heavy-lift, long-range vessels," Kyal said. Actually, there was more, which was what Brysek was taking him to see, but he didn't want to go into it just now.

"Sounds intriguing," the first said. "I hope you post it when you find out more."

"You'll know as soon as we do," Kyal promised.

He and Brysek carried on along the main corridor from the elevator vestibule to a room that contained Terran electronic hardware and a power conditioning and distribution panel fed from the surface supply. Irg, the communications specialist, was standing with a couple of the engineers in front of a countertop on which tools lay scattered in front of a pile of boxes that included oscilloscopes, a waveform generator, a signal analyzer, and other instruments. Beside it all, a piece of Terran equipment stood connected by a tangle of wires. The screen on the front of it was glowing and showing lines of text.

"It's amazing," Irg said as Kyal stepped forward to look more closely at the blockish, upright Terran characters. He recognized them as English—which was to be expected, of course, if Triagon had been an American installation. "You could almost think it came out from the assembly shop yesterday."

"What have we got here?" Kyal asked.

"Just rudimentary stuff so far," Brysek said. "But there could be volumes of information in there. Some of the devices look like storage crystal recirculators."

"If we can unravel the coding," Irg added.

"How that going?" Kyal asked curiously. The possibilities he could imagine were tantalizing.

"We're working with a hookup to Sherven's people on *E6*, and they've got some high-power crackers and crunchers at the other end of the laser link to home," Brysek said. He indicated a Venusian monitor standing on a portable worktable to the side. "Some of what they've managed to extract is here." Kyal moved across. The monitor was displaying a split screen showing a copy of the original Terran text above, and the corresponding translators' renderings below. "That seems to be some kind of an inventory list," Brysek commented.

"Can we scroll it?" Irg said to the engineers. One of them dragged a scroll bar on a control screen, causing the lines of text in the two windows being displayed on the monitor to roll off the top. Irg stopped them in places to point out and remark on some of the curiosities. Many of the lines of the translation were still blank. A table of line entries and numbers appeared. A translator's comment noted that it seemed to be a list of machinery and parts. Something in the Terran original caught Kyal's eye. A line near the top carried the characters MASSEY MODEL 236-B TRACTOR. Something about it was familiar. The last string, TRACTOR, had appeared on a label he'd seen at the refurbishing shop in Rhombus, where they had looked at the Terran machinery. "I've seen that word before," he said, pointing.

Irg located the matching entry in the translation below. "It's showing a generic. Some kind of mover," he said.

"I think that word means something more specific," Kyal said. "An agricultural engine."

Another of the engineers looked surprised. "Agricultural? Out here at Luna? Were they planning on planting trees?"

"Some of us are beginning to think this might have been a staging base for onward migration to somewhere else," Brysek told him.

"Oh, I hadn't heard that."

"That's my point," Kyal said. "It was driven by chemical combustion. Or at least, the 'tractor' that I saw down on Earth was. What use would that be on Luna?"

The theory was arousing astronomers' attention, since if true it could point to the existence of other parts of the Solar System having once been habitable. Mars was generally held to be the most likely candidate. The trouble was that the Terrans had sent robots and a couple of small manned missions there, and everything pointed to its having been as dead then as it was now.

Kyal had noticed that all the screens carried headers containing a word in a large font that the translations gave as "Providence." "It looks like a general name for the whole set of lists," he remarked to Brysek. "Could it be a catalog title or something?"

"Kyal doesn't miss much," Irg commented.

"It's more than just the catalog title," Brysek said, moving forward. "The same word appears in other related contexts as well. It seems to be more of a code word for the program that these lists relate to."

"Program? You mean the evacuation program from Earth?"

"Not exactly. 'Terminus' covered that. This seems to relate to a specific part of Terminus—a program for collecting together a comprehensive stockpile of equipment and supplies. It seems to have been a large operation."

"Hm." Kyal looked back as the monitor screen scrolled some more. The next frame listed tools and implements. "The kinds of thing you'd take with you if you were planning on moving on someplace," he mused.

"It's looking like it, isn't it?" Brysek agreed.

Lorili called later, when Kyal was back in the surface huts, pondering over the day's developments. Yorim was on the far side of the room with some others who were watching a movie from home telling a story cast in a Terran war setting. Although the thought of mass killings and destruction was abhorrent to most Venusians, the subject nevertheless held a macabre fascination that drew large audiences.

"Live?" Kyal said, surprised, when she appeared on the screen of his phone. They usually communicated in text. "I was just thinking about—"

"Well, I've got something special to tell you, so I decided— Oh. What? . . ."

"What's special?"

"What were you—"

"You said you had something to tell me." They were out of synch already. Kyal grinned. "We'll have to do this the formal way. Over."

"I didn't want to— Oh, yes, okay . . . Look I didn't want to load this on you before, but I've been having some personal problems down here." She stopped. He waited. "Oh, er over."

"Yes, I had kind of gathered there might be something like that from some of the things you said. . . ."

"Well, it's going to . . . No, wrong. Go ahead."

"So what's the latest? Over."

"It looks as if it's going to get worse. Well, no, it already has. Do you remember that person I told you a little bit about when we were at . . . Paris, I think it was. Over."

"The control freak? The one you had the hard time with on Venus? Over."

"Yes, him. He's here in Rhombus and thinks he can turn the clock back. That might sound trivial, but it's a major hassle already. And it's not going to stop."

"There's no reason you have to put up with—"

"He's been at the apartment causing disturbances and— What? Over!"

"Sorry, my fault. I started to say, there's no reason why you should have to put up with it. It's a public nuisance. Call the provosts in. Over."

"I would but there might not be any need. This is the big news. It's looking as if I might be moving up to *Explorer 6*! I've been talking to our chief here, Garki Nostreny, about setting up a sequencing lab in *E6* to look at some of those Terran bodies you've found there. The frozen deep tissues are practically intact. No decay or bacterial action. We've never found anything like it before. It's a biochemist's dream. It will give me a big chance to test a genetic theory I've been working on. Nostreny is for it, and he's proposed it to Sherven. The whisper from *E6* is that it's looking as if it will go through. So I'll be that much closer to Luna and Triagon. Over."

It sounded like good news indeed. "Does it mean you'll be coming out here to collect them, then?" he asked. "Over."

"I was hoping I might be able to, but it won't really work out. I'm going to be too tied up with equipment and administration and getting things organized on *E6*. Mirine—you know, my assistant— will be moving up with me too. She'll be going on to Triagon to take care of that. Although I might be able to find some excuses later to take a trip or two out there myself. Anyway, I just wanted to let you know. Over."

"It might be quite a surprising home from home if you do make it. They just got one of the Terran elevators working today. And it's looking as if there might be a chance of getting into some of their computers too. The way everything's preserved here is amazing. It isn't just your dead bodies. So you don't have an actual date yet? Over."

"Not until it's official from Sherven. But Nostreny knows about the situation—the personal problems, I mean. So things should move quickly when they do. Over."

"Well, let's hope Sherven feels the same way as your chief does. Keep me posted. How's everything otherwise? Over."

"Oh, much the same routine. We had an interesting thing happen today in the graphics section One of the—" Lorili paused. "Oh. Look, Kyal, I've just got a priority one incoming alert from Iwon. He doesn't do things like this lightly. I'd better take it. I'll text you more later. You've heard the exciting news anyway. Okay? Over."

"Sure. I hope it's not bad news. Take care. Over. Out."

Kyal looked across at the group clustered around the screen. Somebody emitted an exclamation of awe and horror. The screen showed a fireball mushrooming into a turbulent cloud, while a voice off screen that was supposed to be Terran shrieked and babbled inanely. "What this?" he called across to Yorim.

"They've just fusion-bombed a slave city." That was what Venusians called the Terran metropolises with their concrete towers of work cubicles, optimized for maximum short-term financial returns. "They had them in parking orbits, ready to be targeted anywhere. Want to come and watch?"

Kyal screwed up his nose distastefully. "No, I think I'll go back to some quiet in the dorm and just read." As he stood up, his mind went back again to the electronics he'd looked at with Bryskek. "You know, I can't wait to see if we can restore some of the Terran music."

CHAPTER TWENTY-NINE

Lorili was not looking forward to meeting Tyarla. She expected it to be a confrontation, and confrontation was not her style. Such experiences tended to be draining, unsettling, and seldom productive. Clearance had come through late in the afternoon from Sherven's office for her transfer up to *Explorer 6*, but by that time Elundi and Iwon had already set things up for that evening. Having made a commitment, Lorili would honor it, naturally; but after that, she just wanted to be away from it all to get on with her work and be free to think about the future.

At the end of the day, she walked with Iwon to the Central District, where he had arranged to meet Elundi, and the three of them proceeded to Tyarla's apartment, which was not very far from Lorili's in another of the outer residential sectors. Tyarla received them wearing a glittery green trouser suit with the flared sleeves and legs that were the current fashion on Venus, her hair worn high in a silver slide. The interior was a colorful riot of purple, lilac, yellow, and black, splashed across compositions of angular mural designs and hanging drapes, with metallic furnishings and ceramic ornaments. Tyarla herself remained cool and aloof, evidently relishing the experience as little as Lorili did. She let them find their own seats around the room and didn't offer anything by way of drinks or refreshment. Elundi introduced his two companions and then began:

"I'm sorry to bring this up again if you're having enough to deal with already, Tyarla. As I said on the phone earlier, yes, it's to do with these things you've said concerning Gaster Lornod." He sighed, as if to convey that this wasn't easy for him either. "Look, I've been following Lornod's arguments for a long time. I think he makes some good points. And when I get interested in a subject I do a lot of research into the background. So I know a lot about the man, his character, and where he's coming from." Elundi shook his head appealingly. "What you're saying just doesn't fit. I've talked to a number of people who know him personally, and they say the same thing."

Tyarla raised her chin defiantly; but at the same time her eyes betrayed insecurity. "He's a politician. They're all alike. Of course there's a nicely groomed public image. I can't help it if your friends were taken in by it. I only know what *I* heard and saw."

"Why should you care?" Iwon put in. "Even if it's true, why bother? Why get yourself mixed up in this?"

"I think the people should know," Tyarla shot back.

Elundi was shaking his head. "One of my contacts talked to you— Karteen Bissel. She says you weren't even able to describe Lornod accurately."

"So—I'm not very good at putting descriptions into words. Is that supposed to be a crime?"

Lorili could see this kind of line going on indefinitely without result. But Elundi abandoned the circuitous route and came directly to the issue. "I mentioned Jenyn on the phone earlier—"

"And I said it's got nothing to do with Jenyn." Tyarla looked at the other two, as if for support. "Why is he bringing Jenyn into it?"

"I work with Jenyn, as you know," Elundi said. "I don't pretend to know him that well, because he's only been back in Rhombus from the Americas for a short time. But he was the one who introduced us, and I think *you* do know him very well from when he was in Rhombus before."

Tyarla sniffed haughtily. "I can't see what that's got anything to do with it, or that it's any of your business."

"You were pretty clearly making it everyone's business at the time," Elundi retorted. Even as he said it, the pained look in his eyes showed he knew that he shouldn't have.

"I don't have to listen to this." Tyarla started to rise.

Iwon tried to be placating. "Let's not get heated. It won't help. . . . Look, Tyarla, this is for your own good as much as anything else. Really. If it is the way Elundi's saying, it will be far better to come clean about it now."

"I don't need you people to tell me what's good for me. I can take care of myself, thanks." Tyarla was on her feet, but as yet she was making no move to show them the door. A part of her, yet, was undecided.

Elundi came back in. "I might not have known Jenyn for a long time, but let me be frank about what I see," he said. "I see a person with problems—ambitions of power and grandeur, totally egotistical. The kind of person who won't think twice about using others to get what he wants, or destroying them through lies, deformation, or whatever it takes if they get in his way. He has no interest in truth, only results. He doesn't care how they come about, or who else might get hurt in the process. It was a quality that the Terrans somehow elevated to a virtue, and he admires it. But it's easy to mistake Terran disinformation and propaganda for being the way things really were. Most of the Terrans themselves couldn't see through it." Elundi made a gesture of finality. "But on Venus things work by different standards. Jenyn will come unstuck. It won't be the way he has promised. Why let yourself go down with him? . . . Yes, I know that having to retract now will be embarrassing. But that would be much better in the long run than where it will lead otherwise."

Tyarla hesitated and looked less sure of herself, sinking back slowly to perch on the arm of a low-backed padded chair with fluffy pink and purple cushions. But her pride wouldn't allow her to back down yet. "What promises are you talking about?" she returned. "Who told you he promised anything?"

"Oh, let's be real," Elundi said, sounding impatient. "There had to be some motivation. What else? It's written across the whole situation."

"I . . . don't know." Tyarla looked up obstinately. "I need to think about it."

It was time for a woman-to-woman input, Lorili decided. After all, that was why she had been brought along.

"There may not be time for that," she said quietly. It was the first time she had spoken. The words and her tone took Tyarla by surprise, causing her to look around sharply.

"Why not?"

"Don't you realize that you could be in danger?"

"What are you talking about?"

"I know Jenyn too. I've known him a lot longer than you have. I knew him back on Venus. I know his anger and his instability, and I don't think I'm under any delusions as to where it could possibly lead. Think about this. If something were to happen to you now, can you see how convenient it would be for Jenyn? He would be free from any risk of being exposed by the one person who would be in a position to do it. And with the situation we've now got, it wouldn't take much for some people to ask who stood to gain from making sure you never got a chance to prove the things you've been saying, and jumping to the wrong answer, would it?"

"Lornod!" The surprise in Iwon's voice made it clear that such an angle had never occurred to him before either.

Lorili nodded. "Especially if it were helped along by a little rumoring, and maybe some convenient 'facts' leaked in the right places."

"Rig the evidence to point to your opposition," Elundi said. "That was a favorite Terran trick. They did it all the time. Jenyn thinks it was brilliant."

Tyarla's gaze darted from one to another of them. "You don't know any of this," she accused. "None if it has happened. It's just speculation, that's all it is. You're making it up."

"It's the way Jenyn operates," Lorili said. "I told you, I've known him a lot longer than you have." She snorted scornfully. "I was young, naive, vain, and full of myself with all the things I thought I knew." She paused just long enough for the unvoiced words *just like you* to assert themselves. "Do you want me to tell you exactly what he promised? Because I can, you know, and I will. Or would it be too embarrassing to be told in front of Elundi and Iwon? So suffice it to say that what he actually delivered was enough to make me want to come this far to get away from it."

Tyarla licked her lips dryly, searching for a way to put the question. "Are you saying that something 'happened' to somebody before . . . back there?"

"No, I'm not saying that," Lorili replied evenly. "But I know him enough to have seen how he works and what he's capable of. I wouldn't put it past him."

"Why wait to find out the hard way?" Elundi interjected.

"There's only one way to be sure of being safe," Lorili concluded. "Come clean and put the truth on record *before* anything can happen. Then the whole situation would be turned around: There would be no case for Lornod to have to answer to; Jenyn would have nothing left to try and cover up, because it would be in the open; and he would have nothing to gain if anything were to 'happen.' But he would have a lot to lose."

There was nothing more to be added. Silence fell while Tyarla shifted her eyes from one to another of them. "Look, if it helps, none of us feels anything against you personally," Elundi said, more to relieve the strain.

"Why do you care?" Tyarla asked finally. She was still stalling.

Elundi pondered, then threw up his hand and made a face. "I guess I'm not like Jenyn. I believe truth and principle *do* matter. If you have to sacrifice them to get the results you want, then the results aren't worth it." Perhaps feeling that he was being a bit pompous, he added in an easier tone, "I suppose I'd never have made a Terran."

They waited. "I'm not admitting to anything, but I'll think about it," Tyarla said. "Give me until tomorrow. I'll talk to you again then." Her tone was final.

Elundi, Lorili, and Iwon looked at each other. They all read from the others' faces an agreement that there was nothing further to be done for now. Elundi rose, and the other two followed.

"Thanks for hearing us out," he said to Tyarla. "We'll leave it with you, then." For a moment Lorili feared he was going to spoil things with a final sermon, but he played it right, left it at that, and moved toward the door. Tyarla went ahead and held it open for them.

"Thanks for caring," she said almost in a whisper as Lorili, who was last in line, was about to step through. Lorili looked at her, hesitated, and grasped her hand briefly before Tyarla closed the door.

Outside, they stood looking at each other, each waiting for the others to find something appropriate. Finally Elundi hazarded, "Drink somewhere?"

"Good idea," Iwon agreed.

"Magic Carpet?" Lorili suggested.

Iwon looked dubious. "Too crowded. I'm not in the mood."

"I agree," Elundi said." How about the Caspian? It should be quiet there at this time."

The nods said the verdict was unanimous. They turned to head back the way they had come, toward the Central District. As they moved away, a figure that had been approaching from the opposite direction and stopped when they came out of Tyarla's door emerged from the shadows of a stand of rhododendrons.

Derlen had told Tyarla that she would stop by later in the evening, but then found herself at a loose end and decided to make it earlier. Also, she was itching to learn the latest on this business that Tyarla had gotten herself involved in. But it seemed there were things going on that Derlen wasn't a part of. Maybe Tyarla would tell her about it now. But when Derlen went up to the door and rang after waiting a few minutes for the visitors to be well gone, Tyarla seemed distracted and not all that pleased to see her.

"Yes, I know I said we'd go out somewhere," she told Derlen, "but something unexpected has come up. Can we make it another time?"

"Well, I guess so," Derlen said. She felt put out and didn't try to disguise it. If something like this were likely to happen, Tyarla could have called her and said so. She waited, but Tyarla didn't invite her in. "What kind of thing has come up?" she inquired.

"Oh, I can't go into it now. Could we just leave things for tonight? I need to be on my own to figure some things out. I'll give you a call, okay?"

No apology. No mention of whatever it was Elundi apparently already thought important enough in Tyarla's life to be involved in. Derlen hadn't been aware of any further dealings between Elundi and Tyarla since the night he had been with Jenyn in the Magic Carpet. As Derlen walked away, she remembered that Elundi had asked her not long ago for Tyarla's call code. He'd said it was because a friend had asked him if he knew any accountants who might be able to help with something or other. She was feeling angry and jealous. Something significant was going on, and Derlen was being left out.

CHAPTER THIRTY

Filaeyus Sherven, Honored Doctor of Science and Philosophy, sat at the desk in his spacious office of shelves and display screens, staring out through the glass wall at parts of *Explorer 6*'s external structures silhouetted against the starfield. Many years ago now, when he was a student in Ulange, he had lodged for a while in the house of a widowed master carpenter, who was renting out a couple of the spare rooms. Sherven remembered a day when he had watched the carpenter taking out a piece from the mounting battens of a cabinet that he was building in a corner of the dining room. "Why are you taking that out?" the young Sherven had asked him.

"Oh, I must be getting careless. I cut the joint a bit slack."

"But it will be on the wall, at the back of everything. It won't show. Who would ever know?"

"*I* would know," the old man had told him.

If the most important part of "education" was acquiring standards to set oneself and cultivating good habits of thought, then those three words, he sometimes reflected, had contributed more to his own than many of the semesters spent absorbing facts about matters he had never had reason to think about since. The key to a settled life was learning to be honest with oneself and honest with the world.

He looked back at the revolting Terran display of gaudy art and self-obsessed, practically unclothed females being presented on one

193

of the screens. Casselo had sent it through as an example of some of the image restoration techniques that one of the labs was developing. It had apparently been devised to persuade people that a cheap concoction of sugar and fruit flavoring was the key to a full and satisfying life, and induce them to purchase it. It seemed that exaggeration, falsification, and skill in the art of making things and people appear to be other than what they were had been much sought-after, highly rewarded professions.

Sherven was disturbed by the reports coming from Venus of growing political extremism and more exposures of distortions, outright lies, and the use of increasingly deplorable tactics. A former colleague there had mentioned in a private communication that investigators of the fire in the offices of the Korbisanian Counselor Weskaw were saying it looked like arson, although they were not making the fact public until they were more sure of their case. And now, closer to home, they had this ugly business about Gaster Lornod breaking out. Sherven didn't like the way things were trending at all.

The source back on Venus had expressed a personal suspicion that the Progressives were behind the arson. Weskaw was an outspoken critic of the movement, and in particular their demand for a direct universal franchise, which he said would be akin to letting popularity votes decide professional accreditation. His continuing to serve on the Korbisanian congress testified that a solid majority of the population there had confidence in the judgment of the Electors who appointed him. Had it been otherwise, those Electors wouldn't have been there—any more than a designer whose bridges fell down or a math teacher whose pupils couldn't transpose an equation. If this was the way things were heading, nothing good could come of it, whatever the anticipated ends. Ends were something imagined in the future; the means was the reality, now. At best it would lower the standards of leadership in the direction of the travesties of government that the Terrans had endured.

The way in which the Terrans had glorified their leaders left Venusians mystified. Perhaps it had been another triumph for the Terran image manipulators. Virtually without exception, from what the exohistorians had made of things so far, they had demonstrated no worthwhile learning, skill, or talent of any kind beyond the ability to insinuate and ingratiate themselves into the public awareness, seize and hold power by force and intimidation, and pander to the interests of influential minorities. The system of appointing them was such that gaining office demanded abilities that were the exact opposite of those that would be required of anyone occupying it, so the accusations of hypocrisy and insincerity that appeared to have been widespread were hardly to be wondered at.

On Venus, those eligible for government were drawn from a pool of qualified candidates who had met some of the highest educational standards demanded of any profession, and gained practical experience through a progression of more demanding public offices. They were appointed by a body of professional Electors, who in turn were elected by the people and accountable to the people for the performance of the governments they delivered, in the same way that any other professional body would be accountable if it chartered incompetents and authorized them to practice. Few things could have contrasted more sharply with the appalling Terran system of mob rule through misinformed masses. Every Venusian citizen got one base vote by right, and beyond that there was a scale for earning additional votes with greater educational attainments. Even the Terrans would never have dreamed of appointing their physicians, engineers, architects, and other professionals without seeing evidence of suitable aptitude and knowledge. How much more important was it, then, for the supreme profession of running an entire country safely and effectively?

Like the Korbisanian Counselor Weskaw, Sherven believed that the body sociopolitic was a growing organism in its own right, guided by the same underlying formative principle that shaped all living things, and as such would mature in its own way, in its own time. Attempting to force it prematurely was like trying to induce a flower to blossom by prizing open the petals before they were ready, and likely to be as effective. Terran culture had brought itself to its final, logical conclusion. In the end, nobody, it seemed, could be believed or trusted. Nothing was what it appeared to be. Small wonder that it had culminated in ruin. Where else was there for it to go?

The thought occurred to him that perhaps the purpose of the universe was to produce worlds on which to conduct experiments in life, which in turn yielded consciousness and generated structures of thought, reason, and intuitive knowledge. Perhaps it had been, then, that the Terrans, while physically robust and versatile, had not been very successful temperamentally. Might Venusians represent a more stable and hopefully longer-lasting model? It was an attractive thought, Sherven's wife, Pidrie, had agreed when he mentioned it to her one evening. She had asked why Vizek should concern itself with conducting such experiments. That was another question, was all Sherven had been able to tell her in reply.

A tap sounded on the door. It opened a fraction, and Borgan Casselo stuck his head in, giving an inquiring look. He was spending some time on *Explorer 6* before returning to his office in Rhombus. Sherven had asked Casselo to join him for lunch, primarily to get an update on developments. "Yes, come in, Borgan." Sherven waved a hand.

"Emitte thought that Frazin might still be here."

"No, he's gone. An interesting theory of his about collective amnesia. What do you make of it?"

"I can't really see it," Casselo said, closing the door. "There's no plausible mechanism for it."

"I agree. I think it was cultural."

"Ah, I see you got the Terran beverage commercial," Casselo said, observing the mural screen. "The imaging people reconstructed it from dried-up fragments. Some clever frequency-spectrum transforms in infrared. Not bad, eh?"

"Not bad at all, as far as the technique goes," Sherven agreed. "I wish I could say the same for the content. I mean, look at those four specimens they've got there. Somewhat spectacular as far as the paint and the body parts go, I suppose, but hardly the brightest lights in town, I'd have thought. The Terrans were fixated on appearances and packaging, weren't they? Everything was phony. No ability to discern the actual substance of anything at all."

"They were taught not to," Casselo said. He took one of the visitor chairs while Sherven tidied up his notes and papers from the morning.

"So how are things at Triagon?" Sherven inquired.

"Kyal Reen has got his side of things together. He seems capable and energetic. I don't think we'll see any problems there. He's gotten himself involved with the linguists and the electronics people out there too, but Brysek says he gets on well with everybody. No complaints."

"Sounds like a chip off the old Jarnor Reen, all right," Sherven remarked. "How about those biochemistry people who moved there from *E6*?"

"They're settling in. I hear that Nostreny down in Rhombus wants to set something up in their old lab space up here."

"Genetic sequencing on the Terran corpses. I've already okayed it. A couple of his staff are transferring up here to take charge of it. In fact they're shuttling up today."

"That was quick," Casselo commented.

"Yes, well, Nostreny talked to me confidentially. Apparently it would relieve a personal situation that's developed down there concerning one of them—the principal. A Korbisanian woman. The other one is her assistant." Sherven arranged his folders into a stack but selected some sheets to keep separate. "They're eager to get on with it, in any case. Can't blame them, I suppose. How often do biochemists get a chance like this? It wouldn't do to be stifling initiative would it, Borgan?—never mind what the Progressives say about us."

"True. But I also think there might be more to it," Casselo said. "If it's who I think it is, there's a personal element in it, between her and Kyal Reen. They met in Russia, when he was on acclimatization leave. One of those instant attraction things, according to Kyal's partner."

Sherven's eyes twinkled. "Oh, really? Well, you get the best out of people when they're in situations like that. They're certainly not wasting much time about it."

"As you said, a touch of the old Jarnor Reen."

"Just before we go . . ." Sherven touched the panel inset to one side of the desk and inclined his head to indicate another of the screens. It activated to show the pyramid-form structure that was being investigated some distance out from the main Triagon base. "What do you make of these latest reports of theirs?" Sherven asked.

Casselo nodded as he glanced over the view. "It seems to be what they say," he replied. "A discharge attractor for some kind of large, long-range vessel. It fits with everything else they've been finding with the other structures."

"Yes," Sherven agreed. "But it's the 'large, long-range' that I was specifically interested in. Have you seen this?" He pushed across the papers that he had kept aside. Casselo picked them up and ran an eye over them. "From a Terran scientific journal that Parigel's group at the Ulangean Institute have been working on." Sherven meant the Ulangean institute for Terran studies, set up to concentrate on such work. "It talks about work that was going on in the American region."

"A star probe?" Casselo read aloud.

"A study for such a program anyway," Sherven said. "And some other references too. It talks about new electrical propulsion physics to harness transgalactic currents." He looked at Casselo curiously. "Maybe they weren't as far behind as we thought, after all. What do you think?"

Casselo turned to the next page. "Did anything actually happen? Or was it just a theoretical exercise?" he asked. "Does it say?"

"Parigel isn't sure. I asked him the same thing. From the limited material they've got to go on, the details are obscure. If it had military potential, it might have been kept vague deliberately."

"Or maybe invented as a cover for what was going on at Farside . . . in case anything leaked out," Casselo mused.

"Yes, that's another possibility, I suppose."

Casselo sat back in his chair and thought for a moment. He nodded toward the Farside pyramid, still showing on the screen. "You know, Kyal did say how he was struck by some of the similarities between that and the things he envisaged in his own speculations about future star travel systems."

Several seconds went by while each waited for the other to voice the implication. "That can't have been their destination, surely?" Sherven said at last. "If Triagon was a staging base to somewhere else, as Kyal has been saying." He was thinking of storage space for lots of equipment and supplies; agricultural machinery; pens for animals; hydroponic setups for what the biologists were now saying they thought were for cloning plant seeds.

"It couldn't have been, surely," Casselo repeated.

And yet, repeatedly, the Terrans had showed themselves capable of making the most amazing advances suddenly, in spite of all their destructive compulsions and craziness.

Casselo was evidently thinking the same thing. "If they did have the technology, maybe another star system makes more sense than anywhere here," he said.

"But is it even plausible?" Sherven asked.

"Their priorities were different. With the focus on military matters and secrecy, there could have been more going on than we've uncovered. . . . Well, obviously there was. I mean a *lot* more. Has Parigel been able to put together anything else that correlates with it?" Casselo motioned with the papers in his hand. "Can we say for sure whether any of the vessels it talks about here were ever launched—or even built?"

"Not really," Sherven admitted. "A major global conflict erupted at around the time it was going on. It seems to have been the final one, involving Euro-Russia and the Muslims against Americans and Chinese. They never recovered as a civilization. Records from after the war are practically nonexistent. Anyway, we can talk about it over lunch. I've asked Frazin to join us."

"Fine."

Sherven was just about to rise, when a call sounded from the desk panel. It was from his assistant in the outer office. He touched a key to activate the channel on voice only.

"Yes, Emitte?"

"I was away for a few minutes. Did Borgan arrive?"

"Yes, he's here."

"I have Chief Provost Huiano, from Rhombus on the line. He apologizes for intruding but requests a moment."

"Certainly." Sherven glanced at Casselo. "Excuse me."

Huiano's features appeared on the desk-panel screen a moment later. "My apologies for the interruption, Director Sherven," Huiano said again.

"There is no need. What can I do for you?"

"It's about the allegations concerning Gaster Lornod."

Sherven sent Casselo an exasperated look. He really could have done without being dragged into this kind of thing. But he had asked Huiano to contact him if there was any further news. "Yes, Chief Huiano?"

"The girl who started it all, Tyarla Yiag . . ."

"What about her?"

"She came in here earlier and has confessed that it was a fraud. She says she was put up to it by a Jenyn Thorgan."

Sherven frowned. "I don't think I know that name."

"He works with Linguistics. He was away in the Americas for a period and has only recently returned. He's already become known here as a militant Progressive activist. He was also a rising star in the movement some years ago back on Venus. It appears that he promised Madam Yiag a prominent and lucrative position with the Progressives if she cooperated. She also claims he threatened her if she refused, but I think that might be to cover herself. There, ah . . .

would also appear to be something of a personal element in their relationship."

Sherven was livid. "This is exactly what I *didn't* want," he muttered to Casselo. "Progressive politics and intrigues undermining the mission's work. They're causing enough trouble back on Venus." And then back to Huiano, "Is she still there?"

"Yes. I asked her to stay here pending your instructions."

"Has she gone public with any of this?" Sherven asked.

"She says not. She came straight here this morning, when she decided to come clean."

"Well, that's something, anyway."

"What do you want us to do?" Huiano asked.

Sherven thought for a moment or two. "Let's keep everything like that for now," he answered. "What I'd like is a closed-door session to try and resolve the whole business in private without a public circus. Have them both, Yiag and this . . . what was his name?"

"Jenyn Thorgan."

"Thorgan. Have them both sent up here on the next shuttle out. We'll hear them out up in *Explorer,* and hopefully get rid of this whole mess. There are other things going on that are what I'm supposed to be here for." He glanced at Casselo and shook his head with a sigh. "And they're a lot more interesting too."

"I will make the necessary arrangements," Huiano promised.

CHAPTER THIRTY-ONE

Elundi sat working through the references to the latest list of word searches requested by the people at Triagon. Their work had been given a high priority. One of the hot items was "Providence," which was thought to be the code word for a Terran program to amass a large inventory of equipment and supplies there. Even Sherven was getting involved, sending memos to various people on his staff querying progress and requesting details. They were excited over a current theory that Triagon might have been not just an evacuation shelter for elites as previously thought, but a staging base for onward migration to somewhere else. Elundi wasn't sure why that should be such a big issue. The problem from the linguists' standpoint was that Terran code designations with military connections were usually chosen from common words in order to be innocuous, which meant that they would also occur in countless other contexts that had no connection with the particular example of interest. Weeding out the irrelevant flags that the search programs listed was a tedious business.

It would be a good application for a decent artificial intelligence system, Elundi thought to himself. Recognizing correct context—what was appropriate; what was relevant—he believed, was the essence of intelligence. It came from that "common sense" faculty that humans recognized in each other as a result of growing up and forming their conceptual associations in the same shared reality, from the physical space they moved around in that inspired so many metaphors of common speech, to their cultural heritage—and computers didn't. He recalled with amusement how the AI pioneers back on Venus had confidently predicted full, human-level automatic translation of natural language within five years. That had been twenty-five years ago, and they were still not even close. Misled by the ease with which programs could disassemble and convert their own artificially created symbolic languages, they had assumed that the meanings carried by natural speech could be extracted from the syntax. But the meanings that humans were able to perceive instantly, even from infancy, were not there in the syntax of the message to be extracted. The words and phrases merely triggered what was already inside the heads of the recipients. Even some of the widely quoted experts didn't seem to have grasped it, and continued to construct ever-more-elaborate syntax analyzers that continued to return wrong, way-out, and frequently hilarious results. But they were five years away from the real thing at most, they assured the world. Doing it the right way was what he would devote himself to when he returned to Venus, Elundi had decided. The experience he was gaining on Earth was ideal preparation for it.

The next item on his screen was from the Terran electronic records that the engineers up at Triagon had managed, amazingly, to reactivate. It was filed under the name of an engineering company that had been involved in the Providence program, and stated that one of their inspectors had flown from Santa Cruz to perform postdelivery tests and was back in the Bay Area by evening. There was nothing sensational about it that would warrant alerting the researchers, but the fact that the record had come from Triagon indicated that the "Providence" reference was in the category that they were interested in. Elundi sent it across for routine incorporation into the consolidation file that Jenyn was working on. On the far side of the table, Jenyn moved his head as the item flag appeared on one of his screens. From the corner of his eye, Elundi was aware of Jenyn turning toward him. He carried on working and pretended not to notice. The air had been cool between them since their confrontation over the Lornod business, and the things Elundi had learned since, in his visit to Tyarla's with Iwon and Lorili, had only exacerbated matters.

"Have you seen any more of this pal of yours in Biochem?" Jenyn asked. His tone was mildly taunting, deliberately nonchalant as if challenging Elundi to come out and say what was bothering him—as if Jenyn didn't know.

"Not really," Elundi murmured without looking away from the screen he was working on.

"I need to straighten things out with that partner of his," Jenyn said, obviously meaning Lorili. "Think you can put a word in for me? You know what they're like when they get funny and sulky. Makes it difficult to talk to them direct. Maybe this friend of yours who works with her could get the message across."

"I don't think it's really any of my business," Elundi said.

"Aw, come on. Just a small favor. I thought you might get them to meet you somewhere, socially. Then I could accidentally show up and—"

"Look." Elundi swung his chair around and faced Jenyn directly across the table. "You're wasting your time. Iwon told me she's fixed up with a physics guy who's not long in from Venus, that she met while she was in Russia. Okay? So why don't you just drop it? I told you, it isn't any of my business. And if you want my opinion, it's a sleazy way to operate. I wouldn't want any part of it anyway."

Jenyn's face darkened as he dropped the game-playing. Elundi braced himself for the row that had been brewing to finally come to a head. But before anything happened, a call-mode tone sounded from Jenyn's terminal. He picked up the handset and said curtly, "Yes? . . . Who? . . . What does she want? . . . Yes, I'll be right out." He got up and left, breathing heavily, without saying more. Elundi returned his attention to his work. This couldn't go on, he told himself. He'd talk today to Girelandi about getting a transfer to another office—maybe another location, even. He thought he was beginning to see why Lorili had decided to get herself up off the planet completely.

The item mentioning Santa Cruz and the Bay Area remained flagged but unprocessed on Jenyn's screen.

Derlen was waiting for Jenyn in the reception area at the entrance to the Linguistics offices. She beckoned him aside, away from the desk, and spoke closely to him in a low voice. "I think you might be in trouble. Can we talk outside?"

Jenyn looked at her searchingly. The interplay of emotions on her face was too confused for him to read. He nodded and followed as she turned back toward the door. Outside was a covered foyer with steps going down to a paved court dotted with a few shrubs in planters.

"Tyarla came to see me late last night," Derlen said. "She told me the story about Gaster Lornod wasn't true. She said she was going to the provost's office to tell them the whole thing." Jenyn drew in a sharp breath. Derlen looked at his face with an expression that was half questioning, half fascination. "She, ah . . . she said that you asked her to do it."

Jenyn swore inwardly. "Is she going to tell them that too?"

Derlen made a slight suggestion of a shrug. "I don't know. I guess so." She watched Jenyn's face, but his mind was already racing, barely aware of her. He was angry at himself. Why had he trusted somebody like that? He'd *known* she was the kind that was all phony and fake and would fall apart. "I tried to talk her out of it. I really did." Derlen's eyes were earnest, but the words had a cracked ring. Jenyn had the feeling that a part of her was relishing it. He sensed a jealousy of Tyarla surfacing that had been simmering for a long time. Derlen was excited by him. He knew the signs. Being defensive would only detract from the image.

"Did she say what changed her mind?" he asked, not bothering to deny anything.

"No. But I was by her place earlier, and I saw Elundi coming out. . . ."

"Elundi? What was he doing there?"

"He was with two other people. They didn't see me. One was a tallish guy, with kind of light hair and a mustache under his nose—you know, like the Terrans had. The other was a woman."

Jenyn looked up abruptly. "Describe her," he said.

"Oh . . . a bit older than me. I didn't really see her face. She had, let me see . . . pants and a dark jacket. But very black hair, long, about down to here." Derlen indicated a point halfway between her shoulder and her elbow.

The woman was obviously Lorili. The other person with them had to be Elundi's friend who worked with her. So Elundi had sat there all morning, acting so cool and disinterested, while all the time he had betrayed Jenyn, probably because Jenyn disturbed his comfort and petty little dreams of burying himself in computer labs when he got back to Venus; because Jenyn made him think about things that mattered.

And as for Lorili, who had already turned on him back at Venus after he'd made her everything she was, and then run away to Earth, and after he had given her a second chance . . . Now she was throwing it back in his face and playing the same tricks behind his back again to get him out of the way to make room for her new infatuation with this physicist.

The rush of anger that he had felt toward Tyarla and at himself for trusting her was gone now, and in its place he could feel a slow rage building deep inside, consuming him slowly like an acid. Nobody did things like this to *him* without feeling the consequences. The first thing was to stop Tyarla getting to the provosts. He would take care of that himself right away. After that, there would be the score to settle with Lorili. He would attend to Elundi later.

Jenyn looked again at Derlen's eyes. They were bright, hopeful. He recognized a willing helper, just waiting the word to step into Tyarla's shoes and take over the glamorous image, savor the hint of danger. "A pity," he said. "I thought Tyarla had more nerve. I guess that's how you find out, eh?"

"What are you going to do?" Derlen asked him.

"Do you want to help?" Jenyn regarded her with an expression that was at the same time both a challenge and a promise. "I don't think you're a phony." Derlen returned a quick nod. "I know who the woman is," he said. "Her name is Lorili Hilivar. She's in the ISA Molecular Genetics lab. She's had a grudge against me since a long time ago back on Venus. I want you to contact her and say you're a friend of Tyarla. Tell her that Tyarla wants to meet her and talk some more. Okay? Then call me and let me know when and where."

"What are you going to do?" Derlen asked again.

"I've got something else I have to take care of first. I'll see you later today. Get moving and track Lorili down for me. Set up a meeting, and then let me know." Jenyn's voice fell. "You're smart. I have bigger things going on back home than you know. You won't regret this."

He watched her leave the court and then turned to go back inside. The thought of confronting Elundi again checked him. He couldn't risk anything developing between them now that might introduce a delay. Changing his mind, he followed the way Derlen had gone and came out onto the street. She was just disappearing around the corner at the end of the block.

Jenyn's anger had crystallized into a cold determination to get even. It was the test of him as a man to be reckoned with. No other consideration mattered for now. He took out his phone and checked the news channel for the latest on Lornod. Nothing had changed since that morning. No new announcements. The important thing was to stop Tyarla before she said anything that would connect him with her.

Moving briskly, Jenyn set off in the direction of Tyarla's apartment. The scheme of how he would play it was already forming in his mind. With Tyarla out of the way, only Elundi and Lorili would know that she had implicated Jenyn—he discounted Elundi's friend, whom he took to be just a go-between. If either of them voiced it, his position would be that Tyarla had set him up out of spite after he refused her overtures to use him as a ticket into the upper ranks of the Progressives. What other motive would she have had for making up the story about Lornod? That left Derlen as the only other person who would know. And he thought he would be able to handle Derlen without too much trouble.

She called him when he was halfway to Tyarla's.

"Hello, Jenyn."

"Yes?" Well, she certainly hadn't wasted much time, he told himself.

"I tried calling this Lorili Hilivar, but her personal code is turned off. So I tried the number at Molecular Bio where she's listed. The guy I talked to was the same one I told you about with the mustache who was at Tyarla's place. He says she's moving out today—something about moving to a new laboratory. He wouldn't tell me where."

"Okay . . . Thanks," Jenyn acknowledged shortly.

"What do you want me to do now?"

Jenyn sighed and thought hard. "There isn't a lot else you can do for now," he answered. "Don't get me wrong—you've done just fine. As much as you could. But right now I have to finish something else. If you can find out where she's going, that would be a big help. Work on that. Otherwise, I'll call you later today. Maybe we can get together."

"Okay, Jenyn."

"Trust me, eh." He winked and shut off the phone.

Lorili, true to pattern, he told himself as he began walking again. Just like the last time, ratting on him and then running away. He was angry for letting himself be taken in by her a second time. Sometimes he could be too forgiving. That was half his problem.

That kind of weakness wouldn't do for the future leader of the worldwide Progressive movement that would one day call the tunes on Venus. It was something he was going to have to work on. But Lorili Hilivar was going to find out. She would find out that he was someone to be reckoned with.

The provosts must have been staking the place and waiting for him. The car drew up from behind him when he was a few yards from Tyarla's door. An officer and two troopers emerged. The officer confronted him, while the troopers stood by, one at his shoulder, the other a yard or two behind Jenyn.

"Mister Jenyn Thorgan?"

"Yes."

"I have a warrant and must ask you to accompany us, sir."

"What am I supposed to have I done? Are you saying I'm under arrest for some reason?"

"Not arrest, sir. But you are required to attend a hearing that is to be held up in *Explorer 6*. The warrant is signed by the mission Provost Marshal, and has been issued on the express instruction of Director Sherven."

"So I'm not under arrest. What if I refuse?"

The officer gave him a look that said he ought to know better. "Then I'm afraid that we would have to insist," he replied.

If he was going to be under this kind of scrutiny, there could be no question of settling any scores for the time being, Jenyn realized. "When is this due to take place?" he asked.

"It isn't exactly fixed yet," the officer answered. "Within the next few days."

"So are you telling me I'm being apprehended?"

"My instructions are to detain you until transportation is arranged for you to *Explorer 6*."

"And what about after I get there?"

"That's not for me to say, sir."

Jenyn thought rapidly. He would achieve nothing being cooped up somewhere down here. At least he might have freedom of movement up on *E6*. It wouldn't be as if he were likely to go very far. "Then let's get on with it now," he said. "I take it I can pick up a few things from my place?"

"We can stop there on the way." The officer stepped back, and the trooper who had been standing by him opened the rear door of the car.

CHAPTER THIRTY-TWO

Kyal and Yorim were in what had become known as the Decoding Lab—the room in the Lower Complex where Brysek had demonstrated the first reactivations of Terran electronic files. The text being displayed on the screen they were looking at was a translation from more Terran records that the engineers had managed to access. The Terran entry had been scanned from a hand-transcribed original that appeared to have been part of an aircraft pilot's log. There was no obvious reason why it should have been stored in equipment at Triagon, since there wasn't any air to fly an aircraft in, and it clearly described coastlines. But electronic storage was cheap, and Venusians were used to finding their own computers accumulating peculiar assortments of information from collections of jokes to family pictures and birthday lists. There was no reason to suppose it had been much different for Terrans, and so nobody attached any great significance to such notes being found in a computer on Luna.

The reason why the item had attracted attention was that its header line contained the word "Providence." The header graphic incorporated another interesting feature too. Besides having a code-word designation, the materials stockpiling program, or whatever it was that "Providence" signified, was also represented by a symbolic icon that appeared on documents and designs relating to it—like a logo. It could only be coincidental, of course, but the icon bore a close resemblance to the Venusian katek character.

All work going on at Triagon that required inputs from the various translation groups scattered around Earth and back on Venus was now centralized in the Decoding Lab. The surroundings were more spacious and less cluttered than the original labs in the surface huts, and Brysek's restoration crews were making them more comfortable all the time. The lighting was up to laboratory standards now, and a canteen had been installed farther along the corridor outside. As the surface huts became steadily more crowded with the continuing influx of new people from *Explorer 6*, some of the staff, including Kyal and Yorim, had moved their sleeping quarters down into the original Terran complex. With the latest improvements to the air circulation system, it was cooler and less stuffy than the huts.

Strictly speaking, being drawn into unraveling precisely what "Providence" had signified was a sidetracking from the original job that Kyal and Yorim had come here to do. But the urge to find out was starting to affect everybody. It was now generally accepted that "Terminus" had meant not just the physical location that the Venusians called Triagon, but was a more general term covering also the whole operation of spiriting away selected people and getting them there.

With regard to "Providence," first impressions had been that it referred to the stockpiling of equipment and supplies as part of the Terminus operation—as preparation for the migration elsewhere. But from later findings it was now beginning to look as if "Providence" had carried a broader meaning too. In a number of references, the word was used in a sense that seemed to indicate a particular place. This led to the suspicion that perhaps "Providence" had not been the code word for just the inventory lists but for the operation that the lists had been a part of—in other words, the migration program itself. Such a grander meaning of the term made it easier to understand, too, why it should have been accorded its own graphic symbol—hardly to be expected for a mere set of inventory lists. But the main allure of Providence having a meaning that meant "place" was that if it could be interpreted, it might reveal the destination that the migrants had left for. Hence, anything pertaining to Providence was of interest.

The snippet from the pilot's log described the descent to a landing approach. A tentative guess was that the flight had been to one of the equipment suppliers or consolidation centers back on Earth that had been involved in the Providence supply operation.

"So what gulf is it talking about here?" Yorim pointed to a line on the screen. He was more thinking aloud than expecting Kyal to have an answer. A note at the top of the page carried the reference *Simulator Test P37-G. Gulf Map, Sheet 172.*

"It has to be the local area—a sheet from a regional set," Kyal replied absently. "There were inlets and bays called gulfs all over the place. Since Terminus was an American project, if I had to guess I'd say somewhere around there."

Yorim rummaged among a stack of map hardcopies lying to one side. "What about the 'Simulator' reference?"

"Who knows?"

"Here." Yorim puled out a sheet and checked over it. "The Americas. A gulf called Mexico looks like the most prominent one in that region."

"Could be."

"What else have we got?" Yorim turned back toward the screen.

The text read:

> 11 o'clock approach midway between La Paz and coast, homing peak bearing checks at 5.778
> Following right-hand shore
> Landfall 0.384
> 1st marker 0.577
> 2nd marker 0.715
> GZ on visual at 0.838. Approach too steep. Almost overshot into High Lake.

"La Paz," Yorim read.

"Something geographical," Kyal murmured. "I'm not sure if it was the name of somewhere specific, or a generic word like 'town.' That's something we'll need to check."

"Coast . . . right-hand shore . . . landfall. We're definitely talking about water," Yorim said.

Kyal turned to refresh his memory from another screen showing a list of Terran signs and abbreviations. "'Homing peak' and 'markers' sound like navigational beacons. I don't know what 'GZ' is. It's a Terran abbreviation for something."

"Do we know anything about this High Lake?"

"There were mountains all the way down the Americas. They had lakes up in them everywhere."

"Yes, but look at the way the translators have written it. It reads more like the proper name of a particular one."

"True. . . ." Kyal tilted his head to one side and then the other, as if changing the angle might cause the screen to present its content in a different light. "I don't think this is going to get us anywhere," he said. "It could have to do with anything. There must have been a whole web of locations down on Earth involved with a project of this size."

Yorim rubbed the side of his nose. "Providence could also have been used as a cover word when dealing with them," he commented.

"A good point." Kyal stretched his arms and sighed. It was just another of the pieces that they had played with but hadn't found a fit for.

At that moment Brysek appeared through the double doors from the corridor. With him was a young woman in light gray ship fatigues of the kind worn on lunar transports. "Ah, this looks like Mirine now," Kyal said, unfolding from his chair. She was small in stature but with a bouncy gait that radiated liveliness and energy. Her face was bright and quite pretty, and her hair neat and bubbly in a style that seemed to go with her personality. She had landed an hour or so previously from the transport that had arrived recently in parking orbit. They stood up as she and Brysek came over. Brysek introduced everyone. The two bio technicians who had come with Mirine from *Explorer 6* were attending to some equipment that had been unloaded and would join the group later.

"Lorili sends her love," she told Kyal. "And she said to tell you it's a big relief to be out of Rhombus. She knows you'll understand." Mirine was obviously referring to Lorili's personal situation, which Kyal imagined Mirine would know something about. That was something they could talk about privately later.

"How is she doing?" Kyal asked. "Is the lab on *E6* getting set up okay?"

"It's exactly what we needed. She wants some samples of the bodies sent there as soon as possible so that she can begin working. And you probably know what she can be like when she gets impatient. So I don't think we're going to get much rest for a while."

"You've joined the right club," Bryskek commented.

"We saw those structures that you're studying—on the way down," Mirine said to Kyal. "Lorili told me about them. It all sounds so fascinating. Are you getting any further?" She looked at the screen that Kyal and Yorim had been working on. "What's this? Is it anything to do with them?"

"No, that's about Providence," Kyal replied. "Our sideline that we've taken up."

"Just about everybody has," Brysek said.

Kyal grinned tiredly. "I don't think this particular item means a lot," he told Mirine. "It's an aircraft pilot's log. It looks like directions to a place down on the surface somewhere that was connected with Providence somehow."

"I'm wondering if Providence might have been used as a cover word down there," Yorim said. "That would maybe mean it was associated with all kinds of places."

Brysek nodded thoughtfully. "Could be, I suppose. If so, it could complicate things a lot, couldn't it?"

"Terrans," Yorim said, shrugging in a way that could have meant anything.

"Some people on the transport were talking about it meaning a destination," Mirine said. "Where they migrated to. Could it have been Venus?"

Kyal shook his head. "It was too long ago. Venus was still uninhabitable when the Terrans became extinct. We don't know where it referred to. That's one of the big mysteries to be resolved."

"Have you heard Sherven's starship theory?" Yorim asked Brysek. He and Kyal had gotten it from Casselo.

"Starship?" Brysek looked surprised.

"The Terrans were working on it," Yorim said. "Sherven has got hold of some of their design studies."

Brysek made a so-so face. "Anyone can do design studies." He gestured at Kyal. "Kyal here has produced a few. I've read them, and they're mind-boggling." As an aside he told Mirine, "They talk about harnessing galactic currents to achieve continual boost over interstellar distances." And then back to Yorim, "But it's not exactly the same thing as flying one, is it?"

"Oh, I agree," Kyal said. It was always good to have someone around with a skeptical side to their nature, like Brysek. It provided a healthy ballast that prevented speculations floating too far from solid ground. Brysek had also expressed reservations that the lists of inventory compiled under "Providence" referred to a stockpile amassed at Triagon at all. He thought that the amounts they had by now established records of were too large to be believable. So what else could they be? A production schedule planned to get a colony started after arrival, Brysek had suggested. If he thought that introducing an interstellar dimension strengthened such a case, he didn't say so.

"Sherven was only speculating," Yorim said. "But he wanted Kyal's opinion."

"What did you tell him?" Brysek asked Kyal curiously.

"Pretty much what you just said youself. Dreaming up studies is a long way from delivering the actuality." Kyal paused and then added, "But they were doing some surprisingly advanced things here at Triagon. And you know, that pyramid we found out there is uncannily like some of the discharge attractor designs that I played with. I have to say that . . . And right now, that's all I'm going to say."

"Anyway, Mirine's technicians will be joining us along the corridor when they've unpacked their stuff," Brysek said. He meant the new canteen. "We thought you and Yorim might want to come along too and meet them. One's a Ulangean. Another face from home for you, Kyal."

Kyal extinguished the screen, and they all began moving toward the door. "So it sounds as if you'll be getting started straight away," he said to Mirine as they walked.

"As soon as we can, anyway," Mirine said. "I don't know about the techs, but I'm going to need a refresher on working in suits first. I haven't been in one since EVA training before the trip out." The Terran corpses in the Rear Annexe had been kept in hard lunar vacuum conditions for preservation.

"How long ago was that?" Kyal asked.

"I came out from Venus with Lorili."

"Oh, I didn't know. No wonder you two decided to stick together."

"She's great to work with."

"Do you have a specialty field?"

"Pathology."

"Hear that?" Kyal looked at Yorim. "Mirine's a pathologist. The right person to be looking at corpses."

"I did the preliminary studies on the deep tissue samples that were sent to *E6*," Mirine told them. "There are indications that the individuals they're from were sick. Some of the findings are consistent with viral attack."

They came into the canteen. A few figures were seated around the room, but the two bio technicians hadn't arrived yet. "How widespread could it have been?" Yorim asked, looking curious.

"We don't know," Mirine answered.

"It couldn't have been a pandemic, could it?" Brysek asked, seeing Yorim's point. "Something to do with what wiped the Terrans out?"

"We've wondered that too," Mirine said.

"But how would something like that get to Luna and spread?" Yorim asked.

"The only way would be if they brought it with them," Mirine replied. "Once inside a closed environment, it would be everywhere in no time."

"Wow," Yorim murmured.

He was obviously still thinking about it as they came to the serving counter to inspect the cook's offerings for the day. "An epidemic loose. People shooting each other." He looked aside at Mirine. "Did you come down in Aluam's elevator? See the bullet marks?"

"Aluam?"

"Aluam Brysek."

"Oh, is that his name? Yes, he pointed them out. It sounds as if maybe it wasn't the luckiest of places to be."

"Does Lorili still have her katek?" Kyal asked Mirine. The Terran icon that stood for Providence had looked like the Venusian good-luck character.

"The one her mother gave her? Oh, you know about that. Yes, she still wears it most of the time."

The pancakes looked good, Kyal thought. He fancied something sweet and not too heavy. While he waited for Yorim to fill his plate first, he reflected that the Terrans' icon didn't seem to have brought them a lot of good luck. Disease loose and violence down underground. Destroyed vehicles up on the surface, with remains of bodies that had been burned and blasted. The same feeling came over him that he had experienced looking at the ruins of the town in the Caucasus, the bleak, featureless hills where Moscow had once stood, and the animals browsing among the forested remains of Paris. It was still and peaceful now. Yet what forgotten events had taken place here out on Luna all those millennia ago that would never now be told?

CHAPTER THIRTY-THREE

The Army general who was known as Polo stormed into the lower communications room at Terminus. His expression was dark with anger. The aide with him was blanching openly with fear. "Get me Oberstein in the ship!" he barked at the controller in charge of communications.

"What did you find?" his adjutant, Glasey, asked. He had been left with a squad to watch the room.

"It's cleaned out down there. They're loaded up already. Except for a roomful of mokofaces."

"Mokofaces! Here?"

"They're in an isolation section," the officer who claimed to be base commander blurted. They had found him in one of the upper rooms, unable to give a coherent account of the situation and seemingly bewildered. "It has an independent air recirculation system, and the door is guarded. They can't get up to this level."

"Fatalities?" Polo queried.

The commander's eyes dropped. "Some . . . They've been moved to the rear lock loading zone. It's evacuated. Open to the outside."

Polo looked away, dismissing the matter as now of secondary importance. "Make sure the ferry doesn't move," he told Glasey, referring to the ship they had just arrived in. "Take Blue, Yellow, and Green squads from our guard and round up anyone else you can move, and secure it. Get all our people back onboard, and have the

217

commander at the pad set up automatic cannon to rake the area on the approach side. Post detachments to secure the elevator approaches here and at the surface. If anyone gets in the way, shoot them."

"Sir." Glasey nodded to two of the staff subalterns to follow him and hurried out.

"I must protest . . ." the base commander began.

Polo cut him off curtly. "This is survival now. I'm in charge here." He glared around the room. "Everybody got that?" A burly staff sergeant straightened up from beside the base commander and looked at him inquiringly. Polo dropped his hand quietly to the pistol holstered at his hip. The commander shook his head, and the sergeant eased back down. Nobody else made to challenge. "Bring all the ground vehicles you've got to the main entrance," Polo told the commander. "Stand down the guards in the access antechambers and muster your staff. Get surplus numbers into suits." It was more to keep them busy. He had no real expectation of getting everyone to the ferry. If Glasey got their own people back onboard, it would be full anyway. The commander stared at him, swallowed numbly, and then passed the orders on to his own subordinates. Polo strode over to the console where an operator was trying to raise the ship. The communications controller moved behind him, watched closely by one of Polo's guards.

Polo had arrived with his staff and entourage less than an hour before. As far as he knew, theirs had been the last ferry to get away— certainly from any of the West Coast bases, anyway. It was all over on Earth. The plague had been confirmed from Finland to Tierra Del Fuego, Tibet to central Australia, and across the Pacific islands. Breakdown was general and universal: rioting, panic, and conflagrations in the cities, unchecked banditry loose everywhere. Weapons were being launched and fired, not in any planned or organized war but simply as part of the craziness that the disease itself seemed to induce, and from the realization that there was no escape. It was if the world was rushing into an unconscious collective decision to get it over with quickly. The disease was characterized in its terminal phase by purple blotches on the face and upper body that became connected by a tracery of lines. It had gotten its name, "moko plague," from the Maori tattooing system.

As far as the rest of the world had been told, the craft that had been undergoing tests and was now in orbit above the Moon was the unmanned star probe that had been conceived and put under development in better times. By the time the official story began being questioned openly, it no longer really mattered. Its current flight after lifting off from Terminus was supposed to have been for a final test of the propulsion dynamics before loading and embarkation. Polo had been told that his rearguard would be the last group of arrivals from Earth to be joining it after holding the launch facilities in California and demolishing any other serviceable vessels there. It was looking as if he had been set up.

Oberstein appeared on the screen, looking sour-faced and grim. Polo wasted no time on preliminaries. "What is this? Terminus is evacuated."

"Simply to make the best use of the time. We—"

"We're coming up now. Put your flight engineer on to fix the docking trajectory and coordinates."

"We are working on a revised schedule. I understand your concern, General. Please bear with us. . . ."

They would need some time to build to full power for liftout. Polo recognized that Oberstein was stalling. "No. This isn't a request or a bargaining session. We are coming up now. I demand that we be received."

Oberstein's face hardened. "You are not in a position to make demands, General," he said icily.

Polo had been expecting it. "You aren't yet ready for liftout," he reminded the deputy to the Director. "The Euro-Russian base on Nearside is equipped with interceptor missiles. If they were to learn the true nature of Terminus, they wouldn't let you get away. They would disable or destroy you."

The face on the screen looked uncertain. Even if it were ready to lift now, a fully loaded ship of that mass would never outrun AMMs in the early phase of exiting from low lunar orbit. "What makes you think they have missiles there?" he demanded. "I have not heard this before."

"It was my job down there to know. Just convey it to the Director," Polo replied. It was pure bluff; but there was nothing else to play.

An operator across the room announced, "It looks like there's trouble up top, sir."

"Let's see it," the base commander said. He had moved to stand closer behind Polo, with the communications controller. The

operator brought images from the surface cameras up onto several
of the wall monitors. They showed confrontations between groups
of armed, space-suited figures. Others were trying to block some
vehicles moving up a ramp from the underground depot at the rear
of the complex. At the same time, the sounds of disturbances and
raised voices began filtering in through the doors to the corridor
outside the room.

Oberstein reappeared. "Are there any mokos among your group,
General?"

"Of course not," Polo replied impatiently.

"Or anyone who has been in contact with them, who could be
infected?"

"No." There had been five suspects, and a few more whose stories
sounded weak. All had been left in California. "Stop these games. I
have ordered a connection to Nearside. The channel is being held
open."

"You will be received as the final complement. Please be quick."

"We're leaving for the pad now." Polo motioned to his own
officers to clear the way and headed for the doors, at the same time
using his phone to alert Glasey. "We're coming up now." He no
longer had any interest in what the base commander and his people
did. They were irrelevant now.

He heard the consternation breaking out behind them as he came
out into the corridor, and those he had just left realized what was
happening. Shots sounded. His men were returning fire. One of
them went down. Polo had unholstered his pistol by the time the
reached the elevator. "At the elevator now," he told Glasey over the
phone.

"We're holding the area, but it's turning bad here," Glasey's voice
replied. "The word's out. They're panicking."

"Thirty seconds."

As Polo and his officers bundled themselves in, a smattering of
bullets from somewhere tore into the elevator car. One of the figures
cried out and slumped against the wall. He was pushed out before
the doors closed. The remainder who couldn't fit in were running
for the stairs. The last thing Polo saw there was a firefight breaking
out between his own men and the base commander's.

They emerged into a scene of tumult and the sounds of shouting
and firing. Glasey's squad was holding the way through to the
surface locks, where two vehicles were attached and a crawler

waiting to move in. Other figures were heading for the suiting rooms in the antechamber area, intending to try and make it to a vehicle outside. Polo's impressions became blurred. A face contorted with malice appeared in his field of view. Polo shot it two times, point-blank. Another figure behind it was gunned down from elsewhere and collapsed spurting blood amid flying shreds of flesh. Glasey was ahead of him, then turning to fire back with a machine pistol at somewhere behind. The door through the lock loomed ahead. Then they were inside. Polo was breathless, his chest pounding. Out of a window he could see the other crawler starting to move. Somebody was standing by the lock door, holding it for several figures backing toward it, firing. "Close it!" Polo barked. "Let's move!" The last defenders outside tumbled in.

The scene outside was confused. Vehicles were being hit and immobilized; figures in suits were bounding on the surface, firing, being blown apart. Who was trying to achieve what was impossible to make out. It was as if the kind of insanity he had seen in the last few days on Earth was breaking out all over again.

The officer sitting next to the driver turned to call back. "Shuttle captain for you, sir."

Polo elbowed his way forward through the crush to front and took the handset. "Reading."

"All aboard and secure here. Fighting is spreading to the pad area. What's your situation?"

"We're in the second crawler that's approaching you now. Direct covering fire on those units moving in to our right, about two hundred yards out. Be ready for immediate launch. We're cleared for the ship."

"Wilco."

It had dawned on the workers around the pad area that they were not going to be included. They had been told that more ferries from Earth would be coming in before the ship now in orbit departed, but that obviously wasn't going to happen, and had never been meant to happen. There was enough other transportation out there to get the ones who were left to the bases on Nearside. What they did then would have to be their problem.

Polo was sweating and shaking by the time he collapsed into a seat in the front cabin of the ferry and buckled up. The inner lock door closed, and the voices of the flight crew rattling out final launch checks came from above. In the seat opposite, Glasey gave an order into a field mike for the automatic cannon placed outside to open up, providing a screen of fire to cover the launch. Polo had never known so few seconds take so long to drag by.

Finally, he felt the vessel moving. Outside, the ground with its scenes of desperation and folly fell away and was replaced by stars. "Climbing and on course as programmed," the captain's voice reported. "We've got them on visual, coming up over the horizon now."

Polo leaned to the side, and craning toward a port he could see it—vast and awe-inspiring, rising like a distant, immense bird from its barren, rocky eyrie. Haven . . . at last. After everything. In the horrors of those past few weeks, he had sometimes found himself wondering if he had invented it in his mind as a dream, a trick of self-preservation to stop himself from going insane. But it was there; it was real and solid, coming to take them into its protective embrace. He fell back in his seat and closed his eyes. Only now did he realize that he was shaking with the release of the tension that he had carried for days. He gripped his arms above the elbows as he sat in the seat and braced his legs firmly so that the trembling wouldn't show. He had brought them all through. The telltale of the all-too human weaknesses that assailed him were not appropriate to the image he had to maintain. He drew in a long, deep breath and released it as a series of quiet shivers. Relief seeped through his body, beginning from his spine and his loins, like liquid percolating cell by cell through a sponge.

The missile from the ship hit the ferry dead center when it was twenty-five miles out. It carried a tactical fission warhead rated at two kilotons. After the flash, the cloud of debris dispersed in moments to be lost in the starfield.

Thirty minutes later, the ship commenced its lift out of lunar orbit.

CHAPTER THIRTY-FOUR

The Rear Annexe of Triagon contained its own air-lock system and an access ramp up to the surface that emerged behind doors recessed into the crags of a broken crater wall on the far side of the ridge running behind the main base facility. Some damaged Terran vehicles had been found on and below the ramp, along with several more bodies that had died violently.

The sixty-eight undamaged corpses had been laid out in several of the rooms farther back. An interior set of locks connecting the Annexe to the Lower Complex had been found closed, and the Annexe open to the surface vacuum. The fluids had sublimed from their eyes and outer tissues, leaving the exteriors in a fragile state of dessication best described as natural "mummies." However, the deeper layers, fast-frozen, shielded from sunlight, radiation, and micrometeorites, and unaffected by any bacterial action, were amazingly well preserved. The best place for preparing and packing the specimens selected for shipment back to *Explorer 6* was right there, in the Annexe, maintaining the conditions under which they had been found.

Mirine was at the bottom of the ramp, helping the two technicians who had come with her from *Explorer 6* stretch a retaining net over the canisters containing the bodies and secure it to the trailer that would carry them to the pad area. The bodies had been sprayed with a protective laquer that set hard in the lunar cold, which would be removed by evaporation after arrival. Yorim had suited up and come through the internal lock from the Lower Complex to see how they were getting along. Mirine would be glad to get out of these foreboding, sepulchral vaults and back there, where there were lights and people and life. Thinking about the macabre role that this place had played, cold and dark, preserving its rows of silent dead for untold millennia, was getting to her. The effect might have been purely psychological, but that didn't make it less real.

Kebrik, one of the technicians, tested the tautness of the net ties. "It's fine on this side," he said over the circuit.

"Here too," Dodra confirmed from the other.

Fenzial, the crew foreman who had been working with Yorim and Kyal since their arrival, was already in the tractor's driving seat. "Who's riding in the back?" his voice asked.

"I will," Mirine said. She looked at Yorim through her helmet while the other two clambered up in front, one either side of Fenzial. "Coming for the ride too?"

"Sure, why not?" He helped her hoist herself up onto the trailer, and she in turn lent a hand for him to join her. It wasn't a question of weight; climbing in suits and with packs was a clumsy business. They found themselves niches among the canisters, and secured safety lines from their belts to anchor points on the trailer's sides. Bumpy rides at a sixth of normal body weight could be eventful.

"All set," Mirine said. The tractor with its load moved away slowly and began ascending the ramp. She checked around again that they hadn't loosened the net in climbing aboard. Yorim had wedged himself into a corner with his arms spread on either side and one leg propped out in front of him, even managing to look comfortable as he presided over the bizarre hearse. He looked as if he could have dropped off to sleep. Mirine couldn't remember meeting anyone so capable of being at ease in any circumstances. His nonjudgmental way of accepting everyone as they were made others around him feel comfortable. He hadn't really bothered to disguise the fact that his main motive in taking a break and coming through to the Annexe had been to get to know her a little better. She felt flattered at the thought.

"Pad calling Fenzial." A voice came through from the lander waiting in the launch area.

"Reading."

"How are we doing?"

"We're finished loading and just coming up to the surface now. Be there in five to ten minutes."

"We'll see you then."

Mirine switched her suit's transmitter from the common circuit back to the channel that she and Yorim had been using to chat privately. "I may have had a stranger ride than this at some time in my life, but if so I can't remember it," she said.

He grinned behind his visor. "At least the gravity makes it easy on the bones where things stick out," he answered. "We've been doing a lot of work outside on the South Field and out at the pyramid. I guess I've gotten used to it."

"Do you have any idea how long you'll be here for?" Mirine asked.

"At Triagon?"

"Out here generally—Earthside."

"Oh, we don't know yet. It depends on what we find. It's open-ended."

"What part of Gallenda are you from?" Mirine asked.

"A small town you'd never have heard of, originally. It's along the coast from Beaconcliff."

"I know where Beaconcliff is. Lorili has a younger brother who plays the polychord. His teacher was from there."

"How long have you known Lorili?" Yorim asked. "Did you grow up together?"

"Only since college in Korbisan. We got to be close friends then. When she accepted the offer from the State Institute to come out here, I thought it sounded like a great adventure and applied for a posting too."

They emerged onto the surface. Fenzial nosed the tractor around, its headlamp beams following the tracks leading out of the gully in the crater wall where the Annexe doors were situated, around the ridge, and toward the pad area. Farside was away from the Sun, and the only light was from the stars, reducing the surroundings to ghostly highlights of crags and detached parts of ridges floating above black slabs of shadow.

"Kyal says she was mixed up with the Progressives back then," Yorim said. "Were you involved in that too?"

"No. It was never my kind of thing. What about you? Dodra thinks you're a Prog. She says she can tell because you're irreverent."

Yorim laughed. "Is that what she said?"

"She says you don't show the right sense of awe and respect toward the revered ways and hallowed customs."

"Oh, a lot of people seem to think that. But politics is all about telling people what they should think and how they ought to be. I guess I'm too lazy. I just let 'em be how they want to be." He thought for a second. "I don't think people ever really change much underneath anyway."

Mirine looked across at him curiously. His face was invisible now that they had come out from the light below in the Annexe. "Do you have anyone waiting for you back there—you know, anyone special?"

"I hang around with a bunch of people . . . but no, not really."

"Oh, I'm surprised. I'd have thought you'd have lots of girlfriends."

Yorim snorted audibly. "It's hard work. I just said, I'm too lazy. And you?"

"No." A short silence followed that needed filling. They were coming out from among the crags and shadows. The boxy form of the lander with its struts and tanks stood white in the pool of light bathing the pad area ahead. "How about Kyal?" Mirine asked. She was fishing on Lorili's behalf and made her voice casual.

"Kyal? No. He's too much like his father—always up to his neck in his work. I was as surprised as anyone by this thing with Lorili. Never seen it happen with him before." Yorim answered matter-of-factly without trying to hide that he knew what she was doing. It singled him out as someone she could be frank with. Mirine felt reassured.

"His father was quite a well-known name in Ulange, wasn't he?" she said.

"That's right. Jarnor Reen. He was one of the big movers behind the Earth exploration effort. A pioneer in electromagnetic propulsion technology too. That's where Kyal's own work follows on from, of course."

"And is that what you do too?"

"Me? Not exactly. I'm more electrogravitics—related, but a different area. It's to do with how gravity emerges as a residual effect of electrical forces. How we go about synthesizing it. That kind of thing."

"I've never really understood it," Mirine confessed. "Somebody told me it's what stops the Sun from collapsing."

"That's right."

"How come?"

"The atomic nuclei distort under the pressure as you get deeper inside. That causes their electric charges to a polarize, creating internal repulsion forces. The Terrans thought it was due to nuclear fusion photon pressure—that the reactions going on in the photosphere happen deep in the interior."

"They seem to have gotten a lot of things wrong," Mirine said. "The main reason Lorili wants to do the sequencing studies on these corpses is to see if she can make more sense out of the timescales. There's just too much in common between us and them biologically. She says they refused to see the evidence for the earlier unstable period in the Solar System—because of what they went through. Admitting it would have been too traumatic."

"Yes, Kyal and Brysek are looking at all that too. There's a guy called Frazin who has a theory that what was repressed came out as their religions, and maybe helps explain why Terrans were so compulsively warlike." Yorim fell silent for a moment. Then he went on, "They were obsessed by bombs. Maybe that was why they made the Sun into one."

They arrived at the pads and switched back into the common circuit while the canisters were loaded aboard the lander. When the last one had been hoisted into the cargo bay and was being fastened down, Mirine moved to the edge of the lighted zone around the pads to look once more over the chilling desolation of the lunar surface by starlight. She and the two technicians would be returning to *Explorer 6* with the load. In her mind, she tried to imagine the last Terrans who had left this very place long ago, heading for where? What story did the mutilated corpses, destroyed vehicles, and other signs of violence tell of? Probably no one would ever know.

A shadow darkened the light coming from behind. She realized that Yorim had joined her. "Bleak and lonely out there," he said.

"That's just what I was thinking. And about the things that went on right here, all that time back . . . Do you think they ever got there—to Providence, wherever it was?"

"Who can say? We only know that they left. If any ship that all this hardware was for were still here on Luna, we'd have found it by now."

Mirine looked up at the shining canopy of stars. In the clarity of the lunar night, their different colors and shades were easily discernible, embedded in places in patches of wispy nebulas, crimson and violet. "Just imagine, their descendants could be out there somewhere right now," she said. "We have Venus to return to— a world with people, towns, a civilization, security. . . . They had nothing, did they? They were heading into a complete unknown. And even if they came back, what kind of prospect would they have faced to come back to? The aftermath of a worldwide war. And if it had been later still, their race extinct. Or was it the war that wiped them out, do you think? Nobody knows for sure, do they? . . . Yorim?" He had moved around so that the light from the pad illuminated his face through his visor, and was staring at her with a strange, fixed expression. "What's the matter?" Mirine asked him.

"Say that again." His voice was odd, distant, as if his mind were racing over something.

"What?"

"About them coming back."

"I said that if they came back, it would have been just to the survivors of a war. Or maybe to nobody at all . . . Why?"

"Before that. You said we have security and things to return to. . . . It's so obvious, isn't it? The same thoughts would have occurred to them too. They would have known that when the time came for them to return, it might be to a world that had been destroyed. So they'd leave behind some means to ensure their own survival, wouldn't they? That huge inventory of equipment and materials! It makes sense now."

"Yorim, what are you talking about?"

"Providence. Maybe it wasn't a stockpile to take with them—or even anything ever brought to Luna at all. *Now* it all makes sense! It was a survival cache that they *left behind*, to draw on if they needed it, and get them started again when they came back! Especially with a major war breaking out. All of a sudden I think those navigational directions that Kyal and I were looking at might be a lot more significant than we thought. They're not talking about any supplier's location or forwarding consolidation point. They point to Providence itself. Providence is somewhere on *Earth!*"

✦   ✦   ✦

Yorim sought out Kyal as soon as he was back inside, and put the idea to him. Kyal was immediately convinced, and together they began reviewing other outstanding questions in this new light. A lot of things seemed to fit. Kyal called Casselo, who was still at *Explorer 6*, and went through it again. Casselo took the matter to Sherven, who agreed that it represented a breakthrough. After discussing it further, Sherven decided to call the principal scientific section leaders and department heads together up on *Explorer 6* for Kyal and Yorim to present their new theory. Casselo set things up accordingly, and Kyal and Yorim booked themselves onto the next transport due to leave Luna.

CHAPTER THIRTY-FIVE

Amingas Quarles had read an article somewhere by a biologist who thought the climate of Earth was better suited to Venusians than that of Venus itself, and predicted mass migrations, the founding of cities and nations, and a general population explosion over the next fifty years. He felt he could believe it too, as he and the pilot who had brought him made their way up the short but steep trail from the sandy flat where the helicopter had landed to the jumble of tents and trucks beyond the scarp of rock above them that was designated Camp 27. The air was bracing and clean, coming in as a breeze over the blue waters visible below to the west. The views had been as clear all the way from the Regional Base two hundred miles to the north, where the office for coordinating geological surveys of the western side of northern America was located.

Uzef, who had been supervising the diggings, was waiting at the top of the trail, with a broad grin showing strong white teeth, which he emphasized with an exaggerated welcoming bow. He was wearing a floppy brimmed hat, stained bush shirt, shorts, and heavy work boots, and had acquired a deep tan from the Terran sun. Quarles exchanged greetings and introduced the pilot.

"You look like one of the natives, resurrected," he told Uzef. "You'll end up settling here. I'd bet on it."

"One could do worse," Uzef said. He turned to lead the way back toward the camp. "How long has it been now? Two months? Three?"

231

"I'm really not sure. I've lost track too. Are we getting old, Uzef? Or us it just the work keeping us busy?"

"Well, you don't look any older, so it must be the work. They say it keeps us young, anyway. Did you have a good flight down?"

"Smooth all the way. Great views of the mountains. There's the man I'd recommend if you decide to get your own chopper added to the unit." Quarles gestured at the pilot. "Knows how to handle one. Someone told me once that flying a chopper is like being on top of a slippery invisible ball, and the thing is trying to slide off one way or another all the time. The job is to keep it there. Well, this fellow has the trick. Is that right?" he asked the pilot.

"It's like everything else, I guess. Just takes a bit of practice."

"Would you like to stop off at the camp first?" Uzef asked. "Cool off with a beer, maybe? Or we can go straight on up."

Quarles drew in a lungful of the air. "Oh, let's go straight on up and see it. I was just thinking to myself how invigorating it is here. No wonder you're looking so fit, out in it all the time. The beer will go down better afterward."

"That's because I don't get chauffeured around in helicopters all the time," Uzef gibed. He looked across at the pilot. "They live too soft a life, you see—these people up at Regional Base." The pilot grinned.

"Well, I don't know so much about that," Quarles said. "You should try coming out and spending some time at the place we've been working in. A mile deep and over twenty across. The Terrans called it the Grand Canyon."

"Yes, I've seen some of the reports. An arc discharge gouge that long. Amazing."

"Running up and down there for a week or two will get you into shape, I can tell you."

"How are things going otherwise up north?" Uzef asked. "Are you finding anything interesting these days?"

"Not so much in the major cities," Quarles replied. "Most of them were targeted in the final war and pretty totally devastated. That Altian that we met, Xervon, he told me they estimated that the Los Angles area alone was hit by at least forty nuclear bombs."

"Vizek!"

"The smaller towns are better when it comes to yielding anything useful. Some of the space bases were farther north too. But I'm not sure what they've been finding there. That's more for the archeologists and archeotechnologists than geologists." Quarles gave Uzef a nudge. "You might be needing some of them up here if this is what you think, eh?"

"Well, let's see what you make of it first, anyway."

They came over a rise of sand and rocks. Quarles halted to take in a general impression before going closer. The peak stood on the far side of a depression that bore the vaguely discernible lines of a dried-up creek bed meandering along its center. It had been taken as a natural part of the ridge and attracted little attention from aerial survey photographs. And then, a couple of weeks previously, Uzef's team had arrived in the area on a ground exploration tour of the coast.

The mounds of sand piled along the base of the peak below a hollowed-out amphitheater showed where the slide had occurred. It had uncovered part of a flat, sloping surface that didn't look natural at all. Further digging and clearing on the south and west faces had established the general form and revealed that it had a layered and ribbed structure.

Uzef tilted his hat forward to shield the glare from the sun and gestured with an arm. "You can see the general lines there, and there. . . . And that digging up there is where we've located the summit. I don't think there's any doubt that it's a pyramid."

Quarles stared, taking it in for a while. "I think you might have a first here, Uzef," he said at last. "None of the ones found so far in the Americas has been this far north. I'm fairly sure that goes for the ones across the eastern ocean on the main land mass too."

Uzef shook his head. "This is much more recent than any of those, Amingas," he said. "From what we've been able to make out, it seems to have had an electrical function." He took off his hat and mopped his forehead with a bright red handkerchief that he took from the pocket of his bush shirt. "You know, if the Terrans had possessed that kind of technology, and I had to guess, I would have said it's a spacecraft discharge attractor."

Nostreny said that Jenyn had been called away in connection with some business that needed attending to up on *Explorer 6*. He hadn't volunteered any more, and since it was really none of his business, Elundi hadn't asked. But it had been very sudden and was certainly very strange. The bad feelings between them over the Lornod affair had been about to boil over after simmering all morning; then Jenyn had received a call on the internal line, got up and left without a word, and not been seen since. Elundi learned later from the receptionist at the front desk that he had left with a visitor. The receptionist's description left little doubt that the visitor had been Derlen. But when Elundi called Derlen to find out what was going on, she had been evasive, said she couldn't meet him, and she hadn't returned his further calls since. Compounding the mystery, Tyarla didn't seem to be available either.

Elundi could only conclude that Tyarla had indeed gone to the provosts, and that she and Jenyn were now involved in some kind of investigation or whatever other procedures had been initiated up on *Explorer 6* as a consequence. He could only attribute the abrupt change in Derlen's behavior to her having formed some kind of involvement with Jenyn that she hadn't told him about. If it pointed to a more fickle side to her than he, in his fond enthusiasm, had imagined, he would rather find out about it now than after an inordinate investment of time, wherewithal, and emotional energy, he told himself philosophically. But she was a great dancer nonetheless.

Iwon was unable to provide any further information other than that Lorili's request for a transfer to *Explorer 6* had gone through surprisingly quickly. Not only was she already there, but her assistant, Mirine, who had gone with her from Rhombus, had just joined her after a detour via Luna. They were setting up to work with some Terran corpses discovered on Farside, and Mirine had gone there to arrange their shipment to *Explorer 6*. In the process, she had brought news of a new theory that was causing considerable excitement there. Iwon wasn't really clear why himself, but apparently Lorili and Mirine referred to it jokingly as Mirine's theory. The essence of it was that the "Providence" code word that everyone had been expressing so much interest in was now thought to refer not to some destination that the Terrans had been migrating to, but a repository somewhere down on Earth. Shortly afterward, a memo came down through the official channels asking Linguistics to make a special compilation of any recent findings and references pertaining to "Providence," for a scientific meeting that was being organized up on *Explorer 6*.

As well as going through his own files, Elundi took it upon himself to check also for any items that Jenyn might have been working on at the time of his sudden disappearance. He came across the piece that he himself had passed over to Jenyn concerning the engineering inspector who had flown from Santa Cruz to perform postdelivery tests and been back in the Bay Area by evening. It had been flagged for inclusion on a report but not processed. If Providence had been on Earth, the reference to "postdelivery tests" perhaps carried even more significance than had been evident then, Elundi noted with interest. In any case, the item clearly warranted action. He attached it to the others that he had collected and forwarded the package to Kyal Reen, which was the name specified on the departmental memorandum.

"I've come across a fascinating snippet that I wanted to share," Emur Frazin said on the screen in Sherven's office aboard *Explorer 6*. "Terran astronomy seems to have originated as a science of ordered, predictable phenomena at around the time of the Greek Thales—the middle of the seventh century 600 B.C. What it could mean is that the Solar System before then was too chaotic for them to put together a coherent picture. So that would be when its catastrophic period ended, and it settled into its present stable condition. It fits nicely with our other findings."

"Hm." Sherven sat back in his chair and stared at the image distantly, while Frazin waited. At length he pronounced, "Very interesting. Let me think some more about it."

"It might help explain the dichotomy of their hypermaterialistic science and irrational religions," Frazin said. "It was an over-reaction. After the period of chaos and terror, when nothing was safe or certain, here was the first indication of stability and predictability in the heavens. Obviously a gift from the deities. The relief and security that it brought were so profound that they sought to impose it on all that made up the world around them, for all time."

"From one extreme to the other," Sherven commented. "It sounds like Terrans, doesn't it?"

"Yes," Frazin agreed. "It became a dogma that they adopted as part of their reaction against dogma, and seemed oblivious to the contradiction."

"Well, as I said, interesting. It might be a good point to bring up at the meeting to hear Reen and Zeestran's new ideas about Providence. I take it you'll be there?"

"Absolutely. I like the sound of it. It would answer a lot of questions."

"So many of us seem to think. Very well, we'll see you there, then. Was there anything else at this stage?"

"No, I just thought you'd like to hear about Thales. It fitted right in with what you were saying the other day. Good day for now."

Sherven carried on thinking to himself after Frazin had cleared down. While the rigidity of Terran science that Frazin had referred to, rooted solidly in intellectualism and materialism, might have been effective—indeed, maybe necessary—for eliminating the flights of fancy and self-delusion to which the Terran mind seemed to have been peculiarly prone, it resulted in a system that by Venusian standards was narrow and restricted. Although the general Venusian system of acquiring knowledge included the methods of induction and experiment that the Terran essentially confined themselves to, it also embraced facets of philosophy, tradition, and what Terrans would have regarded as "metaphysics" as respectable sources to draw on—or at least, sources not to be dismissed out of hand. From the Terran scientific extremist way of viewing things, Venusians would have been regarded as more tolerant toward the "intuitive" and "spiritual"—aspects of existence that were not only dismissed as unreliable by many Terrans, even prominent ones, but denied any reality. No doubt, that went a long way toward explaining their attempts to construct a materialist explanation for life. Well, if Lorili Hilivar thought she could find anything that argued for such a case, he'd certainly be willing to listen. But it didn't seem to Sherven to be a good way to bet.

The call tone from the desk panel interrupted. "Provost Marshal Huiano from Rhombus," Emitte's voice said.

"Yes, of course. Put him through." Huiano's features appeared on the screen that had framed Frazin's. "Not necessary," Sherven said before Huiano could voice formalities. "What can I do?"

"It's concerning Jenyn Thorgan."

"Oh, yes." Sherven felt a twinge of discomfort. He had intended getting on with the business as soon as Thorgan and the Yiag girl were brought up from the surface, but all these other developments had distracted him from taking it any further. "Is he complaining? I can't honestly say I'd blame him. We have been somewhat tardy over this."

"More a case of defiance and not a little ill-concealed anger," Huiano replied. "The provost captain up on *Explorer* is asking when we'll get something moving. He's having a hard time of it. Thorgan is demanding to know who is saying what about him, and where the evidence is. I've talked to him and explained that this isn't a trial but simply an inquiry that we'd rather not turn into a public spectacle. But that just makes things worse. He insists he should be under no restriction and allowed to move freely about. I just wanted to check with you first, Director."

Sherven pulled a glum face. "Well, as I said, after all the fuss, we have been a bit slow over the whole thing, haven't we? What's your opinion on it?"

"He hasn't been charged with anything, and technically he is not under arrest."

"What do the regulations say?"

"Nothing that really anticipates this kind of situation. They're open to interpretation."

"Hm." Sherven rubbed his chin. "I don't see any reason not to comply, really. Do you? Refusing would serve no purpose except get us some bad press in the long run. Let's go along with it but make sure he knows that he will be expected to present himself at the appointed time."

"I agree," Huiano said. "We've got better things to do than be guarding people."

Sherven snorted. "In any case, it's not as if he can get lost in many places up here, is it? Just make sure that his name can't get on any boarding lists for flights out."

"Right away," Huiano promised. He looked relieved. "It will make things pleasantly quieter for my people up there for a while, too."

CHAPTER THIRTY-SIX

On disembarking from Luna, Kyal and Yorim were taken straight from the docking ports to Sherven's office in the Directorate, which was where the meeting was being held. Around a dozen of the mission's scientific figures were assembled in the conference space adjoining the windowed area where Sherven had his desk, when Emitte ushered the two arrivals in. They included Sherven and Casselo; Lorili's departmental head, Garki Nostreny, who had come up from Rhombus to represent the microbiologists; and Emur Frazin. Kyal sat at one end of the long table, facing Sherven at the other. Yorim took the empty seat across a corner. Frazin, whom they had last seen aboard the *Melther Jorg* at the end of the voyage out from Venus, raised his balding head with its short beard from some papers that he was arranging, and nodded at them cheerfully.

"Good to see you again, Emur," Kyal said. "Your name keeps coming up. You seem to have gone straight into the thick of things here."

"There's enough to be done," Frazin agreed. "You haven't exactly been idle yourselves. Why else are we here?"

"Fascinating ideas about Terran mythology," Yorim said, referring to Frazin's recent work.

A bespectacled, wispy-haired figure was looking at Kyal from Frazin's far side. "Have you said hello to Lorili yet?" he asked. "I'm the person she worked with down in Rhombus up until a few days ago."

"Garki Nostreny?"

"Yes. A privilege to meet you."

"Oh. No, mine entirely. She's mentioned you many times. No, we came here directly after docking. That's the first thing on the list later."

"I'll have to stop by her new lab myself before we go back, to see how it's looking," Nostreny said. He'd just had time to introduce a fair-haired woman next to him as Acilla Jyt, a translator, also up from Rhombus, when Sherven called the meeting to order.

In keeping with his characteristically terse style, he went through the formal introductions, reiterated the subject matter from a summary note that he had circulated in advance, and handed the proceedings over. Since Yorim had been the first to suggest the idea, Kyal had conceded that his was the first right to present it. Yorim, however, was happy to defer to the senior partner. Addressing prestigious groups wasn't really his style, he said. He'd let Kyal do it. With the pace of events, Kyal had been able to provide only a few sheets of background information to supplement Sherven's note, instead of a more comprehensive overview as he would have preferred. Since not everyone present would have had reason to follow them events in detail, he began by outlining the order of events so far.

"We have established that the code word 'Providence' is associated with a large inventory of supplies and equipment. It showed up first in the Terran records recovered at Triagon, and later in related references found in various places down on Earth. Our first thought was that it referred to a stockpile of materials accumulated at Triagon as part of the 'Terminus' evacuation program. But then it became evident that many of the items contained in the lists wouldn't have been any use there." Kyal turned up his palms and looked around the table. "Combustion-driven agricultural tractors . . . Seed stocks . . . What good would they be on an airless moon? Weapons . . . For use against whom?"

Nobody had any comment at that point. He continued, "The lunar constructions that Yorim here and I came from Venus to investigate indicated that the Terrans were developing an electrical form of space propulsion technology—something they had previously been thought not to possess. This led to the suggestion that Terminus had perhaps meant more than just an evacuation program—that it was the staging operation for a migration elsewhere. Then the linguistics people began finding instances of 'Providence' carrying a geographical connotation—as if it were associated with a particular place. The pieces seemed to fit. We had Triagon on Luna as the departure point for a migration; a stockpile of materials that wouldn't have been suitable for Luna; and those materials being talked about in connection with a specific place." Kyal looked around, inviting the obvious completion.

Casselo voiced it. "The place where the migration was heading." Heads here and there around the table nodded, intrigued.

"These weapons." The speaker was a young exohistorian called Lewen, whom Sherven had introduced as working closely with Frazin. "Couldn't they have been just a provision for their own internal security? I mean . . ." He looked around with a wry expression. "We are talking about Terrans, after all."

"Not really, if you look at the kinds of things it lists," Kyal replied. "There was practically enough there to start one of their wars. It had to be a contingency against possible external threats."

"Was it going to be a migration, or an invasion?" somebody quipped.

There were no further points. Kyal resumed, "But as more was discovered, the idea of Providence being supplies for a migration started to look less credible. The amounts were too vast—more than they could believably have transported to Luna."

"More than Triagon could have held," Sherven murmured. He had been one of the first to express doubts.

Mellios Chown, a geographer based on *Explorer* 6, who was cataloging Terran place names, asked, "Why would they have to take all of it? Maybe in a situation like that you'd hoard large stocks of everything you could get while it was available, and be selective later about what you actually wanted to take with you."

"Why ship all of it to Luna?" Yorim queried. "It would make more sense to do the selecting first."

Casselo added, "And if they did do the selecting at Triagon, where's all the stuff they didn't take? It's not there."

Chown bunched his mouth and nodded in a way that said there was no arguing with that.

"It's funny how often the obvious is the last thing to occur to us, isn't it?" Kyal said to the table.

"Oh, not really," Sherven remarked breezily. "It's for the same reason that something you've lost always turns up in the last place you look: Who's going to carry on looking after they've found it?" It produced a few smiles.

"Well, it was Yorim who finally saw the obvious," Kyal said.

"Only because of something Mirine said," Yorim put in.

"Mirine? You mean Lorili Hilivar's assistant?" Nostreny looked astonished.

"Yes," Yorim confirmed.

"Well, who would have thought it?" Nostreny waved vaguely to take in the table. "Is she aware that this is all her doing?"

"You know, I don't think she is," Kyal said.

"Oh dear. We'll have to put that right," Sherven told them.

Kyal came to the point by motioning with the copy of Sherven's summary note that he had been toying with while he spoke. "What we're proposing now, instead, is that Providence was not an exotic supply program for beginning a new life somewhere else at all, but a survival cache that had been left *back on Earth*. That does away with the problem posed by the sheer volume of it. And when you put yourself in the position of the Terrans, it makes perfect sense. If the reason for the Terminus program in the first place was to escape the consequences of a war that threatened to be globally devastating, what kind of prospect would they have faced coming back to? Wouldn't one of the first provisions of any competent planner be to make sure they would have the means to survive and get started again?" Kyal glanced at Lewen, the exohistorian. "And there's your reason for including some heavy-grade weaponry. You wouldn't know what to expect from the survivors." Lewen nodded without comment.

A planetary physicist called Hiok observed, "So the possibility of migration isn't ruled out." He sounded as if he hoped not. "A survival cache set up back on Earth could just as easily have been to provide for a forced return from anywhere, not just a planned return from Luna."

"It's not ruled out," Casselo agreed. "There's just no reason for introducing it."

Nostreny shifted in his chair, rubbed the back of his neck dubiously, and looked at Sherven. "To be honest, I was never really keen on that starship idea, Fil. Even if they did have a more advanced propulsion technology than we thought, as Fellow Reen said, at best it seems they were still *developing* it. Why in secret, and why on the back of their moon, I don't know—but that's Terrans.

Would they have entrusted themselves to something like that? I don't think I would have. It just sounded too far-fetched."

"We have records of several star-probe studies," Sherven replied. "And there is some evidence that they were engaged in active development." It was one of his pet ideas, and he wasn't going to let go of it lightly. But his tone was resigned.

Hiok took up Nostreny's point. "Unmanned probes, yes. But that's a very different matter from supporting a viable human colony. And as far as I'm aware, we don't have any proof that they ever actually launched anything."

"That's true," Sherven had to admit.

Hiok gestured apologetically. "And even if they did, there wouldn't have been enough time for them to receive any reconnaissance information back. They would have been going blind into something completely unknown. Is that really credible?"

"Not for us, probably," Sherven said, and left it at that.

Yorim came in again. "Nothing specifically connects the star-probe studies with the electromagnetic work at Triagon," he reminded everyone. "They could have been coincidental. If Terminus was a migration program, it could still have been to somewhere in the Solar System that has changed radically. We think the Solar System has remained essentially unchanged since the time of the Terrans, but it's not certain."

"Right," Hiok said. "We know they made a couple of manned visits to Mars. Maybe there was more going on there than we've realized. Perhaps we should be thinking about looking at Mars more closely." He sent Sherven an inquiring look.

"Perhaps," Sherven agreed neutrally.

"The Terrans' records show it as being not very different from the way it is now," Casselo pointed out.

"I'm still not convinced about the idea of them migrating *anywhere*," Nostreny said. "I mean, why take all the risks associated with going out somewhere totally unknown, when all they had to do was wait it out and go back to Earth? It doesn't make any sense to me—especially if, as we're now hearing, this whole Providence thing was a survival cache waiting back there for them anyway."

"We're only saying that its being a survival cache on Earth doesn't rule migration out, Garki," Casselo reminded him.

"I know, I know. I was just making the point," Nostreny said.

Kyal waited until they had settled down again. "All of those possibilities are valid. But the crucial point is this. *If* any Terrans did in fact return to Earth, they would have formed a colony that existed somewhere—for a while at least—*after* the final war, which is where all the records that we have at the moment cease. So, if we can locate where Providence was, the chances are that it will give us a source of invaluable information on the last days of the Terrans—maybe far more complete and of better quality than the fragments we've been forced to work with up until now." He paused to let them take that in.

"It might give us some clues on what exactly did wipe the Terrans out, finally," Lewen mused, half to himself.

"A good example," Kyal agreed.

An assortment of odd looks, exchanged glances, and then murmurs greeted him as one by one the others saw the implication of what he had been leading up to. He sat back, allowing them to reflect on it. Lewen frowned at his hands, then looked along the table. "If they did return, wouldn't we already know about it?" he said.

"How so?" Kyal invited.

"I'd have thought there would be evidence of it. The place would have been opened up. With all the orbital reconnaissance and aerial surveys we've done over the years, wouldn't we have found it by now?"

"I'm not so sure we would," Kyal replied. "Think about it. If you were leaving a world that was on the verge of a major Terran-style war, would you want it to be common knowledge where you had left your cache of supplies and equipment for when you come back? Of course not. It would be the first place that survivors would raid and loot. So you'd make sure it was well hidden, probably in some out-of-the-way area. And you certainly wouldn't advertise it with lights and signs. But you've got a point. If we can find where Providence was, its condition will tell us if anyone returned to it."

"Not necessarily." Chown came back in. "Even if it were opened up, it could still have been by survivors from the war who just stumbled on it."

"That's possible," Kyal agreed. "But if was opened by the people who set it up returning, I'd expect there to be a good chance of finding evidence that would identify them."

"The only way we'll ever know is by locating Providence," someone else said. "That has to be the first priority. Fellow Reen is right."

Reactions were becoming positive. It was time to move things along, Kyal decided. "And here's something that might give us a start." He used his phone to bring up on the central wall screen a copy of the pilot's log that he and Yorim had first looked at in the Decoding Room at Triagon, with the reference: *Simulator Test P37-G. Gulf Map, Sheet 172*

And text:

11 o'clock approach midway between La Paz and coast, homing peak bearing checks at 5.778
Following right-hand shore
Landfall 0.384
1st marker 0.577
2nd marker 0.715
GZ on visual at 0.838. Approach too steep. Almost overshot into High Lake.

"This was recovered from some reactivated Terran electronics at Triagon," he informed the company. "They appear to be flight notes made by the pilot of an aircraft. From the mentions of coast and shore, it evidently describes somewhere on Earth. And from the header, it's connected with Providence. At first—when we thought Providence was part of the Terminus program on Luna—we didn't attach any great significance to this item. Our guess was that it referred to a supply or collection point somewhere that was involved in the general Providence operation. But if Providence was located somewhere on Earth, this could have a whole new significance."

All eyes turned back toward the screen as the listeners took in its content from this new perspective. "You're saying this could refer to the location of Providence itself," Emur Frazin said eventually. It was the first time he had spoken. This latest turn had evidently aroused his interest.

"Right," Kyal confirmed.

"A moment ago it was a—what did you call it?—a supply or collection point for onward shipping somewhere," Lewen pointed out. "Why should it suddenly mean the location of Providence?"

"It might not," Kyal conceded. "But at least it becomes a possibility that didn't exist before—if Providence wasn't on Earth."

"Uh? Hum . . . Okay."

"However, there's more. Look at the header. At first we had no idea what the reference to 'Simulator' might mean. Now this is speculative, I agree, but consider a further possibility. We've just agreed that whoever the group of Terrans were who set up Providence, they would have gone to great lengths to keep it a secret and conceal its location. They wouldn't surround it with lights and navigation beacons. But obviously the pilots ferrying in the supplies would have to be able to find it." He turned his head to look with the others toward the screen. "I think that's maybe what we have here. Notice it says 'Testing.' These could be notes made in the course of developing a simulator program for finding Providence." The others, clearly attracted by the argument, were already searching the screen for more clues.

"Where's this gulf that it talks about?" Acilla Jyt, the linguist, asked. "The Persian Gulf, maybe? It figured prominently in much of what was going on around that time. Half of Terran politics and wars seemed to hinge around it."

"Unlikely," Lewen said. "As you say, it was a permanent war zone. Nobody would choose an area like that for something this crucial and secrecy-sensitive. It would be in friendly territory. Terminus was built by the Western powers. I'd look on the other side of the planet—the Americas."

"That's what we thought too," Casselo agreed. He had already been through this remotely with Kyal and Yorim.

"The most obvious gulf in that region is the one they called the Gulf of Mexico," Kyal said. "As yet we haven't found anything connecting Providence with it. But it seems promising all the same. La Paz is a Mexican place name."

"This is on the right track," Sherven interjected. "The kind of thing we need to be looking for."

"Actually, La Paz would be more accurately described as Spanish," Acilla Jyt cautioned. She didn't seem to have any suggestion at that stage as to how the fact might be material.

Chown looked at the screen again for a few seconds, then to Sherven, and finally along at Kyal. "I might be able to contribute something right now," he offered. "Large parts of the southern American continent were Spanish speaking, I believe."

"That's correct," Jyt said.

"The city of La Paz was the capital of the country they called Bolivia. Moreover, it was close to a lake called Titicaca, which was at the highest altitude of any lake anywhere. Come to that, I'm fairly sure it still is—but I'd need to check."

"The High Lake," Sherven read from the screen.

"Yes. You see, it ties in," Chown said.

Casselo brought something up on his phone and consulted it for a moment. "Let's have a look, then," he said, entering a code. A map of the region came up on another of the wall screens. He entered more commands, and La Paz and Lake Titicaca appeared, annotated in red.

"So where's the gulf?" Yorim asked, looking over it. The most conspicuous inlets that might have qualified were all on the eastern seaboard, whereas the places Chown had indicated were over on the opposite side of the continent.

"There's only that coastal indent about halfway up," Chowm admitted. "It would be around the border between the countries of Chile and Peru. That could have been it, maybe. I've never come across it as being called a gulf. But that's something that needs to be looked into, obviously."

The meeting finally broke up on a note of optimism. While groups were still continuing to debate some of the issues, Sherven steered Kyal over to one side. "You know, you really are more of a generalist, just like your father," he said. "I like your ways of thinking and working. How would you feel about the idea of taking charge of this whole question? It's going to need a somebody at the middle of it who can talk to all the specialists and coordinate their inputs. You seem to have a flair for it. I can see this Providence issue becoming central to a lot of what we have going on at present."

It sounded attractive. Kyal was already intrigued by the Providence riddle in any case. "Do you mean in parallel with the Triagon work?" he asked.

"I'd say that's pretty well completed," Sherven replied. "As far as the essentials go, anyway. Others can work out the details. I was thinking we could set you up here for a while, aboard *Explorer 6*." His eyes had a faint, mischievous light.

"I could almost answer that now," Kyal said. "Do I take it you'd be talking about including Yorim Zeestran too?"

"Oh, I'm sure that could be accommodated," Sherven assured him. "Perhaps we can discuss it over lunch. Are you joining us? We've got a table reserved in the Patagonia."

Kyal smiled apologetically. "If you don't mind, Director, I'll duck out this time. I, ah, have some personal matters that have been waiting long enough. Yorim can stand in for me, if that's acceptable. You can take my answer as affirmative."

Sherven didn't argue. "Very well, then. We'll see you back here later, I trust? Now that we seem to have made some headway, I'd like to get someone along from the news service to put a public bulletin out about it. Would you mind saying a few words?"

"I'd be happy too, of course."

"And you're sure about the offer I just mentioned? If so, I might mention that as well. Would that be in order?"

Kyal had heard that while Sherven sometimes took a while to make his mind up about things, once he did, he could move amazingly quickly. Lorili's transfer up to *Explorer 6* seemed to be an instance. He could see no reason to change his mind. "If Yorim feels the same way, then by all means go ahead," he replied.

Sherven turned to someone else who wanted his attention, and Kyal took the opportunity to detach himself. He went through to the outer office where Emitte was usually stationed, but it was empty. Taking advantage of the privacy, he took out his phone and called Lorili.

"You made it!" she exclaimed, looking delighted.

"Yes. And I'm free at last. Sorry I couldn't call sooner, when we arrived. They rushed us straight through to the meeting."

"I guessed it was something like that. How did it go?"

"Just fine. Meet me for lunch and I'll tell you all about it."

"The general cafeteria would be good," Lorili said. "You know where it is?"

"Not really. I've only just got here. The last time I was on *E6*, my feet hardly had time to touch the decks."

"Where are you?"

"Sherven's office in the Directorate. That's where the meeting was."

"Okay. Then this is what you do. . . ."

CHAPTER THIRTY-SEVEN

Kyal had never felt any true sense of closeness in the few years that he had been married. It only really dawned on him in later years that he was supposed to have. The example had been there for him in the shape of his own parents, sure enough. But he'd found himself forced to admit later in life that preoccupations with science, his work, and other things had prevented him from seeing it.

Once, long ago, when he had been traveling in another part of Ulange and stayed overnight in a hotel, he remembered observing an elderly couple in the dining room at breakfast. The way they talked and seemed to know each other's thoughts had left an impression on him of two people who had shared a life of contentment together, and who probably couldn't have imagined its being any other way. He had envied the completeness that he sensed in their existence. He had never felt that kind of closeness, even potentially, in the few relationships that had followed his marriage. But in a strange way, even after knowing her for such a short time, he was already feeling that way toward Lorili. And even more exhilarating was his sensing that it was mutual: a feeling of easily and naturally "belonging" with someone. He hadn't realized until he headed for the cafeteria how much he had been looking forward to seeing her again since the day of his rushed departure from Rhombus with Yorim.

She arrived looking as striking as ever with her long black hair contrasting against the light tone of her skin, but still wearing a white lab coat that in her hurry she had neglected to take off. Kyal came forward, smiling, from where he had been standing waiting near the door. They started to hug, and then both turned it into a kiss on the same impulse. The cafeteria was self-serve. After chattering about nothing in particular, and mildly inanely, while they collected dishes and loaded a tray, they settled down at a side table by a rail overlooking the Central Concourse in *Explorer 6*'s main superstructure.

"I hope you feel suitably honored," Kyal told her. "You know, I turned down a lunch on Sherven in the Patagonia for this."

"Oh, I'm mortified! Then I'll have to try all the harder to make it worth it, won't I?"

"I don't think you'll need to strain yourself on that account. So how's the new lab going here? Are you getting everything set up okay?"

"It's going well. We inherited some good people who were there before."

"And Mirine?"

"She's fine. I left her in a sterile room, thawing out corpses and cutting incisions."

Kyal made a face. "Sounds wet and messy. I'll stick to watts and amps."

They fell silent while they sampled the cafeteria's offerings of the day. Kyal had decided to try a deep-fried Terran fish. It was quite good. "How's the salad?" he inquired.

"Tasty. And welcome—the first I've eaten today. . . . So, tell me about Sherven's meeting."

Kyal related the morning's events, not forgetting to mention that Mirine had received due credit for her inspiration. Lorili hadn't known that Nostreny was up from Rhombus to attend. She hoped he would stop by before he returned and Kyal confirmed that Nostreny had told him he would. He summarized the case for Providence having been somewhere on Earth and described the reactions. Lorili followed attentively, clearly finding it fascinating. In conclusion, Kyal went through the points that had led Chown to propose a location for Providence on the western side of southern America.

"I'd be curious to see the translations that you're getting these things from," Lorili said when he had finished.

Kyal shrugged. "Sure. There's no reason why you shouldn't. I'll send you a set of copies."

"Would you? Thanks so much." She ate in silence for a while and then cocked her head as a new thought struck her. "There are old pyramids there, aren't there—in the southern part of the Americas?"

"Are there? I hadn't heard about them."

"All overgrown in jungles and places like that. Could they be anything like the one that you and Yorim looked at near Triagon?"

"I don't know. I'll have to look into it," Kyal said. After a pause, he added, "I wouldn't have thought so, though. They were probably from the older civilizations that existed there before the Europeans and Late Americans. So if I had to guess, I'd say they were probably more like the ones Yorim saw in Africa."

Lorili reflected for a moment, then dismissed it with a shrug. "Maybe," she said.

Kyal looked at her curiously while he ate. "You didn't waste much time moving," he commented finally. "Or Nostreny didn't, or Sherven. Whoever . . . I take it that the business with Jenyn had a lot to do with it. What's the latest with him?"

"You remember the person I told you about, who works with Jenyn in Linguistics: Elundi Kasseg?"

"Right. The guy who's concerned about all this Gaster Lornod stuff. "

"He's a friend of Iwon's. That was how he got in touch. Jenyn had mentioned my name. They took me to see the girl who started the business."

"Tyarla . . . Yig or something, wasn't it?"

"Yiag. It seems that she's mixed up with Jenyn. He put her up to the whole thing. It was just like I've seen before, all over again. . . ." Lorili pulled a face as if she were experiencing a bad taste and shook her head. "Can we go into this some other time, Kyal? It's too good a day to start bringing it all up."

"Of course." Kyal glanced at the clock display above the cafeteria door. "I'm going to have to cut it short and get back soon anyway," he said. "Let's celebrate with a nice dinner tonight—in the Patagonia. I'll pick you up at your lab. How would that be?"

"It sounds just great. I ought to be getting back to give Mirine a hand, too. We're in Room C-23 down in Molecular Bio labs. It's a bit complicated to give directions to."

"Don't even try. I don't know *E6* well enough yet for them to mean anything anyway. I'll find it."

"You can take your time," Lorili said. "We'll probably be working late. There's a lot to do."

"Just as well," Kyal said. "I don't think those people up in Sherven's office will be going their own ways in a hurry either. So it probably suits both of us." He looked at her mischievously for a second or so. "But before we go, I suppose I should give you the good news."

"What's that?"

"I was talking to Sherven just now, after the meeting ended. He wants us—Yorim and me—to take a new position coordinating the Providence work that I was talking about. It would mean we'll be based here, on *E6*. How about that?"

Lorili stopped with the drink that she had been about to finish poised in midair, and stared at him. "Here? You're going to be moving here?"

Kyal nodded. "I thought you'd like it."

"And you've been sitting there all this time since we sat down, holding out? That's mean."

"Okay, you've found out. I have a dark side."

"But it can't be final yet if you've only just talked to him. When should we know for sure? Any idea?"

"Well, maybe you're not the only one around here who can move fast. Sherven's putting out a public news bulletin this afternoon on the new Providence theory. He might make some mention of it then."

"That soon?"

"If Yorim is agreeable. They're supposed to be talking about it right now, over lunch."

"I couldn't imagine you and Yorim splitting up," Lorili said. She thought about it for a moment longer and shook her head. "There won't be any problem with Yorim. He's easygoing enough. If it meant going to Mars as this person you were telling me about at the meeting was saying, Yorim would just shrug and go along with it."

"So you see, it did bring you some good luck . . ." Kyal began. "Oh, you're not wearing it. Where's your katek?"

Lorili looked down, putting a hand instinctively to her neck. "Oh, I take it off when I'm working in the lab. See, I was in such a tizzy to see you again that there, I forgot it. It seems to work remotely though, doesn't it?"

"Did I tell you that the Terrans' sign for their Providence program looks like it?"

"Yes, in one of your mails. Isn't it strange?"

"It's even stranger now, when you think about it," Kyal said.

Lorili looked at him curiously. "In what way?"

"Well, the katek is also a symbol for homecoming, yes? Remember the legend I told you when we first met, about the Wanderers?"

"Okay."

"Well . . ." Kyal tossed out a hand, "if Providence was a survival cache that the Terrans left back on Earth, then it would have meant homecoming for them too, wouldn't it? So how about that? A double coincidence."

Kovark worked as a general help in the kitchen of the Patagonia staff restaurant on *Explorer 6*. Fidira was a machine tender and stitcher in the fabric cleaning and repair shop. They both liked the sound of the Progressive agenda as the way of rising to better things. If you helped the movement, then when the time came and the right people had the power, the movement would help you. That seemed like a fair enough deal. Kovark, in particular, admired the image he had formed in his mind of the proud, unbending, militant Terran rebel, and had no qualms about the use of force as a political expedient. Jenyn had long ago recognized that such people would make good shock troops and had been working hard to organize and educate potential loyal lieutenants for the times that lay ahead. Right now, however, what he needed was cooperative witnesses. And what made these two ideal was that in their surface leaves down at Rhombus, they had found their way to some of the "interesting" parties that Tyarla talked about. They had even seen her at one or two of them on occasion.

Jenyn talked to them on some seats set around an alcove in front of the public network booths on one side of the Central Concourse, where he had been using the directories to check names and contact details of other Progressive supporters located on *Explorer 6*. The background noise from the concourse area gave them privacy, and the alcove was screened by a planter filled with Terran flora, and reasonably secluded.

"It isn't public knowledge yet, but what's going on is that she's saying I was behind it," Jenyn told them. "I've had to come up here from Rhombus to defend myself. You don't need to know all the details, so I'll just say it's a grudge she's been carrying since the time before I went to the Americas. She thinks she's doing Lornod a favor that he'll be grateful for when his name is cleared and I'm out of the picture. That's where she's really aiming."

"Sounds like a pretty crazy way of taking out a grudge," Fidira said. She had mirror-streaked hair and face doodles—the latest from Venus.

"Yeah, well, she's a pretty crazy kind of person," Jenyn agreed. Kovark snorted knowingly. "But the problem is, we have big things about to happen all over—down at Rhombus; across in the American settlements and bases; back on Venus." Jenyn gestured expansively. "I can't afford to have this kind of thing hanging over me, even if it is fabricated. But it could take me down all the same, and the news ghouls are slavering. I need to be able to kill this dead once and for all—for the movement's sake. Especially now, when it's all about to happen." He looked at them meaningfully. "That could make things pretty good, one day, for anyone who helps the movement out at a time like this."

Korvark nodded knowingly. He looked willing but puzzled. "What can we do?" he asked.

Jenyn's voice dropped. "The only way you can fight this kind of thing is with the same weapons," he murmured. "This Tyarla wants to start spreading smears? Okay, I'm not happy with it, but she's not giving us any choice. We have to defend ourselves accordingly."

"I'm not sure what you're saying," Fidira said.

"I told you a minute ago that she's doing it to work off a grudge against me," Jenyn said. "But all I've got against her is my word. What it needs is someone else, better still, more than just one"—he gestured at each of them in turn—"to back me up. Look, you saw her at a couple of these parties, right? All we need is a couple of words to the effect that you heard her say she was going to make Jenyn Thorgan sorry. Something like that. You don't have to be specific about when she said it. In fact it might come across better if it were a little vague. More natural. And if *two* of you say you heard it . . ." Uncertainty registered on their faces. "It would only be stretching things a bit," Jenyn told them. "It was there in her head for sure. And with some of the states I've seen her in, she wouldn't know what she'd said anyway." He looked from one to the other.

"Well, I don't know. . . ." Korvark said hesitantly. "I mean, it's kind of a personal thing you're asking here. Those kinds of parties aren't exactly the kind of thing you go around telling everybody about."

Jenyn nodded. "I understand. Think of it as being for the movement. A small thing to put up with. A month from now it will all be forgotten anyhow." He waited. Korvark vacillated. "We'll make it worth your while," Jenyn said. "I know the right people. Trust me."

"How much might we be talking about?" Korvark asked.

"Aw, say a couple of hundred, maybe? . . . Two-fifty?"

Fidira met Jenyn's eyes searchingly. He gave a almost imperceptible nod of affirmation. She nudged Korvak's arm with an elbow.

"He needs help here," she urged. "Where's the Terran warrior? Do you think they would have thought twice about it?"

Korvark flushed, and Jenyn saw she had touched a nerve. "Okay," Korvark told him. "You can count on us."

"Terrific. You won't regret this, either of you."

"What exactly do you want us to do?"

"I'll call you about that shortly, okay?"

Korvak nodded, firmly now. "Okay."

Jenyn braced his hands on his knees. "You probably need to get back. And I know I have things to do. I'll be in touch."

He stood watching while they disappeared back out onto the main concourse, then turned and went back to the row of network booths and sat down in an empty one. He still had his list of Progressive follow-ups to be completed. Before returning to that, however, he checked the Earth-local news channel for anything new regarding Lornod. The topic seemed to be quiet just at the moment. A line in the new announcements box said something about Providence, which was the last thing Jenyn had been working on down in Rhombus. He selected it out of curiosity. A clip began playing of a commentator talking about a statement released after a scientific meeting that had taken place that morning, to the effect that Providence was now believed to have been somewhere on Earth. It was evidently a matter of some excitement. Still absorbed in his own thoughts, Jenyn watched absently as heads talked about a secret survival supplies dump, interspersed with shots of the Terran installation on lunar Farside and a map showing the southern half of the Americas. Then Sherven, the Scientific Director, was summing up with a routine pep spiel about significant new findings ahead, and appointing somebody to a new position on *Explorer* 6 to coordinate the work. As Sherven was speaking, the camera backed off to bring into view another figure who had been waiting alongside him—a man, maybe in his late thirties or early forties, with lean, ruggedly formed features, but drawn around a sensitive mouth, mirthful eyes that seemed to be finding the business fun, and dark curly hair.

Jenyn sat up sharply. He had seen that face before. The immediate associations that he felt were negative and disturbing. Sherven was saying, ". . . Master of Engineering Kyal Reen, son of the distinguished Ulangean electromagneticist and philosopher Jarnor Reen, who was a leader in initiating the Earth exploration program. Also joining us here along with Master Reen will be a colleague of his from Venus, who has been working with him on the investigation of Terran electropropulsion constructions on the lunar Farside: Fellow of Applied Sciences, Yorim Zeestran." The camera angle widened again to take in a younger, yellow-haired figure with a short beard, standing the other side of Reen. "One of the questions . . ."

It was the same Yorim that Jenyn had met in Rhombus, who had joined the group on the trip westward to the Mediterranean coast. Reen was the person who had arrived to join him in the launch area back at Rhombus, when Jenyn had followed him. Lorili had been with Reen.

The scientists were evidently in a jovial mood. "Oh, I think Kyal has other, very good reasons for wanting to move to *Explorer* too," one of them quipped—short and squarely built, with a dark beard. A caption popped up saying BORGAN CASSELO.

"She's purely a coincidence," Reen said, smiling. The banter moved on to other things.

Jenyn muted the sound and sat back heavily in the chair. The picture replayed in his mind of Lorili and Reen embracing before Reen departed with his partner to catch the shuttle. He could no longer hide from himself that his obsession to reassert himself with Lorili had stemmed from the jealousy he had felt since that moment. When Derlen tried to call her, the friend of Elundi's who worked with Lorili had told her that Lorili was moving to a new laboratory, but he wouldn't say where. And Sherven was talking about reassigning Reen to a job in *Explorer 6*.

On a hunch, Jenyn killed the news channel and brought up a directory showing the organizational structure of departments and personnel in *Explorer 6*. He found the section for scientific offices and laboratories, went to the heading BIOLOGICAL, and began searching under Molecular Biology. "Hilivar, Lorili, F.Exp.Sci.(Biochem)" was a new entry listed in Molecular Genetics & Cell Biology Laboratories, Room C-23.

His breathing became labored and shaky as he stared at the screen. He could see the picture clearly now: her scheming with Elundi and his friend; the clandestine visit to Tyarla's; a way out already planned. Even after he had been prepared to forget her earlier treachery back at Venus and give her a second chance, she had stabbed him in the back again and run away to her newfound lover with a famous name—one of Sherven's clique, doubtless with a direct ticket into the Establishment. So much for the worth of loyalty and principle.

The same cold but relentless rage began taking hold of him again as he had felt after listening to Derlen down in Rhombus. Once again, he saw his carefully laid plans and ambitions, the result of years of work, about to come apart because of the same person. He worked a fist savagely into the other hand. *No!* he felt some force that was arising inside him saying. She would learn that he was not someone to sit by and let her get away with it, but a person to be reckoned with. It was a test of himself also. He would prove to himself that he was capable of the boldness and the nerve that his vision for the future demanded.

Jenyn closed the directory and brought up in its place an index of *Explorer 6* layout and construction plans.

CHAPTER THIRTY-EIGHT

As Kyal had predicted, the attendees from the morning's meeting were in no hurry to break up after the news interview, but stayed on, debating different angles and using the conference-area screens in Sherven's office. The sense of significant new findings about to unfold intensified when it was discovered that there had indeed been a town called Santa Cruz in central Bolivia. But the directions that Elundi, down in Rhombus, had supplied in connection with the Terran engineer who had flown from Santa Cruz to Providence couldn't be made to fit. Late in the afternoon, Elundi called back in response to a request that Casselo had sent for confirmation. Kyal went through the problem with Elundi again, while others followed or continued with their own discussions around the room.

"The engineer flew from Santa Cruz to Providence, then back to wherever this Bay Area was."

"That's what it says," Elundi confirmed from a screen adjacent to the one displaying the map of western south America, which included Bolivia.

"And 'Bay Area' would imply the coast."

"Yes."

"Which we're saying appears to be the west coast."

"Yes."

Kyal sent an appealing glance to the others around him. "Which means Providence would have to be somewhere east of Santa Cruz.

259

It's supposed to be in the region of this 'High Lake,' which we think was Titicaca. But Titicaca is *west* of central Bolivia and Santa Cruz, not east."

Elundi sighed audibly. "Yes, I know. There has to be something wrong here. Look, all I can do is go back to the original sources and double-check the translations. You'll have to leave it with me."

"Fair enough," Kyal said.

"Eleven o'clock," Chown reminded him.

"Oh, yes." Kyal looked back at the screen. "And there's another thing we'd like you to look into, Elundi. Going back to the pilot's notes, is there anything to indicate why it says eleven o'clock? What was so significant about the time of day?"

"I assumed it was to identify the particular flight," Elundi answered. "You know—as one of a series. But I'll see if I can find anything else."

"We'll be waiting to hear from you," Kyal said. Elundi cleared down.

Sherven sauntered back in from attending to some matters with Emitte in the outer office. "So what did our friend down in Rhombus make of it?" he asked Casselo.

"He insists it's as he stated. But he's gone away to double-check his sources," Casselo replied. Sherven nodded in a way that said he'd expected as much.

"It's definitely not this Mexican gulf," Chown said. "I'd say we can forget about the east coast."

The language situation was more confused than had been the case when dealing just with the installations on Luna, where English seemed to have been the universal rule. Earth's patchwork of regional and national tongues was bewildering compared to the simple pattern of spreading and divergence that could be traced on Venus. Besides there being no comparable long history of conquests and assimilation, the geography of Venus, especially on account of its inhospitable equatorial belt, was not conducive to large-scale migrations and the mixing of populations.

"Could this 'Bay Area' that the engineer was talking about be a reference to part of the lake?" Sherven suggested. "One end of it or something? Nothing to do with the ocean at all."

"You've still got the pilot's notes," Chown reminded him. "They describe shores and a coast."

"And landfall," Casselo said. "That doesn't sound like a lake to me."

"How far can we trust these translations?" Sherven wondered aloud. "I remember once, a couple of years ago, one of the physics catalogers was trying to index Terran transuranic elements. There was one called plutonium. Half the references he'd compiled turned out to be to some silly fictional dog."

Kyal drew himself away and glanced at his watch. It was already past the time that he had said he would collect Lorili from her lab for dinner. On the far side of the archway from Sherven's conference area, the office itself appeared to be empty. He reached for the phone inside his pocket and began moving toward it. Just then, Yorim caught his attention from where he was sitting at a screen with Acilla Jyt and beckoned him over with a nod. Kyal repocketed the phone and changed direction to join them.

"Why are we looking in the Bolivia-Peru area?" Yorim asked.

"Because it's where La Paz and Santa Cruz were," Kyal answered.

"Look at this." Yorim gestured at the screen. It showed part of a western coastline running northwest to southeast, with a narrow, south-pointing peninsula running parallel to the mainland for some distance.

"What is it?" Kyal asked.

"It's an enlargement of part of the northern continent. That seems to be where the Americans had most of their space and military industries that were on the western coasts."

"But I thought they spoke English up there."

"Acilla says maybe so, but there was a lot of Spanish influence on place names. So we thought we'd have a look through what's been found. And she's right. There's quite a lot."

"So what have you got?" Kyal asked, getting interested.

Yorim gestured again. "See this inlet. It's between a long, thin peninsula to the west, and the mainland to the east. The Terran name for the inlet was the *Gulf* of California. And guess what. There was a town that used to stand down near the tip of the peninsula, on the western side of the gulf. Want to know what it was called?"

"La Paz," Acilla supplied before Kyal could say anything.

Kyal stared at the screen. Something told him this was making more sense already. "Is there any indication of a Santa Cruz up that way as well?" he asked.

"That's the next thing we were going to check," Yorim replied.

Sherven had come over, accompanied by Casselo. "What are you three looking so excited about here?" he asked Kyal.

"Maybe we've been looking in the wrong place," Kyal said. "Look at this. Acilla has found another La Paz in the north. It's not anywhere down around Bolivia and Peru at all . . ."

Molecular Genetics and Cell Biology was located in the lower levels of the Biological Sciences laboratories, which formed part of the main body of *Explorer 6*, beneath the high superstructure. To the rear of the complex was a conveyor tunnel that connected to the docking port area. On one side of the tunnel ran a maintenance passage giving access to various heating, ventilation, plant, and electrical compartments located behind the laboratories. *Explorer 6* was an orbiting scientific base, not a place frequented by the general public. The people who occupied it were not disposed to trespassing or vandalizing; on the other hand, the nature of their work made them of a kind who would typically find it frustrating to have to deal with locks and codes all the time. Hence, security issues were not a paramount consideration in *Explorer 6*. The subject was not a high priority for Venusians in any case.

Avoiding the front approaches to the laboratory complex, Jenyn made his way to the freight storage bays in the docking section and located the door through to the maintenance passage from a hardcopy he had made of the local plan. He was wearing an engineer's coverall that he had found in a locker on one of the higher levels. No clear intention had formed in his mind. A mixture of slow, simmering anger, gnawing jealousy, and the need to prove himself had taken control.

The passage was illuminated by pilot lights, its lines of converging perspective accentuated by the ducts, pipes, and banks of cabling threading through a succession of diminishing support frames into the distance. A catwalk running above, with metal stairways descending at intervals, served a higher level of machinery compartments and hatches. The whole space acted as a sound resonator and conduit, carrying a melange of subdued throbbing and humming from distant parts of the structure. Jenyn moved woodenly but purposefully past the doors and bulkheads, driven by a force from deep in his psyche that had subordinated the conscious part of his mind to the role almost of a spectator.

The location codes stenciled on the walls told him when he had reached the service doors for laboratory section C. One of them carried identification as giving access to rooms C-15 to C-25. Jenyn tested the lock and bolt, and they disengaged freely. The space inside was in darkness. Jenyn eased the door open and stood to one side to let light through from the passage behind. He could make out a narrow space filled with machinery housings and switch boxes. There was another door on the far side, with a small glass window. He stepped through and closed the door behind him. The light beyond the window in the door ahead was low, but enough for him to see his way across to it. Cautiously, he brought his face close and peered through. Beyond was what appeared to be a storage space, and farther back, glass walls partitioning off clean areas containing white countertops with items of metal and glass laboratoryware, instrument trays, and computer panels. There didn't seem to be anyone around.

He moved on through, turned to close the door, and recoiled almost screaming out aloud with fright from the gruesome figure grinning at him from just a few feet away. Its head was skull-like, with empty eye sockets and exposed teeth, but still possessing veils of what had once been flesh, shrunken and frayed into a grotesque gray mask. The rest of the body was the same, withered and flaking like a disembalmed mummy, glinting in macabre highlights from some kind of oil or preservative. Only then did Jenyn realize that it was on the far side of one of the glass partitions. He closed his eyes, breathing deeply and shakily until he felt the adrenaline rush subside.

When he opened them again, his vision had adjusted better to the gloom. There was brighter light ahead. He moved toward it, between the cubicles of glass walls, to find himself looking out at a more open laboratory area. Lorili was standing at one of the benches, with a younger girl. Jenyn felt his composure slipping and his anger rising again. A vein in his temple was pulsing. Beside him was a table supporting a glass-topped sterilizer cabinet. By the light coming from the lab area, he could see the tray of surgical instruments inside. He wasn't sure yet what he meant to do. But he wanted to see her scared. To watch her grovel, and plead, and beg . . .

"Oh, I suppose it will take me a while to get used to being shut in up here again," Mirine said as she added a fixing solution to the tissue samples she was preparing for microscope slides. "And we were just getting to know some good people down in Rhombus."

"It won't be forever," Lorili promised.

"And then there were the travel tours. I liked them. Earth has so many contrasts. I haven't seen half the places I wanted to yet."

"They say the ice caps are incredible. I want to see the Antarctic before I go back."

"And the climate is so wonderful! It makes home seem like a hot, foggy swamp."

"Well, most of it is." Lorili finished marking the labels for the tray and pushed it across.

"You know, I think I'm beginning to agree with the people who say we're better adapted for Earth," Mirine said. "Isn't it strange? Why would that be, do you think?"

Lorili had wondered the same thing herself. "Maybe because Earth is so much older," she suggested.

"Do you think a lot of people will decide to move here?"

"That's what they say."

"I'm beginning to think that maybe I could go for it. Some of the images of Terran cities make our towns look like factory complexes with dormitories. But I suppose the people who founded ours just had to make do with the best spots they could find." Mirine noticed the clock display on one of the instrument panels. "Oh no!"

"What?"

"I've just realized the time. Have we really been that busy? I'm supposed to be meeting Yorim in the cafeteria. He's probably there already."

"You'd better run along then," Lorili said.

"What about these slides?"

"There isn't much to finish with this set. I'll take care of it. The rest can wait until tomorrow."

"You're sure?"

"Absolutely. I was about ready to call it a day myself, anyway."

Mirine peeled off her work gloves and turned away to rinse her hands in the sink to one side. "I thought Kyal was collecting you," she said over her shoulder.

"He *was*. But you know what they're like when they get together. I'll probably have to go up to the Directorate and drag him out."

"Well, don't end up falling out over it."

Lorili smiled to herself. "I don't think that's likely," she said.

"You're really getting serious. I never thought I'd see it."

"Hmm, hum . . ."

Mirine dried her hands, slipped off her lab smock, and exchanged it for her jacket hanging on the wall. "Well, don't you go forgetting as well. And they only arrived here today! How can you?"

"Call it dedication. And don't worry so much. I'll be right behind you."

"Okay. Good night, then. See you tomorrow . . . or maybe later?"

"Maybe. Say hi to Yorim for me, anyway."

Mirine disappeared around a section of dividing wall in the direction of the front part of the lab. A moment later, the sound came of the door leading to the entrance lobby closing, and then silence fell. Lorili returned her attention to the tray of slides.

Mirine's memory could sometimes be very short, she thought to herself as she worked. Only the day before, Mirine had been saying how good it felt to be back amid the familiar surroundings and security of *E6* after the bleakness of the lunar Farside. She had told Lorili that she was still haunted by visions of Terrans fighting each other and dying out there. Coming back with a cargo of desiccated ancient corpses hadn't helped her composure either. Lorili thought back over some of the things Kyal said about Emur Frazin's theory of Terran collective amnesia, and their addictive violence being an acting out of repressed terrors that they had disguised as myth, and which had formed the origins of their psychopathic religions. Were Venusians inherently more stable and rational? she wondered. Or was it just a case of having been through different experiences? Hopefully that was something the genetic studies would help answer. While her mind played with its speculations, she glanced toward the glass-walled clean rooms at the rear of the lab area, where the first group of treated corpses were thawing.

And she almost died on the spot. The tray she was holding dropped with a clatter on the benchtop. One of the dim, shadowy forms behind the glass was moving.

The reaction was reflex. Of course it couldn't be a Terran corpse. But before she could recover, the door through the partition from the rear area slid silently aside, and the figure moved out into the light. It was Jenyn. Lorili hadn't even known he was up in *Explorer 6*.

Already off balance from her fright, Lorili's mind reeled helplessly. She backed away between the benches as he advanced. "What are you doing here?" she whispered, shaking her head in protest. But she could already see from his expression and the fixed, chillingly depthless look in his eyes that he was past reasoning with. She knew from past occasions that Jenyn had an ugly, sinister side that could turn him into a different person when it surfaced, but she had never seen it as extreme as this. And then cold, sickening fear overcame her as she saw that he was holding a dissecting scalpel.

"What do you want? Don't be insane, Jenyn."

"You . . . betrayed me." His skin had a glazed, clammy sheen. His voice sounded dull, almost slurring. He moved toward one end of the bench. Lorili retreated around by the wall, keeping the bench between them. She looked around frantically for something she might defend herself with, something to throw. At the end of the room there was a rack with glass bottles. She tried making a dart toward it; Jenyn moved with sudden, surprising swiftness and cut her off. She backed away again, without the protection of a bench between them now. His face twisted into a crooked grin. Light gleamed off the scalpel's razorlike edge. Lorili stumbled over a pedal bin and fell against the bench. For an instant, all she could do was hang onto the edge to prevent herself from going down. Jenyn sprang forward.

The lab stool flying in from the side entangled his legs. Jenyn pitched forward over it, clutching at Lorili, and they fell together, grappling in a heap. Kyal threw himself across from the corner around the dividing wall and grabbed Jenyn from above to pull him off. As Kyal heaved Jenyn away, Lorili drew herself clear. Kyal moved himself between them and turned to face Jenyn, his body tensed, arms extended defensively. But the onslaught didn't come.

Jenyn straightened up slowly, clutching the middle of his body. There was a strange look on his face, the color already draining from it visibly. He moaned. Then Lorili saw the blood running down from between his fingers. The scalpel had been driven deep into his abdomen. Kyal moved forward warily and reached out to steady him. But Jenyn had no fight left. "We need somewhere to set him down," Kyal said, catching Jenyn as he sagged.

"The chairs out front." Lorili nodded in the direction that Kyal had appeared from.

"I can manage him," Kyal said. "You'd better call for some help."

CHAPTER THIRTY-NINE

The captain from *Explorer 6*'s provost office took notes while Mirine gave her version of as much of the background as she knew. She and Yorim had come in response to a call from Kyal. Casselo had joined them. They were sitting in the waiting area outside the Emergency Room in the Medical Wing. Jenyn had been taken in and was undergoing surgery, and Lorili was being checked after experiencing the effects of delayed shock.

"It must have been devastating," Mirine said. "She had no idea he was up in *Explorer* at all. The last time she'd heard from him was down in Rhombus."

"Do you have any theory as to what might have driven him to something like this?" the captain asked.

Mirine sighed and shook her head. "I can only presume that he lost his head over this Lornod business. From what Lorili told me of what happened before we left, he seemed to imagine that she was responsible. But all she did was go and talk to the girl who had been spreading the story, when Iwon and the guy who worked with Jenyn asked her to. Jenyn must have gotten wind of it somehow and read too much into it. . . . That's all I can think of."

"Thank you. You've been very helpful," the captain said.

"I dread to think what might have happened if Kyal hadn't shown up when he did," Casselo said.

"You can thank Filaeyus Sherven for that," Kyal told them. "He practically threw me out of the office and told me to go and collect her for dinner as I'd promised. I'd gotten totally involved in something Yorim had come up with."

"And Acilla," Yorim said.

"Oh, of course."

"So what happens now?" Casselo asked the provost captain.

"That's not for me to say, sir. I'll pass a report on to the Provost Marshal down in Rhombus, and he will take it up with the directors. We don't have much precedent for this kind of thing."

At that moment the doctor who had attended Lorili earlier came out from the inner rooms. Everyone looked at her expectantly. "Lorili is fine," she informed them. "But she's sedated and could use a good night's rest. It would be best to let her stay here overnight, where we can keep an eye on her. We'll call you in the morning to let you know the situation. Very likely you'll be able to come and collect her then."

The others exchanged nods and looked relieved. "How about the other fellow?" Casselo inquired.

The doctor drew a breath with an expression that said the matter wasn't trivial. The scalpel went in pretty deep and caused some nasty internal damage. Nobody really knows what was on it, so we're taking full precautions against anything infectious. He'll be with us for a while longer. What happens then will be up to his department." She nodded to indicate the provost captain, who was putting his papers away in a folder. "All done here?" she asked him.

"As much as we can cover for now." He looked at Casselo. "Could I trouble you for a few departmental details? I need them for some forms up in the office."

"Of course," Casselo said.

"We could do it now, or tomorrow if you prefer. It would only take a minute."

"Oh, let's get it out of the way now. I've got more interesting things to get back to tomorrow," Casselo said. They stood up to leave.

"I'd better be getting back to my patients," the doctor said. "Call us in the morning."

"Thanks," Kyal told her, and was echoed by the others.

"I'll see you two tomorrow, then," Casselo said to Kyal and Yorim. "Let's just be thankful that it wasn't worse news." He turned to follow the provost captain out. Kyal acknowledged with a wave, waited until they were gone, and then looked questioningly at the other two.

"Where to now?" Yorim asked.

Kyal shrugged. "You tell me."

Yorim pursed his lips and rubbed his beard, which was now looking quite established. "Well, as the hero of the hour, I suppose I should stand you a drink. Also, you could probably do with your own brand of sedative and relaxant. How does that sound?"

"My kind of doctor," Kyal said. "Do we know anywhere in this place yet?"

"There's a recreation area with a bar just off the cafeteria on the Central Concourse," Mirine informed them.

"Sounds good," Yorim agreed. "You coming with us?"

"Sure," Mirine said

"Show us the way, then."

They left the Medical Wing via a broad thoroughfare that came out on a terrace overlooking the Central Concourse. From there they could descend either via stairs or by using the elevator. To Kyal, *Explorer 6* had more the feel of being back in Triagon than anything reminiscent of the cramped interior of the *Melthor Jorg*.

"I wouldn't think any of this is going to reflect well for the Progressives," Yorim commented as they walked.

"Does Lorili say much about them to you these days?" Kyal asked Mirine.

"Not really. I don't think she's as enamored by them as she used to be—not the extremist position anyway."

"Hardly surprising, considering," Yorim commented.

The recreation area was fairly busy when they arrived. A lot of people seemed to have decided to make an evening of it, and there were a number of ship's fatigues denoting off-duty crew. A corner was cleared for dancing, but it was empty just at the moment. Nearby, a group of figures were standing around some kind of game or entertainment that was in process. Kyal and Marine found an empty table, while Yorim ordered at the bar.

"The dancers are quiet," Mirine said, looking around.

"Not for long, I'm sure. You'll have to get Yorim up there."

"I'm still getting to know him." Mirine looked interested. "Does he dance, then?"

"Oh, he's fantastic," Kyal assured her, keeping a straight face.

She was just trying to keep up a brave front, Kyal could see as her smile faded. Even as he thought it, she said, "I do hope Lorili will be all right."

"Master Reen, I do believe," a voice declared behind them. Kyal looked around and up.

"Ari!"

Arissen, the zoologist who been one of the party on the trip out, had detached himself from the group by the wall and come over. "I've been ignored in better places than this, you know," he said.

"I had no idea you were even up here."

"Up on some staff business for a few days. I thought you and Yorim were going to Luna."

"We're just back from there today. Ari, this is Mirine, who was there too recently. Arissen was with us on the voyage out."

"Charmed," Arissen said, bowing his head.

"A pleasure."

Kyal looked across to the bar. "Here's Yorim coming now. Hey, Yorim, look who's here."

"Say, Arissen! And you don't look any older. How's life with the animals?"

Arissen shook his head. "This planet! It's unbelievable."

One of the group that Arissen had left called over. "Arissen, it's your shot. Are you still playing?"

"Oh . . . Take my turn, will you? I've just run into a couple of friends from the ship."

"Okay."

"What's going on over there?" Kyal asked.

"An old Terran game that somebody's discovered. Something more to feed the Terrabilia mania back home, no doubt. Anyhow, how are you two doing? I've been following some of it in the net posts. So those things out there on Farside really turned out to be interesting, eh?"

"It looks as if they were into space electromotives, all right," Kyal said. "In fact there was a big meeting about it here today. That's what we're back for."

"Yes, I saw you on the news with Sherven this afternoon. Sounds like a new job. Congratulations."

"Thanks."

"You too." Arissen looked at Yorim. "Were the Terrans into electrogravitics as well?"

"Not as far as we know. Kyal and I just stick together."

"Have you managed to get down to the surface yet?"

"We had the regular week after arrival. I got in with some people who were touring some parts along northern Africa. Got to climb a pyramid. Kyal preferred old bombed Terran cities. How about you?"

"I've been farther south. The rain forests. Talk about diversity!"

Kyal saw that Mirine was looking distant and only partly listening. The affair in the lab was still troubling her. Probably it was because she had left Lorili only minutes before it happened. "Ari, why don't you show us this Terran game?" he suggested. "Mirine looks as if she could use some livening up." He ushered her to her feet and waved her over behind Arissen before she could object. Yorim picked up his glass from the ones he had set down, and followed.

"Three new recruits," Arissen informed the rest of the company as they arrived.

"Come and join in the fun," one of them invited.

They were taking turns to throw short, fat-bodied darts fitted with tail flights at a circular board divided into numbered sectors. Arissen explained that the game was believed to have been derived from early target practice with bows and arrows. The original Terran scoring rules were not known, so the players had invented their own. Eventually the game in progress ended, and the newcomers were given a chance to try their hand. Mirine went first, squealing with surprise and frustration when her first two darts missed the board completely. But at least she was brightening up a little, Kyal saw.

"It's not as easy as it looks," Arissen commented. "You need a double to start. That's the outside ring. We know that was one of the Terran rules. Go for one of the big ones. Twenty's the best."

"Where's that?" Mirine asked, searching around the board.

"Twelve o'clock."

"What?"

Arissen grinned. "Another Terranism. Right at the top. It's from their clock dial. They used it to indicate directions."

Mirine considered the prospect. "A double? You mean that little tiny rectangle right at the top there? I can't even hit the board."

"Just try for the number," a girl to the side suggested. She looked around at the group. "That's all right for first-timers, okay? A new rule."

"Can I start if I just hit the board?" Mirine joked.

"As long as it's somewhere in the numbers," someone answered. Mirine threw the dart.

"Eight. And a treble!"

"Is that good?"

Kyal was staring hard at the board, replaying in his mind what Arissen had said. He shifted his gaze to Yorim, who was watching the next player. Yorim saw him from the corner of his eye and turned his head.

"What?"

"Did you hear what Ari said? They used their clock dial to indicate directions." He waited a moment for Yorim to make the connection, then said, "Eleven o'clock?"

Yorim turned to face him, the game forgotten suddenly. "The pilot's notes! It wasn't the time of day at all."

Kyal was shaking his head. "We should have known. Terran pilots and military people used a twenty-four-hour system. It would have said eleven hundred or twenty-one hundred if it had anything to do with time."

Curiosity equal to Kyal's own was written all over Yorim's face. "Want to go and check it out?" he said.

"Right now?"

"Why not? We can use the net booths that we came past back there across the Concourse. And wouldn't it be something to show Sherven in the morning."

Mirine had come over and was looking at them. "Did you see that? I got a treble. This could be fun. . . . Hey, what's up?"

"I think maybe we've hit more than a treble," Kyal told her.

"To do with directions on Terran maps," Yorim said.

"Are you two at work again?"

"It's important," Kyal said. "There are some net booths back across the Concourse that we just passed. We need to use them to check something. Do you want to come too, or stay here with these people and learn the game? We can stop back for you later."

"After the things I've heard, it could be all night," Mirine said. "I'd better come with you."

"We have to leave," Kyal told Arissen.

"Already? You've only just arrived."

"Something came up that we want to look into. All your fault, Ari."

"Me? What did I do?"

"You can be such an inspiration at times. Don't give up on us. We might be back later."

CHAPTER FORTY

The fit was perfect. Superposing a line oriented with respect to north at an angle corresponding to eleven o'clock on the conventional Terran clock dial matched the direction of the long Californian Gulf. Rereading the pilot's notes in this context produced a course right up the center of it.

The next morning, Kyal and Yorim presented their finding to the members of the previous day's meeting who had decided to stay on—which meant most of them. But it was in a general library and conference facility on a lower level of the superstructure. Sherven had ended the occupation by evicting them from his office. Casselo disappeared for a while, leaving the others in the throes of shifting their attention to the Californian gulf area. One of the new facts to emerge was that there had indeed been another Santa Cruz on the western coast of the northern continent, six hundred miles farther north from the head of the gulf. If they were on the right track, it followed that Providence would be somewhere inland from it. However, the terrain in that direction was a rugged region of high mountains giving way to canyons and deserts on the far side, and the population centers had been virtually annihilated in the final war. How to pinpoint a location that had in all likelihood been picked for concealment and then camouflaged was a daunting prospect.

When Casselo returned later in the day, he called them together around one of the display consoles. "This has only just been filed," he informed them. "I didn't know about it myself until earlier today, when I checked for anything new from the region."

The screen showed a selection of shots of excavations in a dry, rocky location, although some of the views showed water in the background. The excavations were centered around a rising feature forming part of a ridge, and had uncovered portions of smooth, sloping surfaces that looked decidedly unnatural. They were evidently parts of a pyramid form. The apex had been uncovered.

Casselo went on, "It's at a geological site known as Camp 27, on the eastern shore of that gulf about halfway up." He looked toward Kyal and Yorim in the semicircle. "It has a laminated, metal-ribbed structure. Doesn't that sound familiar?"

They glanced at each other. The similarity to the discharge attractor found near Triagon was obvious. There had to be a connection. "Some kind of test prototype that they tried on Earth, before they built the one on Farside?" Kyal ventured.

"Could be," Yorim agreed.

"Now look at this," Casselo said. He activated another screen to show the map of the Californian gulf that Kyal and Yorim had introduced that morning. The pilot's notes appeared in an inset. Casselo recited them as he entered commands to add the details in sequence. "Eleven o'clock approach." A red line appeared to one side of the map, oriented at the same inclination as the lie of the gulf. "Midway between La Paz . . ." A circle appeared, showing where the town had once stood on the eastern side near the tip of the peninsula. ". . . and the coast." He moved the line horizontally across until it was centered in the position indicated. The gulf narrowed toward the north. About halfway up, the coastline closing from the east fell more or less into alignment with the red vector.

"Following the right-hand shore," Chown, who was among those present from yesterday, read from the notes in the inset box.

"Yes," Casselo confirmed. "But now watch this. Here's the pyramid at Camp 27." A triangular icon appeared. The red line slanting upward at eleven o'clock from the midpoint of the gulf's mouth passed right over it. "Coincidence?" Casselo asked. Murmurs of interest came from all sides.

Yorim turned to Kyal with an astounded expression. They had probably seen the implication before most of those present. It meant that the Camp 27 pyramid probably hadn't been some kind of prototype at all. The facts were more likely the other way around:

The construction on *Luna* had been the prototype, to develop the technology before building the final version down on Earth.

Casselo read the expressions on their faces. "Does it mean what I think it means?" he asked. The voices subsided as one by one the others realized there was more to this than everyone appreciated. "Care to spell it out for us, Kyal?" Casselo invited.

"A discharge attractor right on the flight path." Kyal glanced questioningly at Yorim. Yorim nodded. Kyal explained, "It wasn't a simulator program to help local supply pilots find Providence. It was for training the crew who would bring everyone back. That's the descent path for a returning spacecraft."

"Which might help explain what the information was doing at Triagon," Casselo said, nodding.

"The wording starts to make more sense that way," Yorim said, reading the screen again. "Nobody could have known who would be piloting the craft when it was time to come back. It would probably be somebody who had never been there. You wouldn't use place names or arbitrary conventions that might change. You'd base the directions on things that would be more permanent, like cardinal directions, major terrain features . . ."

"La Paz is a place name," Chown pointed out.

"Yes, but it also says 'Testing,'" Kyal said. "I think Yorim could be right. If this is from when they were still developing the program, it could just be a bit of loose terminology by somebody involved in trying it out."

Chown mulled, then rocked his head from side to side. "Mm, well, okay, maybe."

"'Homing peak bearing' seems clearer now," Hiok, the planetary physicist said as he read over the text. "It says it checks as a directional pointer. What does 'five point seven seven eight' mean?"

"The Terrans used a three-hundred-sixty-division circle," Chown murmured, half to himself. Venusians did too, as it so happened. The number offered such a convenient choice of divisors as to make it an obvious circular measure.

"To four significant figures?" Casselo queried dubiously.

"Can we be sure it means degrees?" Acilla Jyt asked. A short silence fell. Hiok pulled a sheet of paper from a pile on the worktop by where he was standing and leaned over it to begin scribbling something.

Finally, Yorim said thoughtfully, "A more universal circular measure would be radians—independent of anyone's system of units."

"That's a possibility," someone agreed.

"What are they?" Acilla Jyt asked.

"Two pi of them make a circle," Yorim said. "Engineer's unit. More convenient for lots of things. Fifty-seven point three degrees."

"Oh."

Casselo took out his phone and flipped it to compute mode. "Five point seven, seven eight . . . Fifty-seven point three . . . " He recited. "It works out at three hundred thirty-one degrees. Where would they start from? North, rotating to the right?"

"Try it," Yorim said.

Hiok did the subtraction mentally. "That would put you twenty-nine degrees west of north." Even as he said it, Casselo added a blue vector to the screen, starting from the same center point at the bottom of the gulf and angling up at twenty-nine degrees west of north. The divergence from the red line already there was barely discernible. Murmurs of astonishment came from around the group, with a low whistle from somebody.

"What do we have along it?" Chown asked.

Casselo composed an input to access the survey files of physical terrain data and display the major peaks. Although the chain running to the west of the flight line, called the Sierras, contained many, the line surprisingly missed all of them. The eyes gathered around the screen searched up and down its length in bafflement. Then Kyal said, "Up there, right at the top." He had to step forward and point. At the very top of the map, right on Casselo's line just before it ran off the edge, an isolated peak stood out conspicuously from the relatively flat surrounding terrain. The Terran name for it was Shasta.

Hiok blinked. "But that's got to be, what . . .?" He checked the scale. "It's something like thirteen hundred miles north from the mouth of the gulf."

"Nowhere near Santa Cruz," Chown said.

Yorim came in. "It doesn't have to be if it's just a directional beacon." He thought for a second longer. "In fact, it could strengthen the case for this not being something they put together for local supply pilots. I agree, you'd never see it from an aircraft anywhere around Santa Cruz. But from long distance at the altitude of an incoming spacecraft, it would be an ideal marker. Short of a radio beacon, you couldn't ask for anything better." Silence from all round greeted his words.

"There's your homing peak," Casselo said.

A number of lakes lay along the path, along with the sites of others identified as having dried up. None stood out as being of any great significance. Of course, there was also the possibility that more had vanished without trace.

As to the two "Markers" that the notes referred to, the general feeling was that these were probably peaks too, marking progress along the descent path. But until the numbers associated with them could be interpreted, little more could be said. Almost certainly they denoted distances, but there was no indication of the units they were expressed in. Unlike the case with circular measure, there was no common standard that immediately suggested itself.

Acilla checked in dictionaries of Terran terms and discovered that "GZ" stood for Ground Zero. Almost certainly, it meant the location of Providence itself. It seemed unlikely that any prominent terrain feature would be associated with a survival cache that was intended to be kept secret. But it was somewhere along that line. If they could only make sense of the distances, they would have it.

The next day, Casselo and Kyal discussed the findings with Sherven. Sherven contacted the scientific director of the Western North America Regional Base and requested a low-altitude aerial survey to be carried out along a fifty-mile-wide corridor centered on a line running twenty-nine degree west of north from the eastern edge of the California gulf, to where it intersected the coastline far to the north.

The first significant result came in a couple of days later: another partly buried pyramid. It was right on the approach path near a place that had been called Yuma, on the Colorado River. From descriptions and pictures sent through by a hastily dispatched ground team, Kyal identified it tentatively as a secondary, backup attractor, a little under two hundred miles downrange from the one at Camp 27. The dimensions and general scale of the setup suggested an incoming craft that was extremely large, arriving from a great distance, or both. This didn't sound like something making the relatively short hop back from Luna. So maybe there had been somewhere else in the Solar System that had changed beyond recognition since the time of the Terrans after all.

CHAPTER FORTY-ONE

Earth!

It was a sight that Zaam had thought he would never see. The legendary ancestral home of the tiny residue of humanity that he had shepherded back after the long exile of their kind. Its form was familiar from images preserved and handed down through generations, but now it was really out there ahead of the ship, shining blue and white against the background of stars—as if it had been waiting.

The attempt to live away from Earth had failed. Contact was lost. Most of the plants, the animals, and the children died. For a hundred or more generations—nobody knew for sure—the colony clung on the verge of extinction, unable to muster the will or the strength to rebuild the facilities necessary for refurbishing the still-orbiting mother ship to make a bid to return. Finally, Zaam's father was born, and he had organized the manufacturing and re-equipping. Tears of joy and final release from the years of strain tickled down the old man's cheeks. The promise that he had inherited was fulfilled. He had brought them home.

As the ship drew closer, the swirls and streaks of color resolved into recognizable parts of continents outlined between the clouds. The long, two-part American hemisphere, although changed a little in places, was easily identified, extending almost from pole to pole. West of it stretched the vast ocean occupying almost half the planetary globe. A flyby followed by a long turn into an eccentric closing orbit to shed velocity brought the farther hemisphere into view, with its vast northern landmass and stubby southern-pointing extension on the western side. After the caustic wilderness in which the generations had struggled and died, the bands of warmth and color adorning the disk from its green equatorial band to the brilliant ice caps spoke of life and vibrancy that none of the ship's occupants had ever in their lifetimes been capable of imagining.

Despite objections from the others, Zaam insisted on going down to the surface with the advance party. He would let nothing deny him this moment. The lander detached from the mother ship and went into an almost polar descent orbit, coming in over the southern ice cap on a northbound trajectory skimming the tip of the southern American continent to the right. The computer projection showed their course coming into alignment with the long, narrow gulf far to the north on the western coast, still hidden from direct view by the planet's curvature. "Disengage descent program," Xoll, the commander on the bridge deck ordered.

"Auto unlocked. Approach vector confirmed," the Flight Officer responded.

It was up to Wirton now, tense and concentrating on his displays at the manual piloting station. He was the best, and had trained assiduously on the simulator for this task. It had to be right first time. After shedding its share of the excess charge accumulated through the voyage, the lander would not have the reserves to regain orbit for another attempt. The others around the bridge watched and waited in a silence broken only by the hum of power coursing through the structure and the swishing of air flowing from the ventilator grilles. A display above the pilot's station showed the directions that had been preserved since the time of the ancestors.

The western American coast unrolled slowly ahead and below, the screen images enhanced from long-range infrared scans. The coastline to starboard receded to become a thin, twisting neck joining the two continents. Ahead, the target gulf crawled into sight over the horizon. A superposed sliding graticule showed Wirton's fine course adjustments bringing their approach over the center point, bearing set on 5.778 radians. Telescopic and infrared revealed a high mountain peak dead ahead at the limit of visibility, standing white above surrounding plains. It had to be the homing target!

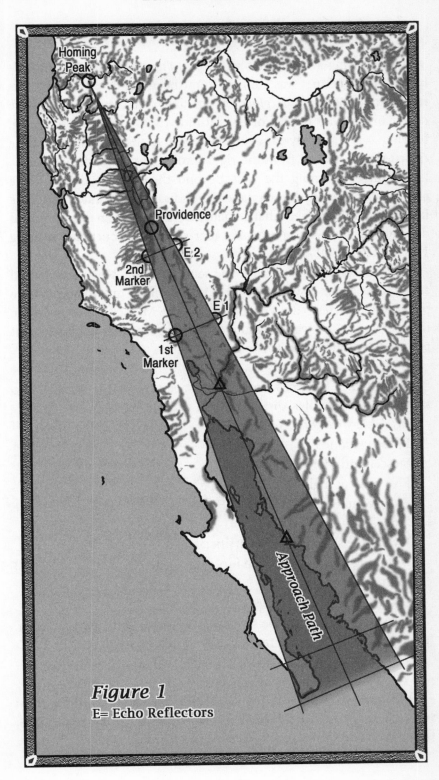

Figure 1
E= Echo Reflectors

The mouth of the gulf rose up and opened out ahead. . . .

. . . stretching away like a blue carpet. The image inside Kyal's all-round vision helmet was coming from the aerial drone that he was remote-piloting from *Explorer* 6, making a test approach up the center of the Gulf of California. Altitude twenty miles, descending, bearing set at twenty-nine degrees west of north. The coastline closed slowly inward from the right until it was immediately below, like a finger pointing the way. Beyond the head of the gulf, the cloud-speckled, red-brown landscape disappeared into haze. He intensified the image enhancement to reveal Shasta standing out dead ahead like a white beacon, radar-echo range currently reading 1,150 miles.

The Marker distances had made sense instantly when interpreted as fractions of the distance from the mouth of the gulf to Shasta. The purpose of the test run was to identify the Marker peaks from the numbers given, by watching and scanning both sides of the descent path as the drone made its run in.

The Flight Engineer's voice came again. "Charge dump echo signature. Thirty miles, directly ahead."

"Available window?" Xoll queried.

"Fifteen seconds."

"Descent profile?"

"Five percent high, within envelope."

"Engage auto retro for seven seconds, then initiate discharge sequence."

Outside the ship, tendrils of artificial lighting snaked groundward.

"Dumping charge. Sequence function positive."

"Course report?"

"On vector," Wirton confirmed.

Zaam, listening from the side, released a slow, quiet sigh of relief. It seemed strange that the radio bands should be so silent.

Kyal was over the Camp 27 pyramid.

"We have you on radar," a voice said in his helmet, coming from somewhere below the drone. "Your altitude is thirteen miles. Descent reads at point zero three six."

"Check," Kyal responded.

Casselo came through. He was following on an external monitor in the same room as Kyal, along with Sherven, Yorim, and a few others. "The shoreline should pretty much stay with you for the next one hundred ninety miles, bulging slightly to the left."

"Got it," Kyal confirmed.

He made final landfall crossing the coast at nine miles altitude, five hundred thirty-two miles after passing over the baseline at the mouth of the Gulf. A quick calculation showed the drone to be 0.384 of the distance to Shasta. Right on!

Over the Yuma pyramid. It seemed odd that the two discharge attractors were not mentioned in the pilot's notes. Maybe they hadn't been built at the time the simulator program was being developed. Another possibility was that the purpose of the run that the notes described had been to test only for the designated Markers.

"You should be getting close to the first Marker now," Casselo prompted.

The drone had just passed the halfway point to Shasta. The terrain below was rounded, featureless desert. Others in the lab were following views from the side-looking imagers tracking the east and west skylines. Just as the distance reading turned over at 0.577, one of the operators reported: "Significant peak to the left now." Kyal turned his head a fraction, which caused the image inside the helmet to shift around. It showed a distinct, isolated mountain standing up above otherwise unremarkable surroundings.

"I have it on the map," another voice came in. "Tagged as San Gorgonio. Seventy miles east of where Los Angeles was. That has to be it."

An instant later the radar surveillance technician announced, "Enhanced echo from the east, directly opposite. Looks like some kind of artificial reflector out there, mirroring the peak."

Everything was going smoothly. The next encouraging sign would be if a similar sequence repeated for the second Marker, which from the pilot's notes should occur at a distance of 0.712.

It did. At exactly that point, the drone was abreast of a peak called Whitney that turned out to be the highest in the Sierra range. And once again, its position was mirrored by a radar reflector located equidistant to the east. It meant that Ground Zero—the presumed location of Providence—should be seventy miles ahead.

"We're on schedule all the way," Kyal said into his helmet mike. "What's the verdict?"

"Is there any sign of this lake?" Casselo asked.

"Not that we can see," someone following on the external monitor screens answered. Kyal scanned the landscape ahead in his helmet image. It was a montage of crumbling ridges and rocky canyons interspersed with flats that could have been dried up lake beds.

"I'd say this is about as well as we're going to do from up here," he reported.

Sherven's voice came over the circuit. "Go for it. See if you can find anything."

It was dry, desolate country. The ruins of some kind of structures almost obliterated by sand passed by to one side. Boulders and creek beds took shape, rushing out and flying by more quickly as the drone came down to surface-skimming height. Kyal eased up on speed. Quiet reigned in the room around him as eyes searched the views coming in from the drone's cameras.

"Point seven," the radar tech's voice said. "We're getting another Marker echo. You should be in visual range by now."

Kyal didn't need to be told. He could already see it—a deep canyon ahead, skirting the base of a mountain to the right that formed the end of a ridge. The interior of the canyon would only be visible from overhead. He circled the drone to the right and around, coming in again on a low, slow run from west to east, following the canyon line.

Ahead, the canyon turned northward below the mountain. It was gouged between steep walls on both sides. Between them, terraces of rock slabs flanked a narrower, inner gorge that looked like a dried-up creek, giving way to mounds of scrubby sand and boulders at the bases of both the canyon's walls, but higher along the south side. In several places, the lines of shapes that were not natural protruded. Although they had been long corroding and disintegrating, Kyal was still able to make out some of them as the remnants of machinery and artificial constructions.

The lander had settled among the sand flats a mile or so short of the indicated zero point. Zaam walked from there with the advance party toward the base of the mountain. The sensation of being outside under an open sky, surrounded by trees and formations of natural rock, and breathing natural air again was a wonder in itself. Above, the golden Sun of Earth seemed to welcome them home with its radiance.

They came to the southern rim of a canyon. Below, almost as the records from old described, they saw a fast-flowing river channeled between rocky shelves, flowing from a bend northward to their right, below the mountain. Excitement rose. If this was indeed the location of the entrance to Providence—which would be below the mountain, there was no sign that it had been found. The roadway serving it had been removed after it was sealed.

After some exploring around, two of the crew members from the lander found a way leading down the side of the canyon. From the floor, Xoll consulted the plans again and looked up at where the concealed entrance should be, with the mountain rising behind. All that they could see appeared to be featureless rock.

One of the officers looked at Xoll with a worried expression. "Is this really the place?" he asked.

"The sign should be around here somewhere," Xoll replied. Once again, groups dispersed from the party to search among the rocks. Within minutes, a jubilant shout came from one of the same two who had found the path down. The others hurried over to converge around the place where they were standing. Carved into the rock, recessed beneath an overhanging sill, was the symbol for Providence, passed down from the long-gone builders:

Xoll turned and clasped both Zaam's hands while the rest of the party looked on. "You did it, Zaam." The commander's voice choked as he struggled to fight down his emotions. "After all our doubts and our complaining. But just like your father, you never wavered. You brought us back."

Circling slowly out again above the flats to the south, Kyal was able to pick out the outlines and remains of several other constructions. Here and there were traces of what might have been the line of a former road. From orbit it would easily have passed as just another piece of eroded devastation from the war of long ago.

He brought the drone back over the canyon again. The northern wall seemed to be intact and unbroken. He followed the line of mounds and rock falls on the southern side to the point where the canyon turned north. Just visible behind the scrub topping the sand mounds was the top of what looked like an opening. Kyal brought the drone down to a point high among the mounds. If the opening extended down to the rock shelf below the sand, it would be pretty sizeable. The edge that Kyal could see was weathered but looked too straight to be natural. He increased power again and nudged the drone to a different angle, revealing a squared corner at one end. The sun was to the south, putting that side of the canyon in shadow, so he was unable to make out anything inside. He cut the drone's engine, shut down its controls, and removed the remote piloting helmet that he was wearing. The others around him were already closing around and showering him with congratulations. A screen above the room displayed the completed flight plan.

"I think we've arrived," Kyal told them. "We won't find out anything more now until we go there."

CHAPTER FORTY-TWO

With the location of Providence finally established, the possibility offered itself of now being able to identify, or find the former site of, the mysterious "High Lake." The Terran records showed that there had indeed been a lake not far to the north. But it had been called Mono Lake. It was Elundi, down in Rhombus, who eventually tracked down how the confusion had arisen.

In Terran English, the prefix "mono" meant one of something, in other words, something that was rare. "Rare" was also used in a different sense to describe a condition of being thinly dispersed, as with the air of the upper atmosphere. As a consequence, a translator back on Venus who was not very experienced had mistaken the word as meaning "high," and used the Venusian equivalent accordingly. Hence, had arisen the misdirection to Lake Titicaca.

A team was sent by helicopter from the Regional Base to investigate the places where radar echoes from east of the flight path had marked the right-hand side of the approach lane converging on Shasta. They found the sources to be metalized reflector surfaces carved into rock features at the appropriate places and angles to mirror the locations of the two Marker peaks bounding the lane on the west.

Another party traveled overland to Providence itself. The opening that Kyal had found in the south canyon wall was, as he had surmised, the top of an entrance. It opened to a tunnel that led

287

beneath the mountain overlooking the canyon, which turned out indeed to be where the Providence survival cache was located. The interior was vast, excavated to accommodate the huge stock of materials, tools, and equipment that had raised doubts about the intended repository being Triagon. The strange thing, however, was that most of the inventory was still there, crated and packaged in preservatives and unused. If the place had been found and opened up by survivors of the war, why would they not have availed themselves of everything that was to be had? On the other hand, if it had remained undisturbed until the evacuees or their descendants returned to reclaim it in the manner intended, it appeared that they had stayed only briefly. If so, why, and where had they gone? Just when it seemed that answers had started coming together, nothing was making sense again. Kyal, Yorim, and Casselo decided it was time to go down and have a look at Providence for themselves.

Lorili looked at Kyal and Yorim despairingly. "It's the same as last time, only the other way around," she told them. "No sooner have I gotten myself posted up to *Explorer*, than you're going back down to Earth. If you're trying to get rid of me, Kyal, it would be far easier to just say so." They were in the docking bay area, waiting to board the shuttle that Casselo had organized to take them down to the Western North America Regional Base. Lorili had come to see them off.

Kyal grinned. "It should only be for a few days—a week at most. You've enough going on to keep you and Mirine busy anyway."

Lorili had long recovered and was back to her normal self. That was more than could be said for Jenyn. Far from healing without complications as had been expected, he had developed some kind of an infection involving fever and delirium. The latest report described purple blotches breaking out on his face and upper body, which was something new to the Venusian physicians. Tests conducted so far on the affected cells gave conflicting results, but some of the data at least were consistent with an infectious agent. The doctors had seen nothing like it before. Their guess was that Jenyn had picked up something from the scalpel that had pierced his stomach, which Lorili had been using earlier to dissect the Terran corpses. Jenyn had taken it from a sterilizer in the clean rooms at the rear of the laboratory where he had entered. The area was normally kept at a small under-pressure to maintain a flow of air inward from the surroundings. It was as well that the medical staff who had treated Jenyn had taken appropriate containment measures. Otherwise a full-scale epidemic might have been loose in *Explorer 6* already.

The likely culprit, then, was thought to be some ancient Terran microorganism that had been carried to Triagon long ago and managed to survive since then in a dormant state under the ultra-cold, totally sterile, lunar conditions. If so, it might help explain the sixty-eight Terran corpses that had been found in the Rear Annexe—undamaged physically but removed and isolated from the main complex. On top of their own planned schedule of work, Lorili and Mirine were going through the results of their Terran gene and protein sequencing studies for possible corroboration and hopefully more information on the agent responsible.

"I think, if the truth were known, we're just being cowards and sneaking away at the right time," Kyal said.

"How do you mean?" Lorili asked.

"All kinds of people back home have found out about Providence already—museums of Terran artifacts, colleges, collectors. . . . We're being deluged with inquiries. Poor Filaeyus is going to have to deal with it."

"I'm surprised he didn't decide to come along too," Yorim said. "Doesn't he ever get tired of being cooped up aboard *Explorer*?"

"Oh, confidentially, I think that's being taken care of," Casselo said. "Pidrie, his wife, is down there at the moment—somewhere in southern Europe, I think. She's been touring around different parts for a while now."

"What's going on?" Kyal asked.

"Checking out likely areas for a home. From some of the things Fil's said, I wouldn't be surprised if they're thinking of retiring here. It's surprising how many people are. There are some fine little communities springing up all over. A lot of people who come out here just don't seem to want to go back to Venus once they're used to it. Families are moving out to join them."

"Mellios Chown was saying there's going to be a huge migration this way over the next fifty years," Kyal remarked.

"You know, I've sometimes thought the same thing," Lorili told them. She sighed. "But I honestly couldn't see many of my folks uprooting. They sit in their foggy towns, breathing sulfur fumes and surrounded by swamps. You try to tell them about cool climates and clear skies, but they just can't picture it. Some of the images of Terran cities that I've seen were like . . . I don't know. Fairylands. Do you think Earth might be like that again one day?"

"I don't know. It's a thought, isn't it?" Casselo agreed.

"But then they had all those wars," Yorim put in.

"I know," Lorili said. "Isn't it crazy? In a world filled with everything they could ask for. But there's no reason why that should have to be the same again."

A call tone came from Casselo's jacket pocket. "Excuse me." He took out his phone. "Hello. Borgan Casselo here . . ."

Kyal moved closer to Lorili along the seat. They only had a few minutes left. What she had just said about Earth echoed a lot of his own sentiments that he hadn't realized he felt. He put a hand on hers reassuringly. She looked up at him and smiled.

"It won't be long," he said in a voice not meant for carrying. "I'll call you tonight, after we get there."

"I was hoping you would."

He paused for an instant. "About living on Earth . . . It wouldn't have to be a case of finding your way on your own, you know." Yorim did a superb job of leaving them to it by getting up and sauntering over to study the flight information displayed next to the boarding gate.

It took Lorili a second or two to register what Kyal was saying. She looked at him disbelievingly. "You mean you too?"

"Uh-huh. One day, maybe. Who knows?"

"Us? . . . Are you saying? . . . You really mean it?"

"It's something we could talk about, anyway."

Lorili's eyes had brightened. "That would be . . . just wonderful." She emitted a short, spontaneous laugh, as if it were too much to believe. "Whereabouts would you have in mind?"

Kyal affected a groan. "Now you're rushing me already. I've no idea. Maybe we should have sent you on the tour with Pidrie."

"No chance. She's the Director's wife. I have a job to do."

"There. And you expect me to know. As I said, it's something we can talk about. Okay?"

She smiled happily and whispered. "Okay." Kyal gave her hand a squeeze. Casselo had finished taking his call.

"That was Amingas Quarles down at the Regional Base," he informed them as Yorim came wandering nonchalantly back. "They'll have a chopper waiting at the landing area to take us straight out to Providence. So we should be there some time this afternoon."

"Not wasting any time," Yorim commented.

"Word's out. It's generating a lot of interest," Casselo said.

"Who's Quarles?" Kyal asked.

"An old friend of mine who's based at Regional. Runs the geology section. You'll like him, Yorim. He's been getting some life into the place, turning it into more of a town. It's going to be another Rhombus. He's already been out to Providence."

"What's the climate like there—in western North America?" Lorili asked.

Casselo bunched his mouth. "Oh . . . dry and sunny, pleasantly mild. Everything from coast to high mountains in a couple of hundred miles. It was a thriving area with the Terrans."

"And got bombed flat for it," Yorim said.

"You're fishing already," Kyal murmured to Lorili out of the corner of his mouth. She bit her lip with a smile but didn't deny it. "What does Director Sherven's wife find to do with herself when she is here?" she asked Casselo instead.

"Grows things, apparently. She's becoming an expert on Terran plants. Fil says their cabin over in Staff Quarters looks like a rain forest. She's got a domesticated feline there too."

"What kind's that?" Yorim asked.

"Like the one Mirine was telling you we had in the labs down in Rhombus," Lorili said. "Small and fluffy; big eyes and whiskers; claws; pointed ears."

"Oh, Lucifer. Right."

"Can we have one?" Lorili asked Kyal. He rolled his eyes.

"What does 'Lucifer' mean?" Casselo inquired.

"One of the old Terran gods, or something," Lorili said. "It was all Nostreny's fault. It used to hang around the trash cans at the back of the kitchens, and he started feeding it. Then it adopted us."

A man wearing a crew tunic emerged from the gate and came over to them. "Ready to board at your leisure, gentlemen," he informed them. "We'll be closing the door in fifteen minutes."

"Well, might as well get comfortable," Casselo said, rising. The others did likewise.

"And I've got things to be getting back to," Lorili said. Then, to Kyal, "Talk to you soon?"

"You've got it."

"Any news on the weather at Regional?" Casselo asked the crewman.

"Dry, sunny, and mild, I believe."

Casselo spread his hands appealingly at the others as if he were waiting for applause.

Lorili's phone sounded just as they began to move. Kyal hung back while she stopped to answer, leaving Casselo and Yorim to follow the crewman through the gate. He stayed out of her personal space while she talked, letting his gaze wander casually over the surroundings, but noticed her expression growing more grave.

"What?" he asked, when she finally snapped the unit shut and looked back at him.

"That was Mirine calling from the lab. The doctor from the Medical Wing has just been on. Jenyn is deteriorating rapidly. They don't think he's going to make it."

"I see." Kyal kept his voice neutral. From what he knew, Lorili should have no real reason to shed tears over it. But on the other hand, he supposed, it was a person that she had known and been close to once. It said a lot for her humanity that she should show some concern.

"And there's more," Lorili said. "Mirine has been comparing some odd DNA sequences that the lab sent over with ones we obtained from the Terran corpses. She says they match."

Kyal frowned. It had caught him when his mind was on other things, and the significance wasn't immediately apparent.

"This has never been found in Venusians before," Lorili explained. "The structure suggests some kind of virus. But if so, it's an extremely unusual kind of virus that somehow gets transcribed into the host DNA."

"You mean like a retrovirus?" Kyal said. He was familiar with that much at least.

"Similar genetics. But retroviruses are passengers. They're not cytopathic like lytic viruses—cell killers. Their mode of reproduction is from mother to child, which means the host has to live to reproductive maturity. If a virus like that killed its host, it wouldn't be viable." Lorili shook her head. Her face had a look of disbelieving horror. "But this one is highly lethal. What that says is that it couldn't have arisen naturally. It had to have been manufactured deliberately. Do you see what that means . . .?"

CHAPTER FORTY-THREE

Amingas Quarles was a big man with ragged, graying, hair, his face weathered and tanned from years of fieldwork under the Terran sun. But his stride was still robust as he led the way from where the helicopter had landed on the open ground above the south side of the canyon. The area was already cluttered with a miscellany of STOL aircraft and vehicles that had arrived overland, alongside which portable cabins and tents were springing up along the canyon rim. Preliminary digging here and there had turned up a few remnants of vehicles, machinery and structures that seemed to indicate it as having been the scene of some kind of activity. Whether it had been due to survivors from the war or returning evacuees wouldn't be known without more detailed studies and dating tests.

"Was there any trace of a ship anywhere?" Kyal asked curiously, as they stood looking around before moving on down.

"No, nothing like that," Quarles told him. "Not so far, anyway."

They followed a trail between rocks and parked vehicles to the canyon rim. Work parties with picks and shovels were widening a path down to the floor, where a small earthmoving machine had penetrated and was clearing away more of the mounds of debris and sand filling the tunnel entrance. "If this place is going to be properly explored and opened up, the next thing we'll need will be a decent access road up to the south-side rim," Quarles told them as they made their way carefully down. "Makes me wonder how they got all that stuff down there in the first place. Maybe there's another way in someplace."

"They'd have erased any pointers to it," Kyal said. "Its location was secret."

As the first views from the drone had showed, there were also remains of machinery and equipment scattered about the canyon floor, some of which had been further uncovered by exploratory digging. There was little evidence of the site being developed into a working center for further expansion in the way that would be expected of returning migrants—or at least returning migrants who had stayed any length of time. On the other had, if it had been war survivors who found the place, why hadn't they cleaned it out? Either way, a riddle remained.

As they approached the entrance, Quarles halted in front of a niche in the rock formed beneath a protruding sill above, and gestured. Carved in a recess, worn and smoothed by the winds of ages, but still recognizable, was the kateklike Terran icon that stood for Providence.

What was left of the two massive steel doors that had once closed the tunnel entrance were now lying partly unearthed outside, twisted and corroded. The entrance itself was framed by beams of concrete, tilted and broken on one side to reveal heavy internal reinforcement bars. The steel frame that had held the doors was recessed back ten feet or so from the line of the canyon wall, which suggested that originally they might have been concealed by an outer covering of natural rock. Like the doors, the frame was torn and buckled, the rock surround in front of it gouged into irregular hollows.

"The way in seems to have been jammed," Quarles said, waving as they passed through. "Maybe by geological distortion. Whoever opened the place up had to use explosives."

"It sounds like people who knew what they were looking for, and exactly where to look," Casselo commented.

The tunnel beyond, lit by temporary lamps strung along the roof, was wide enough and high enough to allow the passage of fairly large vehicles, and had a raised walkway running behind a rail on one side. An air pipeline that the Venusian engineers had brought in for ventilation farther inside ran along the floor. Despite its regularly spaced buttresses of thick metal ribbing, the tunnel was visibly canted in places. At one point it had suffered a fall that had been dug through and shored with props and cross-members sufficiently to walk through, but the passage would have to be enlarged before anything sizeable could be brought out.

They emerged from the tunnel through another set of doors into a space that had corridors leading off to the sides and an even broader gallery extending away ahead of them with large doors spaced at intervals along both sides. "Where do you want to start?" Quarles asked them.

"What is there?" Casselo asked back in turn.

"Those doors going away in front there are the storage vaults," Quarles answered. "They were the most readily accessible from the entrance tunnel. But clearing a way through the caved-in part of the tunnel back there took time, so we haven't gotten around to exploring all of the place yet. There are elevators in those side chambers—not working yet, but there are stairs too. We've got a couple of levels below where we are now fitted out and supplied for accommodation. So whoever it was who found the place had a guesthouse ready for them on arrival. I guess that's what it was designed that way for."

"Sounds like Triagon all over again," Yorim commented.

Kyal was thinking the same thing. "A lot bigger, though," he replied.

Quarles went on, "And then up above, we've got what seem to be control rooms for services and so on, and admin offices. That's the most recent part to be found—we didn't know there were any stairs going up until this morning. Everybody thought it was just mountain. They were still fitting lights up there when I left for Regional to come and pick you people up."

"Let's have a look at the stuff in the vaults first," Casselo decided. "Then we can go up and see what your people are finding in the control rooms. I've seen dormitories and canteens before."

"Fine."

It was all far vaster than Triagon. Most of the contents of the vaults were still packed away in crates and canisters for preservation. But after the fragmented oddments that until now had been all there was to try and build a picture from of the lost world, the small part that had been opened up was enough to cause amazement. There were engines and generators, pumps, lifting gear taken out of grease packing in sealed containers, all cleaned, gleaming, and looking as if they had just been manufactured. Along with them were all manner of tools, agricultural implements, accessories, and fastenings.

The hall adjoining contained construction machinery, well-drilling equipment, earth diggers and scrapers, along with bays of fuel drums, maintenance fluids, and parts. Some technicians had even managed to get a land tractor started and were taking turns at gingerly trying to figure out how to drive it in a clear section of the service gallery outside the vault. "There's a small fleet of trucks and all-terrain cars farther along that way," Quarles said, waving an arm. "We could make good use of them ourselves if we can get them going. There are never enough vehicles at Regional for what you want." The whole place was a trove of Terran culture that would keep the archeologists and technohistorians busy for years.

The phone clipped to Quarles's belt sounded. He answered it. "Hello, Emmis." In an aside he muttered, "Our man upstairs in the control room," and then louder, "What's up?"

"I'm told that you're back," a voice from the phone replied.

"Right. Have been for a while, in fact. I'm down in the warehouse with Borgan Casselo and his two friends from *Explorer*, showing them what we've got so far."

"I think you need to get up here," Emmis said.

"That sounds ominous."

"Not so much ominous. Impossible."

"We'd just about finished a quick, once-over tour." Quarles raised his eyebrows at the others and inclined his head to indicate the direction back out from the vault that they were in. "What is it?" he asked into the phone as they began moving.

"You'll have to come and see. I'm still not sure I believe it."

"Where do we find you, Emmis?"

"Take the stairs past the elevator on your left as you come out from the wide gallery. Two levels up from the entrance tunnel, there's an exit door with a Terran *E* on it. Go through, follow the corridor right, through some double doors, and it's one of the rooms to your left. The Terran characters *E-18* are painted on a column outside, but I'll have someone watching for you at the door."

"We're on our way now. . . ." They came out into the wide gallery, immediately flattening themselves against the wall as the latest novice driver hurtled by in the Terran agricultural tractor, followed by alarmed shouts from behind for him to slow down and steer away

converging upward to the left, with a pair of bars bridging the angle between them. The Venusian symbol of good fortune and homecoming.

He turned his head toward Yorim, who was also staring at the icon with a strange look. "There's our katek, Yorim," Kyal murmured. Their eyes met disbelievingly. He knew that the same thought was going through Yorim's mind too.

They had seen the same form only recently somewhere else. The two sides of a landing corridor converging on the mountain called Shasta, barred by two approach Markers. How could this ancient sign, preserved by the Terrans who had braved unknown trials and dangers to come home finally to Earth, have become a symbol dating back to the earliest times of Venusian history, standing for those same things? Not by coincidence, surely. There was only one way.

Casselo was giving Emmis a puzzled look. "I thought you said on the phone that you've only just found this place," he said. "What are you reading? How could you have gotten that much translated already? I mean . . . who translated it?"

In answer, Emmis turned around the sheet he was still holding and slid it across the table. Three pairs of eyes stared at it in mute befuddlement. Some of the letter forms and spellings were quaintly odd, and Emmis had cheated a little in his rendering of the wording. But it was readily recognizable for what it was, even to a nonscholar. Simply, the question of translation didn't arise. There was no need for any. The documents carefully stored and preserved by the last humans to depart from Earth were written in one of the earliest dialects of Venusian.

CHAPTER FORTY-FOUR

Earth was dead. At least, all human life had long ago ended. As far as could be ascertained from the conditions observed from the orbiting mother ship, it must have happened not long after the migrants from Terminus departed. And now their descendants had returned to find only that Earth was still lethal for humans. Many of the party who landed and opened up the cache of supplies at Providence that they thought would provide them a new beginning soon succumbed to the sickness before it was recognized as the same sickness that had prevented their ancestors from returning to Earth long before.

Those down on the surface who were still unaffected couldn't remain there. But neither could any of them remain indefinitely in orbit. And there could be no going back to the world they had finally mustered their last reserves of strength and resourcefulness to get away from. They had already learned that it was impossible to grow and flourish there.

But a strange quirk of fate gave them one other, slender chance. For whatever reason, it seemed that the timescales that their ancient Terran ancestors had based their geological and planetary sciences on had been in error. Long-range instrument measurements and observations from the mother ship showed that the planet Venus was already exhibiting recognizably Earth-like properties. It was still hot and inhospitable there, and if they could make it, life would

301

surely be rough and perilous with few pleasures or comforts to relieve the hardships. But were they not all descendants of the ultimate in human survivability? In any case, they couldn't stay where they were, and there was nowhere else for them to go.

Using materials from the stores at Providence and with special equipment and engineers sent down in a smaller, chemically driven shuttle, they improvised launch and recharging facilities for lifting the surface lander back to orbit. They took with them what they could from Providence that looked like being the most useful. The rest, they left behind to the winds and the sands, and to time. Xoll tried to joke wryly that somebody might find it and be able to use it one day. The others were too weary even to smile. How could such a thing ever be possible? But they left a record of their passing here, of who they were, and their story. So the universe wouldn't simply carry on evermore existing, as if they had never been.

After burying the last of those who had died and lifting off successfully, they remained separated in orbit for a quarantine period to make sure they were carrying no more incubating cases of the disease. Then, with all the survivors finally back together again aboard the mother ship, Zaam marshaled his followers and exhorted them to make the last, supreme effort.

CHAPTER FORTY-FIVE

In what proved, with macabre appropriateness to be their ultimate achievement in more senses than one, the Terrans created genetically vectored viruses that could be targeted against specific ethnic and racial groups, and turned them loose. But something went wrong. The different strains somehow mutated and interacted—exactly how would probably never be known—and all human life on Earth perished as a consequence.

And so Sherven's theory, which had seemed so far-flung, turned out to be correct after all: The Terrans *had* migrated to another star system. Their own account found at Providence confirmed it. They called their new world "Eden," after a mythical idyllic realm in early Terran fable, which perhaps told of the touching hopes they had for their future there. But the name was ill-chosen. The colony was not viable in the long term, and in the end their descendants came back.

It was true that although tiny in numbers, the community created on lunar Farside in the form of the Terminus program had concentrated some of the most potent talents of the race. But even so, the revelation was stunning, adding a new order of magnitude to the picture the Venusians had already formed of what Terran resilience and tenacity had been capable of. Exactly how the migration had come to take the form it had was unclear, since the records left by the descendants who eventually made the voyage back were fragmentary in that respect. They gave the impression that conditions at Eden had been too arduous for the earlier generations to pay much attention to past matters, and much of the historical detail had been lost. It could have been that the technical enterprise evidenced by the structures on Farside had been conceived as a contingency escape plan of interstellar dimensions from the beginning, in case such a measure should become necessary. Possibly, it had been improvised in desperation as the only available expedient from the prior work on unmanned probes when it was realized that Earth was uninhabitable. Either way, there was nowhere else in the Solar System to go.

But only for the time being, maybe.

Perhaps the supreme irony was that if they had held out long enough where they were, they, or almost certainly their descendants of within a generation or two, could probably have returned to Earth safely. But the people selected for evacuation to Terminus had not been of a kind characteristically disposed to sitting and waiting. Impatience and an impulse to bring about some kind of action *now* had been a trait of the stronger-minded Terrans too.

After further studies of the viral sequences obtained from the Triagon corpses, and postmortem analysis of the agent that had infected Jenyn, the Venusian scientists concluded that without human hosts to perpetuate the strain, the population of synthetic viruses would have been reduced by natural biological processes and died out fairly rapidly. It was possible that a less virulent mutant strain might have found a lodgement in some Terran primate species, but unlike the original synthetic virus that had been targeted at humans it would have been susceptible to natural immunological suppression, and in the end the result would have been the same.

But there was one place on Earth where a dormant residue of the original virulent form could remain and be unaffected. By opening up the sealed environment of Providence, the returnees had reactivated a remnant that had existed there ever since those earlier times, and been infected just as had Jenyn by the residue preserved in the freeze-dried corpses at Triagon. The rest of the world out there all around them had in all probability long ago eradicated all traces of it. After all, that Earth that they had returned to was the same one that Venusians were living on today, with the same kind of biosphere, and it was clean.

But they hadn't known. The chronicles from Providence described how they saw the same sickness that had wiped out everyone on Earth and found its way to Luna, breaking out among those who had landed. It wasn't a situation that permitted the luxury of time for extensive testing and deliberation in the way the Venusians could afford. They had to assume the worst, that it was still out there, everywhere. So they took what they could and got themselves back up off the surface before everyone was infected.

And what were they to do then? By rights there should have been nothing left open to them.

Yet through a fluke that none of them had expected, there was one possibility. The final entry in the records recovered at Providence told as much as had been known and decided when the craft that had landed there lifted off to rejoin its orbiting mother ship. The conditions that long-range observation and measurements from the ship had detected on Venus did not seem to be as the models handed down from the sciences of former days predicted. It was cooler, with atmospheric characteristics and chemistry that appeared compatible with a livable environment, and it had acquired a respectable axial spin. There was no mention of the presence of Froile—which answered the question of how much its capture had contributed: effectively none. It was the result of electrical effects, as Yorim and most of the Venusian astronomers had maintained.

What it must have taken for that last remaining handful to make the effort after all they had been through, most Venusians were thankful they would probably never know. But that side of Terrans that inspired awe had still been there. Whatever it had taken, they had risen to it, and had made that effort. And the result was Venusians reading their story today, still speaking a language that was closer to the words it had been written in than theirs was to that of their distant ancestors who had migrated to Eden.

As well as minimal stocks from Providence, they took with them livestock and plants from Earth that they hoped they would be able to introduce. This explained the presence on Venus of organisms with the quadribasic form of DNA, and the paradox of why they seemed to be more advanced as a group than the hexabasic types, which were more widespread and should have afforded a greater potential for flexibility and complexity. In a way that Lorili's hypothesis had anticipated, the hexabasics were native, and had evolved to a degree that was appropriate to the present conditions on Venus; the quadribasics—which included Venusians—were imported Terran varieties and their descendants, from an older, more mature world.

What happened after then had to be filled in by conjecture, but it seemed that their travails had still not yet ended. Even the chance to rebuild from such slender beginnings amid the harshness of Venus's swamps and lava fields was denied. Before the exhausted and bewildered arrivals could even consolidate in their new, hostile environment, Froile appeared in the sky above them, bringing convulsions and climatic upheaval to complete the ruin of the last shreds of their civilization that they had managed to save. They reverted to a primitiveness from which it had taken centuries to recover, losing all traces and memory of their origins in the process. Only versions of those events enshrined in mythical form had survived to be passed down from what present-day Venusians had thought were the earliest days of their race. The parallel to the far more devastating catastrophes reconstructed as having taken place in the Terrans' own early history was obvious and sombering. What set the two epochs of happenings apart, other than the difference in severity, was that the forefathers of the Venusians—being products of an advanced scientific culture themselves, whatever else they might have lost—hadn't taken recourse in the vengeance and judgment of supernatural gods to explain them.

The first inclination among the Venusian researchers was to accept the capture of Froile at just such a moment as one of those unfortunate coincidences that nature seems to come up with from time to time to test the mettle of its creations. However, further calculations on long-range spacecraft electromagnetics by Kyal and Yorim, in conjunction with information gained from the Providence records about the craft that had made the voyage from Eden, suggested that there might have been rather more to it than just coincidence. Kyal was always suspicious of coincidences anyway.

An incoming vessel from another star system could acquire an enormous electrical potential difference with respect to anything local in the Solar System. The builders of Providence had provided a primary discharge attractor at Camp 27 and downrange backup at Yuma, but such provisions could only be based on guesses of what would be required, not on whatever the returning ship had actually experienced. And even if the guesses had been close, after all that time there could have been no guarantee that the constructions built in response to them still existed.

A copy of the narrative from the craft that had made the landing at Providence talked about "dumping" the *residual* charge when they were on their final approach. Searching back further turned up the log of the mother ship that had made the voyage back from Eden. Its course into the Solar System had been on the far side of the Sun from where Earth was at the time, crossing the interior of Earth's orbit. On the way, it had tracked and course-matched to an orbiting minor body that it had coupled to electrically and shed a large part of the extraneous charge accumulated in the interstellar medium. The interaction would also involve transferring much of the ship's incoming momentum, which would have perturbed the receiving body's path. Sensitive nonlinear dynamics were involved, meaning that its new direction could have been just about anything, and for the likely ranges of velocity and mass that such an body would possess, the imparted velocity change came out in the order of several hundred to maybe a couple of thousand miles per hour— modest enough, and with the possibility of added electrical effects arising from its acquired charge, to make a capture scenario by Venus plausible. The ship's log described the object as "elongated and knobby."

Their error over the virus might have been the supreme irony, but this was the final one. Having abandoned Earth to make that one last effort, and left behind them most of what had been provided to help toward making a fresh start, *they themselves* had already set in motion the destruction of whatever fragile toehold on Venus that they would be able to establish.

It had been there all along, but wrapped in terms that had caused generations of Venusians to read it as meaning anything except exactly what it said. "The Legend of the Wanderers," Lorili recalled, when Kyal told her about the latest findings. "How did it go, again? The ancestors of long ago, who didn't like the ways of the world, went to the end of it. It got a bit garbled there, didn't it? The 'end' that it talked about was Terminus. And then they left to go and live on the Sun. Well, not *on the* Sun, but *at another* sun, I suppose. And wasn't there something about rising from the dead?"

"Some versions say that," Kyal agreed. "But the more usual line is that they came eventually to the Place of Death but escaped from it. We know now where that was: Providence." He went on, "When they returned, the Wanderers had annoyed the local inhabitants by frightening their dog away. So when they caught it again, they made it their watchdog in the sky, to make sure the Wanderers stayed home from then on."

"And Froile was born out of hurricanes and floods, when the sky fell, and the seas moved over the land," Lorili completed.

It all fitted.

CHAPTER FORTY-SIX

Kyal and Lorili stood by the window wall of Sherven's office. Beyond the glass, exterior parts of *Explorer 6* stood out as geometric shapes of reflected Earthlight against the slowly moving starfield. Sherven and Casello were in front of the curved desk with its side panel, sharing the view. Yorim and Mirine were there too, standing on the far side of the room, where screens flickered and glowed in the battery of displays alongside the arch leading through to the conference area.

Below the superstructure, the *Melthor Jorg* was docked once more. The time had come to go home. Locating Providence had proved to be a short-lived task, and its further exploration was now in other hands. Kyal had a program of professional commitments to attend to following the later developments, and Lorili needed to tidy up family matters. They would return after being married on Venus. Their home, they had decided, would be in on the western coast of North America, somewhere near the rapidly growing town that the Regional Base was transforming itself into, and already referred to unofficially by its Terran place name: Pasadena. And if Lorili was going back, it was only natural that her assistant since the early days should be going too. At least, that was what Mirine said. Yorim and Mirine hadn't announced any definite plans, but the general feeling among the others was that Kyal and Yorim were as inseparable as the two women, and it wouldn't be very long before the four found themselves in close proximity again.

In the meantime, Casselo would be returning to Rhombus after his sojourn on *Explorer 6*. Sherven was making no secret that he was wrapping up official duties and would soon be retiring to southern Europe. This didn't mean an end to his involvement with scientific matters concerning the Terrans, but on the contrary, a shedding of administrative responsibilities in order to be able to devote more of his time to them. Although they would all doubtless continue to communicate and meet from time to time over the years ahead, the moment was poignant in marking the end of an extraordinarily fruitful period of discovery from which they had all drawn, and to which they had contributed in that peculiar, mutually enhancing rapport that can be generated by unusually creative people working closely together. It was the kind of experience that graced the lives of a few privileged people perhaps once, and for most, never at all.

The Venus that they would be going back to had undergone its own experience of transformation and realization too. The hardline following of the Progressive movement had wilted; at the same time, the traditional merit-focused establishment was broadening its stance and committing to reexamining some of its ways with a view to providing more in the way of helping hands toward the needy, or simply unlucky. The reactions from both sides were an expression of the universal horror that had come with the realization of what the extinction of the Terrans implied.

Compared to Venus, the Terrans had been given a garden. But the knowledge that they had amassed through centuries of effort and dedication in developing their sciences and their industries, that could have carried them outward to plant other gardens among the stars in the ways some of them had dreamed, they had turned instead to their main preoccupation of destruction and killing. Aggression and a history of "settling" differences by organized violence—it never settled anything—had been the culprit. Venusians heard the same readiness to resort to force in the demands of the Progressive extremists. And the accessories had been the Terran hierarchies of power by which the few commanded the obedience and labors of the many. Venusians saw beginnings of the same thing in the institutionalized favoritism and privilege that were appearing in their own governing system. On both counts, they were resolved not to emulate the ways that had brought about the downfall of the Terrans.

"It must say a lot for the people up in the mother ship that they not only waited, but sent down help," Lorili said. They were recapitulating some of the outcomes from it all—a way of prolonging the moment before the two departing couples left to join the waiting ship.

Sherven rubbed his chin. "Oh, I don't know that they could have done differently. Could you? After they'd been together all that time through the long voyage back?"

"And from what I read of it, that elder, Zaam, doesn't seem like the kind they would lightly have abandoned," Casselo agreed. "He was the one who got them there."

Sherven moved to the window and stood looking out with his hands clasped behind his back. Below, the bulk of the *Melthor Jorg* hung against the backdrop of void, lit up by the lights of supply craft and service platforms preparing the ship for its departure.

"So it turns out after all that we are indeed the Terrans' direct descendants," he said. "The reason we're not comfortable on Venus is that it isn't ready for our kind yet." Kyal caught Lorili's eye and gave her an approving nod. She smiled but didn't say anything. Sherven went on, "Where Terrans came from in turn is an open question. I still think it's pretty clear that by its very nature and laws, the universe is preprogrammed to produce air-breathing, oxygen-fueled, carbon-based life on aqueous planets, very much like ourselves, wherever the conditions are right. How it came to be that way, and why, only Vizek knows. I don't believe this Terran fable of unguided matter being able to organize itself in such ways mindlessly, for no reason. In denying the universe its soul, the Terrans denied their own. That was what made them what they were, and what ultimately brought them to the kind of end that befell them."

Sherven turned from the window to face the others again, spreading his arms sideways along the ledge behind him. "So let's, for a moment, consider some of the deeper implications that pertain to us directly. Many Venusians have admired what they perceived as the Terran spirit of self-assertiveness and their refusal to submit to injustices. Those are noble thoughts, and let's not belittle them. But I would urge an element of caution in taking their praises of themselves too literally, because we know that they habitually distorted reality to a degree we would find untenable when it suited their purpose." He ran his gaze briefly over the listening faces. "But having said that, I have to agree that there's a part of the heritage we owe to them that makes me proud."

Nobody interrupted. Their faces were solemn. Kyal realized that Sherven was speaking for all of them. He had never expressed positive sentiments regarding the Terrans before.

Sherven continued, "We seem to be a more stable version of what they were: more disposed to cooperate than to compete; to protect weakness rather than exploit it; mutually supportive, where they were adversarial. And I think there are good reasons why this should be so. Consider the two selection processes that occurred to produce very different populations. The Terrans were descended from the few who survived its early catastrophes and its terrors, which they interpreted as the wrath of supernatural beings who judged human actions. Hence emerged a world driven by brutality, ferociousness, and cunning, stemming from irrational beliefs in gods. The result was thousands of years of bloodstained history, culminating in the use of horrific weapons that all but wiped them out." Sherven gave a slight shrug. "Well, as far as Earth was concerned, they *did* wipe themselves out.

"But by this quirk that we now know about, a handful were saved to go through the saga that we have no doubt only glimpsed. They also constituted a selection from which a world would develop, but this time a world of a very different kind. For one thing, these were not technologically primitive like the early Terrans who gazed up, terrified, at the events and apparitions filling their skies. Their line was from what had been a socially selected elite to begin with, who went on to found a starfaring colony that endured, even if it was unable to flourish and spread. When they suffered the lesser calamity caused by Froile, they may have lost their technology and history, but they retained enough rationality not to be carried away by notions of magical gods dispensing retribution. Thus, they avoided the fear and superstition which lay at the root of so much evil on Earth.

"And second, instead of resorting to conflict and rivalry to seize what they could of was left, they brought to their situation the tradition of a spacefaring community and colonizing venture, where the crucial qualities were cooperation and the ability to contribute— the values of life that the Venus we see today represents."

"And which will flourish on Earth too one day," Casselo said. He glanced at the clock display above the screens and then pointedly at Sherven. It was time. Sherven nodded.

He came forward from the window and moved from one to another of the four who were leaving, clasping the shoulders of each with both hands as a gesture of farewell. "A safe and a pleasant journey to you," he told them. "You have all played an invaluable part in work here that will never be forgotten. I look forward to the day when we will be able to welcome you back."

"It won't be long," Kyal said. "And thank you for everything too, Director."

"A life that adds one brick to making the world a better place than you found it is a life that was worth living," Sherven told them all. "Remember that we represent a unique and precious combination that the Terrans contributed to, but which they could never have equaled. That is why the recent trends back home disturbed me. Our culture has no room for the kind of divisiveness among ourselves that destroyed Earth. We have experience of governing our affairs in ways that they never knew. I believe we will command the wisdom to make things succeed this time, by working in combination instead of in conflict. That's as it should be, and has to be. The Universe is vast and dangerous, as our ancestors who tried to live at Eden discovered. Living well and securely with it will demand the best that all of us have to offer. Let us use our heritage wisely. One day, we will go back to the stars. And this time it will be to stay. It's a debt that we owe to those last children of Earth, who left here long ago."

CHAPTER FORTY-SEVEN

They sat in the midships cabin on C-Deck of the *Melthor Jorg*, watching the disk of Earth on the wall display screen, shrinking slowly and looking like a mottled blue-and-white marble. Its moon was partly visible behind, like a bright bump on one side.

The paint on the cabin walls was new, and the floor had been resurfaced. It seemed long ago that Kyal had sat here with Yorim on these same seats, surrounded by a different circle of faces, looking at the same view. But it had been growing larger then. So much had happened since. Then, it had been an enigmatic world of unanswered questions, tragedy, and mystery. There would always be unanswered questions; but now it felt familiar, and in a way, friendly. It would be good to see Venus again, Kyal thought, but he was already looking forward to the day when they would return. The future Scientific Director designated as Sherven's successor was already talking about developing Luna as a construction center and experimental facility for long-range space exploration technology. There would be much to do.

Yorim spoke from where he was sprawled in one of the chairs to the side, next to Mirine. "So what's first on everyone's list of things to do back home?"

Kyal looked at Lorili, shrugged, and made a face. "I hadn't really made a list. We've been too busy. What's on yours?"

Yorim waved a hand vaguely, as if he were raising an imaginary glass. "Oh . . . look up the old faces. See what's new in the neighborhood. Stay away from politics." He didn't seem to have any clear ideas either. Kyal watched his face, still taking in the screen. The look in his eyes seemed wistful. Kyal could almost read his thoughts: picturing Mediterranean beaches and ancient pyramids under blues skies, standing solid and immutable in the sun. He smiled faintly and felt inwardly reassured. Yorim would be coming back.

"Well, one thing you have to do is meet my folks," Mirine told him. "They say they're organizing a big welcome-home party. Our family has great parties."

"Sounds good to me," Yorim said neutrally.

"Do you realize we've never been anywhere we could dance yet? And Kyal says you're a terrific dancer."

"He did?" Yorim stared across. Kyal remained expressionless and kept his gaze averted. Lorili snickered to herself.

"What's that place you were telling me about in Rhombus that had lots of parties and a bar, and dancing?" Kyal asked Lorili.

"The Magic Carpet?"

"That's the one. Amingas Quarles was telling me they're going to open something like that in Pasadena."

"Oh, there are going to be all kinds of places opening up there," Yorim said.

"Next to a lake," Kyal went on. "And they'll have a dining room over the water, with boats. They think the lake might be a bomb crater that goes all the way back to the Terran war."

"A bar. That sounds like a good idea." Yorim looked more interested. "We're going to have something like twelve weeks to get through again. Fancy checking out the place up on E-Deck, and seeing if it's still the same? Remember that Korbisanian cocktail the guy used to mix on the way out? I wonder if he's still there."

"You're making me thirsty. I'll try one," Mirine said.

Yorim unfolded from the chair and sat up. "That settles it then."

Kyal wasn't in a hurry. He and Lorili hadn't had a moment alone all day. Twelve weeks was twelve weeks. "You carry on," he told them. "We'll catch up."

Yorim stood and helped Mirine to her feet. "See you there, then," he said. As they moved away, he said to Mirine, "You know, if we've got all this time on the way back, you ought to think about writing a piece for the magazines about those Terran corpses. . . ."

Kyal sighed luxuriously relaxed back in his chair.

"Nice to be alone at last?" Lorili said.

"It's nice to have friends too. But sometimes . . ." He left it unfinished. Lorili shifted closer and rested her head against his shoulder. "Mm, you smell nice," he told her.

"A scent that I got when we were in Europe. They make it in one of the settlements there. Plants that you don't see on Venus. They need lots of sun. And we're so much closer to it. Funny, isn't it."

Something bright and metallic hanging from Lorili's neck was resting on the arm between their chairs. Kyal reached with a hand and turned it over. "Your mother will be pleased," he said. "Still wearing your katek."

"Of course. Look at the good fortune that it brought me."

Kyal studied it absently. Two converging lines spanned by a pair of bars. A sign from a vanished world, that had once meant Providence. The landing approach of an incoming spacecraft. "And it worked for her too," he said. "It's bringing you back home."

Lorili lifted the katek from his fingers, looked at it for a moment, and then took his hand. She turned her head and gazed at the image of Earth, still shining on the screen. "No, it will have worked when we come back again together, Kyal," she told him softly. "That's our home now. It always was."